THE DEAD OF DECEMBER

RYAN BOWMAN

PRAIRIE REBEL PRESS
www.prairierebel.com

The Dead of December

Copyright © 2014 by Ryan Bowman

www.ryanjbowman.com

For information address Prairie Rebel Press:

Prairie Rebel Press

www.prairierebel.com

First Edition

ISBN: 978-0-9939389-0-0

Chapter 1

Twenty minutes into the midnight tour, his first shift back after a three-day weekend, and all Gerald Dawes could think about was knocking off.

As he stared through the grimy glare of the driver's side window, he yearned for the solitude and comfort of his queen size bed. Instead, here he was, exhausted and miserable, first on scene at another domestic, dreading what awaited him beyond the weather-beaten door of 101 Winchester.

Same shit, different day, Gerald thought.

Even from a distance, he could see the place was a typical Crookston eyesore. The peeling paint. The rusty eaves. A ragged patch of dead grass that looked as if it hadn't been cut since the spring.

The shit-brown shingles were cracked and curling at the corners, the stout brick chimney jutting from the slanted roof like a smoking cannon. Beyond the surrounding treetops, a single, low-hanging cloud clung to the starless Detroit skyline, carrying with it the greyness of burnt coal and the threat of snow.

"Haven't we been here before?" Nick Reese said. He was leaning forward in the jump seat, his elbow resting against the dashboard.

Gerald killed the engine and cracked his knuckles against the worn plastic of the steering wheel.

"Haven't we been to em all?"

He opened his door and stepped into the silence of an abandoned neighborhood without waiting for an answer. Other than a half-dozen rustbuckets parked along the crumbling curb, the street was empty.

Nick climbed out of the cruiser and they walked toward the yellow bungalow, their heavy boots slapping against the concrete with every synchronized step. As they followed the cracks of the sidewalk and climbed the sagging staircase, Gerald noticed a sliver of light framing the window in the center of the front door. The rest of the house was dark.

"Seems pretty quiet," Nick said. "Maybe they worked it out."

Nick took a step forward and knocked on the wooden door.

After about thirty seconds of silence they heard movement inside and the door creaked open. The narrow slice of a black man's face peered out at them. Late twenties, early thirties. His hair was braided in cornrows, his eyes glazed over and slightly bloodshot.

"Evening, sir," Nick said. "We're with the police. Somebody here called us?"

While Nick talked, Gerald stood to the side and surveyed what he could of the interior.

The black man remained silent, still hiding behind the door, his face fixed in an expression of defiance.

"Was it you that called us, sir?"

The man glanced at Gerald. Back at Nick. Shook his head.

"Somebody else here call us, maybe?"

"Ain't nobody else here."

"You're alone?" Nick took a small notepad out of his chest pocket. "This is one-oh-one Winchester, ain't it?"

"Uh-huh," the man answered. "This one-oh-one, but it's like I said. Ain't nobody else here."

Gerald and Nick exchanged a quick glance.

"Says he's alone, Ger. You believe him?"

Gerald shrugged. "All I know is we get a call from dispatch fifteen minutes ago saying there's a situation at one-oh-one Winchester. We get there and this guy answers the door, says he's alone."

Gerald peeled his eyes from the man and glanced at the floor just beyond the crack in the door, confirming what he thought he'd seen when they first arrived.

"Only there's these shoes inside. Small red things, got heels on em. Like they're for a woman." He looked back up at the black man. "So either our guy here wears women's shoes with heels on em, or he's lyin to us."

Nick's turn.

He shifted his feet until he was facing the man head on and squared his shoulders. "So which is it, guy? You a fruit, or you a liar?" He crossed his forearms across his chest. "Personally? I'd rather be a liar, but that's just me."

"Or," Gerald jumped in, "maybe you just forgot someone else was here. You've had a couple pops, smoked a little reefer? The

2

memory ain't what it used to be, you know? You just forgot. It happens."

The black man glowered back at them but said nothing.

"So we'll ask you one more time," Nick said. "Nice and slow, so there's no chance of confusion or nothin like that. Is there – "

He was interrupted by a banging noise from inside the house. A hollow thud, faint but unmistakable. All three of the men heard it at the same time, and none of them moved.

Suddenly, the black man's face disappeared and the door slammed shut. Before either Gerald or Nick could react, they heard the crack of the deadbolt.

"Go round back," Gerald said, reaching for his holster.

As Nick took off down the stairs and around the side of the house, Gerald scanned the front. Other than the door, the only entry point was the large rectangular window next to it. Smashing through wouldn't be a problem, but Gerald didn't know what – or who – was on the other side. Before he could look for another option, he heard shouts from the back of the house.

Gerald reached for his Glock and felt a familiar wave of nervous energy. He scrambled down the porch and ran along the outer wall of the house, his body pulsing with adrenaline. When he reached the rear corner, he leaned his shoulder against the stucco, rested his finger on the trigger and stepped around the edge of the house.

If the black man had put up any kind of a struggle, there wasn't any sign of it. He just lay there, silent, face down on the dirty pavement, his body sprawled out like a crooked crucifix. Nick's knee was planted in the small of his back.

Gerald took a breath and holstered his gun. He crossed the backyard and knelt at the black man's side, adjusting his bony wrists so Nick could cuff them. They patted him down and emptied his pockets. Nothing but a lighter, a Budweiser bottle cap and some loose change. Gerald stood up and inhaled a long gulp of icy air, the blood pumping through his body.

"You all right?" he asked Nick.

Nick nodded. "I got Carl Lewis here. You go check inside." Gerald brushed the dirt off his knees and looked down at the black man, who was still lying flat on his stomach, his hands cuffed behind his back.

He gathered a wad of saliva in his mouth and spit. It landed inches from the man's head.

"Nice try, asshole."

Gerald wiped his mouth with the back of his hand and headed toward the house without looking back.

Chapter 2

"This better be good." Kelvin Jackson was sitting at the edge of Sugar's bed, his voice equal parts anticipation and annoyance. "All this buildup and shit."

Sugar Sinclair was sprawled out across the hardwood floor of his bedroom, reaching around Kelvin's dangling legs for the shoebox he had hidden there. When his fingertips found cardboard, he dragged the box toward his body until it was close enough to grab.

He emerged from beneath the bed, wiped the dust off his baggy jeans and jumped up beside Kelvin. He placed the Nike box on the heavy grey blanket between them and covered it with both of his hands.

"You can't tell no one about this." Sugar was two years younger than Kelvin and had always revelled in holding the older boy's attention, the way he was now.

Kelvin sighed and rolled his eyes. He made a move for the box, but Sugar pulled it away just in time.

"Promise?" Sugar was clutching the box tight against his chest.

"Whatever," Kelvin said. "Just get on with it already."

Sugar placed the shoebox back on the bed and lifted the lid. Other than the background beat of a Fifty Cent tune coming from the three-disc changer on his dresser, the room was silent. He reached inside the box and pulled out a black, rolled-up sweatshirt, pushed the box aside and placed the sweatshirt between them as delicately as if he were handling a live grenade.

Watching Kelvin out of the corner of his eye, trying to read his dark, expressionless face, Sugar couldn't believe how much his friend had changed in the past year or so. The older they got, the more noticeable the age gap between them seemed to become.

Kelvin, who had always been the same height as Sugar growing up, was now a full head taller than him. He was still all arms and legs though, his bony shoulders swallowed by his grey Fubu hoodie, his skinny neck poking out like a turtle.

Even more noticeable than his change in appearance though, was his behavior. The outgoing, fun-loving Kelvin that Sugar had grown to look up to was nowhere to be found, rubbed out by the years and replaced by somebody colder, harder, more distant. He still liked to joke around, but his humor was darker now, and his laugh had an edge to it. His smile, still as contagious as they came, seemed less natural and there was a vacancy in his coal black eyes.

Looking into those eyes now, Sugar wondered if he'd made a mistake inviting him here.

"Come on already," Kelvin said. "I don't got all night."

Shifting his focus back to the bundled sweatshirt on his bed, Sugar slowly pulled the sleeves back until they lay flat across the bed and the shiny black handgun was fully exposed.

For what seemed like minutes, both of them just sat there. Sugar had seen Kelvin briefly acknowledge the gun, but now he was looking right at him, his thin face neutral and impossible to read.

Sugar had found the gun three days earlier, when he'd been looking for a CD in Reggie's room. It was one of the few times he'd actually built up the courage to enter his brother's room since he was killed, and he was on edge. So when he climbed up on the chair and ran his hand along the top shelf of the closet and felt the gun there, he nearly died of a heart attack.

His immediate instincts told him to leave the room and pretend it never happened. But there was something about the feeling of sleek metal against his skin that excited him. So instead of listening to that instinctual voice inside his head, the one he'd always obeyed without question, he listened to the louder, unfamiliar voice and he took it.

For the next two days, the gun had sat under his bed, Sugar dying to show it to someone. So when he saw Kelvin on his way home from school this afternoon, surrounded by all his friends, making everybody laugh, Sugar saw an opportunity to prove he wasn't as straight as everybody thought he was, to show he wasn't just Reggie's little brother.

And now, here they were, sitting across from each other, the gun between them and the room suddenly hotter. Sugar felt Kelvin's eyes on him, too uncomfortable to meet them.

Finally, Kelvin reached out and wrapped his long skinny fingers around the grip of the pistol.

"Shit, man." At the sound of Kelvin's voice, Sugar allowed

himself to breathe. "All this buildup over a fuckin heater?"

Sugar didn't know what to say, surprised by the disappointment he felt as Kelvin continued turning the gun over in his hand, examining it as casually as if it were a toy.

"It is a nice one, though." Kelvin's elevated voice gave Sugar renewed hope. "Same kind the pigs use."

Sugar gave Kelvin a smile he hoped seemed natural.

"Where you get this shit?"

"Found it over in Shaughnessy Park," Sugar lied. "Just walkin by and saw somethin under a tree. It was in a paper bag."

"It loaded?" Kelvin asked.

Sugar answered with a shrug, too embarrassed to admit he didn't know how to check.

Kelvin gripped the gun in front of him and Sugar watched as he pressed a button behind the trigger with the thumb on his right hand while pulling down on the butt with the thumb and forefinger of his left.

"This here the mag," Kelvin said as he pulled a sleek, black canister out of the grip, the sound of metal on metal making Sugar's pulse quicken. He tilted the canister downward and, with his thumb, began popping out bullets until a small pile of bronze lay in the center of the bed.

"Four shots," Kelvin said.

Sugar watched as he scooped the bullets up and pushed them one by one back into the mag. When all of the bullets had disappeared, Kelvin picked up the gun and slid the canister back inside the grip until Sugar heard a hollow click. Kelvin slid the top of the gun back and released it and there was another click, this one louder and more metallic, like a deadbolt sliding into place.

Kelvin extended his arm, offering the gun to Sugar. "Loaded and ready to go," he said. His mouth was set in a thin smile and Sugar sensed a shift in his mood, though he couldn't tell if it was good or bad.

Sugar reached for the gun tentatively, as if it might burn his hand. But when he grabbed the grip it felt cool and smooth against his clammy palm and the gun seemed even heavier than the first time he'd held it. The excitement he'd felt the other day was still there, but it was different this time, laced with fear and uncertainty.

A wide smile broke across Kelvin's face and he started to laugh. Sugar wanted to laugh along but felt self-conscious with the gun in his hand, thinking maybe he was holding it wrong or something.

"Little Sugar Sinclair packin heat. Shit man, who woulda thunk it?"

Sugar felt his face flush and couldn't contain his smile. Packin heat: he liked the sound of that.

He stood up and strode across the room with the pistol in front of him, pointed it at nothing in particular. When he caught a glimpse of himself in the mirror on the back of his bedroom door, he turned toward it, lifted the gun and aimed it side-arm, the way they did in movies and rap videos, cocking his head to the left and steadying the gun on the reflection of his chest.

"Be careful with that shit." Kelvin's tone was stiff, but he was still smiling.

Sugar took one more look in the mirror – at the excitement in his eyes, at the gun in his hand – and wondered what it would be like to pull the trigger. What it would sound like, what it would feel like.

"Anyway, I'm out." Kelvin got up from the bed and grabbed his winter jacket off the back of Sugar's chair. "Big party at Pork Chop's tonight. Gonna be crawlin with bitches."

As Sugar stepped aside and Kelvin walked past him, he felt the entire night drain into a sewer of loneliness and abandonment in the bottom of his stomach. Like he'd somehow been taken advantage of but was too naive to understand how.

"You comin or what?" Kelvin was looking back at Sugar, one foot out the door, one hand on the copper knob behind him. There was indifference in his voice, but Sugar thought he read something in his face that said he wanted him to.

Before Sugar had a chance to answer, that familiar voice of caution was knocking again, throwing at him all the reasons not to go. He didn't go to parties. It was too late. It was a school night. It was Kelvin Jackson.

Screw it, he thought. What's the worst that could happen?

"Yeah," Sugar said. "Sure."

"Come on, then." Kelvin clapped his hands together and

gestured with his head toward the empty hallway. "Let's bounce."

Sugar took a step toward the door but stopped, suddenly aware of the gun still in his hand. He walked to the bed and grabbed the shoebox.

"What you doin?" Kelvin said.

Sugar turned around and for an awkward couple of seconds looked back and forth between Kelvin and the gun. Finally, he tossed the empty shoebox back on the bed and slid the gun into the front pouch of his hoodie.

He followed Kelvin out of his bedroom, the voice in the back of his mind nothing more than a distant whisper.

Chapter 3

"Do you have to?" Leslie Sanford's pleading tone told Clarence she already knew the answer but thought she might be able to change it.

"Sorry," Clarence said as he dried himself off in front of the floor-to-ceiling mirror. "Gotta put in the long hours now so I can have time off at Christmas. The schedule should be back to normal in the new year."

"Here," she said, grabbing the towel from him and rubbing it across his lower back. "You always miss that spot."

Clarence turned around and looked at his wife. Even in her ancient U of M sweatshirt and her tear-away track pants, she still got him going. Seven years and two kids later she still had that flawless mocha skin, that lean, athletic body.

Clarence grabbed the towel from Leslie's hands and dropped it at their feet, leaning his body into hers. They touched lips and found each other's tongues as he ran his hands from the base of her neck down her narrow back. When they landed on her ass and he began guiding her toward the bed, she playfully swatted his wrist.

"What do you think this is, a drive-thru special?" she said. "Unh-uh, boy. You want a piece a this, you best be puttin in some time."

Clarence laughed and strolled over to his side of the walk-in closet. He grabbed a fresh pair of boxer-briefs, his newest pair of black pants and a blue dress shirt before making his way to the foot of the king size bed.

"Anyway, it shouldn't be too late tonight." He was pulling his pants on, one leg at a time. "A couple hours, tops."

Clarence put his shirt on, the Egyptian cotton soft against his skin, and buttoned it from the bottom up. He tucked it into his pants and reached for one of the black leather belts hanging on the inside door of the closet. He walked back to the mirror and took a final look at himself: black socks, black pants, royal blue dress shirt, top button undone, no tie. A thick chain hung from his neck, the same fourteen-carat gold as the watch on his left wrist. Both were gifts from Leslie for their fifth anniversary.

10

"Oh, stop it," Leslie said. "You spend more time in front of that mirror than I do."

Clarence found her eyes in the mirror and gave her a small shrug. "What can I say? It takes work to look this good."

Leslie reached for the pile of pillows on the bed, grabbed a fluffy orange one and tossed it at him. It hit him in the chest and fell to the carpeted floor.

"That's it," Clarence said, locking his eyes on Leslie and stalking toward her with heavy, determined steps, his hands curled out in front of him like one of those dinosaurs from Jurassic Park. "You brought this on yourself."

He made a growling sound and slipped his arms around her waist, lifting her into the air and suspending her there for a moment before tackling her to the mattress. He nibbled on her cheeks and her neck and Leslie shrieked and laughed as they rolled among a multi-colored flurry of pillows and comforters.

When he was out of breath, Clarence rolled over on his side and unravelled his arms from beneath her. Other than their labored breathing, the room was silent.

Clarence reached up and, with two fingers, brushed the hair from the side of her face. He stroked the smooth skin of her cheek with the back of his hand.

Her face was glowing bronze beneath the frosted overhead lamp and he took in that small crescent mouth and those rich brown eyes, slightly sloped at the corners and always looking as if they held the most important secret in the world and were saving it just for you.

Lying there, in the folds of the blankets and the piles of pillows, Clarence felt like a kid again. No obligations, no responsibilities, no stress. It was as if he and Leslie were the only two people in the world and all that mattered was that they loved each other and they were together.

As he tried to lose himself in the moment, to drown himself in the pools of her eyes somewhere, Clarence became strikingly aware of how rare moments like this had become. He found himself wanting to hang on to it, desperate to preserve the purity of it for as long as he could.

He turned his hand over and ran his fingertips across her

eyebrows and along the bridge of her nose and the contours of her cheekbones, brushing them across her lips and finally landing on her chin.

"I know I tell you every day Les, but I love you. I love you so much."

The corners of her eyes crinkled and she smiled the most innocent, heartbreaking smile he'd ever seen. She shifted her body and leaned into him, her head coming to a rest just below his jaw.

"All these long hours? All this overtime? I'll make it up to you." Clarence propped himself up and slid to the edge of the bed. "I promise."

Leslie nodded. "I know you will, Clarence. It's not me I'm worried about."

She hopped down from the bed and stood in front of the dresser mirror, dragging a brush through her tussled hair. "But what are you gonna tell the kids? It's movie night."

Clarence took a deep breath and looked at his watch. "Do you mind covering for me this time? I really need to get going."

"Seriously?" Leslie sighed. "You're gonna put this on me again?" "Please? Tell them I'll see them at breakfast. I'll even make my famous blueberry-chocolate chip pancakes."

Leslie exhaled and tilted her head as if she had no choice.

"Fine." She placed her brush back on the dresser before finding his eyes in the mirror and smiling. "But only because I'm such a sucker for those pancakes."

Clarence watched his wife walk past him, her footsteps padding down the carpeted stairs, her voice echoing throughout the house as she called the kids' names, and he was suddenly overwhelmed by a swell of shame.

He turned off the lights and stood in the darkness for a moment before leaving the room and following her down the stairs.

Chapter 4

By the time Gerald and Nick were back on the streets it was going on eleven-thirty. They'd taken their time at the Eighth Precinct, dropping off the suspect and shooting the shit with the intake officers. Every night it was the same, and every night it went without saying: they were in no hurry to get back out there.

The night had grown windy and miserable, the streets even quieter than usual. There was nothing out there but scattered trash, a few stray cats, the odd parked car. Even the corner boys and the cart people seemed to be in hiding.

The heat registers were pumping at full blast and there were fresh coffees in the cup holders, still steaming, the aroma mingling with the smells of older, staler coffee and an assortment of Little Tree air fresheners hanging from the rear view mirror.

Both men sat in silence, staring out the windows. Thinking, or trying not to. For what seemed like the thousandth time, what should have been a routine call to a domestic dispute had ended up in an arrest. And a call to the hospital.

The banging from inside the house had turned out to be a young black woman, nineteen, maybe twenty. She was locked inside a closet so small she couldn't even sit down, had most likely used her head to bang on the door. When Gerald had found her, he was surprised she was still breathing.

The left side of her head was gouged with a long bloody gash and her left eye completely swollen shut. Her naked body was covered in bruises darker than her chestnut skin, her wrists and ankles bound crudely with neckties. A sport sock was jammed in her mouth, duct tape wrapped around her head holding it in place.

Apparently ex-boyfriend had come over drunk and wasn't in a very good mood. He went on to rape her, beat her, drink some beer, and rape her again. She was already tied up and gagged when Gerald and Nick got there, so all the asshole had to do was shove her in the closet and lock the door.

Who had made the nine-eleven call was still a mystery. There wasn't a landline in the house, and the woman didn't have a cellphone on her. A neighbor, most likely. Whoever it was probably saved the girl's life.

As much as Gerald hated when they caught one like this, he knew it hit Nick even harder. Maybe it was his youth, or maybe his inexperience. Maybe he was more naive than Gerald, or just more sensitive. Maybe all of the above. But whenever something like this happened, it was as if Nick took it personally.

Gerald still hadn't decided if it was a strength or a liability, wasn't sure whether he pitied Nick or admired him. One thing he did know is that he envied his partner's faith in humanity – the way he always expected the best of people, the way he came out here every day and did his job for the right reasons, as best he could. Not because he needed the paycheque and had no idea what the hell else he'd do with himself.

"Talk to me, Nick. What's goin on in that head of yours?" Gerald didn't particularly want to go there again, but it had become part of the routine.

"Nothing, really. Just thinking."

"About?"

Sometimes Nick would talk about it, other times he'd keep to himself, let it brew up inside and act like nothing happened. Gerald felt exhausted and found himself hoping for the latter.

The Crookston Gerald saw as he stared out the window, the Crookston he and Nick had been patrolling for the past ten months, was a brittle shell of the neighborhood he had grown up in. In less than twenty years, it had devolved from a working class community with promise to a prison for the poor, twenty thousand life sentences with no chance of parole. Home to a desperate and disconcerted population that was mostly young, mostly poor and mostly black.

That was the problem, Gerald figured as he took in the decrepit neighborhood around him. So many blacks in such close quarters. Not that Gerald considered himself racist; two-thirds of the DPD were black, and he'd never had a problem with any of them. Hell, he'd even consider some of them friends.

But when you threw poverty into the equation, blacks in this country didn't stand a chance. All the unemployment and the prostitution and the pre-teen pregnancies, the drugs and the alcohol, the gangs and the violence.

And although he no longer recognized the area he grew up in, Gerald still felt an indescribable sense of duty to protect it. As

14

recently as his childhood, Detroit had been a city of progress, one of the economic and industrial hubs of the world. Now it was the murder capital of America, a giant exposed scab on the face of the country it had helped define. From surplus to scarcity. From progress to poverty. From riches to rags.

With his gun on his hip and his badge on his chest, Gerald sometimes felt he had the means to make a difference, to provide the vaccine. The longer he patrolled this degenerate wasteland of a beat, though, the more he'd come to accept the hopelessness and the helplessness of it all. He could arrest a dealer, a rapist, a murderer, slap the bracelets on em and lock em up. But for every one he got, he knew there were a hundred he didn't. The best thing they could do with areas like Crookston was to leave em be and let em kill each other off.

Taking in the abandoned streets and the darkened houses, Gerald thought of all the lives they'd swallowed, all the futures they'd extinguished. All those kids – the next generation of drug dealers and crack heads, the rapists and the murderers of tomorrow. They didn't have a chance. From the cradle to the grave, maybe a few years behind bars in between.

"Just that scumbag, you know?" Nick was still staring out the window, his voice quiet and even. "How someone could do that to another person? I mean, crime is one thing. I get that." He turned around and Gerald could feel his eyes on him. "Did you see her face?"

A series of vivid images flashed through Gerald's mind like a slow motion slide show. The blood so dark it was almost black. The various shades of blue and purple and yellow surrounding her lifeless eyes. Horrible, no doubt. But no worse than all the others he'd seen over the years.

Over time Gerald had learned, had forced himself to learn, how to push it to the back of his mind and regard it as an unfortunate side effect of The Job. The things that used to shock and repulse him barely registered now. The truth was, he no longer saw these people as human. Not the criminals and – in most cases – not the victims either. He told himself this was just the life of a beat cop in Detroit with eleven in.

"He'll get what's coming to him," Gerald finally said.

15

"Karma's a real bitch."

"Karma?" Nick said. "We both know that guy'll be back on the streets before she's out of the hospital. Back home, drinking his beer, smoking his dope. Beating the shit out of helpless women."

"Probably true." Gerald pulled the cruiser forward and hit a streak of greens, the familiar neighborhoods fading in his mirror as he coasted west toward the freeway. "But we both know jail doesn't help people like that, man. Just makes em harder, just feeds the hate. What can you do?"

Nick scoffed. "You're right, Ger. Just let em all free. Let em run wild until the entire world is one big Crookston. Let karma take care of things."

"It were up to me, we'd cut the fucker's hands off," Gerald said. "He starts kickin people? Bye, bye legs. Eye for an eye, man. That's real justice."

Nick was looking out the window again, the bill of his police cap profiled against the dark glass. Still, silent. Gerald not sure if he was even listening to him anymore.

"Knowing what you know now," Nick said. "You think you woulda signed up for this?"

Gerald shook his head. "No one would, man. Why do you think we get free donuts?"

Nick kept staring out the window, but Gerald noticed the slightest of smirks cross his face.

"Thanks," Nick said after a minute or so. "For . . . you know."

"Don't mention it," Gerald said.

All part of the routine.

*   *   *

As Gerald reached the tracks behind the high school, the season's first snowflakes began to fall. Through the glow of the headlights they looked transparent, dissolving into nothingness the moment they hit the windshield.

"Great," Gerald said.

"What?"

"This." Gerald jerked his head toward the distant city lights beyond the slick windshield. "Winter."

16

"What?" Nick said. "Three years we've been partners and not once have I heard you complain about winter."

Gerald shrugged but said nothing.

"You're telling me you all of a sudden got something against the snow, the lights, the holidays? You got a problem with Christmas, too?"

Gerald didn't answer. Thinking now about how recently the sun had hung in the sky late into the evening instead of setting at suppertime. How recently the T-shirts and shorts had been replaced by gloves and parkas. How on Thanksgiving day it was seventy degrees, Janet and him at her parents' place in Dearborn, sitting in the backyard, hand in hand on the swinging bench, their nieces and nephews running around and tossing the football without a care in the world.

Gerald wondered what his wife might be doing at this exact moment. Where she was. What she was thinking. Did she even miss him?

"OK, but what about that first day of spring?" Nick was leaning forward in his seat now. "You know, the one where the sun beats down, the snow starts to melt, everything turns to slush. You got the window down and the radio up, you're in nothing but your T-shirt, the girls walking around in tank tops and dresses and you know playoffs are just around the corner."

"What about it?" Gerald said, suddenly wanting nothing more than to turn the cruiser around, go back home and climb beneath the covers.

"It's just . . . all I'm saying is you can't have one without the other, you know?"

Gerald shook his head. Asking Nick what the hell he was talking about would only encourage him, so he decided to let it go.

The snow was coming down steady now and everything glistened with a thin layer of white powder, making it seem somehow brighter outside. Gerald sat back in his seat, listening to the rhythmic swishing of windshield wipers on glass, and thought, it might be a quiet night after all.

Chapter 5

Natasha Stokes lived in a single-story house not far from where she worked. It wasn't much, but compared to some of the others on the street, it stood out as one of the nicer ones. It had belonged to her grandfather until he died of a stroke in '95 and left it to her mother, mortgage-free. Last summer, with her brother and her sister out of the picture, it had been passed on to Natasha by default when her mother fled to Missouri with her prick of a boyfriend.

"You sell, I get half," was the last thing her mother had said to her before she left. Back when the place was actually worth anything.

From the day she moved in, the place seemed too big for just one person. The high ceilings and the airy halls had a way of making Natasha feel lonely and sometimes got her thinking about packing her bags, maybe joining her sister in the city or buying a one-way ticket to some place new. She'd never been outside Michigan and often wondered what life was like beyond serving coffee in a dirty diner and suffering through long, snowy winters.

But that all changed the afternoon she met Clarence Sanford.

In the three short months since he first stepped foot into Pearl's, tall and handsome and perfect in every way, her life had taken a complete one-eighty. She could still remember the nervous way he'd flirted with her, how he fumbled over his words and didn't know where to put his eyes. And then the surprise, the relief, the initial fear she felt a few weeks into it, when she realized it was more than just a wave of passion. That he wasn't just another distraction, another way for her to validate herself and give her pathetic life meaning. And that to him, she wasn't just a piece of meat or another conquest.

Clarence was older than most of the guys she'd been with, more mature. And besides looking like a young Denzel, he had a real job. Money in the bank and a fancy sports car. And he was funny, polite, educated, respectful. He was perfect.

In the beginning, it hadn't bothered Natasha that he was married. In a way, she actually preferred it. She was the independent type, not jealous or possessive, and she liked to have her own space. As long as she got her two nights a week with Clarence, it was the best of both worlds.

But lately, Natasha had found herself wanting more. She'd started feeling jealous and possessive, and she no longer enjoyed having her own space unless Clarence was there to share it with her.

For the first time in her life, Natasha could say she was in love and actually mean it.

Chapter 6

When the affair had first started, Clarence told himself it would be a one-time deal. A single mistake that he would feel guilty about for a while but could in time deal with, could some day forgive himself for and move on from.

But as Clarence inched the Infiniti forward, mindlessly flipping through the satellite radio stations, he wondered how that single mistake had turned into nearly three months of single mistakes. All his life, he had considered himself one of the good guys. And then, all of a sudden, just like that, he wasn't.

The lanes in front of him opened up and Clarence headed north over the bridge, watching as the comforting lights of suburban life disappeared behind him, and navigated the increasingly silent streets toward Natasha's.

Little more than ten miles from his own neighborhood, Crookston seemed like a whole other world. Four squared miles of barren land pockmarked by burnt-out buildings and boarded-up houses, it resembled the aftermath of a successful and devastating air raid. Clarence had himself been raised in a working class community, but he couldn't remember it ever being this dismal. At least where he grew up, he'd had neighbors. Around here, there were just as many abandoned houses as there were inhabited ones.

Clarence knew that when he'd married straight out of college he was giving up the typical life of a twenty-something – self-exploration, meeting new people, trying new things. And at the time, he'd been fine with it. He'd been with Leslie since his freshman year and knew she was the one. Beautiful, inside and out. Talented and driven. Everything he'd ever wanted in a woman. He'd considered himself lucky when he found her and he vowed to himself to never let her go.

Following the wedding, everything had gone according to plan. Michael was born within eleven months of the honeymoon and Sonia followed exactly two years later. Clarence landed a promotion and they bought a cozy $200,000 home in the suburbs of Lexington Heights. By the time he'd turned thirty, Clarence had accomplished everything he'd ever dreamed of.

But over the years, he began experiencing an increasing level of lament. Life was cruising along and it seemed he'd never really gotten a chance to catch his breath. Initially, he'd condemned his thoughts as selfish and mercenary. The more he fought them though, the stronger they got. He couldn't shake the feeling that something was missing in his life, some invisible void that he couldn't quite explain.

Then, one steamy afternoon in September he had met Natasha Stokes. What had started as an innocent stop for a bite to eat in an unfamiliar part of town ended with the most passionate and sensual encounter of his life. Clarence felt things he hadn't felt in years, maybe ever. Parts of him came alive that he thought no longer existed. And after spending that first afternoon with her, Clarence realized with exhilarating clarity what it was he'd been missing: he had forgotten what it felt like to want something.

*　　*　　*

Natasha's street was lined on both sides by ancient oaks, their newly naked branches quivering in the wind. Clarence found a spot behind a rusty green Pontiac without plates and stepped out of the car. As he pulled up the collar of his wool coat and crossed the street, he saw a group of young men huddled next to a tree like football players, the glowing tips of joints jutting from their lips.

When they took notice of him they grew silent and Clarence dropped his head. He moved toward the far edge of the sidewalk, careful to keep his eyes on his shiny black shoes the entire way to Natasha's stoop.

She came to the door wearing tight dark jeans and a light green low-cut sweater. Her long black hair, which usually hung past her shoulders, was tied back in a tight braid and reminded Clarence just how young she truly was. As far as he could tell, she was wearing no makeup other than a faint score of eyeliner, no jewelry other than a small diamond studding the left side of her nose.

Clarence stepped inside and his face tingled in the warmth of the house. When Natasha leaned forward to greet him with a hug, he hesitated for a moment before bending down and embracing her. He inhaled the usual medley of citrus and vanilla and fought the involuntary instinct to pull her closer.

21

He slipped off his shoes and coat and walked into the living room that had become so familiar to him. Contrary to the rundown exterior, the inside of the bungalow was actually respectable. The furniture was outdated, and there was far too much of it, but the paint was relatively fresh and the blond parquet floors were still in decent condition. Clarence took a seat on the sand-colored sofa and stretched his legs across the coffee table.

"Long day?" Natasha took a seat beside him and squeezed his forearm.

"Brutal." Clarence shook his head, thinking, And about to get worse.

"Nothin a few beers can't take care of." Natasha rubbed his thigh and walked toward the arched doorway leading to the kitchen. As Clarence watched her, he couldn't help but be mesmerized by the rhythmic swaying of her hips, the youthful tightness of her body.

Before she got to the kitchen, he stopped her. "No thanks, Nat. I actually won't be staying long."

She turned around and stared at him, the momentary crease in her manicured eyebrows signalling confusion. She shook it off with a smile and moments later returned with a bottle of Bud in each hand. She placed them on the coffee table and sat down beside him, close but not touching.

Clarence pulled his feet from the table, leaned forward and twisted the caps off both bottles with a sigh before handing her one. As he took a long swig of his own, he closed his eyes. His mind was swarmed simultaneously with the ways to go about this and the excuses not to.

"It feels like I never see you no more, Clarence. We agreed to at least two nights a week." She sounded more hurt than angry.

Clarence took another sip of his beer and wished the words would just come to him. You started this, he thought, it's up to you to finish it. He waited for the alcohol to enter his system and looked at Natasha's face, her delicate skin the color of dark chocolate.

He turned away and stared at the TV screen, dark and empty except for the dim orange reflection of a lamp. He forced himself to think about Leslie, hoping the guilt and the shame might spark a moment of resolve.

Leslie. She had always been so trusting of him, so

understanding. She wasn't even mad about all the nights he'd had to "work late." She just shrugged it off and said it was time they'd have to make up for.

Like a Band-Aid, he thought. Quick. Firm. Now.

Head still down, voice barely above a whisper: "I can't do this anymore."

He stared down at his lap for a moment, tracing the beads of moisture along the beer bottle with his fingers, picking at the damp label. No movement beside him, no sounds. Maybe he hadn't said it loud enough. Or maybe the thought never left his head at all.

A full minute and still nothing.

Please don't make me say it again, Clarence thought. He finally raised his head and turned slowly toward Natasha. His mouth was half open when he saw the shiny streaks of tears on her cheeks.

He wanted to look away but couldn't, wanted to say something but didn't. The tremor started in her jaw and made its way down to her shoulders and her arms until her entire body was shuddering. She leaned forward, burying her wet face and muffled sobs between his chest and his shoulder. He closed his eyes and held her tight as she continued to cry.

Chapter 7

When the president had put Crookston on the map by publicly labeling it the armpit of America a few years back, Sugar could tell from the reaction of the grownups that he was supposed to feel personally offended. But wandering the neighborhood, especially at night, it was difficult to defend the only place he'd ever called home.

Everywhere he looked, the streets were pocked with potholes and smeared with oil stains. The curbs were lined with skeletons of old cars and overturned trash cans, the yards littered with broken bicycles and remnants of half-finished construction projects. Other than the flickering of the overhead street lamps and the ghastly shadows they cast, the streets were swallowed by complete darkness.

Sugar shivered. The wind had picked up and the temperature had dropped below freezing. Both he and Kelvin had their hooded heads lowered and their hands shoved deep in their pockets. Sugar was wearing his heavy Exco hoodie with the fleece inside, the closest thing he had to a winter coat. He regretted leaving his gloves at home.

So far, they had walked the streets mostly in silence. Sugar was having trouble keeping up with Kelvin's long, determined strides, part of him wanting to keep pace, another part wishing he could shrink back and get away without being noticed. The farther they got from Sugar's house, the more uncomfortable he became. Sure it was late now, after eleven, but that's not what worried Sugar. The knot in his gut had more to do with the gun he had in the pouch of his hoodie, the gun he now regretted showing to Kelvin.

For as long as Sugar could remember, Kelvin had been fascinated with making the news. Over the years, he'd done so about a half dozen times; he'd even graced the front page once for setting an old, abandoned auto body shop on fire. His name was never mentioned, of course – that would defeat the purpose. Kelvin was all about getting away with as much as he could without getting caught. Getting caught would mean jail time, and you can't make the news when you're behind bars.

As they crossed Franklin, Sugar tried telling himself he was being paranoid and childish. Besides, what would Kelvin think of him if he bailed?

"Haven't seen you around school lately," Sugar said, finally building up the courage to speak.

"Nah, man," Kelvin said without looking at him. "School's for tools. No offense," he added as an afterthought. "Rather be out here makin the green. Sittin round a classroom all day ain't gonna put these clothes on my back, y'know what I'm sayin?"

Sugar looked at Kelvin: the black coat with the fur collar, the navy NY baseball cap tilted sideways, the baggy Rocawear blue jeans hanging low and bunched up at the bottom, tucked behind the tongues of his tan Timberland boots – the kind Sugar had always wanted but couldn't afford. And all of it topped off with the sparkling studs in each of his ears and the thick silver chain hanging around his neck, centered with a flashy pendant embossed with the initials KJ in tiny sparkling diamonds.

Sugar knew that Kelvin had been dealing drugs for a while now; he was the one who got Reggie into it. Sugar could still remember two summers ago when they started disappearing for hours at a time and coming back with video games and CDs, designer threads, the newest kicks. Sugar never asked where they got the money for all this stuff, didn't need to. Dealing and running were a way of life around here. It had been that way since Sugar's dad was a kid, it was that way now, and it would be that way as long as there were addicts who wanted drugs and kids who wanted cash.

Despite the opportunities, Sugar'd never gotten into the things Kelvin and Reggie had. Never tried drugs, not even weed. He'd tasted alcohol once, but never gotten drunk. He'd never been in a fight, he'd never stolen anything, and he'd only cut school twice in his life.

"I dunno," Sugar said. "You never think about college?"

"College?" Kelvin turned around and laughed. "Boy, you heard of the Crookston Curse?"

Sugar nodded. He'd been hearing about it all his life.

"Crookston Curse," Kelvin continued. "You male and you grow up in Crookston, there ain't but two ways you end up. In jail, or in the dirt."

Bleak as it sounded, Sugar couldn't argue it. His father, his mother's father, and at least two uncles that he knew of were all currently behind bars. Reggie, another uncle and at least a half dozen of his schoolmates were dead. And that was just the people he knew personally.

As much as he heard about the Crookston Curse though, Sugar never completely bought into it. Maybe it was the optimist in him, or maybe he was just naive, but he didn't believe you had to end up in jail or dead just because of where you came from. Sugar believed there was a third way, that you could make something of yourself, that you and you alone controlled your destiny. Not fate, and definitely not some stupid curse.

"College?" Kelvin said again. "College ain't no option for guys like us."

"You don't think we have a choice?" Sugar immediately regretted the question.

"A choice? Yeah, we got a choice. Eat or be eaten, man. Life ain't no motherfuckin Disney movie, kid. This be it." He spread his arms wide, as if the world didn't exist beyond these darkened blocks of darkened houses.

Kelvin had quickened his pace again and Sugar was a couple steps behind. He picked up his pace and caught up just as he heard voices and laughter up ahead. Seconds later, a group of four guys walked around the corner and made their way toward them. Sugar felt himself shrink and instinctively move to the far edge of the sidewalk.

"Yo," he heard Kelvin shout at them when they were within a couple of steps. "What's crackin, boys?"

The group approached Kelvin, fist bumps all around. Now that they were closer, Sugar recognized all of the boys, but couldn't put a name to any of them. Probably from school, or maybe just around the neighborhood. They were all dressed the same: baggy coats, baggy jeans, assorted caps of various sports teams, and white kicks. One of them held a paper bag at his side. He raised it to his lips, pulled the paper back, took a swig and passed it to Kelvin.

Kelvin took a sip and wiped his mouth with the back of his hand, passed the bottle back.

"What's goin on?"

"Not much," said the tallest. "Headin over to Pork Chop's."

"Supposed to be off the hook," Kelvin said. Sugar was standing behind him, watching the older boys as they talked, trying

26

to avoid eye contact with them.

"You comin?" The tall one took another swig and passed it off to one of his friends.

"In a bit. Gotta swing by my place and change." Kelvin jerked his head toward Sugar and for the first time the other boys acknowledged him. "This my boy, Sugar."

Sugar felt his cheeks burn. He peeked around Kelvin's shoulder and gave them a slight nod. Two of them nodded back while the others went on ignoring him, passing the bottle back and forth. Sugar looked back at the ground.

"You Reggie Sinclair's little brother, huh?" One of the boys who had nodded was pointing at him.

Sugar looked up and bobbed his head awkwardly, feeling both proud and pained by the association.

"What up, bro. Me and Reggie was homies. Marshawn." He extended his fist and Sugar took a step forward and bumped it with his own. "This Kenard, Mackie, Darryl."

Sugar gave them all half smiles without making eye contact.

"Anyway," Kelvin said. "Me and Sugar got places to go, people to see." He winked at Sugar and gave him an exaggerated smile. "But we be by later, a'ight? Give me one more hit."

The boy with the bottle finished his drink and gave it back to Kelvin. He tilted his head back and pulled the bottle to his mouth. Took a gulp and shook his head.

"Want some?"

He had the bottle extended to Sugar. All eyes were on him and he could feel the blood gathering in his cheeks. He looked around from one boy to the next. Time seemed to stand still. He felt his mouth go dry but couldn't swallow. Finally he shrugged and reached for the bottle.

He wrapped both hands around the paper and raised it to his lips. He could smell it before he tasted it, strong and sweet. He opened his mouth and tilted the bottle back until he felt liquid hit his tongue. It burned like hell but he felt the stares of the others, so he kept the glass bottle pressed against his lips and managed to force down a full sip. It took everything inside him to not spit it out. Harsh and bitter, how he imagined a bottle of Pledge might taste, with the faintest aftertaste of flat Coke. His lips and his tongue burned and he felt a tingling sensation all the way from the top of his throat to the deepest part of his stomach.

He passed the bottle back to Kelvin and again looked at the boys, feeling a bit more comfortable now, not quite so invisible. Kelvin took one more quick drink and passed it on. He clapped Sugar on the shoulder.

"Let's bounce. Have fun at the party, boys. And don't be leavin me all your sloppy seconds, neither."

They all laughed.

"We'll save Pork Chop's mama for ya," one of them said. They all laughed again and headed off in the direction Sugar and Kelvin had just come from.

Sugar could feel the alcohol floating around in his stomach and his head, a dizzying sensation like the time he rode the roller coaster when he was a little kid. As he followed Kelvin, his steps felt lighter and the cool night seemed warmer now, the dark and empty streets more alive somehow. There was a bounce in his step and all the anxiety of ten minutes earlier had all but disappeared. What was there to be worried about, anyway? He was out for a night of fun with Kelvin Jackson. Kelvin Jackson, who had called him his boy.

As they turned the corner and headed toward Kelvin's place, it started to snow. Sugar looked up to see one, then two, then hundreds of perfect white snowflakes tumbling from the darkened sky. They were soft and wet and disintegrated the moment they hit the street, like tiny white water balloons. Sugar lifted his head and tried to catch them in his mouth as he walked, the sensation cool and tingly as they landed on his still-burning tongue.

Within a block, the snow started coming down harder, the flakes bigger, and Sugar stopped to look up at the suddenly bright sky. The moon was hanging directly above him like a giant white globe and the streetlights, veiled by slanted sheets of white, looked like halos.

"Yo, check it out." Kelvin snapped Sugar out of his dazed reverie. Sugar looked at him, disoriented from the spinning lights and the swirling snow and wasn't sure what Kelvin was excited about. All he saw was a set of headlights up ahead, moving slowly toward them.

"Where's the gun?" Kelvin asked. His voice was high with urgency.

Sugar had completely forgotten about the gun.

"Quick!" Kelvin screamed. "Gimme the gun!"

The headlights were getting closer, wide and angular. They beamed a brilliant white with a tinge of blue and momentarily blinded Sugar. Before he knew what was happening, Kelvin was at his side, arms waving. He was almost shouting now.

"Come on, man. The gun! Where's the gun?"

In the midst of his confusion, Sugar finally managed to get his hands in the muff of his hoodie and locate the grip of the gun. It was stiff and icy against his bare hand, and before he could do anything else Kelvin snatched it from him.

"Come on," he said. "Just be cool, follow my lead."

The approaching car was mere feet away now, its headlights glaring through the snow, its engine humming, its slick rubber tires gliding across the wet, black street. Sugar could see now that it was a sporty silver two-door with chrome rims and sleek curves. He didn't know much about cars, but he knew it was a nice one.

They were at an intersection with a four-way stop and Sugar could see the red glow of the brake lights bounce off the pavement as the car began to slow down. Kelvin stood at the corner, next to the stop sign, and lowered his head. He held the gun at his right side.

Don't stop, Sugar wanted to yell at the driver. Keep on going. He wanted to wave his arms and jump up and down and warn the driver, but he just stood there, frozen in time and space, silently regretting what was about to go down. He didn't want any part of it, but he knew with a pang of finality that it was too late.

Just as the car reached the stop sign, Kelvin made his move. He ran in front of the car with the gun at chest level, pointing it directly at the center of the windshield. He moved around to the driver's side of the car, the gun trained on the vehicle. Sugar stayed where he was, his feet planted to the pavement, his knees shaking. He couldn't see through the tinted windows if there were any passengers.

"Get out the car!" Kelvin yelled, the gun at shoulder-height now, pointed downward, directly at the driver's side window. "Get out!"

29

For a couple of seconds nothing happened. Sugar saw the red of the taillights disappear and thought for a moment the driver was about to take off. Would Kelvin actually shoot? Something deep down told Sugar he might. Bracing himself for the skidding of tires, the deafening gun shots, the ensuing scene from Grand Theft Auto, Sugar took a step back and tried to dissolve into the concrete wall of the building behind him. To his surprise though, the next thing Sugar saw was the driver's door open. A tall black man in dress clothes stepped out of the car with his hands in the air.

Kelvin steadied the gun and pointed it at the man's chest.

"Turn around!"

The man obeyed, and without a word he put his hands on the top of the car. Kelvin patted him down and grabbed something from his back right pocket.

"That it?"

The man didn't answer. His hands were spread out across the roof of the car and he had his head down.

"That all you got?" There was no panic in Kelvin's voice. As cool and calm as if he were asking for the time.

The man bobbed his head, ever so slightly.

"Get your face against that wall. And don't turn around." Kelvin looked over at Sugar and pointed with his chin toward the car.

Sugar willed his legs to take a step, and then another. He kept his head down and shuffled his feet. He slid in the passenger side door, trying to catch his breath and calm his shaking limbs. Moving as little as possible, he risked a look out the side view mirror and saw Kelvin leading the man toward the wall. He looked away, unable to watch what might, what he hoped and wished to God wouldn't, happen next.

After a minute or so of unbearable silence, the driver's door opened and Kelvin jumped inside. He had a smile on his face and tossed a black leather wallet on Sugar's lap.

"Go through it," he said. "Take the cash, the credit cards, whatever else he's got."

Kelvin put the car in drive and pulled away from the curb. Sugar was tempted to look back but he kept his eyes on the road in front of them. Finally, when he felt himself breathe again, he steadied his trembling hands and reached for the wallet.

Chapter 8

Clarence turned away from the brick wall and looked down the dark, empty road. There was no sign of his car; the road where its tire tracks should have been was covered by a layer of freshly fallen snow. It was coming straight down in perfect sheets now, and had covered the ground in a wide white carpet as far as he could see.

When the original shock of the gun in his face had dissipated, Clarence controlled his breathing and tried to come up with a plan. He realized that along with his wallet being stolen, his cellphone had been in the car. The last time he remembered looking at a clock it had been pushing midnight.

As he looked around, Clarence knew it wasn't the kind of place he could knock on a door and be invited in to use the phone while they took his coat and put on a pot of coffee, telling him to make himself at home and engaging him in small talk while he waited for his ride. He also knew it was the privileged, tainted influence of his life that made him think this way, but he couldn't help it. The thoughts were there, and he knew they weren't entirely unfounded; he grew up poor and he knew the way of the world better than he'd like to admit.

With no money and no phone, he was defeated with the realization that he had no choice but to make his way back to Natasha's. He'd use her phone and call for a cab, maybe the police. All Clarence knew was that he needed to get home.

He brushed the snow from his shoulders and tugged on his collar until the wool scratched against the back of his bare neck. He bunched his hands into fists and slid them into the warmth of his deep pockets. As he made his way down the unfamiliar streets there was a feeling deep inside him, beneath his skin, that he couldn't quite identify. It pushed its way down to the pit of his stomach and churned and pulsated and felt like it would never go away. There were traces of fear, he knew, and there was definitely a sense of anger over what had happened – anger at the punks for jacking his car, yes, but also a deeper, more internal anger at himself.

But that wasn't entirely it. Anger made you want to hit something, it demanded release. This feeling consumed him, made him want to disappear within himself. It was the same feeling as the time he'd been arrested at nineteen for possession, the same feeling he got lying in Natasha's bed after the first time.

Clarence felt shame.

He felt shame for letting it happen and he felt shame for how much it scared him, how much he'd let those little hood rats rattle him. They had a gun, he tried to reason with himself. It was dark, no one else was around, it was Crookston, they had nothing to lose. He gritted his teeth and clenched his jaw, shook his head at the empty street and his empty excuses.

When that gun was shoved in his face and he'd begun to shake uncontrollably and he'd gotten out of the car and turned around and spread his hands on top of the car and handed over his wallet like a bitch, and marched toward the cold brick wall like a prisoner in some concentration camp and closed his eyes and stood there facing that cold brick wall until he knew for sure that they were gone, Clarence had given up a piece of himself. And like his youth, like his virginity, he knew it was a piece that he'd never get back.

Clarence knew there was a time he wouldn't have let things go down the way they had. There was a time when he wouldn't have bowed out like that, when he would have stepped up, like a real man, and done what needed to be done. Even if he wouldn't have been able to save his car, he would have at least been able to hold his head high knowing that he salvaged his pride trying.

But those days seemed like a lifetime ago. And tonight, when he saw that gun in his face, his reaction reinforced just how much he'd changed, just how distant his past had truly become. Tonight he didn't think about his pride, or his ego. Didn't even think about his car. All he could think about as he stared down the barrel of that gun was seeing his family again. If he knew it meant getting to go back home to his Leslie and his Michael and his Sonia, he would have given up not only his car and his wallet, but also his job, his house and the clothes off his back. But still, it didn't make the pill of shame any easier to swallow. It was still bitter, jagged and unforgiving as it slid down his raw throat and rooted its way in his core.

Head down, Clarence picked up his pace. His dress pants had gotten crisp and felt like slices of frigid steel as they rubbed against his shins and knees. The snow-covered concrete was slick and he had to take small, deliberate steps in his Oxfords. Making his way through the empty streets that he hoped would eventually lead to Natasha's, all he could think about was getting home, seeing his family, getting a good night's sleep, putting this day behind him and waking up tomorrow to start a new one.

Chapter 9

The contents of the wallet were fanned across Sugar's lap like a collection of baseball cards. Forty-four dollars in cash. A Visa Gold, an American Express, a Blockbuster card, a gym membership and a driver's license that belonged to a Clarence Sanford – born in seventy-two, address in Lexington Heights. Some business cards for one of the big real estate companies with Sanford's name on them, and three pictures: one of Sanford with a good-looking woman, and individual headshots of a young boy and an even younger girl.

Sugar handed Kelvin the cash and the credit cards, which – along with a Nokia cellphone that was sitting in the center console – he pocketed. Kelvin pulled the gun out from the waistband of his jeans and handed it to Sugar.

"It's all right, man," Sugar said. "You keep it."

"Just hang on to it for now. I got nowhere to put it."

Leaning back in the driver's seat, Kelvin looked completely relaxed, comfortable even. He was so low in the black leather he was almost lying down, one hand on the steering wheel, the knuckles of the other gently rapping against the tinted window. He'd tuned the radio to Hot 102.7 and cranked it.

The system sounded good; clear, sharp tweets and subs that made the bass vibrate to the bone, but Sugar found it difficult to concentrate on the music. He was too nervous, gripping the sides of the seat, his stomach in knots, looking over his shoulder every couple of seconds. How could Kelvin be so calm right now? Sure, he'd probably done this before, but still. Sugar looked at the gun for a moment and shook his head before putting it in his hoodie.

"You never boosted before," Kelvin finally said with a smile. A statement, not a question.

Sugar shook his head without looking at him. He always heard about kids from the neighborhood stealing cars, joyriding them till they ran out of gas and ditching them. He was pretty sure Reggie used to do it too.

"Relax, man. Enjoy it." Kelvin smiled again and tapped the leather steering wheel with his open palms. His head was moving, slow and rhythmic, in time with something by Ludacris. "When's the last time you can say you been in a G35?"

It was true. Sugar had never been in a ride like this, not even close. The nicest car he'd ever ridden in was probably the old purple Pontiac Firebird with the yellow rims that his Uncle Al used to drive. A mid-eighties model with rust along the bottom of the doors and around the wheel wells, a spider web crack across the windshield that he never remembered getting fixed. Growing up, he and Reggie would always fight over the front, a low bucket seat scarred with soda stains and cigarette burns. She may not be a beauty, Uncle Al had always said, but she definitely a beast. Then he'd rev the engine and pop it into gear and they'd take off with the engine growling and the tires squealing.

But as Sugar looked at the glowing colors of the instrument panel, the modern digits and dials on the radio console, the spotless and stylish upholstery, this car made that Firebird look like the old piece of shit it was. This thing probably cost more than most people made in a year, Sugar thought, and definitely more than his apartment was worth. But what did it matter? It wasn't his, and it wasn't Kelvin's neither. It belonged to some real estate agent from Lexington Heights, a man with a wife and two kids.

Sugar leaned back in the leather seat and tried to take Kelvin's advice and relax, but he couldn't do it. In the past fifteen minutes he'd drank alcohol and he'd stolen a car. He had a gun in his pocket. What was he thinking? He wanted to just go home and climb into his bed and pretend this whole horrible night never happened. Maybe Kelvin would drop him off at home. Unlikely, but worth a shot.

"Where we goin?" Sugar said, trying to sound casual.

Kelvin shrugged. "Nowhere in particular," he said. "Just cruisin." After another moment of thought, he added: "Maybe we could swing by Pork Chop's. Arrive in serious style, y'know what I'm sayin?"

Sugar waited a few seconds, not wanting to sound eager or overly anxious.

"Think you might be able to swing by my place on the way, drop me off?" Paused, waited. "I'm not feelin too good."

Kelvin shook his head and chuckled. "You really need to learn to lighten up, man."

The snow was really coming down now, so dense that Sugar

couldn't see the road more than half a block ahead of him.

"What you so worried about, anyway?" Kelvin said.

I'm worried that we're driving around in a stolen car, Sugar thought. About getting caught, getting arrested, getting charged, going to jail, having a record, being known as a criminal and having my life as I know it come to an end.

He thought about saying it all out loud. Instead he just sat there, clenching his jaw and trying to mask his fear and frustration.

"I know what'll help," Kelvin said when Sugar didn't answer. He moved his left hand to the wheel and reached in his pocket with his right. He pulled out a small Ziploc baggie of weed – some loose bud at the bottom and a couple of pre-rolled joints. Kelvin unzipped the bag with his teeth, pulled out a joint, put it between his lips and resealed the baggie before shoving it back in his pocket. When he pulled his hand out of his pocket again, it held a silver Zippo.

Great, Sugar thought. He watched as Kelvin moistened the joint, raised the Zippo, and sparked up. Like his chain, Kelvin's Zippo was embossed with "KJ" across the front. For several seconds the dancing flame of the lighter lit up the entire car, making it seem somehow smaller in there, more remote, like a world completely cut off from the onslaught of flurries and the consuming darkness outside the windows.

Kelvin puffed on the joint and after a couple of seconds put his head back and released a ribbon of grey smoke toward the ceiling. The leather and cologne smells of the car were immediately replaced by the sweet, earthy scent of the pot. Sugar knew the smell well and, to be quite honest, didn't much mind it. But in this context, under these circumstances, all he could think about was the ever-increasing charges waiting for them when they got pulled over. Possession of a firearm, underage drinking, grand theft auto, and now possession of an illegal substance.

Kelvin drew another puff, the ember at the tip of the joint glowing darker, redder, the tapered tip of ash growing longer the deeper he inhaled. The smoke was so thick now, Sugar could taste it. It dried out his mouth and burned his eyes, but the nausea in his stomach had seemed to subside and his nerves seemed to finally be in check. The sharp pain in his head had been replaced by a dull fog, a welcoming sensation that was more soothing than painful and seemed to slow down his racing brain.

After exhaling another mouthful of smoke, Kelvin offered the joint to Sugar. Sugar refused by putting up his hand and shaking his head.

"Come on," Kelvin said. "It'll take the edge off. Chill you out some."

"I'm OK. Seriously."

Kelvin shrugged. He took another hit and turned up the radio. Like Toy Soldiers, by Eminem.

"Boy sure can spit," Kelvin said. "No Tupac, but not bad for a white boy. And from the D, no less. The boy be representin." He shook his head and mouthed the words to a couple of bars.

Sugar looked out the windows and, seeing nothing but the falling snow, finally allowed himself to relax.

He put his head back and lost himself in the music and the cloud of white smoke filling the car, watching the neighborhood float by as they headed back toward the familiarity and comfort of Sugar's place. The streets and the houses and the buildings looked different under a fresh blanket of snow. Cleaner, newer, more peaceful.

Kelvin took a left down Tennyson, a street of identical row houses with tiny front stoops and slanted roofs. Dusted with snow, the squat houses had no age, no history. It was as though someone had taken a giant brush, dipped it in white paint and stroked it across the entire neighborhood, temporarily cloaking the crumbling walls and whatever went on behind them.

The only signs of life on the street were the occasional flashes of television through the front windows. The car seemed to be moving slowly, casually. Kelvin had the windshield wipers on now, clearing the snow in time with the music. He was still smoking the joint, which had burned down to half its original size. Puff, inhale, exhale, repeat.

As they neared the upcoming intersection, Sugar looked to the left and saw something that made him bolt upright. At first, he thought it was just his overactive imagination, his paranoia getting the better of him. Maybe the weed having an effect.

But when he planted his palms on his knees, strained his neck and squinted his eyes for a better look through the snow-streaked windshield, he knew he wasn't seeing things. Up ahead, to the left, protruding just beyond the intersection was the familiar black nose of a police cruiser. Just as Sugar was about to say something, scream something, he felt the car slow down.

"Shit," Kelvin mumbled. He dropped his joint hand to his lap and sat up straight. He kept his eyes forward and spoke to Sugar with a calm and even tone.

"Just be cool," he said. "I'm going the speed limit, they got no reason to pull us over."

Kelvin continued to slow down until he reached the stop sign perpendicular to the cops. Sugar kept his eyes forward, locked on the white lettering of the stop sign ahead, and tried to channel Kelvin's composure. How was he still so calm?

Sugar hoped the cops would somehow not see them, thought that maybe if they were quiet enough and inconspicuous enough they might go unnoticed. For what seemed an eternity, the car sat there, the pulsing sensation of pumping blood filling Sugar's head and body. He looked down at his hands and saw that he actually had his fingers crossed.

Kelvin had turned the radio off and other than the steady hiss coming from the air vents, the car was silent.

Finally, Kelvin put his foot on the gas and Sugar felt the car pull forward. He wanted to tell Kelvin to floor it, to get them the hell out of there as fast as he could, but he knew it would only draw attention. He sat frozen to his seat and finally risked a look over his shoulder half a block later. Nothing behind them but a pair of twin tire grooves cutting through the snowy street, following behind them like a set of railway tracks.

*   *   *

Alone in the darkness of the cruiser, Gerald's thoughts crept back toward Janet. The harder he tried to fight them, the stronger they got, smothering him to a point bordering claustrophobia. He cracked his window and took a deep breath. The crisp, cool air hit his lungs and made its way up to his head. When the stabbing pulse finally began to dissipate, he caved and stole a look in the rear view mirror.

In the faint light shining through the passenger window, Gerald saw a version of himself that was becoming less recognizable every day: older, duller, softer yet somehow harder. The gaunt, pasty skin and the pale blue-grey eyes with the perpetual bags beneath them had him looking like a man a decade older than his thirty-six years.

He turned away in disgust, just in time to see Nick making his way back to the vehicle. His black uniform blended in with the dusky night, only the glare of his chest badge and the white of his face visible in the darkness.

Nick swung the door open and Gerald was hit with a blast of cold air and the faint smell of burnt rubber.

"Buy the entire place?" Gerald nodded toward the paper bag in Nick's hand.

"Damn near," Nick said. "We're on this beat much longer, I'll be putting the old man's kids through college."

Nick reached in the bag and handed Gerald a bottle of V8. Then he pulled out a bottle of water, unwrapped a Snickers bar and took a bite before spreading the Free Press across his lap.

Gerald opened his drink and downed half of it in a single chug before easing the cruiser back onto the road. As the snow continued to accumulate, Gerald couldn't help but think how many accidents there would be between now and morning. Every year, the same thing: the first little bit of snow and ice on the ground and people forgot how to drive.

"So. What's going on in this wonderful city of ours?" Gerald glanced down at the paper, which was open to the Business section. He was anxious now for conversation, anything to keep his mind off Janet.

Nick shrugged and answered through a mouth full of chocolate and caramel. "Same old. More layoffs, another plant closing."

"Nice," Gerald said. "Merry Christmas to you, too."

"Thank God for crime, right Ger? Job security long as we need it."

"Nothin to worry about in this city, that's for sure."

They reached the stop sign at the corner of Albert and Tennyson and Gerald drained the rest of his tomato juice. He was about to pull forward when he saw a set of headlights bouncing off the dark windows lining the street. He kept his foot on the brake, watched the beams as they approached the intersection.

As the vehicle came into view it began to slow down for the stop sign, its brake lights glowing red against the snow. Gerald hit the wipers and saw it was a silver sports car, sleek and shining beneath the snowflakes and the streetlights. As it idled at the stop sign, Gerald saw the driver give the cruiser a half glance before quickly looking away. Gerald could make out the face, but barely: young and black. After a couple of seconds at the stop sign, the car inched forward and pulled ahead.

"See that?" Gerald asked.

"What?" Nick didn't bother looking up from the sports pages spread across his lap. "He run the stop sign?"

"No." Gerald shook his head and turned left, in the direction of the fading taillights. "Brand new Infiniti."

"Driving foreign's not a crime, Ger. Should be, maybe, but we can't be pulling everybody over for not driving a Ford."

"Not the car I'm interested in." Gerald began to accelerate. "How many young black guys you know in this area can afford an Infiniti?"

Nick folded the paper shut and peered out the windshield.

By the time Gerald crossed Carson, the Infiniti was about a half block ahead of them. It was moving at about the speed limit, seemingly in no hurry to get wherever it was going. The brake lights flashed every now and again, looking like two red eyes glaring through the blowing snow.

"I'm just gonna follow him for a bit," Gerald said. "See where he takes us."

*   *   *

Kelvin rolled down the window and tossed the roach. The blast of cool air was invigorating. It woke a part of Sugar's brain that he'd forgotten about, that had seemingly been put on pause without his knowledge. His senses kicked into gear and with sudden clarity he realized that all of this was real.

"Stop looking back," Kelvin said. Still calm, still poised.

40

It felt like they were crawling, the houses passing by in slow motion. It took Sugar everything he had to keep his eyes forward. They drove on, still in the direction of Sugar's place, the heat still blowing from the registers, the vents still hissing, the snow still falling. They'd gone a full block since seeing the cop car and were still the only vehicle on the road. As they approached another stop sign, Sugar saw a flash of light in the side view mirror and instinctively looked back.

There, in the middle of the rear windshield were two bleary circles of light, small and dim but unmistakable. Like the hungry eyes of an animal on the side of the road at midnight. And although he was too far away to see the car they came from, he knew.

"They're following us," Sugar said, unsure if it was out loud or just in his head. His pulse was racing and his heart was beating fast and hard against the inside of his chest.

Kelvin shot his eyes toward the rear view and Sugar saw his jaw tense. "Don't worry bout it. I'll turn at the next street. Just relax. And stop looking back."

Sugar forced himself to take a deep breath. He dug his fingernails deeper into the leather of the seat, sweat forming on his back and forehead despite the cool breeze coming from Kelvin's window. Sugar tried his hardest to not think about getting caught, about what would happen if they did. Against the black of his closed eyelids all he could see was steel bars, long and strong and permanent.

He knew he had no one to blame for this but himself, and all because he'd been trying to impress Kelvin with that stupid gun. Sugar promised himself that if he got through this, he'd never try to impress anyone ever again. He'd go back to his life of homework, video games and hanging with Deon. It might be lame, it might be boring, but it was his life. It was what he wanted.

As they approached the next intersection, Kelvin turned on his signal and, after coming to a complete stop, took a right. Sugar gripped the headrest and glued his eyes to the empty space behind them. Waited. For a few long seconds, nothing. Then, just as he was about to turn around and take a breath, he saw the lights.

*   *   *

41

The Infiniti continued straight for another block. As it approached a four-way intersection, the brake lights shone red and the right turn signal blinked orange. The car came to a complete stop and turned, its taillights disappearing around the corner. By the time Gerald made the turn, he saw that the Infiniti had put some more distance between them.

"I'm gonna get closer," Gerald said to Nick, the Infiniti definitely speeding up now. "Get ready to run the plates."

Gerald pressed the toe of his boot on the pedal until he got to within a couple car lengths. He squinted through the tumbling snowflakes and fought off the glare from the cruiser's headlights. When he was close enough, he read the plate numbers to Nick, who entered them into the computer.

After a few seconds of clicking, "Belongs to a Clarence Sanford, thirty-three years old. Registered address on Pine Ridge Road."

"Where's that?"

"Over the bridge, Lexington Heights area."

Gerald glanced at the computer screen to see the image of a black man with a shaved head, a square jaw and a firm set mouth. Even from the headshot, Gerald could see he was a big man.

"Priors?" Gerald asked.

Nick hit some more keys and nodded. "Possession and resisting arrest, back in '91. Released on bail, no time served." He scrolled down the page.

"Nothing since. Not even a parking ticket."

"Just hasn't been caught," Gerald said. Guys like this get a slap on the wrist and they go on dealing, he thought. Bring their drugs into poor areas like this and drive back to their fancy houses in their fancy sports cars. Retreated and sheltered in their own community, immune to the effect their drugs are having over here, insensitive and oblivious to the lives they're destroying.

"That was fifteen years ago." Nick was looking at him. "Maybe he's gone clean."

"Don't let the address fool you, man. You can take the rat outta the hood, but you can't take the hood outta the rat." Gerald maintained his distance from the car, which was still gradually picking up speed. "Hundred bucks says a search of that car turns up either a shitload of product or a shitload of cash."

Nick looked away and stared out the windshield, his pale face worn and expressionless.

"You don't have a reason to pull him over, Ger."

Normally, having a sheet and being out this late in the pouring snow would have been reason enough. But he could read Nick's mood, could hear the fatigue in his voice and thought, not worth it. Not tonight.

*　　*　　*

The cruiser was behind them again and seemed to be picking up speed. The snow was still coming down hard but Sugar could see the cruiser more clearly. It was definitely gaining on them, only a few car lengths behind now. The headlights were coming in through the rear windshield, bouncing off the mirrors, nearly blinding. Sugar felt exposed, as if he were caught in the beam of a giant spotlight. He knew Kelvin was talking to him, but he couldn't concentrate on what he was saying. Then he felt a hand on his shoulder, pulling him forward.

"Stop looking back," Kelvin was saying, still tugging on his shoulder, harder now, until Sugar finally turned around.

But Kelvin didn't sound so calm anymore. Sugar heard something new in his voice; it was a little bit higher, more urgent. His seat was pulled forward now and both hands were gripping the wheel.

There was another stop sign coming up and Kelvin didn't seem to be slowing down. Just as he reached the intersection, he accelerated and Sugar felt the rear end of the car swing out behind them. He heard the engine rev and the tires spin, searching for traction on the icy road.

They turned the corner going way too fast and just as Sugar thought they would spin out, the tires caught and they were flying. He recoiled in his seat as the blinding white lights turned the corner behind them and got bigger, brighter, closer. They were shining through the windshield, reflecting off the mirrors, filling the interior of the car. When the lights couldn't possibly get any bigger, any brighter, any closer, they were accompanied by flashes of red and

43

blue and the piercing scream of sirens.

*   *   *

Gerald slowed down and dropped back as they approached Gilbert Park. He hit the wipers, the big white flakes disintegrating like ashes at the edge of a fire. The Infiniti was still going right around the speed limit, the driver no doubt aware of the cruiser on his tail. The roads were getting icy now, a slick layer of frozen snow overlaying the pavement. As the car in front of him continued forward, closing in on a stop sign now, it didn't appear to be slowing down. No brake lights, no turning signal.

Gerald felt a familiar quiver in his gut and tightened his grip on the steering wheel. The car was only a few feet from the intersection now, still no sign of stopping. As the car reached the corner, Gerald saw a quick flicker of red lights and watched as the car's back tires slid out, shooting a wave of snow into the air, the car ending up perpendicular to the cruiser in the middle of the intersection. Tires still spinning, it straightened itself out and shot to the right, one second in the intersection, the next second gone.

Gerald felt his heart jump and hit the gas, taking the turn wide, using the emergency brake for added control. When he next saw the Infiniti, it was smaller and fainter, its lights dimmer. It had gained more than a full block on them and seemed to still be accelerating. Gerald floored it and leaned forward in his seat, locked his eyes on the fading taillights.

"How bout now, Nick? This reason enough to pull him over?"

"Oh yeah," Nick said, sitting up straight with his palms on the dash, his voice tinged with excitement. "Do it."

Gerald didn't even try to hide his excitement as he hit the misery lights.

Chapter 10

The Infiniti's engine was humming at a higher pitch now, the urgency of its tone increasing in time with the glowing RPM needle. The snow outside was swirling in all directions, dizzying and disorienting. Sugar watched his neighborhood pass by in a blur; the houses and the lights were smeared and surreal, like some trippy abstract painting.

Pull over, he wanted to scream. Give it up, I can't stand this anymore, what have you gotten us into, let me out. But his tongue was heavy and his throat dry, his lips glued together with fear.

There was a parked car up ahead, the reflection of the Infiniti's headlights bouncing off its bumper, getting closer by the second. At the last possible moment, Kelvin jerked the wheel and Sugar's mirror cleared the rear corner of the parked car by a couple of inches. Sugar closed his eyes and gripped the sides of his seat. He felt the tires slide and the rear of the vehicle rock back and forth several times before Kelvin regained control.

"I'm pulling over up here," Kelvin said. "When I stop the car, get out and run. I'll go that way, you go through there."

He was pointing at a row of houses to Sugar's right.

"If they catch you, you weren't with me." His voice was firm and controlled.

Sugar couldn't think straight. He felt as though his mind were separate from his body, that he was watching all of this from some hidden level of his consciousness. He could see himself, but couldn't feel his body, as if his head was floating and his limbs were detached from the rest of him. All he could feel was his heart, pulsing, rushing, racing.

The police lights had faded, the sirens were background noise. All he could hear was the incessant drumming between where his ears should have been.

He glanced over at Kelvin and saw his thin face glowing red, his cheekbones gleaming with fresh sweat. His jaw and his eyes were set like concrete, unflinching. Without warning, he wrenched the steering wheel again and reached for the e-brake. Sugar felt the car buckle and begin to slide. Through the windshield he could see the world spinning, white in every direction, a flash of light, more white. Then a thud. The jolt snapped Sugar's head against the passenger window and for a moment his world went black. He opened his eyes to a blast of cold air and blurry lights.

Kelvin was gone. Across the street already, head down, shoulders hunched, the white soles of his sneakers kicking up snow as he ran. He cut across a yard, slipped between two houses and disappeared. Sugar was alone.

The cop car had come to a stop, ten or fifteen feet back. The strobe of red and blue sliced through the dark of the night, hazy behind the falling snow. For a moment the cruiser just sat there, Sugar knowing he had to get out, but his limbs not listening. Finally, the driver's side door of the cruiser swung open, followed by the passenger's.

Sugar focused on the door handle next to him. He pulled it until he felt the door pop open, pushed it until he felt another rush of frigid air. He finally willed his body out of the car and allowed the adrenaline that had been gathering in his bones to take over.

Chapter 11

Crouched behind a shrub, Sugar looked around the empty backyard. He was out of breath and his body felt as if it was about to explode. A rotting fence surrounded the yard, the slats too high to see what was on the other side. His house was only about a block away, he knew, but to get there he'd have to risk going back to where they'd ditched the car. Where the cops were.

He ran his hand along the fence until he felt a latch. The wood was stiff and groaned as he pushed the gate open. He found himself in a back lane covered with a frosty layer of fresh snow. Before he could decide which way to go, he heard the crunch of snow behind him.

Shit, Sugar thought. He hadn't closed the gate behind him. He scrambled to his right, trying to stay in the shadows along the fences and not slip. He kept his legs pumping, every second creating a little more distance between him and the yard. He ran harder, faster, fighting the urge to look back. He could hear someone shouting now, telling him to stop.

As he approached an intersection, Sugar hesitated and risked a look back. From what he could tell, the cop was tall and slim and definitely in good shape. He had to disappear. And fast.

He spotted a fenceless yard across the lane and decided to go for it. For a couple of seconds he'd be exposed, but he didn't have much choice. He took one more look back and began pumping his legs as hard as they'd move. Suddenly, just as he began to hit his stride, he hit a patch of ice and felt his left foot slip from under him. He landed on his side with a thud, his shoulder and hip smacking the pavement below. He winced at the pain and lay there for a moment. When he tried to get up he felt a slice of pain across his lower back and knew it was hopeless.

The cop was getting closer now, his shouts louder. Sugar slowly turned his head and saw a silhouette, dark against the fresh snowfall, maybe twenty feet away. But the figure wasn't running anymore. It was moving toward him in the middle of the lane, cautiously, one steady step at a time, the profile of an arm reaching out towards him.

Even with the adrenaline pumping, the pain in his leg and

shoulder was too intense for Sugar to stand up. He closed his eyes and he knew that at fifteen years old his life was over. He wouldn't be the first in his family to graduate high school, after all. He wouldn't get the chance to prove everybody wrong and make something of himself. He wouldn't ever know what it was like to have a girlfriend, or to have sex. This was it. Lying in the middle of a back alley. No way out.

Then he saw it. The butt of the gun, poking out of the muff of his hoodie. With all the anxiety and the fear over the past few minutes, he'd forgotten all about it. But there it was. Cold and hard and metallic.

Lying on his side, with his back to the cop but his head still facing him, Sugar reached into his hoodie and found the grip of the gun. He wrapped his fingers around the butt and felt a pulse against his palm, as if the gun was flowing with electricity. He shielded his abdomen beneath his free arm and pulled the gun from his hoodie. A glance over his shoulder told him the cop was only about ten paces away now.

"Stay right there, kid," the cop said. "Put your hands where I can see em." His voice was firm but somehow comforting. He sounded young.

Maybe it wouldn't be so bad to just give it up, Sugar thought. Maybe he'd get off easy. He wasn't the one who jacked the car, after all, wasn't the one who held up the driver. But he knew he couldn't tell them who he was with. Because no matter what else happened, Sugar Sinclair was no rat. He knew what happened to rats, and he'd be better off in jail. No, Sugar thought as he tightened his grip on the gun. This is the only way.

Sugar curled his finger around the trigger. In one quick motion he pulled the gun from under his left arm, aimed it in the direction of the cop, nowhere in particular, and squeezed. He panicked when it didn't fire immediately and squeezed harder. Finally he heard a loud pop and felt his arm jerk back. He watched as the cop's hand reached for his hip. Sugar squeezed the trigger again and again and again. Four shots, he heard Kelvin's words as he emptied the cartridge.

Sugar watched in horror as the cop crumpled to the pavement. He closed his eyes, tried to block out the ringing in his ears. Once again, he felt as though he was outside of himself, floating above the world like he was in a movie or a video game.

When he opened his eyes, the body was still there and everything was silent. He wasn't sure where he'd hit him, or how many times, but he knew the cop was dead. He looked like a wounded snow angel with his arms and legs spread across the ground, the pools of blood surrounding his motionless shoulders like wet tar. His gun lay by his side, black and shimmering under the light of the moon.

Sugar struggled to his feet, unable to put much weight on his left side. He shoved the gun back in his hoodie and looked around the alley, which seemed to go on forever in either direction. Both sides were lined with backyards and the odd detached garage. His left leg was throbbing now and he decided he had a better chance of hiding than running. About fifty yards ahead, he saw something.

He limped away from the dead cop, his body sore and heavy. When he reached his destination he pulled the green tarp back, revealing an old Ford sedan, its blue paint chipped and decimated by years of rust. Please be unlocked, he thought as he tugged on the handle. It stuck at first, but after a couple of pries it popped open. He slid onto the cold vinyl of the back seat feet first and pulled the door closed as quietly as possible. He cranked down the window a crack and pulled the tarp back down over the car, enveloping himself in complete darkness.

Chapter 12

Gerald crossed the icy road, one tentative step at a time, his Glock trained on the rear windshield of the Infiniti. Both doors were open, the faint interior light illuminating the snow surrounding the vehicle. The car appeared empty, but he didn't want to take any chances.

As he approached the car from behind, he could see it was still running. A small trail of grey exhaust spilled out of the chrome tailpipe and the engine hummed with the low, steady growl of a lion. He made his way around to the driver's side of the vehicle and peered inside. Empty. He holstered his gun and called for backup.

Slipping on a pair of gloves, he reached across the steering wheel and turned the car off. The interior was ripe with the potent smell of pot and a slight tinge of aftershave or cologne. He flipped on the overhead light and scanned the car with his flashlight. The back seats were empty, the shiny leather crisp and clean and looking as though they'd never been sat in. Nothing in the front seats, either. Poking out beneath the passenger side seat, however, he saw something black. A wallet. He circled the car and, leaning one knee on the cold, wet concrete, saw that it was open and its contents were spread across the floor. Some business cards, some memberships, and there, lying on the carpet, a driver's license with the same photo he'd seen on the computer. Clarence Sanford.

Gerald began to stand up when the beam of his flashlight caught something else, small and rectangular and metallic, beneath the driver's seat. Before he could walk around the car to check it out, he heard the shots. Four quick pops, all fired within a couple of seconds. Definitely a handgun. From the direction the passenger had gone, the direction Nick had gone. Gerald scrambled to his feet and reached for his gun.

He stood still and waited. No more shots. No screams. Nothing at all. He scanned the empty lawns and began to run in the direction the shots had come from, looking between the houses along the way. When he reached the end of the street, he turned right.

When he reached the alley he turned right again, and he saw it immediately. In the middle of the lane, not a hundred yards away, a

50

black corpse against the white of the snow. He couldn't make out much more than the shape and the size of the body, but he knew right away.

For a second Gerald's heart stopped. He stood there, staring down the lane, frozen. When he could finally move, he approached his partner's body and checked for a pulse he knew he wouldn't find. The body was still warm and there was blood everywhere. Nick's face was expressionless, his eyes still open and his mouth slightly agape. His skin was drained and gaunt, its whiteness in stark contrast to the pools of blood surrounding it. His gun was by his side.

From what Gerald could tell, he'd been hit twice. There was a dime-sized hole in the front of his uniform, just above the heart. If that one didn't kill him, the other definitely would have. It was clean through his throat.

Chapter 13

Clarence was crossing the street when he heard the unmistakable crack of gunfire. First one shot, quickly followed by three more. He stopped in the middle of the road and looked in every direction. No people, no cars, no nothing. Nothing but snow.

He couldn't tell which direction the shots had come from, but they sounded close. He felt the blood rush through his arms and legs, felt his heart quicken, half expecting to hear more shots. None came. He heard a solitary dog bark in the distance and the streets returned to their eerie silence, as though nothing had happened.

He was getting closer to Natasha's now, within a couple blocks. Clarence picked up his pace, something in the back of his mind telling him he knew who had fired those shots. He put his head down and started to run, the clicking and echoing of his soles the only sound in the quiet streets.

*　　*　　*

In a state somewhere between shock and frenzy, Gerald allowed his instincts take over. He reported Officer Down to dispatch, scanned the area for footprints and, finding nothing but a fresh layer of snow where they would have been, began working his way down the back lane. Despite the chill of the night, sweat was rolling down the sides of his face and he felt alert and focused. When he reached the next crossroad, he glanced to his left and then his right. For a moment it looked clear, but he had to do a double take. There, almost a full block away, he saw motion.

Gerald crossed the road to the opposite sidewalk, moving as quickly and quietly as he could to keep up with the figure.

"Freeze!" Gerald yelled. "Put your hands up and stay where you are!"

The figure stopped, turned around.

"I said put your hands up! Now!" Gerald crossed the street again, his gun trained on what he could now see was a black man, tall and well built.

"Officer, I – "

"Now!" Gerald kept his gun pointed at the man's chest as he

moved towards him. He was about a head taller than Gerald and had forty or fifty pounds on him. He was well dressed – a black wool coat, black pants and shiny black dress shoes. His hands were at his sides and he was shouting.

Approaching him one careful step at a time, Gerald's initial instincts told him the guy was too old to be the driver of the car, and too big. But it was definitely the man from the computer screen, the man from the driver's license.

And Nick was dead. Lying in a pool of blood back there. It wasn't a time to take any chances.

*   *   *

The voice behind Clarence stopped him in his tracks. His first instinct was to run, but as the man got closer he could see it was a cop.

Thank God, Clarence thought.

"Officer," he said. "I – "

Cut off. The cop was yelling at him to shut up and get on his knees. Clarence could see now there was blood on the cop's uniform, and he had his gun out. He was holding it shoulder-high with both hands, the gleaming barrel aimed directly at his chest. What he noticed most though was the cop's eyes. Even in the dark, he could see dark grey eyes threatening to pull the trigger at any second.

"On your knees! Now!" The cop yelled as he moved towards him, gun still pointed, eyes still flashing. "Now!"

Clarence put his hands above his head and slowly kneeled on the cold concrete, one leg at a time, the wet snow soaking through the thin cotton of his pants. His eyes never left the cop.

"On your stomach!"

The cop was standing over him now, close enough to touch. Clarence could see he wasn't a tall man, five-ten maybe, but the veins in his neck bulged and the bulk of his shoulder muscles showed through his uniform.

"Officer," he said again, trying to remain calm but knowing his trembling voice betrayed him. "I'm just – "

"I said shut up and get on your stomach! I will not tell you

53

again!"

"But officer. My car – "

Clarence felt a stab of pain in his stomach and he fell to the sidewalk. Then a sharp blast across the side of his head and his world went black.

* * *

Gerald was standing over the black man now, kicking him again and again and again. You killed Nick, he thought with each boot. You killed my partner.

He kicked and kicked and didn't stop until he thought the black man might be unconscious. Through the sweat dripping down his face he could see that the man's arms no longer covered his face and his legs had stopped writhing.

He bent over the man and steadied himself on his knees, out of breath, the cold night air burning his throat with each greedy gasp. He wiped his face with the sleeve of his uniform and closed his eyes until the world was no longer spinning. There were sirens wailing in the distance now, no more than a couple of blocks away.

After rolling the man on to his stomach, Gerald dug his knee in the center of his back, applying as much pressure as he could. The man's lips twitched and there was the faint sound of his staggered breathing, but the man remained silent. Still mounting him, Gerald pressed the gun against the back of his head with one hand and unclipped the cuffs from his belt with the other. He pulled the man's arms behind his back and cuffed his wrists.

Gerald got to his feet and looked down at the man lying there, motionless, eyes closed, face smeared with fresh blood. It took everything he had to keep from smashing it in with his boot.

* * *

In the distance, Clarence could hear the muffled sound of voices. Everything around him seemed a million miles away. His face felt numb and there was a warm spot on his right cheek. He tried opening his eyes but they were too heavy. The voices grew clearer suddenly and he felt people grabbing at his limbs, pulling and lifting, but the darkness remained. When Clarence finally regained consciousness, sore and disoriented, the outside world around him cast in shadows, his hands were cuffed and he was in the back of a police car.

Chapter 14

Standing on the Reeses' doorstep, sweat seeping through his dirty, bloodstained uniform, Gerald couldn't rid his mind of Ruth Stevenson.

He could still remember with vivid clarity each of his seven house calls from over the years, but she was his first – and by far his worst. The single mother of a drug addict who'd been found face down in a ditch with his pants around his ankles, a belt around his neck and a needle in his arm.

He could still remember her face as it transformed from disbelief to utter anguish, as she battled through the denial and the bargaining stages, until finally succumbing to a fit of uncontrollable rage. And how she began throwing things, punching, hitting, kicking. And how he had let her. How that familiar feeling of guilt had consumed him again and he felt somehow at fault, somehow responsible for what had happened to her son. So he let her wail on him until she'd exhausted herself, absorbing every punch and every kick, crouched in the fetal position, his forearms shielding his face.

This house call, Gerald knew, would be even worse. He'd taken the long way to Nick's cozy suburban bungalow, driving ten under the speed limit on the empty freeway, agonizing for the entire thirty-minute ride over what he was going to say and how he was going to say it.

Nick's dead. No way. It's Nick…he was shot, he didn't make it. Not a chance. No matter how he said it, he couldn't make the words sound true.

But when Virginia Reese came to the door and saw him standing there, he didn't end up having to say anything. He could tell from her face that the moment she opened the door, she knew.

*   *   *

"How?"

They were sitting across the kitchen table from each other, Virginia leaning forward in her chair, hugging herself, not looking at Gerald or anything else in particular. It was the first either of them had spoken. Aside from the rhythmic dripping of the coffee maker, the house was silent.

Gerald looked up at her. Her long blond hair hung carelessly around her narrow face, which was damp with tears. Her normally blue eyes were cloudy and rimmed with red.

"He was shot."

She bowed her head and closed her eyes. A minute or so passed before she spoke again.

"How?"

"We were chasing a couple of suspects on foot. One of them must have had a gun."

Virginia sniffled, still not looking at him.

"Were you there?"

"I heard the shots from about a block away. By the time I got to him, he was – " Gerald paused and looked down before he finished his sentence. "He was already gone. I'm so sorry, Virginia." Gerald immediately regretted saying it, the words coming out so small, so meaningless.

"Did you catch him?" It was the first time she looked at him.

Gerald took his time, not sure how to answer. He remembered kicking the black man over and over and that it had taken all of his self-restraint to stop at that. Wanting so bad for it to be one of the guys from the Infiniti.

"Gerald?" Virginia was leaning forward, looking at him with hope in her eyes. "Did you catch him?"

Gerald reached across the table and took her hand in both of his. He looked her in the eyes and felt the duty to tell her what she wanted to hear.

"Yeah, Virginia, we did. We got him."

She squeezed his hand and closed her eyes.

"Thank you, Gerald," she whispered. "Thank you so much."

For a moment it looked as if she might start crying again, but after a quick shake of her head she stood up and walked over to the counter where she grabbed some mugs from a cupboard.

"Black?" she asked.

"Yeah," Gerald said as he looked at his watch. 1:45. "Thanks."

She brought over the two steaming cups and put one in front of him. When she was back in her seat on the other side of the table she let out a sigh.

"Did he suffer?"

Gerald pictured the hole in Nick's throat. All that blood. Even though he would have bled out quickly, it was unlikely he died instantly. He would have been in pain, probably in shock. Gasping frantically for air that just wouldn't come.

"No," Gerald lied.

She gave him a weak smile and sighed again.

Gerald reached for his cup and took a sip. The coffee was hot but tasteless.

"Jesus, Gerald. Being married to a cop, you always have this fear, you know, but you never really think it's possible. Every time I hear sirens, every time there's something on the news. Every time he's not home and the doorbell rings I think this is it, this time it's really happened." She paused and shook her head. "And this time…this time it's really happened."

Gerald remained quiet. He'd heard it a million times. Every time he was late getting home, Janet would be all over him. In the early years of their marriage it seemed to Gerald like a worried wife trying to come to grips with the danger of her husband's job. But over time it became more and more personal. Janet's concerns became more about her. How could he put her through this? How could he be so selfish? The rational discussions became heated arguments. Gerald became more defensive and eventually withdrew completely. She just didn't understand The Job. Nobody did.

He looked at Virginia sitting there, head down, eyes lost deep in her coffee mug, and couldn't help but think of his wife. She was probably sleeping this very moment. In a warm bed, lying on her left side and breathing softly the way she did. Her feet twitching every now and then the way they did. She'd be dreaming, maybe a soft smile across her lips. She'd be a million miles away from here, away from all of this.

"What am I gonna do? How am I gonna tell the kids?"

Gerald shook the thoughts of Janet and took another long sip of coffee.

The kids. They had been the ones that flashed through Gerald's mind when he first saw Nick's body lying there. Before Virginia, even. Casey and Abby. Four and two. Both born since

Nick had joined the department.

Gerald focused on a group of family pictures on a cabinet against the kitchen wall. Head shots of each of the kids and one of the whole family, together in a park somewhere. Or maybe their backyard. The sun shining and not a cloud in sight. They all looked so happy, big, natural smiles on all four faces. Nick and Virginia looking at each other, the kids straight into the camera. Both of them had dark features and looked more like their dad than their mom. Casey with those big brown eyes, his head tilted back, the same way Nick did when he laughed or smiled.

Damn it, Gerald thought as he looked away from the picture, tears of his own welling deep in his chest now. Damn it all.

He fended off the unexpected surge of emotion and looked back at Virginia, unable to meet her eyes. Her skin looked taut and there was no color left in her face. She was biting her lower lip and picking at her fingernails. He finally managed to speak for the first time in what seemed like hours.

"You're gonna tell them their daddy died a hero, doing the right thing. And even if he's not here anymore, he's proud of them and he loves them very much. He'll always love them."

Virginia closed her eyes. Her lower lip trembled and she covered her face with shaky hands, but to Gerald's surprise no more tears came. When the moment passed she slowly rose from her chair and Gerald knew it was time for him to go.

Chapter 15

Small and cramped and cold and dirty. The holding cell was exactly the way Clarence remembered it. He sat on the concrete floor with his back against the concrete wall, trying to slow his racing mind and figure out exactly how it was he had arrived here.

The suffocating stench of body odor and urine, not to mention the relentless pain in his head and ribs, wasn't making it any easier. Between the aching in his lungs when he inhaled and the burning when he exhaled, he wasn't sure which was worse. And though he hadn't seen it yet, he knew his face was a bloody, swollen mess. He could feel the golf ball-sized lump on his right temple and his jaw was stiff. The cold, metallic taste of blood was still fresh against his tongue.

The heavy fall of footsteps from the far end of the corridor broke Clarence away from his thoughts. He shifted tenderly to face the door of the cell and looked up to see two men on the other side of the steel bars. One, a guard, all smug and self-important with his pressed uniform and his over-sized ring of keys. The other just as tall as the guard and wearing a finely cut suit which he filled out rather well – his lawyer. His being black was of no surprise to Clarence; in fact, he would expect nothing less from Rodney. He was always going on about how brothers had to stick together. Especially in a racist city like Detroit, a racist country like America.

Rodney Gregg was Leslie's older brother and a long-time friend of Clarence. He worked in finance and Clarence had been sure he knew a quality lawyer. When Rodney picked up after a couple of rings, he said he'd have help on the way within minutes. No questions other than to ask Clarence where he was and if he was OK. That was Rodney. All business, all the time. Clarence thanked him and told him he'd fill him in tomorrow, when all this was over. Oh, and by the way, if Leslie happens to call, please, please don't say anything. Rodney hung up without answering and Clarence wasn't sure if he'd heard him.

"Clarence Sanford," said the suit with an extended hand. "Byron Sapp."

Clarence shook his hand through the bars while the guard flipped through the ring for the right key.

"Thanks for coming," Clarence said. "I really appreciate it."

"No problem. Anything for Rodney."

The guard led them down a narrow hallway lined with closed doors and put them in a room at the end. Other than a table and four folding metal chairs around it, the room was empty. Once inside, Sapp put his briefcase in the center of the table, turned to the guard and said, "Thank you. I'll have a moment alone with my client if you don't mind."

The guard appeared as if he was going to say something but stopped himself. Instead, he turned around and left the room without a word. Sapp turned to Clarence and seemed to be sizing him up. Clarence felt his gaze stop on his face, unsure what to say, waiting. Sapp seemed like a man who enjoyed being in control and that was fine with him. As long as it meant he'd be getting out of here as soon as possible.

Sapp took a step toward the open door and looked around the corner. Satisfied they were alone, he motioned for Clarence to take a seat in one of the chairs and closed the door behind him.

"How much have you told them?" he asked, still standing.

Clarence couldn't remember much of the ride but was pretty sure he couldn't have carried a conversation if he'd wanted to.

"Nothing."

"Have they questioned you yet?"

Clarence shook his head and looked down. "They haven't said more than two words to me. Just that I've been arrested. For murder." The words sounded surreal as he said them out loud.

"All right," Sapp said. "Tell me everything. From the beginning."

Clarence thought back to the point he'd been carjacked. From then on all he could remember with any clarity was doubling back to Natasha's, hearing gun shots and getting attacked by the cop. He remembered trying to tell the cop about his stolen car, but wasn't sure how much of it actually got out. He had been too scared to think straight. It wasn't so much the gun as it was the cop. He'd come out of nowhere, fresh blood smeared across his uniform and those greyish blue eyes flashing wild. That face was etched in Clarence's memory, burned there like a recurring nightmare.

"I had just been carjacked. I was thinking about what to do, who to call. Before I could figure it out this cop comes out of nowhere. He's waving his gun at me, telling me to get on the ground. He was crazy. I didn't know what – "

Sapp cut him off mid-sentence.

"I said from the beginning." He stared at Clarence like a disapproving father. "Listen, Clarence. I'm on your side here." He put his arms out to his sides as if to convince him of it. "But if I'm going to help you, I need to know everything. I need the truth."

Clarence nodded his head but found it suddenly difficult to look his lawyer in the eye. Instead he focused on Sapp's shoes. The polished leather looked out of place against the dull concrete floor. He swallowed hard, the aftertaste of blood filling his mouth.

"Look, Clarence." Sapp finally made his way over to the table and sat down. "What you say here is confidential. It's between you and me. You have my word."

"I was at a friend's," Clarence said. He looked up at Sapp, wondering if he understood his intentional vagueness. He could tell from the way his lawyer looked back at him that he did. He nodded his head, urging Clarence to continue.

"Anyway, she lives out in Crookston. I was actually there to tell her that we couldn't, ah, we couldn't be friends anymore. We ended up talking most of the night and it was getting late, so I left."

"What time was this?" Sapp now had a small notepad spread open across the table.

"Just after eleven, I think. No later than quarter past."

"And this friend. She can confirm this?"

Clarence felt like a scolded schoolboy who'd been caught cheating on a test. He nodded.

Sapp scribbled in his pad and raised his eyebrows. Clarence's cue to continue.

"So like I said, I get outside and walk over to my car. I get in and drive a couple blocks when this guy runs up to my car and starts waving a gun in my face. He tells me to get out of the car, takes my wallet. Then he tells me to face the wall and count to sixty."

"Did you get a good look at him?"

Clarence shook his head. "It all happened so fast. He was a young guy, black, dressed in dark clothes. He had a hood pulled over his head. From what I can remember he was tall, skinny."

"Was he by himself?"

Clarence shook his head again. "There was someone else, but I didn't get a good look at him. He was off to the side."

Sapp wrote as Clarence spoke.

"So anyway, I have no cellphone, no wallet, and all of a sudden I hear gun shots. Close. I start walking in the other direction and the next thing I know, this crazy cop starts yelling at me. He has his gun pointed at me and I swear to God he's ready to shoot."

"How much time has passed? From the time you left your friend's house to the time you see the cop."

Clarence tilted his head back and tried to remember. It had all happened so fast. "Fifteen minutes, maybe twenty."

"And this cop," Sapp said, taking a break from his scribbling. "Did you see where he came from? Was his gun already out or did he pull it when he saw you?"

All Clarence could remember was that the cop seemingly came out of nowhere. He was pretty sure the gun was already pulled though. He didn't recall seeing the cop reach for it. He said as much to Sapp.

"So the next thing I know," Clarence said, "I'm on the ground. This cop is above me, yelling at me to stay down. He's waving his gun and I'm thinking this is it. He's gonna kill me."

"Do you remember seeing anybody else this entire time? Anybody walking around, any other cops? Anything at all?"

Clarence shook his head.

"OK. Then what happened?"

"So I'm lying face down in the snow, not wanting to risk looking up. I'm trying to tell him about my car but he's not listening. He's just yelling and waving his gun around like a madman. And then he starts kicking me."

Sapp's eyes moved reflexively towards Clarence's head.

"Is it bad?" Clarence asked. He raised his hand to his temple, tenderly gauging the swelling with his fingertips.

"Pretty bad. Speaking of which," Sapp grabbed his briefcase and pulled out a small digital camera. "Go stand over there." He motioned toward the wall on the far side of the room.

Clarence took a few steps and Sapp put his hand up.

"Right there. Now turn your head to the left." He snapped a

couple of shots. The flash was strong and Clarence felt disoriented for a moment. "Any other visible marks? Bruises, cuts, anything like that?"

Clarence had checked earlier and found nothing superficial. "I don't think so," he answered. "My ribs feel like they might be broken, but there's no external bruising. Not yet, anyway."

"First thing tomorrow we'll have you examined. These animals are going to pay. We'll talk about that part of it later, though. For now we have to nail down the facts."

Clarence nodded and moved toward Sapp, leaned over his shoulder.

"Do you mind?" he said. "There's no mirrors in the holding cell." Sapp pressed some buttons on the camera and showed him the tiny screen. Clarence looked at the bump above his eye and gingerly ran his finger across it.

"So then what happened?" Sapp said.

Clarence sat down again and closed his eyes, trying to recall what had happened next. "I must have blacked out at some point. All I remember is being kicked over and over."

He remembered the vulnerability he'd felt during the onslaught of the cop's boots to his head and body. Feeling dominated and defenseless.

"The next thing I know, I'm in the back of a cop car. My hands are cuffed and I have no idea what's going on. It all seemed like a dream."

Sapp shook his head and gave Clarence a look somewhere between sympathy and pity.

"I was in and out of consciousness for most of the ride," Clarence continued. "By the time we got here, I still wasn't exactly sure what was happening. I knew I'd been arrested and that we were at the police station, but not much more."

Once inside, he remembered handing over all of his possessions – a couple singles and some loose change from one of his coat pockets, a half-empty pack of Mentos. He was fingerprinted and had his picture taken. All of the awful memories from the first time he was booked flooding back and Clarence telling himself repeatedly that was ancient history, part of another life. Before he'd gone straight. Before Leslie, before the kids.

"Had they read you your rights at this point? Told you what the charges were?"

Clarence nodded his head. He remembered there had been two officers with him. Both were around thirty with medium builds and short brown hair. They could have been brothers. Clarence asked them what he was being arrested for. Murder, they told him. He wasn't sure he heard them right and had to ask again. Murder, they said. Same thing we told you twenty minutes ago. And since you can't seem to remember anything, you also have the right to remain silent. Anything you say can and will be used against you in a court of law.

"When they told me I was being arrested for murder I thought for sure it had to be a dream. I mean, murder?"

Sapp hesitated before asking his next question and, for the first time since meeting him, Clarence thought his lawyer seemed nervous.

"Clarence," he began. "It isn't just murder you've been charged with." He paused again. "Did they tell you who you're accused of killing?"

Clarence shook his head. They hadn't told him anything more. Not that he could remember, anyway. The way Sapp was tiptoeing around it though, he wasn't sure he wanted to know. In the silence that followed, the steady background buzz of the overhead lights seemed louder. He could swear he heard his heart beating in his chest.

Sapp cleared his throat. Then, "You're being charged with the murder of a police officer, Clarence. This is a very serious allegation."

For the second time in less than an hour, Clarence felt like he was stuck somewhere between a nightmare and a Law & Order episode. A police officer? He was too jarred to ask any questions. He stood up and walked aimlessly around the room. Feeling weak in the knees, he returned to the table, put his head down and planted his face in his hands. He'd never felt so defeated in his life and he hadn't even done anything wrong.

Though he knew that wasn't entirely true. His thoughts turned to Leslie and he felt another stab of helplessness.

When he'd been put in the room with the telephone and told he had one call, she should have been the easy first choice. He knew deep down that she would probably still be up, sitting with her back against the headboard and a book spread open across her arched knees, waiting for him to get home. But no. He knew that if he called Leslie there would be too many questions with answers he didn't want to give.

Now, here he was. Sitting in an interview room at the Eighth Precinct with Byron Sapp, the lawyer friend of his brother-in-law. He'd been charged with the murder of a police officer, the throbbing in his head and the aches in his body getting worse by the minute.

"So what do we do now? How are you gonna get me out of here?"

"In a couple minutes we'll go to the interview room. They'll ask you some questions, probably the same ones over and over again. Try not to let it get to you and just tell them what you told me. From what you've said there can't be a whole lot of evidence against you."

"Then what?"

"They'll have to decide if they're going through with the charges. If not, you're free to go."

"And if they do go through with them?"

"Then," Sapp said, "you'll be arraigned. They'll formally charge you and we'll enter our plea. Not guilty, of course."

Clarence stared at the wall, empty except for a marked-up calendar and a round white clock that read 2:50. He was pretty sure the answer to his next question wasn't the one he was hoping for. Maybe he was looking for something to hold against Sapp, a way to relegate some of the guilt he was feeling to somebody else. Or maybe he just needed to hear it to believe it.

"Will I get to go home tonight?"

Sapp repositioned himself in his chair. He straightened his lips and averted his eyes. His head shook from side to side ever so slightly.

"If," he began, "and believe me Clarence, this is a big if. But if you're charged? Unfortunately, you'll be spending the night in jail."

Chapter 16

When Sugar got home, the digital clock on the microwave said three-fifteen. The scene waiting for him was the same as it was every other Wednesday, aka Welfare Day. The kitchen and living room were littered with empty beer cans and two-for-one pizza boxes. The air was stuffy and thick with the familiar smell of cigarette smoke and microwave popcorn. The TV in the corner of the room emitted a barely audible hum, the laugh track of some old comedy rerun.

And there, sprawled across the old red sofa, was his mother. As usual, more passed out than she was asleep. One arm pinned beneath her body and the other hanging off the side of the sofa, dangling like a rope, her chipped red fingertips grazing the dirty beige carpet.

Sugar stepped around the mess and turned off the TV. In the silence of the room he could hear Ma's breathing, heavy and unsteady. He grabbed a grey wool blanket off one of the chairs and laid it across her motionless body. The bitter coldness of the night had snuck in through the thin walls and the old windows and given the whole place an airy chill. As he reached across her body, he could smell the stale odors of beer and smoke on her hair and skin. He tucked her in tight and moved her head beneath another blanket he'd rolled up as a pillow. She groaned as he moved her head, but her eyes remained closed. He kissed her on the cheek and made his way up the stairs.

As Sugar flicked on his bedroom light and swung the door closed, he caught a glimpse of himself in the mirror. The reflection was blurred by fatigue, the face staring back at him reminding him of someone he once knew but hadn't seen for ages. He searched the dark brown eyes, looked for an answer that refused to come; all that stared back at him was hollow darkness and the piercing glare of shrunken pupils. He shook his head and gave up, made his way toward his bed.

Taking the gun from the pouch of his hoodie, he cupped it in his hands, as if it were a wounded bird. He'd thought about ditching it somewhere along the way home, but couldn't bring himself to touch it, preferring to convince himself it didn't exist. But now, alone in the silence, its presence filled the room. There it was. The gun that he'd found on the top shelf of Reggie's closet, the gun that at the beginning of the night had four bullets in it, and now had none. The gun that was so recently foreign to Sugar, but seemed now like it had been a natural part of him for as long as he could remember, an extension of his body.

He finally grabbed the empty shoebox, placed the gun inside and slid it under his bed. He turned off his light, stripped off his damp clothes and fell back on his lumpy mattress. He lay there in the darkness, his body numb and exhausted, unable to slow his mind long enough to think straight.

When the room finally stopped spinning, he tried desperately to convince himself it was all a dream, that the entire night was some horrible nightmare that was finally coming to an end. He fought the visions of the gun, the body, the blood, forced them out of his mind until they were nothing but colorless outlines, shades of grey in his subconscious. He climbed under the covers and told himself that tomorrow everything would be OK. That the next time he opened his eyes everything would be back to normal.

Chapter 17

Gerald stood in front of his open refrigerator and stared inside. The last time he ate was around suppertime the day before, going on twelve hours now, but he didn't feel hungry. He was too drained, too exhausted to even think about food. The weight of the day was beginning to settle at the base of his neck, the dull throb extending to his temples and his back and his shoulders. Flashes of a battered woman in a closet, a car chase through the suffocating snow, Nick's lifeless body, a massive black man lying defenseless on the ground, all cycled through his mind in heavy rotation, vivid and relentless.

There was still something in those replays of arresting the suspect that stirred up an unsettling feeling inside of him, scratching at his subconscious. But as the late hours of the night made way for the early hours of the day, and he grew wearier, the feeling was becoming easier to ignore.

Nick was dead. Nothing else mattered.

He grabbed a tin of tomato juice and poured himself a full glass. The drive home had been a blur. All he could remember were the all-night party stores he'd driven past. The neon lights and flashing signs enticing him, tempting him to pick up a bottle and enter a state of oblivion, offering him an escape from the fog that had so completely consumed him over the past several hours.

Gerald hadn't had a drink in almost six months. Not that he was one of those pathetic saps who marked the days on a calendar or carried around a bottle cap attached to his key chain or anything like that. But the day he'd stopped drinking was as clear to him as his own birthday, burned deep in his mind. July 23, 2005. It was the day his life as he knew it was stolen from him. The day that had ruined him far more than any amount of alcohol ever could.

Gerald closed the fridge and flinched. Staring at him, smiling at him, was a photo of Janet.

It's all your fault.

The last words his wife had said to him before she left. The words that seemed to come out of nowhere but had been building up for longer than he'd like to admit. Just waiting there, perched at the tip of her tongue, ready to pounce at a moment's notice.

Deep down, on some level, he had been expecting them. And

then they came. Janet, standing at the front door, the green of her eyes washed over with grey and downcast in defeat, her small, pained voice barely above a whisper.

It's all your fault.

Gerald couldn't remember exactly what had happened next, just that she was gone and he was alone. It must have been planned though. Her red canvas suitcase was already packed and she was out the door before he had a chance to say anything. What would he have said? What could he have said?

He'd simply watched out the window as her sister's minivan reversed down the driveway and disappeared at the stop sign at the end of his street. That was nine days ago. He hadn't heard from her since.

Tomato juice in hand, Gerald turned his back on the memories and wondered when he had begun feeling like a stranger in his own home. There was the new fridge, the new stove, the new dishwasher, all in spotless stainless steel; the new granite countertops, complete with matching backsplash; the dark chestnut floor, newly finished and sleek as a skating rink. All of it so sterile and cold beneath the overhead lights.

Standing there, alone in fifteen hundred square feet of emptiness, he was overcome with a sudden sense of isolation. Like he was the last man on earth, trapped in this oversized kitchen with appliances and countertops he didn't want and didn't need. For the first time he was able to see his kitchen, his house, his entire life, for what they truly were: one big distraction. Upgrade after upgrade, project after project, all the while trying to make their house feel more like a home without their son. Trying to overcompensate for his being gone with all of these things. As if Charlie could simply be replaced by a crystal chandelier or a teak wood dinette set.

Gerald downed the rest of his juice and placed the glass on the countertop. The clang of glass against granite reminded him it was all real. This night had really happened. He was still alone. All of these things were still here. His son still wasn't.

He killed the kitchen light and walked past the bathroom and into the laundry room. He stripped off his uniform shirt, sodden with sweat and damp snow and crusted blood. Nick's blood. Or maybe the black man he'd stomped. Maybe a bit of both. Along with his pants, his socks and a generous pour of liquid detergent, he tossed the shirt in the washer, set the dial to hot, dropped the lid shut and hit the Start button.

He made his way back down the hall, through the dark dining room and up the hardwood stairs, his heavy hollow steps echoing off the walls. When he got to the top, he walked slowly toward the first door on the left.

Since the day Charlie had gone missing, Gerald had entered his bedroom exactly once. It was the Sunday afternoon, eight days later. Gerald could remember the day because he'd just come home from church for the last time. And also because it was the day he decided to accept that he'd never see his son again.

While Janet and most of his family and friends still had hope, his was swallowed up in a sea of search parties and television interviews and replaced with the acceptance that Charlie was gone forever. When Gerald had entered his only son's room that day, he did so believing it would be the first step in the healing process. That seemed like forever ago now, and he didn't feel any further along today than he did the day after it happened.

The doorknob felt cold to Gerald's touch, and a familiar uncertainty passed through his veins. He got the sense that he was embarking upon a journey he didn't know if he'd return from, one he didn't know if he wanted to return from.

He waited a moment before turning it all the way, fighting off the memories as fast as they came.

Like when he used to come in here to tuck Charlie in and he'd be under the covers, blanket pulled up to just below his chin, bedside lamp still burning. Like in the later years when he already had his eyes closed, Gerald knowing he was pretending to sleep but not letting on because he could remember doing it himself as a kid and understood there were certain times you just didn't want to talk to your parents, or sometimes people in general. Like the rare time he'd climb up on his bed with him and read him a story or tell him about something that happened at work he thought his son might find interesting or cool. Like the nights he'd open his door a crack, long after he'd fallen asleep, and just watch him.

Gerald entered the room and stood for a moment in the darkness. The curtains were pulled tight across the double window on the far wall, the only light the faint glow from the hall light behind him. It cast an ominous shadow across the carpet, dividing the room in two. One side was bathed in eerie dimness, the other in complete and utter blackness. When he flicked on the lamp it was like turning on the light to a whole other world.

Gerald and Janet had decided after some time had passed to leave the room exactly as it was. Not as a memory, Janet insisted, but so it's ready for him when he comes back. For Gerald, it was a form of denial. Even though he knew his son wasn't coming back, keeping the room the same would make it seem like it never happened.

The yellow walls were, like Gerald's growing up, covered in sports paraphernalia: team pennants, wrinkled posters, cards of various players from various sports, mini hockey sticks hanging from nails, a plastic basketball hoop taped to the back of the door. The Red Wings, the Tigers and the Pistons were all equally represented; like the rest of the city, Charlie had no use for the Lions anymore. On top of the toy chest at the foot of his bed, atop of a red and white crocheted blanket Janet's mother had made for him, sat his aluminum baseball bat and the old leather mitt Gerald had passed down to him.

To Gerald's left was Charlie's bed. A twin mattress beneath a thin comforter adorned with red and blue race cars and a slightly heavier one, plain blue, folded at the foot. On the back wall, under the window, sat a dresser and a desk in matching oak. The tops of both were tidy and free of clutter, just the way Charlie liked it. His computer sat on one side of the desk, a short stack of CDs on the other, the rolling chair tucked neatly underneath.

To the right of the room was a closet with a sliding door, one half open, revealing Charlie's clothes. Colored T-shirts hung from plastic hangers, along with coats for the different seasons and some button-up shirts he'd wear for family gatherings and school picture days. And there, in the middle of the closet, Charlie's most prized possession. The Red Wings hockey sweater Gerald had gotten him the Christmas before he disappeared. The name Yzerman and the number nineteen stitched across the back.

Thinking about his son now, it was hard for Gerald to picture his son wearing anything else. And he knew the only reason he wasn't wearing it the last day he saw him was because of the weather. Normally it wouldn't matter – summer or winter, rain or shine – that jersey would be on Charlie's back. But that day the heat had been unbearable. Gerald could still remember the blaze of the early morning sun, pushing the temperature to eighty before it had even broken the horizon.

Head spinning, Gerald sat at the edge of the bed. Not even six months ago, his family had been pared down from three to two, and now it was down from two to one. He'd managed to create another casualty. In that room of dissolution and neglect, the loss of Janet suddenly struck him harder than it had in the days since she left. The burden of his mistakes were suddenly heavier, the sting of her departing words suddenly sharper.

It's all your fault.

Gerald extinguished the bedside lamp as he had done for his son so many times and collapsed. As his back gave way to the cushion of the mattress, he wished it would swallow him whole, suck him away into some black hole or some void in the universe where mistakes were forgotten and regret didn't exist. A place with no memory. Maybe Janet would be there, and Charlie too, and things would be the way they used to be. Before the mistakes. Before the regret. Before the blame.

He closed his eyes and allowed himself to be taken over by the unfamiliar darkness of the unfamiliar room. Suddenly cold, he pulled the blankets up to his chin and prayed for the darkness to take him away.

Chapter 18

The interview room was small and stuffy. Three of the pale white walls were bare, the other taken up by a large rectangular two-way mirror. Clarence and Sapp sat on one side of the old wooden table, two detectives in white shirts and dark ties on the other. Clarence was by far the biggest of the four men in the room, but under the illumination of the overhead fluorescent lights and the scrutinizing gazes of the two detectives, he felt frail and vulnerable.

The homicides had already introduced themselves, explained that Clarence was being investigated as a possible suspect in the murder of one of Detroit's finest and offered Clarence a drink. Coffee, soda, whatever he wanted. Very casual about it all. Both men seemed subdued and in no hurry, as if they had nothing better to do at three in the morning.

They'd started by asking Clarence where he'd been on the night in question. Less than four hours ago, and the detectives were already referring to it as the "night in question." One of them did most of the talking. His name was Clifford and he was the bigger of the two. White, mid-thirties, average looking, his only distinguishable feature a sliver of white scar tissue at the corner of his mouth. He wore a gold-plated watch and a gold wedding band on his left hand. He leaned back in his chair and offered a big toothy smile from time to time.

The other guy was about the same age, but Clarence couldn't remember his name. Something Hispanic. Short black hair and a compact build, all muscle and testosterone. His rolled up shirt sleeves revealed the hairiest forearms Clarence had ever seen and he had at least a couple days' worth of dark stubble on his face. He was leaning forward, his elbows on the table, his intense eyes focused squarely on Clarence.

"And where did you say it was you were coming from?" Clifford, the white one, asked.

As he did with Sapp, Clarence hesitated, searching for a way to avoid the question. Finding none, he told them about Natasha and, with some prompting and prodding, the nature of their relationship. The looks the detectives gave him – disappointment from Clifford, disgust from the Hispanic – compounded his shame to the point that he couldn't look at either of them.

"And this lady friend," Clifford said, looking sidelong at his partner. "How long were you…how long was this going on?"

"A couple months," Clarence said to the table.

"A couple months. And this lady friend?" Another furtive glance at his partner. "She'd corroborate all this?"

Despite his innocence, Clarence felt nervous. It was as though they were trying to trap him somehow, make him change his story or mess up a detail. He nodded.

"Sorry, the tape recorder couldn't hear you. That's a yes?"

"Yes."

"OK, so let me get this straight. You're over at this Natasha's place, you leave shortly after midnight. After a night of…talking. You're driving home, minding your own business, next thing you know you're getting carjacked by two kids with a gun. They make you get out of the car, they take your wallet, and you're left standing there while they take off in your car. So far, so good?"

Clarence nodded.

The detectives stared at him, waiting.

"Yes." Clarence's voice felt raw in the dryness of the room and he regretted not asking for a water. Requesting it now would show weakness.

"OK." Clifford turned a page in his notebook and clicked his pen. "Then what happened?"

Clarence took his time, not wanting his anxiety and discomfort to come through in his answers. He turned and saw their reflections in the mirror. Four dark figures, still as statues. He wondered if anyone was on the other side, figured there probably was.

"I decided to go back to Natasha's and call for a cab. I had no cellphone, no cash. I didn't know where else to go."

"So you're walking back to Natasha's. It's what now, twelve-fifteen, twelve-thirty?"

Clarence shrugged. "Sounds about right."

"Then what?"

"So I'm just walking along, almost jogging. It's cold out and it's late and I just want to get home. All of a sudden this guy, this cop, comes out of nowhere and starts yelling at me to get down."

"How'd you know it was a cop?" Clifford was still asking the questions, the other detective still staring a hole through Clarence.

"At first I didn't. Then I saw the uniform, the gun. I tried to tell him about my car but he just kept yelling at me, telling me to shut up and get on the ground." Clarence shuddered at the memory of how close he'd felt to death when the gun was aimed at him.

There was a moment of silence in the room, Clifford leaning back in his chair with his arms folded across his chest. The partner was still propped on his elbows, looking both threatening and bored. Clarence wasn't sure if he was supposed to keep going or wait for the next question. A part of him felt like they were toying with him, like a pair of cats playing pass with a dying mouse.

"Why'd you try and run?" Clifford finally asked.

"Run?" Clarence looked at both detectives, then at Sapp.

"When Officer Dawes initially approached you in the street he told you to stop, to stay where you were." Clifford looked at his partner. Hispanic didn't notice; his eyes were still fixed on Clarence. "So why'd you run?"

Clarence raised his hands in disbelief. He looked at Sapp again, back at Clifford. "I didn't."

"That so?"

"Yeah," Clarence said, a little hotter than he'd intended. "He was yelling at me to get down from across the street and I got down."

Clifford folded his hands on the table and nodded, took his time leaning forward.

"Can I tell you something, Clarence?" He didn't wait for a response. "I've been doing this a long time, man. I mean, a really long time. And in my experience? The more honest you are up front, the better things are gonna be for you in the long run.

"Alex and me," he shot his thumb towards his partner, "we got all night. In fact, we're getting paid O.T. to be here right now." He leaned back again, and pointed his index finger in Clarence's direction. "But you? You got one opportunity. One chance to come clean and answer our questions and cut the bullshit."

"But I – "

Clifford cut him off. "We know you tried to run, we know you resisted arrest." He motioned toward Clarence with a bob of his head. "How do you explain that nasty bump on your head? You think our officers just go around hitting people on a whim? You didn't try and resist arrest, how'd your face end up lookin like you went ten rounds with a heavyweight?"

At that moment Clarence realized with dreadful clarity that it was his word against a cop's; he didn't stand a chance. He clenched his jaw and it sent a shock of pain through his temples. There was a deep burning in his chest, like it was ready to explode. He held his tongue and looked over at Sapp, who hadn't said much of anything since they'd entered the room.

Meeting Clarence's eyes and likely reading the helplessness there, Sapp cleared his throat and spoke.

"I appreciate you boys trying to get the facts straight, really I do. But we've been in here almost half an hour now and you have yet to present one piece of evidence implicating my client for the crime of which he's been accused. Unless you are willing, or more to the point, able to bring forth some evidence, I think it's time we all move along here. You've wasted enough of my client's time already. He has a family to get home to."

"Yeah." It was the Hispanic detective speaking for the first time. "We can see your client here is a real family man. Rendezvousing at all hours of the night with lady friends."

Clarence felt the detectives' eyes pierce his body, a new wave of vulnerability washing over him.

"Now, now Alex," Clifford said. "Maybe when you're married you'll understand that sometimes you need a little something on the side just to keep you sane. You get tired of the home cooking once in a while, ain't that right Clarence?"

Clifford continued, turning toward Sapp.

"And Mr. Sapp. Since you seem so intent on evidence," he looked down at the notebook in front of him, circled something with his pen and turned the pad towards Clarence. "This number mean anything to you?"

Clarence recognized his license plate number immediately and sighed. "It's like I told you. My car was stolen."

"Right," Alex said, snapping his fingers. "The kids with the gun."

"Look," Clifford said. "Let's try this a different way.

"Our officer says he saw two men get out of the vehicle, your vehicle, and run. Maybe this other guy, whoever it is you're with? Maybe he's the shooter. But as it stands right now, all we got is gunshots, the body of a police officer and your car. Try and see this from our side, Clarence."

"Who were you with, Clarence?" Alex again. "Help yourself out here. Give us a name."

Clarence looked down at his lap and tried to control his breathing. Fortunately Sapp spoke up before he was forced to.

"This is ridiculous," Sapp said. "You can't even prove my client was in the car."

"Physical description," Clifford said. "Both men who ran from the car were identified as black males. One short, the other tall." He sized Clarence up. "Looks like the glove fits."

"Circumstantial at best," Sapp said. "And definitely not enough to charge my client with murder."

"Eye witness testimony," answered Clifford, a smug look of complacency on his face. "We both know how valuable it is in the courtroom, counsellor. Especially that of a credible source. A police officer, say."

Clarence sat there in silence, only half listening to the back and forth banter between his lawyer and the detectives. He was preoccupied with the sinking realization that he would be spending the night in jail. Hard as he tried though, he was unable to conjure the hate and the anger that he knew he was supposed to be feeling. Over the past couple of hours, he'd been a victim of police brutality, wrongful arrest and undue process. He thought about the cop with the fury in his eyes, the kicks to the head, the handcuffs, the taste of blood in his mouth, but it was no use. All he could think about was Leslie; all he felt was guilt and shame.

"What about motive? Something more substantial?" Sapp was saying now, the intensity of his voice at a level Clarence had yet to hear. "The murder weapon, maybe? You're grasping for straws here and you know it."

"As for motive, it's obvious. Your client didn't want to be arrested again. I'm sure he told you about his record." Clifford glanced at his notes and continued. "Possession with intent to distribute, resisting arrest. Another charge looks bad, so he shoots the cop chasing him. No arrest, no problem. Except he gets caught.

Big problem."

Clarence had not, in fact, divulged the information of his previous arrest to Sapp, so he was surprised when his lawyer addressed it.

"First of all, the arrest of which you speak was fourteen years ago. My client is a reputable and contributing member of his community with no history of violence. Your motive is razor thin. You may be able to keep him over night, but the judge will release him at the arraignment." Sapp began gathering his papers and looked apologetically at Clarence.

"Speaking of which," he said, "I would like to request it be expedited, based on the seriousness of the charge."

Clifford glanced back down at his notepad. "Scheduled for ten thirty tomorrow morning." He got Clarence's attention and winked. "You better get some sleep, Clarence. It's been a long night."

Both detectives smiled as they stood up. They waited until Clarence and Sapp exited the room and followed them out, closing the door behind them. Clarence dragged his feet down the long narrow hallways and past the other interview rooms with his head down, ignoring Sapp's words of encouragement.

He reached his holding cell and walked inside, waited for the clang of the steel bars behind him and the patter of the jailer's footsteps to disappear down the concrete corridor. When he was finally alone, he fell to his knees and began to cry.

Chapter 19

Natasha Stokes laid a stack of crumpled bills on the ticket counter. Fifty-two dollars in all; the amount for a one-way trip to Cincinnati. Waiting for her ticket to be printed, she glanced at the clock above the clerk's shoulder and felt the sudden need to yawn. Just after 7 a.m. and she hadn't been to sleep yet. With shaky hands she took the envelope from the girl behind the counter, picked up her single duffel bag and made her way through the empty lobby of the terminal to her platform.

As she leaned back against the steel bench, Natasha could feel the weight of the previous night in her bones. After Clarence had left, she'd sat on her couch in stunned silence for what seemed like hours. First came the denial, followed by the anger. She had been somewhere between self-pity and acceptance when she heard the gunfire, the four pops jolting her from her seat.

The sound of shots in her neighborhood was common enough, but these ones were close. By the time her fear had passed and she managed to get up and look out the front window, the street was quiet again and all she could see was the white snow, falling from the sky and covering the streets like confetti. Probably just some kids playing around with a gun, she figured, settling quickly back into her seat on the sofa.

Over the next several hours, Natasha had waged war with the thoughts in her head. Maybe Clarence leaving her was a sign to get out of Detroit once and for all, the catalyst she had been waiting for, the spark that could ignite her new life. Then again, maybe it was just bad luck, another bump in the road. One of those life lessons you were supposed to learn from. She paced from room to room, knocking off the remaining beers from the six-pack in her fridge as she went.

One minute she'd be packing her bags, the next she'd be emptying them. One minute she'd be circling cities on a map, the next she'd be throwing the map across the room. Three hours and four beers later, it came down to a coin toss. Heads she would stay, tails she was gone. Who was she, anyway, to make an important life decision like that? Twenty-five years old, and what did she have to show for it? A part-time job in a dirty diner making minimum wage and measly tips; an old decrepit hand-me-down house from her long-dead grandfather; a handful of failed relationships and no real friends to speak of. No, she thought. Your way has gotten you nowhere.

She leaned against the kitchen table and rested the quarter on her thumb and stared at it for a moment before flicking it. She watched as it rotated through the air and landed with a solid ping on the hardwood floor by her feet and rolled beneath the kitchen table. She let it lay there for a moment, trying to decide which she was hoping for. After a couple of minutes, she realized she honestly didn't care either way. She crouched down, placing a hand on a chair to steady herself, and reached for the quarter. Staring up at her, in the dimness of the kitchen, was the profile of an American eagle. Wings spread wide, talons gripping a scroll.

Her last couple hours in the only house she could remember ever living in went by slowly. She packed a red and black YMCA gym bag with as many clothes and toiletries and books as she could. What didn't fit, she left behind, sentencing her unwanted belongings to grow old and perish with the rest of the memories there.

She took a final walk around the place, looking at everything a little bit differently knowing it was the last time she'd ever see them. She noticed things she never had in the thousands of times she'd walked by them: the small crack in the lower left corner of the bathroom mirror, the slight rattle coming from the heat register in the main hallway, the faint smell of shoe polish coming from the front closet. She wrote a letter to her sister and left it on the kitchen table. Finally, she sat on the old blue reclining chair her grandfather used to fall asleep in and waited for the sun to rise.

Natasha felt herself nodding off, finally succumbing to the heaviness of her eyelids and the comfort she found behind them, when she saw the bus pull around the corner and park between the concrete pillars in front of her. She heard the grinding of the brakes and the hiss of the front door, and she knew it was time. She stood up, heaved her bag over her shoulder and walked outside. The snow was blowing in every direction, grainy pellets peppering her cheeks and forehead, the stinging sensation against her skin waking her up.

The driver took her ticket and helped her with her bag. She climbed the stairs of the bus, found an empty seat near the back, reclined it as far back as she could and closed her eyes. As she felt the bus pull away from the terminal she silently said goodbye to her old life. She didn't even feel the urge to look out the window.

Chapter 20

Sugar's throbbing head woke him just before eight o'clock. He was hit with the acrid smell of dried sweat coming off his sheets and pillows, his dreams instantaneously coming back to him in jagged fragments. The gun. The bullets. Kelvin Jackson. The stolen car. The cops. The shots. The body. The blood.

He kept his eyes closed, fearing that if he opened them it would all become real, that the monster of a nightmare he'd just endured would become a real, living thing. If he continued lying there, eyes closed, cut off from everything, maybe he could ban it from his consciousness, rid it from his memory. But the sounds and the sights kept playing through his mind, as real and graphic as the dreams that had robbed him of any real sleep.

Finally the knives in his temples became unbearable and he slowly lifted his heavy eyelids. The old wool blanket that served as his curtain was pulled tight across the window but slivers of the outside world stabbed through at the edges, the early morning sunshine bathing the bedroom in a faint and translucent light.

He peeled the sweaty sheets from his body and sat at the edge of his bed, looked around the room. The silhouettes of his crumpled clothes lay sprawled across his bedroom floor, scattered like casualties on a battlefield. The eerie green glow of his digital alarm clock showed 8:05. Less than five hours since he'd crawled beneath the sheets.

Sugar stood up, flipped on the light and avoided looking at his bed. He knew what was under there, but as long as he didn't see it, it didn't exist. He went to the bathroom and jumped in the shower, cranking the water as hot as he could handle it. He soaped his body from head to toe and scrubbed every reachable surface as hard as he could, not stopping until his muscles hurt and his skin felt raw. He cranked the tap even further and felt the water scald his skin until his body went numb and he couldn't feel anything at all. When the water finally started running lukewarm, he stepped out of the shower, dried off and brushed his teeth without wiping the fog from the mirror.

Back in his room, Sugar grabbed his hoodie and slipped on his Nike high tops. He took one more look at the bed and hesitated before closing the door and making his way downstairs. First period started in forty minutes.

*   *   *

Redford High was a large, uninspiring brick building between Logan and Cowley. It looked every bit its eighty years and then some. The rows of oaks and elms surrounding it, even older than the building itself, were either dead or dying. Their gnarled, exposed limbs sagged outwards, plastic bags hanging from the branches like flags of surrender. Cracked and fallen branches were scattered across the schoolyard like shrapnel, alongside paper coffee cups, greasy fast food wrappers and cigarette butts.

As Sugar approached the scarred metal doors he was calmed by a feeling of familiarity. The memories of last night immediately began to fade, the details growing more distant. For as long as he could remember, school had been Sugar's sanctuary, the only place he felt safe and the only thing in his life that felt certain. No matter what was going on at home, the front doors at Redford always opened at exactly 8:30. The first bell rang at 8:55, the final bell at 3:00. Six periods of security and escape. While most kids his age skipped class and treated school as an afterthought, Sugar lived for it. While they looked forward to summer break, he would spend his holidays counting down the days until classes started up again.

He struggled with the weight of the heavy brown door and made his way across the scuffed floors. The halls appeared larger and echoed louder by the day, the outdated and undersupplied classrooms growing increasingly empty. Graffiti, both old and fresh, covered the faded white walls and the prison-grey lockers. Sugar walked toward the east wing stairwell and took in the familiar, ever-present stench of marijuana when he reached the landing.

When he reached the tenth grade commons, Deon Dressler was waiting at his locker. Same as every day, standing there with his scrawny shoulders against the locker, his hands deep in the pockets of his baggy khaki pants. White buds dangled from his ears, the wire disappearing down the neck of his too-big Nike sweater. He didn't notice Sugar until he was right beside him.

Deon pulled out his ear buds, letting them hang loose down the front of his chest. They greeted each other with their complicated and ever-expanding handshake, a series of slaps and bumps and snaps and pounds so fast and fluid that an observer would have no chance of replicating it no matter how many times they tried. As usual, Deon had a smile on his face and was bobbing up and down.

"Hey, man. Do anything last night?"

On the walk that morning, Sugar had decided to play it cool. Tell absolutely nobody about last night, not even Deon. Give himself some time to think things through.

Sugar began dialling his combination lock, avoiding eye contact. "Not much, man. Just chilled."

He popped his lock open, grabbed a binder and two textbooks from the top shelf and closed the locker. They made their way down the hall, through and around the other students, ignoring them and being ignored back, Sugar comfortable with the anonymity and dissociation.

"Why you limping?" asked Deon.

Sugar suddenly became conscious of the discomfort on his left side. He slowed down, but ignored Deon, pretending not to hear his question.

"You hear the shots last night?"

Sugar felt his face flush. He hoped Deon didn't notice and dropped a step back.

"Nah," he said. "Didn't hear nothin."

Deon stopped and stared at him. "Serious?"

Sugar looked at his feet, shrugged.

"Four, five shots," Deon said, excitement in his voice. "Po-po was there, lights, sirens, everything. It was crazy, man. Whole damn neighborhood looked like a carnival."

Sugar shrugged again. "Heavy sleeper, I guess."

"Anyway," Deon lowered his voice now, leaned in toward Sugar. "I hear it's a cop got capped."

Sugar felt his shirt collar tighten and his mouth go dry.

"Where...where'd you hear that?" He managed to avoid meeting his friend's eyes and tried his best to keep his voice casual. He started walking again, faster now.

85

"All over the news." Deon caught up to Sugar. "They caught the guy right away."

Sugar stopped, felt the hallway shift.

"What?"

"The guy that shot the cop," Deon said. "They pinched him."

Sugar closed his eyes. Everything went red behind his eyelids, then black. His head started to spin and he lost control of his breathing.

"Sugar? You OK, man?"

Sugar could hear Deon's voice, weak and muffled, like it was coming from another room. He fought the clawing inside his skull and the clench in the back of his throat and forced his eyes open. He walked over to a row of lockers and crouched.

"Sugar?" Deon was right beside him, looking down at him with worried eyes. "What's wrong?"

"Nothing," Sugar managed, shaking his head. It took everything he had to feign a smile for his friend. "Probably just hungry. I didn't eat breakfast."

Deon looked at him like he'd lost his mind, but he didn't say anything. He reached into his backpack and pulled out an apple.

"Here," he said.

"Thanks." Sugar took the apple and reached for Deon's outstretched hand, pulling himself up. Back on his feet his legs quivered, but he managed a step forward, followed by another.

"Let's go," he said, clapping Deon on the back. "Don't wanna be late for class."

Chapter 21

Gerald was neither deep in sleep nor fully conscious. As he lay there with his eyes closed he was aware of a sound, vibrating just beneath the surface of his foggy mind. The incessant chime of a grandfather clock striking the hour, or church bells in the distance. He opened his eyes to blackness.

Where was he? What time was it? He strained his eyes as they slowly adjusted to the darkness of the room. What looked like a desk stood in one corner, the silhouette of a dresser in the other. Slowly, the room began to take shape, the details of last night falling in to place one by one in reverse order, like a movie stuck on rewind: collapsing in Charlie's bed, exhausted; sitting at the kitchen table with Virginia Reese; finding Nick's body; the car chase. All of these things seemed so long ago already, as if they'd happened in another lifetime.

The chime sounded again, louder this time, and Gerald realized it was the doorbell. He slowly pulled the blankets back and padded barefoot across the cool carpet. He slid his hand along the wall until he hit the plastic light switch. Standing in his boxer shorts, still half asleep, no other clothes in sight, he followed the hall to his own bedroom, pulled on a pair of jeans and an old fleece sweater and made his way down the stairs.

The living room was dark and airy. He walked over to the big bay window and parted the full-length drapes. The murky hue of the sky, somewhere between black and blue, told him it was still the early hours of the morning. Everything outside was covered in a thin layer of snow, a coat of frost covering the windshield of his Taurus. On the street, parked along the curb at the foot of his driveway, sat a Lincoln Town Car with tinted windows.

He briefly considered pretending he wasn't home, going back upstairs and burying himself in a pile of pillows and blankets for the rest of the week. Instead, he answered the door, immediately recognizing a pair of plainclothes detectives on his porch.

"Morning, Gerald," John Clifford said. The dark pockets under his eyes and the firm line of his mouth gave his face the solemn look that could only follow a night of death. "How you holdin up?"

Gerald shook both men's hands and shrugged. "Tell you the truth, it hasn't really sunk in yet, you know? Doesn't seem real."

Clifford and Alex Ramos nodded in unison, faces worn but sincere.

"Nick was a good cop," Clifford said.

"A good man," Ramos added.

The three of them stood at the front door in silence. The air outside was cold and crisp. Gerald inhaled a refreshing mouthful and let it out with a sigh. His breath passed his lips and hit the icy air, floated and curled like a puff of smoke and vanished.

"Anyway," he said. "Come on in. I'll put on a pot of coffee."

*　　*　　*

In the light of the dining room, Gerald could tell from the taught skin and the patches of sparse stubble on the detectives' faces that they hadn't been to bed yet. The three of them sat around the dining room table and sipped steaming coffee in silence, not in much of a hurry to say anything. Gerald was fine with that; it gave him time to gather his thoughts.

"Well," Clifford finally said, his voice scratchy with exhaustion. "Reason we're here Gerald, is that we've been assigned Nick's case."

Gerald nodded, not at all surprised that they'd landed it. He wasn't sure how long John Clifford and Alex Ramos had been partners, but he couldn't remember a time when they weren't. They were known and respected throughout the department for their skills, particularly in the box. Combined, they were said to have more confessions and a higher close rate than any other homicide team in the state.

Clifford continued, "And aside from being the arresting officer in Nick's case, you're also our only witness at this point. So this visit is just due diligence on the part of the department. A formality."

"Fair enough," Gerald said. Then, "So how can I help?"

"We've gone over the report you made last night, but I was hoping you could maybe give us a verbal account of how it all went down."

"Sure," Gerald said.

He cradled his chin in his palm and closed his eyes. There was something about last night he was unable to pinpoint, something instinctual telling him he didn't want to; as if he were holding a key that didn't quite fit in a door he wasn't sure he wanted to open. He momentarily considered forcing it, but instead opened his eyes and retreated, not yet ready to step inside for what he might see.

"I know how difficult this must be right now, Gerald. Just take your time."

Clifford's voice reminded Gerald there were other people in the room. He cleared his throat and began from the time he and Nick had first seen the Infiniti. Clifford listened intently, jotting shorthand in his yellow notepad, nodding in approval every now and then. Ramos was quiet as a ghost, hands cupped around his mug, his tan complexion blending in to the neutral tones of the room around them.

Gerald took his time, recounting as many details as he could. He told them about the chase, the gunshots, finding Nick's body. When he got to the part about seeing the suspect in the streets, he felt a thud of discomfort in the cavity of his chest and froze up.

"What happened next, Gerald? What did you do when you saw the suspect?" Clifford urged.

Gerald remembered the man standing there, hands in the air, eyes full of fear and confusion. He remembered the pleasure he'd taken in seeing him so scared and the satisfaction he got wiping that fear off his face, making him pay over and over and over again for what he'd done to Nick. Covered in Nick's blood, the image of his lifeless body sprawled across the snow, Gerald had wanted so badly for the black man on the sidewalk to be Nick's killer.

But now, without the anger and the adrenaline coursing through his body, those discomforting thoughts that had been mulling through his subconscious, that nagging itch he couldn't quite reach, that key that didn't fit in the door, all of a sudden gave way to a revelation of such finality and clarity he thought he might vomit.

He'd arrested the wrong man.

Gerald closed his eyes again to keep the room from spinning. He took quick, sharp breaths to get the oxygen flowing to his head.

89

"Gerald? You with us?"

Gerald forced his eyes open and looked at the detectives. They seemed more distant somehow, as if the tabletop between them had grown wider and the room around them larger. Their outlines were blurred, their faces blotched with bright spots beneath the radiance of the chandelier.

"Yeah," he said. "Sorry. What was the question again?"

"The suspect. What happened when you saw the suspect?"

"Well," Gerald said. He wondered how much to tell them, how much they already knew. "From a distance, I was convinced it was him. The guy from the car, I mean. Black male, tall, dressed in dark clothing. He fit the profile. But…" Gerald trailed off, not sure which direction to take it.

"But?"

When Gerald had decided to become a cop, his plan had been simple. Cruise the beats, do the tours, put in his twenty-five and get out. He'd still be relatively young, and with a fifty percent pension and his house paid off, he'd be set for the rest of his life. He could play more racquetball, watch more hockey, maybe take up golf or buy a small building and open up a gym.

But a wrongful arrest on his record would confuse things. It was a suspendable offense at the very least, and may even cost him his job and have legal consequences. He considered keeping his doubts to himself, letting the chips fall where they may and lawyering up with the union if and when it came to that. But he'd been around the system long enough to know that the truth always had a way of exposing itself.

"Well, when I caught up to him I wasn't so sure anymore, you know? I just – I wasn't a hundred percent certain it was the same guy." Gerald felt some of the weight of his revelation fade away; it was out in the open now.

Clifford exchanged a quick glance with Ramos.

"What?" Gerald said.

"How certain can you be?" Clifford asked. He looked as if he were expecting an answer he didn't want to hear.

"It was dark, it was snowing, my adrenaline was pumping." Gerald shook his head.

In the silence that followed, the three men looked around the room, down at their hands, up at the ceiling, anywhere but at each other.

"Why?" Gerald asked. "What?"

The detectives looked at each other again, longer this time.

"Well," Clifford began. "Sanford, the suspect, he claims he was carjacked about thirty minutes before the arrest. We thought it was just some bullshit story he made up."

Of course, Gerald thought. The suspects fleeing Clarence Sanford's car didn't look like Clarence Sanford because they weren't. The reason the driver took off was because the car was hot.

"I fucked up." Gerald stared into his black coffee, flicked the mug with his fingernails and another moment of silence fell over the room.

Ramos leaned back in his chair and for the first time since coming inside, spoke.

"Listen, Gerald. We're not here to judge. We're here to find Nick's killer." Ramos looked down as he said Nick's name. "You tell us it was the same guy, it was the same guy. But if Sanford's innocent…"

Ramos didn't finish his sentence. Didn't need to. The significance of what it meant was obvious, the weight of it consuming the entire room. If Sanford was innocent, Gerald realized for the first time, Nick's real killer was still out there. The justice he had felt as he stomped and cuffed Sanford, the relief in the face of Virginia Reese when he said he'd gotten the bastard, it all meant nothing.

"Look," Clifford said. "You're not a hundred percent he's our guy, we just treat it as an open investigation. CSI finishes at the scene this afternoon and we see what they find. Who knows, maybe they have enough for us to go in another direction."

"In the meantime," Ramos said, "we keep Sanford in custody on the possibility he is our guy. Based on the evidence at the moment, the arrest is perfectly legit. Besides, the guy ain't exactly a saint, you know what I mean? Keeping him locked up ain't anything off our backs."

Gerald looked at his hands and nodded.

"Gerald," Clifford said. "You can't beat yourself up over this. You did what any other cop in your position would have done."

"You did the right thing," Ramos said, pulling back a white shirtsleeve and glancing at his watch. He stifled a yawn and stretched his arms above his head. "In the meantime, we should get moving if we want to get to the arraignment."

Clifford folded his notebook closed and clicked his pen.

"Why don't you come," he said to Gerald. "We can go over your statement again in the car."

Gerald's body felt as if it were fused to the chair, his mind as if it were on the verge of melting. He managed only a meek look up at the detectives, now on their feet, wondering if he looked to them as defeated as he felt.

"Come on," said Ramos, standing now, rolling the knots of fatigue out of his neck. "I know a great breakfast joint on the way. Best waffles in the city."

Chapter 22

Clarence entered the courtroom through a side door to the left of the judge. The room was small, its dark ceiling and wood-panelled walls adding to his exhaustion and giving him a heightened sense of claustrophobia. All the people in there didn't help. It was standing room only, the dozen or so rows of benches occupied, three of the four walls lined with uniformed police officers and reporters clutching notepads.

Clarence could hear the soft hiss of their voices conspiring against him and kept his head down, ducking the contempt and hatred projected by their accusing faces. Then, amid the suits and the uniforms, three rows back on the aisle, he caught a glimpse of Leslie and Rodney. He had no idea his wife and brother-in-law would be here and his immediate response was to look away, pretend he didn't see them. Too late.

Hands folded neatly on her lap, Rodney's arm slung around her shoulders, Leslie was staring straight at him. The sleepless night was written all over her face: eyes red and puffy, skin dry and ashy, hair unwashed and slightly matted. Her lips were parted in a slight gasp of disbelief, likely a reaction to his face. Despite the overwhelming shame he felt upon seeing her, he forced himself to give her a weak smile. For a fleeting moment it looked as if she would look away, but she returned it and he felt himself flush, the sympathy behind it almost too much for him.

As Clarence crossed the room to the bench reserved for defendants, he could feel every set of eyes in the room burning a hole in his back. He took a seat between Byron Sapp and another lawyer from his firm, a white man introduced to him that morning as Jake Burnett. Burnett appeared to be no older than Clarence, but he carried the confidence of a seasoned partner. His handshake was solid and firm, his voice deep and assured.

There were two tables facing the judge's podium – one directly in front of them, the other off to the right. Two video cameras sat perched on tripods in opposite corners of the room and there was a clerk sitting behind a small table next to the podium, as well as a stenographer. A bailiff stood against the far wall, a thick-bodied black man with his meaty hands resting on his hips, his eyes scanning the courtroom like a hungry predator looking for its next meal.

Sitting on the hard wood of the straight-backed bench, separated from the first row of spectators by only a waist-high partition, Clarence kept his eyes forward, struggling to keep them open. They were dry and heavy, the slicing white lights hanging from the panelled ceiling only making things worse. The only thing keeping him from drifting off were the thoughts of his wife; how she'd reacted when she heard the news, what she'd told the kids, how much she knew. If the smile she had given him was any indication, she didn't have any idea about Natasha. He considered stealing a glance back at her, yearning for the solace of another smile, but was roused by the baritone voice of the clerk.

"Ladies and gentlemen, please rise for the honorable Judge Barlow."

Bodies shifted, papers shuffled, throats were cleared. Clarence felt a tug on his elbow and rose to his feet along with Sapp and Burnett and the rest of the courtroom.

Judge Norman Barlow entered through the back door and approached the bench with a sluggish waddle. He was a short man with a long nose and grey, thinning hair parted to one side. Perched atop his bench and scanning the room with beady eyes and thin purple lips set in a scowl, he reminded Clarence of a vulture.

"Good morning," began the judge, his tinny voice transmitted through the small microphone in front of him. "All right. I can see we have a packed house this morning, so please, I ask that you all maintain order and hopefully we can get through this as quickly as possible. Please be seated."

More shifting, more shuffling. The judge waited for the commotion to die down and looked to the row of defendants before continuing.

"We are gathered here today for arraignments on activities deemed criminal in the state of Michigan. The court will advise you all of your official charge, at which time you will be able to enter your plea. A plea of guilty will admit you have committed the crime with which you've been charged and an appropriate sentence will be imposed. A plea of no contest will neither admit nor deny the charge but will state you are foregoing the process of a trial. Based on the evidence presented by the State, the court will decide your guilt or innocence. A plea of not guilty will result in a trial at which the State has the onus of proving your guilt beyond a reasonable doubt. You will appear before a jury of your peers and they will decide, based on the evidence, your guilt or innocence. As a defendant in a criminal case you have the presumption of innocence until proven guilty.

"OK," he continued, shifting his beady eyes towards the bailiff. "I guess we're ready to proceed."

The bailiff looked down at a clipboard and spoke without looking up. "Clarence Sanford."

Sapp nudged Clarence's forearm with his own and, again, they stood. There was a sudden rumble of whispers through the courtroom.

"Silence," said the judge, speaking to the court but staring directly at Clarence, his lips barely moving. "Outbursts in this courtroom will absolutely not be tolerated."

He let the words hang there for a moment before proceeding, his pebble eyes still glued to Clarence. "You're Clarence Sanford?"

Clarence tried to swallow, nearly gagged at the sand paper dryness in his throat. "Yes, your honor."

"Very well then. Mr. Sanford, you are charged with the first-degree murder of one Nick Reese. The charge is punishable by up to life in prison. Do you understand the charges against you?"

"Yes, your honor," Clarence managed.

"And how do you wish to plead?"

"Not guilty, your honor."

More murmurs, indecipherable. But louder this time, and more intense.

"Order!" snapped Barlow, his warning accompanied this time by the sharp crack of his gavel. "For the record, a plea of not guilty has been entered. The preliminary hearing is hereby set for three weeks from today, Thursday the fifth of January at 9:30."

He looked down at his desk, jotted something down. "And has the prosecution notified you of your rights, Mr. Sanford?"

"They have, your honor."

"Very well. Is there anything else?"

Clarence was about to shake his head but Sapp's voice

stopped him.

"Good morning, your honor. Byron Sapp on behalf of Mr. Sanford."

The judge shifted his eyes over to Sapp and stared at him, seemingly annoyed. "All right."

"Your honor, I would like to address the matter of bail."

"Bail, Mr. Sapp? You must be well aware that the nature of the offence your client has been charged with does not warrant bail. Not today, and not ever." He shook his head in disappointment. "Request denied. Anything else?"

"But – "

"Request denied, counsellor. Is there anything else?"

"Nothing further, your honor."

"Very well then. Mr. Sanford will be remanded to custody effective immediately." Barlow scanned the courtroom once more before making conspiratorial eye contact with the bailiff. "Next."

As the bailiff called out the next name, Sapp led Clarence to the rear exit, Jake Burnett following close behind. Staring at the back of his lawyer's head, Clarence shuffled past the stenographer, past the bench and past the beefy guard, who still had his hands on his hips, his eyes hungrier than ever.

When he reached the door in the corner, Clarence raised his head and looked back. As his eyes scanned the dark uniforms and expensive suits lining the wooden walls, he felt his body cease up and his legs suddenly lock. Against the wall, next to the exit, forearms folded across his chest, stood the cop who had attacked him the night before. With his street clothes and his combed hair, under the bright lights of the courtroom, he looked like a different man. In fact, Clarence didn't even think he'd have recognized him had it not been for the eyes. Even without the fury and the rage behind them, those steel grey eyes were unforgettable. And now they were staring right at him, locked in a death grip on his own. Clarence felt time stop, transfixed with either horror or hatred – he couldn't be sure which. He was unable to move, unable to breathe, until Burnett bumped into him and abruptly sent him stumbling forward a couple of steps.

By the time he regained his balance and glanced back at the wall, the cop was gone.

Chapter 23

Sugar sat at his desk near the front of the classroom, the unrest in the hollow of his stomach raging more violently by the minute. He had lost all concept of time and space; the entire day to this point had been nothing but a blur of lectures he'd listened to but hadn't heard. His notebooks and textbooks remained in his backpack, untouched, his mind confined to a carousel of images and memories from the night before. Sometimes they were vague and drawn out in shades of black and white and grey. Other times he'd actually feel the weight and the coldness of the gun in his hand, hear the hollow pops of the shots, see the crimson blood staining the white snow surrounding the cop's body.

During lunch hour, Sugar had slipped Deon, retreated to the library and asked the librarian for a copy of the Free Press. He folded it close to his chest and walked with his head down to a quiet corner cubicle along the back wall, behind the periodicals. He looked around anxiously until he finally built up the nerve to open the paper, Deon's words playing over and over in his head. They caught him.

To his relief, the front page was plastered with a story about the sale of a nuclear plant. He flipped through the rest of the paper, page by page, section by section, dreading what he might find. But by the time he reached the last page, and had gone through the entire thing a second time, there was nothing about the murdered cop. He put his head down and didn't raise it until the buzzer signalling the end of lunch sounded.

Now, here he was, sitting in Mrs. Ralston's English class but not really there, detached from the room and everything going on around him. Mrs. Ralston scrawling on the blackboard with yellow chalk, her back to the class. A few of the thirty or so students around him listening, others dozing or whispering across the aisles to one another, or doodling in the margins of their notebooks. They were all outside of Sugar's bubble, separated from him by an invisible barrier.

The clock at the front of the room said 2:45. Fifteen minutes to go. But until what? Sugar thought. The school day would end, but there was the rest of the afternoon. And then the evening, and the night, and then tomorrow. His life would become one never-ending burden; minute after minute, hour after hour, day after day, taken hostage by the ceaseless thoughts of what he'd done.

Wrestling his mind back into room 204, Sugar became aware of how clammy his hands were, how heavy his head was, how nauseous his stomach. The yellow scribbles on the blackboard in front of him were nothing but maze-like squiggles, the board itself one big wave of black. Mrs. Ralston's voice sounded as if it was coming from a loud speaker, fading in and out, the whispers and scratching of pens around him distant and unattached. Suddenly the room began to shift and Sugar felt like he was on a boat.

He gripped the wooden edges of his desk and closed his eyes, tried to regain some balance. The black-yellow behind his eyelids remained steady and, for a moment, his world stopped moving. He flattened his hands on his desk and everything became still. He took a breath and opened his eyes. Too soon. Before they had a chance to focus on anything, he was hit with another blast of nausea, the unexpected impact on his stomach so severe it nearly winded him.

He jumped out of his chair, knocking it to the floor behind him.

He ran out of the classroom and turned right down the hall, his shoes squeaking, the steel lockers and the tiled floor swirling around him. He made it to the boys' room, pushed open the orange metal door of the first stall and made it to the toilet just in time.

He kneeled down and gripped the rim of the cold white bowl, the stench of bathroom burning his nostrils, and he puked. Slumped over a floating pile of vomit, he retched again and again, heaving until nothing came up but foul tasting bile and his stomach felt empty and sore from all the clenching.

When he was finally finished, Sugar got to his knees and wiped the remains off his lips with the back of his hand. His head was still throbbing, though the pain behind his eyes had subsided and the world around him no longer spun. He stumbled to the sink and turned the single metal faucet with a shaky hand. He ran the water cold and splashed it on his face.

Somewhat refreshed, he headed straight for the front doors and made his way across the schoolyard. A thin layer of fresh snow crackled beneath his feet and a bitter wind whistled through the naked branches of the trees, pelting him with swirls of grainy ice pellets.

Covering his face with his hands, Sugar crossed Cowley. Halfway down the block, he considered taking a right at Ferndale, walking up the front steps of the cop shop, stepping inside and telling them everything. Maybe he could plea down, cut a deal the way they did on TV, and get out while he was still young. But as quickly as the thought entered his mind, Sugar shot it down. The reason he couldn't turn himself in was the same reason he had shot the cop in the first place. Sugar Sinclair would not, could not, willingly go to jail. Truth be told, if it came down to it and the Crookston Curse was in fact legit, he'd rather die than get locked away.

So instead of turning right at Ferndale, Sugar kept going straight. The cold had begun to seep in to his hands and his feet and he ached for the warm comfort of his bed. He began walking faster, kicking at the white powder with his Nikes as he went. When he reached his housing project, he saw someone sitting on the front stoop of his corner unit and stopped short. The figure had a hood over its head, and it was facing the other way, but Sugar knew immediately who it was. At first he thought about pretending he didn't see him and turning right back around. But Kelvin Jackson looked up, caught his eye, and, before Sugar knew it, was on his feet and moving toward him, tall and thin and lanky, that unmistakable gait in his step.

"Sugar!" Kelvin shouted. He was approaching with long, determined strides and didn't stop until he was within inches of Sugar. He reached out and gripped Sugar's arm, the abrupt motion catching him off guard and nearly knocking him off balance.

"Sugar," Kelvin said again, the long fingers of his right hand clenching Sugar's bicep. "We need to talk."

*   *   *

By the time they got to Kelvin's place, Sugar was shivering – partly from the relentless wind and partly from the uncomfortable anxiety that had burrowed its way into his bones. Kelvin had walked with such urgency and purpose that Sugar had struggled just to keep up, neither of them speaking a single word during the six-block stroll.

Sugar stepped inside without removing his shoes, not that it mattered; the place was filthy. There were cans and bottles and food wrappers strewn about the room and it didn't appear Kelvin owned a garbage can. The linoleum floor had so many stains on it you couldn't even tell its original color.

"Take a seat," said Kelvin, pointing to a long green sofa along the wall.

Cautiously, Sugar stepped around the milk crates serving as a coffee table and slid a pile of crumpled clothes aside to make room for himself. He sat down and allowed himself to sink back into the worn cushions. He felt tiny and exposed in front of Kelvin, who was hunched forward in an old rocking chair, his forearms resting on his thighs, his long fingers dangling between his knees.

"What happened last night?" Kelvin said. There was an edge in his voice, cold and threatening.

Sugar wasn't sure how much Kelvin knew, but the fact that he'd tracked him down and dragged him back here wasn't a good sign. He crossed his arms and forced himself to finally look up. The casual, easygoing Kelvin from the night before was gone. His big brown eyes were stuck in neutral, his thick lips and angular jaw set tight. There was a wiry alertness in the way he sat, shoulders sloped slightly forward, big black hands clenched in front of him now, like cannonballs waiting to explode.

"I know you shot that cop, a'ight? I don't know how it went down, and straight up, I don't give a shit." He paused, waited until he had Sugar's full attention. "Who knows?"

"No one," Sugar said, swallowing the lump forming in the back of his throat. "I swear."

Kelvin leaned back in his chair, as if deciding whether or not to believe him. "Good," he finally said. "Where's the gun at?"

"At home. Under...under my bed."

"A'ight. You gonna go home and wipe it off. Use bleach and a toothbrush, scrub it real good. Then, get rid of it. Throw it down a sewer or some shit."

Sugar nodded.

Kelvin shifted in his seat and leaned forward again. He

seemed calmer now, the youthful energy slowly returning to his face.

"Listen, Sugar." He was looking directly into his eyes as he spoke. "Not a day goes by I don't think about Reg, y'know that? All this time later and I still hear his voice sometimes, I still see his face."

Sugar felt something within him stir. A deep and distant part of him that remained for the most part concealed, off in the darkest, most secret corner of his soul, had been awakened. Like the first spark of a fire, it wasn't much – just enough to remind him something was there, a potential warning sign of something bigger yet to come. He found it impossible to hold Kelvin's gaze and looked away. Down at his Nikes, at his hands, finally at the Tupac poster hanging above the flat screen TV. He felt the warmth of the room rise and work its way beneath his clothes.

The day Reggie had gotten shot was still seared in Sugar's memory. A Tuesday afternoon in August, warm and humid after a morning of steady rain. One minute they'd been walking side by side to the corner store for some penny candies, the next minute there were shots and his brother was lying in a pool of his own blood on the sidewalk. It had been a drive-by, the car gone before Sugar could get a look at it, the shooter never caught.

For the most part, Sugar was over it. He could usually talk about it without getting too emotional. But other times, when he hadn't thought about it for a while, it could catch him off guard. It would seem like it happened just yesterday, and he'd feel his throat lump up and have to fight back the swelling behind his eyes that he knew preceded tears. Looking at Kelvin, he knew that if he opened his mouth he wouldn't be able to speak. So he just sat there and nodded.

Kelvin eventually sat up in his chair and grinned, the mood in the room growing suddenly lighter.

"Reggie was like a brother to me, like family. And that makes you family, too. We gotta have each other's backs, you know what I'm sayin?"

Again, Sugar could do nothing but nod.

"Good," said Kelvin as he got to his feet, his heavy boots sounding like thunder on the linoleum floor of the small room. "So

101

last night? It's our little secret. Matter of fact, last night never even happened, right?"

"Right."

Kelvin started toward the front door and Sugar followed.

When they reached the front door Kelvin put his hand on Sugar's shoulder. "We straight, right?"

Again, Sugar nodded.

"Good."

Kelvin opened the front door and Sugar stepped outside, into the falling snow.

Chapter 24

The nameplate on the solid oak door was at eye level, white block lettering on a matte black background. The two lines of text read: Harriston Graves, Chief of Police.

A few hours after returning home from the arraignment, Gerald had been sitting alone in his living room, immobilized by the weight of the past twelve hours, when he got a call from the man himself. With his deep no-nonsense voice, he had asked if it might be possible for Gerald to stop by police headquarters that afternoon. There was a matter of urgency he'd like to discuss regarding Officer Reese's case, and the sooner he could get there, the better. Gerald had told the Chief he'd be there within the hour and hung up the phone.

Now, here he stood. Palms damp with sweat and throat coated in sand paper. He raised his right hand and knocked, the sound of bone on wood heavy and hollow.

Several seconds later, the door swung open and Harriston Graves stood before him with his hand extended. "Gerald. Glad you could make it."

Gerald, he had called him. Like they were old buddies, the best of friends. The truth was, Gerald had met the Chief only twice, neither time warranting more than a brief handshake and a curt nod. As far as Gerald knew, Graves had only two rules: always address him as Sir, and speak only when spoken to.

After Gerald shook his hand, Graves stepped aside and motioned for him to enter. When they were both inside, he closed the door behind them and led him to the wide mahogany desk in the center of the office. Aside from the desk, the only other furniture in the room were the chairs on either side of it. Three of the pale white walls were covered in plaques, maps and bookshelves, the fourth by a single window looking out at tall grey buildings.

Graves nodded toward the empty chair in front of Gerald.

"Take a load off, Gerald. Make yourself comfortable."

"Thank you, sir." Gerald slid the chair across the thick blue carpet and sat down. Waited. Looking at Graves, it was hard to believe the chief was only a couple of years shy of his twenty-five. His blue eyes and high forehead were etched with only the slightest of creases, and while his hair had a touch more grey than it used it to, he still had that tank of a body that suggested he spent hours a week at the gym.

A computer monitor sat on one side of Graves' desk, his overflowing inbox and slightly more manageable outbox took up the other. He pushed a small stack of manila file folders aside to make room for his elbows. He gave Gerald a weak smile and clasped his hands together.

"Now first off, I just want to say how sorry I am for your loss here." Graves looked down at his folded hands and shook his head as he said it. "Nicholas Reese was a fine officer. A fine, fine man."

Gerald remained silent, thinking how much Nick had hated when people called him Nicholas.

"And I want you to know that you'll have the full support of the department during this difficult time. Anything you need, Gerald. Anything at all."

"Thank you, sir."

"Can I get you anything to drink? Coffee? Tea maybe? I don't touch the stuff myself, but if you need anything I can have Charlotte bring it over right away."

"No, sir," Gerald said. "Trying to cut back myself."

"Good man. Stuff'll send you to an early grave." He straightened in his seat and gave Gerald another smile. "And Gerald. There's no need for the sirs in here. Just you and me. Please," he said, "call me Harry."

Gerald nodded. There were no armrests on his chair and he was having trouble finding something to do with his hands.

"Now, I'm sure you know why you're here." Graves said.

Gerald nodded again, his tongue too swollen to talk, even if he wanted to.

"I spoke with Detectives Clifford and Ramos this morning and they brought to my attention some concerns you have about the suspect you arrested last night. That you might be having…doubts."

It sounded like more of a statement than a question, so Gerald waited for him to continue.

"Sometimes after a traumatic event like last night emotions can run high, your mind can play tricks on you. You mix up facts, forget details, things like that. Happens all the time." He gave

104

Gerald a casual shrug of his shoulders and a reassuring grin.

"Yes, sir," Gerald managed. For the thousandth time, he spoke the words in his head. For the thousandth time, he felt the pang of shame they brought and considered the irrevocable consequences they carried. "It's just that the more I think about it, the more I think I might have made a mistake."

"That's just it, Gerald. You're thinking about it too much. Like when you're standing over a three-foot putt and you think about it too hard? You over-analyze it? You miss every time."

"I understand that sir, I do. It's just that – " Gerald paused. "It's just that the physical description doesn't fit."

Graves tilted his head. His lips got a little tighter and he let out a small, low chuckle.

"Your partner'd been shot. Everything happened so fast. It's understandable for you to question whether you got the right guy. Natural, even.

"Look, Gerald. We're on the same side here. You, me, the entire department, we're all on the same team. It's our job to get the bad guys off the street. Far as I'm concerned, that's exactly what you did last night. Far as I'm concerned, you got the right guy. We have your back on that."

"Did he confess?"

"Not yet. Hired himself a hotshot lawyer and, from what I hear, he didn't do too much talking. Kept going on about getting carjacked. Real original."

"Is it not a possibility? I mean, it would make sense given the – "

"Officer Dawes." No more chuckling, no more cordiality. No more Gerald. "An innocent officer of the Detroit PD was killed in the line of duty last night. We've arrested a suspect with a record, and all of the evidence is pointing in the right direction. The way I see it, we have an open and shut case here. The criminals in this city are already laughing at us. How do we look if this guy goes free? An arrest saves the time and the manpower of a lengthy investigation and we save the embarrassment of an unsolved murder."

"All due respect sir, but what if it turns out he is the wrong guy?" Graves sighed.

"You're a damn hero, Dawes. Why do you have to make this

so difficult?"

Gerald didn't answer. He knew the system was one big, greasy wheel and that he was nothing but a single spoke. He had no choice but to go along for the ride. If he resisted, the spoke would simply bend and snap and the wheel would continue turning without him.

Graves leaned back in his chair and exhaled again. "It's just the stress of it, Dawes. This second-guessing, these doubts you're having. Your partner was killed out there, in the streets, on the job, and you made a very high-stress arrest. Nothing but stress."

He looked Gerald in the eye and made sure he could see the threat behind them.

"So effective immediately, you're being placed on stress leave. With pay, of course. As long as you want, minimum eight weeks. When you feel you're ready to come back, ready to re-join the team, you let me know. Do you understand what I'm saying to you, Officer Dawes?"

"Yes, sir."

"Good." Graves got up from his chair, signalling the end of the meeting. "Oh, and Officer Dawes. The department asks that you keep your...doubts to yourself. For obvious reasons."

"Of course," Gerald said. His limbs were quivering and he had to use the back of the chair to support himself as he stood. He hoped Graves didn't notice.

"Well then," Graves said with a cock of his head and a quick smile, not even attempting to mask its insincerity. "It was nice to see you again. I only wish it might have been under more pleasant circumstances." He stepped around the desk and reached out his hand.

Gerald stared at it for a moment, before turning his back on Graves and walking out of the room without shaking it.

Chapter 25

"Fifteen minutes starts now," said a uniformed officer before he closed the door. There was another guard standing in the corner, a squat man in his thirties with orange hair and a matching goatee, neatly manicured and shaved close to his face. His hands were resting on his hips, just above his belt and holster.

Clarence, Leslie and Rodney were seated on rolling chairs around a small circular table in the center of an otherwise empty room. Leslie hadn't taken her eyes off of Clarence's face, taking in the swelling and the bruising like a concerned mother. She hesitated and reached across the table, grimacing as she stroked his cheekbone with a single finger.

"No contact," said the guard from the corner. His tone was indifferent, the words just another line of the script he had undoubtedly mastered over the years.

Leslie pulled back and Clarence found himself instantly yearning for another touch, tender, sympathetic, undeserved. Instead, he sat there, swamped by guilt, ashamed that he could barely make eye contact with the woman he had been married to for seven years.

"Does it hurt?" she asked.

"Not too bad," Clarence said. "Not like yesterday, at least."

She pursed her lips and shook her head, the small room overflowing with her empathy. Clarence wondered how much she knew, what Sapp had and hadn't told her.

"How are the kids?" he asked, desperate to rid his mind of the circumstances which had led to him sitting here, ankles shackled, prohibited from touching his own wife.

"They don't know anything yet," Leslie said. "I told them you got home late last night and left for work early this morning. Got them off to school and came straight here." She looked down at the laminate table, as if searching its scratched surface for answers. "I don't know what to tell them, Clarence. How do you tell your children their father's in jail?"

Clarence reeled at the bluntness of the question. The thought of lying to the kids had crossed his mind – just tell them he had to go out of town on business for a while and hope he was out sooner than later. As quickly as they materialized, however, the thoughts were suffocated by the realization that it was dishonesty and deceit that had buried him in this hellhole to begin with.

"We have to tell them the truth, Les. Tell them there's been a mistake and I've been arrested. That I'll be out again as soon as they fix it." As he spoke the words, he knew how hard it would be on Michael and Sonia. How could they even begin to understand how one day their father was reading them bed time stories and the next they couldn't see him because he was locked up in jail?

Leslie looked from Clarence's eyes to those of her brother, who was nodding in agreement.

"I don't know if I can do it," she said. "How…" Her voice trailed off, muffled by her trembling hands and the onset of quiet sobs.

"You're not alone, Les." Rodney was leaning towards her. "I'll be there with you. We can do it together."

Leslie nodded without removing her hands from her face and for a couple of minutes the three of them sat in silence. Clarence became aware of the officer supervising them from the corner. His hands were folded behind his back now, his face firm and expressionless. He must see this kind of thing every day, Clarence thought. Goes with the territory. People crying and attempting to deal with the fact that their world has just been turned upside down, their lives uprooted from normalcy and tossed around like trees in the aftermath of a violent hurricane. Clarence envied the officer's apathy, his ability to go on standing there as though nothing had changed. He envied the numbness and the desensitization he must have acquired over the years.

"So," said Rodney, finally breaking the silence and turning to Clarence. "Byron says they don't have much in the way of evidence. He's very good, Clarence. From what he tells me, you have nothing to worry about."

Great, Clarence thought. Then why am I still here?

"If anyone should be worried, it's that crazy cop. Police brutality if I've ever seen it."

Rodney's voice was rising and Clarence stole an uneasy glance at the guard. He was still standing with his shoulders against the wall, hands behind his back, disengaged.

"I mean this guy's gonna pay, Clarence. Who the hell does he think he is? This is twenty-first century America, man. You can't just go around beating innocent citizens." His voice had risen and his face had darkened. "We're gonna start with his badge and go from there. Take it to civil court and – "

Leslie cut him off by grabbing his forearm and shaking her head. "Not now, Rodney. Please, don't do this now."

Rodney gathered himself and adjusted his shirt collar, loosened his tie. He leaned back in his chair and put his hands flat on the table. "You're right, I'm sorry. I just can't stand the institutional racism in this country. We got brothers in government, brothers in politics. We think we're making progress, moving forward, but then something like this happens. May as well still be out there in the goddamn cotton fields."

Clarence felt a sense of vindication rising within him. In the past twelve hours, he hadn't been able to muster any strength to attack his situation head on. But in Rodney he had an ally, a supporter, a voice. Rodney was emotional enough for the both of them, an ample enough excuse for his not having to be.

Leslie was the next to speak, her eyes dry again, the smudges of makeup from her face smeared on the heels of her outspread hands. "Any idea how long you might be, you know, how long until they figure this out?"

After he had exhausted the whys and the hows, this was the very question that had contributed to Clarence's sleepless night in the holding cell. No matter how he looked at it, or how long he dwelled on it, he couldn't come up with an honest answer. All he knew was that it was out of his control.

Whether it was due to the silence that followed her question, or perhaps her ability to read the hopelessness on his face, Leslie shot her head back and forth between Clarence and Rodney with wild eyes like a trapped animal searching for a way out. There were new tears forming at the corners of her eyes, a slight tremor working its way across her face.

"They will figure this out, right?" The optimism she was trying to convey was swallowed whole by the uncertainty in her voice. Then, with slightly more conviction, "The truth will come out, Clarence. It always does."

Just then, the door swung open and the uniformed guard poked his head in and clapped his hands together. "All right, folks. Time's up."

The three of them rose and made their way to the open door. Rodney paused before stepping outside and embraced Clarence.

"You take care of Les and the kids for me, Rod," Clarence said into his ear.

Rodney nodded and clasped Clarence's shoulder. "Of course."

Clarence moved toward Leslie and held her tight, as if it might be the last time.

"I love you, Les."

The guard at the door gently tugged at Clarence's wrist with one hand, Leslie's shoulder with the other.

"I love you, too," she said, the guard between them now, Rodney out in the hall.

As they were nudged out of the room, Clarence took one final look back. The orange-haired officer was still in the corner, hands behind his back and a look of indifference plastered across his face, staring straight ahead as if nothing had transpired over the past fifteen minutes. Nothing at all.

Chapter 26

"Where were you?"

Sugar's mother was sitting at the kitchen table with her head in her hands, a half-smoked cigarette dangling from her dry, cracked lips. Her face appeared gaunter than normal, her short black hair a tangled nest of disarray. She was wearing her fluffy pink housecoat with the bleach stains on the elbows and a baby blue cotton blanket draped across her lap. Despite the appearance of just having woken up, a can of beer sat on the table next to her ashtray. She took a sip from it as she looked across the room at Sugar with glossy eyes.

Sugar looked from his mother to the same mess he had come home to the night before. Aside from the TV being back on, everything was as he left it when he went to bed.

"School," he said and went over to give her a hug. As usual, she turned her head and gave him little more than a brief poke in the chest with her knobby shoulder before pulling away. He nearly gagged from the pungent stench of her breath. He walked over to the fridge and found a loaf of Wonder bread and a jar of peanut butter on the top shelf.

"Find a job yet?" For a couple of months now, Ma had been urging him to find work. To help out his poor mother, to do his part, to be a man.

"Not yet, Ma." Sugar answered with his back to her.

"Not yet," she repeated. "Not yet don't pay the bills, Sugar. Not yet don't put food on the table."

"I know, Ma. I'm workin on it." He found a clean butter knife in the cutlery drawer and spread a thick layer of PB between two slices of bread. He took a bite and went over to the table, pulled out a chair and sat down across from his mother.

"Coulda fooled me." She squinted her eyes as she took a long silent pull of nicotine, followed by a swig of beer. "It's time you made a man of yourself Sugar, started providin for your family. The way Reggie done."

When Reggie had first been killed, his mother hadn't even been able to speak his name. She'd retreated into an isolated state of grief and denial, sequestering herself in her bedroom, coming out only to use the restroom and take the occasional shower. She only ate when Sugar or his aunts would bring food up to her and all but force it down her throat.

Eventually she'd started leaving her room, at first for minutes at a time, then for hours. Her grieving mechanism shifted from isolation to alcohol, and she would curl up on the couch with her bottle and her red plastic cup and lose herself in a world of drunkenness and reality TV. But still, she'd refused to speak the name of her slain son. In fact, for a full year after he was killed, Reggie Sinclair had not existed. Not as a son, not as a brother, not even as a memory.

It was only in recent months that she had started speaking of her eldest. And when she did, it was either with glowing adoration or in direct comparison to Sugar. Lately it had been the latter. Never mind that he had dropped out of high school. Never mind that the money she spoke of came from dealing drugs and hustling. Sugar had to be more like Reggie.

When Reggie had still been around, Sugar knew he would always be confined to wandering through life in the shadows cast by his older brother. And he was OK with that; as he got older, there was even some joy in it, a certain level of pride. But what he hadn't counted on was, two years after Reggie had been taken from them, to still exist solely as a shadow. To know that no matter how bright he shone, he would forever pale in comparison to his dead brother.

Sugar picked up his sandwich and walked over to the sink without a word. He couldn't stand to face his mother when she was like this, knowing that if he turned around and saw her, sitting there with her dirty hair and her can of beer, he would resent her. The way he had the time she'd forgotten his thirteenth birthday. Or the times she'd accused him of stealing money from her purse when he hadn't. Or the times she'd hit him.

So he just stood there, staring out the dirty kitchen window at the blowing snow and the fading daylight. He fought back tears by clenching his jaw and holding his breath, the way he'd taught himself over the years. He spread his palms across the counter and waited for his mother to either instigate him or leave the room; he knew from experience it would be one or the other. It would depend on how many of those beers she'd had already. Or how bad her hangover was.

As he continued to stare at the greyness of the afternoon, he finally heard the grinding scrape of metal on linoleum. He closed his eyes and tensed his body, but heard nothing more for what seemed an eternity. Then, finally, the barefooted patter of his mother's footsteps leaving the room, and he allowed himself to breathe.

Alone in the kitchen, Sugar became aware of the coolness of the room and zipped up his hoodie. He tilted his head back and allowed himself to draw several deep breaths, in and out, in and out. He could hear the high-pitched buzz of the old refrigerator and the faint murmur of the television coming from the living room. He took one more bite of his sandwich and threw the rest in the garbage.

Back in his room, Sugar removed the shoebox from beneath his bed and carried it under his arm to the bathroom. He carefully placed the gun in the sink, plugged the drain and ran the hot water. He stared into the sink, the gun growing seemingly larger and larger the more water surrounded it. It was like one of those expandable dinosaurs he used to play with, the ones that would start out as tiny little things the size of his finger and grow to a hundred times their original size and get all slimy when he put them in a bucket of cold water for a couple of nights. Only this wasn't a toy. This was the gun he had used to a kill a man less than twenty-four hours ago. Why did it seem so much longer? Why did that gun and the unthinkable thing he had done with it seem like they had been a part of him for as long as he could remember?

When the sink was full and the gun had grown to the size of a football, Sugar turned off the water, dropped to his knees and opened the cupboard beneath the counter. Toilet paper, a few hand towels, an unopened bar of soap, a half-empty bottle of glass cleaner, a crusty jar of petroleum jelly, a box of Band-Aids, dozens of loose Q-tips, an old blow dryer he didn't remember ever seeing before, a white plastic cup. Everything but bleach. He rummaged around some more, tossing things to the side and piling them on the bath mat behind him, and finally settled on a spray bottle of Tilex hiding way at the back. He unscrewed the top and dumped what was left in the sink. Then he found an old toothbrush, the one he used to scrub his white kicks when they got dirty, in the top drawer.

He quickly dipped his hand in the scalding water and pulled

out the gun. He laid it flat on the counter and began scrubbing, starting with the grip and working his way toward the barrel. He worked his wrist as fast and as hard as he could, until the air around him smelled of disinfectant and his fingers cramped up. He grabbed the grey towel hanging from the back of the door, slid it over his hand like a glove and flipped the gun. When he finished with both sides, he wrapped the towel around the gun and carried it to his room, out in front of him like a stinky diaper. He looked around his bedroom for his backpack and after a moment of confusion, remembered he had left it behind when he bolted from English class.

He slid his closet doors open and found a red nylon bag with a drawstring. He opened it and dropped the entire bundle inside. He zipped it back up, threw it over his shoulder, slipped on his Nikes and headed downstairs. When he reached the landing, he peeked into the living room long enough to see a dense cloud of grey-blue smoke hovering above the lamp in the corner and recognize a McDonald's jingle coming from the television. He snuck across the hall and tiptoed across the kitchen. Just as he reached the door and had his hand around the knob, he heard his name over the din of the television. He paused and thought about answering, telling his mother he'd be home in an hour and that he loved her. Instead, he stepped outside, closing the door behind him as quietly as he could.

Chapter 27

By the time Victor Anton entered Goldie's Bistro and took a seat in the booth across from Gerald, it was forty minutes past their scheduled meeting time.

Anton was Wayne County's lead prosecutor of the criminal division. Based on Gerald's only previous contact with him, a meeting regarding an assault on which he'd been the arresting officer, he pegged Anton as an arrogant, pretty-boy prick. Seeing him now, sitting across from him in his navy tailored suit and his narrow pink tie, forty minutes late, one leg femininely crossed over the other and revealing patterned socks that went halfway up his calf, his opinion was reinforced.

The waitress arrived at their table and Anton ordered a cappuccino before slowly raising his eyes and acknowledging Gerald with a slight raise of his too-perfect eyebrows. Gerald pursed his lips and gave him the warmest smile he could muster.

"Thanks for meeting me," Gerald said.

"Not a problem, Officer Dawes. I was actually planning on contacting you in the next couple days. So, what can I do for you?"

Gerald was aware of the risk he was taking going behind Graves' back like this, but at this point he knew it was a risk he needed to take. With each passing minute, each wasted hour, the case against Nick's real killer was growing colder.

"Well, I'm not sure exactly," Gerald started. "There's just a few details about the case I wanted to go over with you. Some – "

"Look, Officer Dawes."

"Call me Gerald."

"All right, Gerald. Look. I think I know what this is about. Chief Graves told me about your little meeting this morning."

The waitress returned and placed a steaming glass mug in front of Anton. He removed the cinnamon stick from the rim and waited for her to leave before continuing.

"Something about second-guessing the identity of the suspect?"

Gerald nodded.

Anton leaned back in his chair and stroked his chin. He lifted the cappuccino to his lips with both hands and blew on it before taking a tiny sip of froth.

"From what I understand, you and Chief Graves already worked this out. It was a crazy night, everything happened so fast. You're just having doubts. It's common, Gerald. I've seen it a million times."

"That's the thing," Gerald said. "It's more than just doubts." He lowered his head as he spoke. "I know it's my mistake and I'm ready to accept the consequences. But I'm positive Sanford's the wrong guy."

Anton gave him a tight smile, but not before Gerald saw a brief clench of his jaw.

"Listen. Gerald. This Sanford guy has a prior. He has no alibi, no witnesses. Everything's working in our favor here. With the logjam of cases on the circuit, I don't waste my time or take risks on maybes. Believe me when I say that this thing's a slam dunk."

"But the investigation hasn't even been completed yet. There might be something there that – "

Anton cut him off by raising his hand. "You're not hearing me, Gerald. The investigation has been completed. Sanford's our man, case closed."

He took another sip of his drink and studied Gerald for a moment. Then he leaned in, lowered his voice.

"Between you and me? Any other case, I'd probably let the investigation run its course. See if any other evidence turns up, due diligence and all that jazz. But that could take weeks, months even. We're talking about a cop killing here.

"We need a conviction, and we need it stat."

When Gerald didn't respond, Anton shook his head and looked at him as if he were a dog that had just shit on a brand new carpet.

"You know how much the testimony of a cop is worth in a case like this? Especially a white cop?"

Gerald didn't answer. He felt sick to his stomach.

"As far as I'm concerned, we've already wasted too much time on this. We've charged Sanford, and that's the end of it. The case against him is a lock." Anton's mouth was set in a hard line, his lips barely moving. "So long as everybody remembers which side they're on."

"So long as I lie on the stand." Gerald tried his best to hold

Anton's gaze, to salvage what little nerve he had left.

"I appreciate that your conscience has kicked in Gerald, I really do. But – "

"This has nothing to do with my conscience, sir. For all I care, Sanford can spend the rest of his life behind bars. This is about – " He felt his voice catch and took a deep breath to try and calm himself. "It's about justice. Nick's killer is still out there."

"Look, I know you're emotional right now. Your partner's just been killed. But you can't allow it to cloud your judgment. Think of all the people involved here, everything at stake." Anton downed the rest of his drink. "What about Nick's wife, what about his children? With Sanford locked up at least they have some closure. You really want to take that away from them? Tell them that we, that you, made a mistake, and that the man who killed her husband, their father, is still out there?"

Anton reached across the table and squeezed Gerald's forearm.

"Relax, grieve, hit the gym. Do whatever it is you need to do. You'll come around, Gerald. You'll see we're doing the right thing here. Just give it some time."

"Yeah," Gerald said. "Whatever you say."

Anton reached in his pocket and tossed a ten on the table. "Oh, and Gerald?"

Gerald forced himself to look up now, used every ounce of self-restraint to keep it at that.

"If you decide to go to the press with this? Or you try and screw me in court?" He was staring straight into Gerald's eyes, his voice cold and threatening. "Your life as you know it is over."

Gerald lowered his eyes and knew there was nothing left to do but nod.

Chapter 28

After meeting with Leslie and Rodney, Clarence had been led down a long, dimly lit corridor on the second floor of Wayne County Jail with his hands cuffed behind his back and shown to his new cell. It was at the far end of the catwalk, the last in a row of ten. The cell contained a single bunk, a small desk, an even smaller seat, a tarnished steel toilet and a matching single-faucet sink covered in rust, all of which were permanently affixed to the concrete walls. On top of the threadbare mattress lay a small pile of laundry: two white sheets, a thin blue blanket, a plain white towel and a matching face cloth. There was also an empty cardboard box, which the guard told him was for his personal effects. All of it was enclosed by three windowless concrete walls and a row of steel bars facing an empty grey hallway.

After showering and changing in to his new uniform – an orange and white striped jumpsuit with the word JAIL stencilled in black across his back and a pair of white canvas shoes without laces and a size too big – he was led to the jail's medical center. After approximately twenty minutes of examinations, the doctors confirmed nothing was broken. Some internal swelling, a few bruised ribs and a nasty cut above his left eye seemed to be the worst of it. Nothing a little bit of time wouldn't heal, the doctor had told him with a half-hearted smile.

Now, he sat alone in a tiny room at the end of his housing unit. The musty air carried a faint smell of disinfectant, and other than two stools and a metal table attached to the concrete floor, the room was bare. The discomfort of the backless stool he sat on made him aware of the weariness settling deep in his bones, the sleepless night gnawing at him, weighing him down both mentally and physically. Not yet noon, he could think of nothing but falling asleep in his bedroom at home. Climbing into the comfortable king size bed among the soft sheets and the heavy blankets and the cool, fluffy pillows, the lights off and his wife curled up beside him. It had been less than forty-eight hours since he'd last slept in his own bed. It felt like a lifetime.

Clarence heard the sharp sound of a buzzer and the door along the far wall swung open. He watched a white man of average height and a few extra pounds walk through it. The man made his way across the room with a confident stride, holding Clarence's eyes the entire way. When he reached the circular metal table, he placed two Styrofoam cups on the table. Clarence forced himself to his feet and shook the man's hand. Up close, Clarence could see fatigue in the man's face, but the smile it wore was warm and honest. Judging by the hint of grey in his dark brown hair and the barely determinable crow's feet at the corners of his brown eyes, Clarence put him in his early forties.

"Dr. Allan Strum," the man said as he crouched into his seat and removed the tote bag hanging from his shoulder. "And you must be Clarence."

Back in the discomfort of his own stool, Clarence nodded.

"Nice to meet you. Coffee?" Strum nodded toward the cups on the table.

"Thanks," Clarence said, reaching for the one closest to him, pulling off the plastic lid and blowing on the black liquid before taking a sip. It was hot and strong.

"Sorry to have kept you waiting. My last appointment ran a little longer than expected."

Clarence shrugged. "Not like I have anywhere better to be."

The doctor gave him a small, tight smile, more with his eyes than his mouth. Clarence saw a flash of awkward uncertainty in the doctor' face, as if he were considering whether to take the joke a step further or to leave it alone. He clasped his hands together and sat up straighter in his seat.

"Anyhow," he began, "I'm what they call an intake counsellor here at the jail. As you may have already experienced, the transition here can be extremely stressful, traumatic even. It's my job to assess the condition of the inmates and assure they get whatever they need to help make the transition as easy as possible. Almost like an advocate," he added with another small smile.

Clarence didn't say anything. He stared at the doctor, stared through him actually, at the grey drab of the concrete wall behind him. Maybe if he detached himself from the situation, it wouldn't be real.

"OK, why don't I start by asking you a couple of questions." Dr. Strum opened his black bag and pulled out a yellow lined legal pad. He opened it across the tabletop, removed a pen from his breast pocket and clicked it open.

"So. How have you found the jail so far? The staff, your cell, any problems?"

Clarence kept his eyes fixed on the wall, listening to the doctor but not hearing him. When he didn't answer, the doctor placed his pen on the table and leaned forward. He sighed a deep sigh and ran his hands across his face.

"Look," he said. "Clarence. I know you don't want to be here, but this interview is a necessary and essential step in the integration process. I've reviewed your file and it's clear you're an educated and reasonable man, so why don't we just – "

"It's all my fault." Clarence was still staring at the wall over the doctor's right shoulder. His words sounded hollow in his head.

"What is, Clarence? What's your fault?" Strum's voice soft and distant.

"I just wanted to get something to eat. Get some supper and go home." Clarence could remember it had been a hot day, the vinyl booth warm and sticky from the sun beating down through the front window of the diner and the overhead fan whirring like a helicopter.

"Clarence? What – "

"I had no intention of going home with her. But the way she looked at me? The way she smiled at me?"

The memory was coming back to him in jagged fragments now. Her faded yellow uniform with the brown, folded-down collar and the sleeves hemmed just above the elbows. The crooked nametag pinned just above her left breast. The spearmint smell of her gum and the carefree way she chewed it. The way she leaned into him when she took his order and the way she touched his shoulder when she brought it to him. The way she sat down at the booth across from him and smiled at him and asked him for a ride home.

Clarence could feel the guilt and the self-disgust coursing through his body, mingling, growing more volatile, more violent, slamming against his insides, nowhere to go but out. "I even took off my wedding ring so she wouldn't know I was married. My wedding ring."

"Who are you talking about, Clarence? Who is she?"

Clarence buried his head in his hands. He was short of breath and felt as though he was going to collapse. He dug his elbows into his knees and rocked back and forth until he felt a hand on his shoulder. When he looked up, he saw a series of floating black spots and the blurred outline of a figure standing over him.

"Clarence? Are you all right? Talk to me, Clarence. Say something."

Clarence's eyelids gave way to the weight again and he saw nothing but black. He dropped his head between his knees and kept it there for what seemed like an hour. He drifted in and out of consciousness, from the concrete interview room to his bedroom at home to the diner in Crookston to his claustrophobic cell. He saw the doctor, he saw Natasha, he saw the kid with the gun, and the cop with the angry eyes, he saw Judge Barlow, Rodney, Leslie. He tried to call out to them, but he couldn't speak. When he opened his eyes again, Dr. Strum was kneeling beside him. There was a look of concern on his face and he held a bottle of water. He handed it to Clarence.

Clarence took a swig, the cool liquid circulating through his veins, bringing him back to life one muscle at a time. When he finished the bottle, he placed it on the table.

"Thanks," he said to the doctor. "Sorry about that."

"Are you all right?"

"Yeah," Clarence said. "I think so. I just, I'm not sure what happened there."

"It's been a stressful couple of days. You're exhausted." Dr. Strum got to his feet and walked back around the table. "Let's continue this interview tomorrow, after you get some rest."

Clarence shook his head. "I'm fine. Let's get this over with."

Dr. Strum, who was in the middle of gathering his belongings, paused. He examined Clarence for a long moment before putting his things down and sitting down on his stool. "You're sure? Because if you're not up to it, we can reschedule."

"No. I'm good." And he was. His mind was clearer, sharper. He was still tired, but his body felt lighter, like it did when he got a second wind on the back half of a marathon.

Strum tilted his head and brushed his fingertips against his chin, apparently deliberating how to proceed. "All right. You were talking about a woman. Something about taking her home? Something about taking off your wedding ring so she wouldn't know you were married?"

Clarence felt a rush of blood to his face, unaware of how much he had divulged to the doctor before he'd blacked out.

"Clarence," the doctor said. "I'm not here to judge." He raised his open palms and spread them in front of him. "I'm here to ask you a few questions, to get to know you a little bit better and do what I can to make this as easy as possible for you."

"I'm not a murderer," Clarence said. He had intended to say it with authority, but it came out as more of a plea.

Strum leaned forward in his seat and gave Clarence a sad shake of his head, as if to say he empathized with his situation but there was nothing he could do about it. For over a minute neither man spoke. Clarence wiped at the sweat beading on his forehead with the back of his hand.

"I'm innocent," Clarence said. The words had gone through his head so many times in the past twelve hours, they seemed to him insignificant and meaningless. Just words. But right now they were all he had. "I shouldn't even be here. My lawyer's gonna have me out of here by the end of the day." Clarence heard his voice crack as he spoke the words, hoping to God with every last cell of his body they were true.

"You say you're innocent, and I'm not here to say you are or you aren't," Strum said. "In my experience? The evidence never lies. The truth always finds its way to the surface. In the meantime, this is it." He spread his hands and looked around the tiny dungeon of a room. "Like it or not, you are, for the time being, a county jail inmate. And as long as you're here, there are certain expectations, certain rules you have to live by."

Clarence only half heard what the doctor was saying, lost in the hopeless realization that this was really happening. Here. Now. To him.

"Clarence?" Strum had his elbows on the table again. "Clarence, look at me."

When Clarence looked at him, he saw genuine pity. The doctor's forehead was creased, his eyes drawn down at the corners. Strum reached across the table and put his hand gently on

Clarence's wrist and said, "Clarence. You'll get through this."

"I just want to go home." Clarence could feel a swelling in his throat, a burning behind his eyes. "Why can't I just go home?"

Strum didn't answer. He removed his hand from Clarence's wrist, lowered his eyes and shook his head. He packed up his notepad, clicked his pen shut, placed it back in his shirt pocket. He picked up his briefcase, got to his feet and shook his head again. Then he walked out of the room without looking back.

Chapter 29

Gerald sat with his hands flat across the granite counter top. Between them sat a bottle of whiskey, unopened. He had been this way for the better part of an hour now, rocking the bar stool forward and back, shifting his shaky hands, approaching the bottle with the black label, retreating. Fighting the urge and the desperation to go there. Reciting the reasons not to.

The assault of the ifs and the what ifs, the hows and the whys, was relentless. What if they had arrived at that intersection two minutes earlier, or two minutes later? What if he hadn't decided to follow the Infiniti just because there was a black man behind the wheel? How going in the opposite direction or telling Nick to chase the driver could have changed everything. How it could have been, should have been, him. Why Nick was the one with all the blood on his face and the gaping hole in his throat. Why he was spared.

Gerald fingered the rim of the rocks glass in front of him. He thought about Nick and Graves and Anton and Sanford. About Janet and Charlie and how his life had gone straight to hell that sweltering summer day six months ago.

By the time he and Charlie had loaded the trunk with their coolers, backpacks and fishing gear, it wasn't yet seven, but the sun was high and hot and they were both sweating. Their destination was Booster Lake, a couple hours north, hugging the Canadian border. The highways were nearly empty and they were making great time. They stopped only once. The stop that in hindsight had changed everything. The stop that if he could do it all over again, Gerald never would have made. That's what he told himself, at least.

It was a small general store off the highway, forty or fifty miles from the nearest town in any direction. It was built like a rustic cabin: thick logs, worn wooden shingles, no windows. The faded sign above the single, timber-framed door was so battered from the sun and the snow that Gerald couldn't even make out the name of it. Charlie stayed in the car, lost in whatever magazine he was reading, Sports Illustrated probably, and Gerald left it running to keep the AC going. He walked inside and spotted the bait freezer and picked up two dozen night crawlers packed tight in mud-filled Styrofoam containers. He also grabbed a package of beef jerky and a bag of salt and vinegar chips. They had sandwiches packed, but he knew Charlie ate sandwiches five days a week, the same low-fat mayonnaise on the same whole wheat, twelve-grain, five-dollar-a-loaf bread Janet insisted on buying. Not that Gerald had a problem with eating healthy, but every once in a while he needed to rebel. Sometimes it was sugar that tempted him – the urgent desire for a donut or an ice cream or a candy bar. That day, it was salt. And just as he pulled out his wallet and was about to pay, he heard another calling. The same one that had been playing games with him for most of his adult life. The one he tended to hear when he was feeling especially upset, or happy, or angry, or celebratory, or anxious, or excited. The one that had become his default answer to most of life's questions.

The glass bottles lined the shelves behind the clerk like an ominous beacon. Given his awkwardness with Charlie and his inability to speak more than two words to him on the entire trip to that point, he decided on his go-to icebreaker: Bombay Sapphire.

As he left the store, plastic bag in one hand, paper in the other, the heat of the day hit him like a knockout punch. He sucked in the heavy humid air and felt immediately as though he was going to pass out. He saw the car, the only one in the lot, emitting a steady tail of exhaust like a mirage against the desolate background. He saw Charlie sitting in the passenger seat, eyes down, still reading.

As he approached the car, his son raised his head. Gerald looked at him and smiled and Charlie responded with a small smile of his own. Gerald thought he recognized a glint of something in Charlie's eyes, but he wrote it off as paranoia. A further reason, he justified, for needing the gin. He was too tense, too uptight; he needed something to loosen the nerves. He popped the trunk and deposited the night crawlers into the cooler. He shuffled some things around and found a spot for the paper bag, but not before loosening the cap, making sure the upright trunk lid blocked Charlie's view, and took a swig from the bottle. The Bombay was dry and bitter and burned his throat. He slammed the trunk shut and hopped back in the driver's seat. "You want some chips?"

Though the rest of the ride was only forty-five minutes, Gerald pulled over twice. Once he used the excuse of checking on the ice situation, the other time he grabbed them a couple bottles of water.

Each sip of the alcohol went down smoother, and by the time they got to the lake he'd forgotten why he'd bought it in the first place. Things were great. He and Charlie had been talking the entire time, discussing everything from school to girls to the Tigers' chances of making the playoffs. Slim to none, as usual. He told Charlie stories about work that he referred to as cool and awesome. At one point he thought he even remembered his son saying they should do this more often. "Next weekend," Gerald had said. "Every weekend for the rest of the summer if you want."

Booster Lake was one of the hundreds of small, remote bodies of water connected to Lake Huron. It was fairly well known on both sides of the border, mainly for its abundance of Northern pike and walleye, but still had the purity of a haven untouched by commercialism. The closest thing to civilization for miles was a white-bearded man in a small shack who rented out canoes and single prop motorboats by the hour, cash only.

The lake was quiet that day, and Gerald and Charlie opted for the deserted shoreline, which was so shallow this time of year that you could remove your shoes, walk out several hundred feet and cast from among the jungle of seaweed and bulrush. Within minutes of his first cast, Gerald was pouring sweat, the lake greedily soaking up the rays and throwing them back at his body like a mirror. He found himself thinking about all the smart people back home, enjoying their air conditioned bungalows or backyard swimming pools, sipping on mojitos and long island iced teas. He needed another drink.

By noon, the bottle in the paper bag was half empty. Gerald felt more and more comfortable with Charlie and reasoned with himself that all of his feelings of inferiority and fears of being like his own father were unwarranted. He was a completely different man; he and his son had a great relationship. Side by side, up to their knees in the greyish luke-warm water, taking turns casting and sharing laughs, they couldn't be happier. To Charlie's delight, they'd even caught a couple of fish; Gerald had hooked a perch, Charlie a twenty-inch pike. Neither were keepers, but Gerald had been able to teach Charlie how to hold the fish behind the gills, how to remove the hook from its mouth and release it back in to the water. Just as his own father had taught him.

By two o'clock, Gerald was feeling it. He couldn't keep track of how many trips he'd made to the car or the multiple excuses he'd fed Charlie for doing so. Sweat was leaking from every pore of his body and he felt as though he might pass out. He decided to rest in the car for a while, just to get out of the sun. You don't mind do you Charlie? Of course not. I'll be in the car if you need me, just for a minute. You can keep fishing long as you want, just remember the sunscreen. Reapply every hour, he slurred.

Gerald reclined the driver's seat and used his rolled-up, sweat-stained T-shirt as a pillow. The sun was still pounding through the windows but all Gerald could feel was the cool air blowing on his sandaled feet and his bare chest. Before he knew it, he was out.

Over the past six months, Gerald had gone over those last couple hours more times than he could count. He wanted, more than anything, to remember his last words to his son. Or his son's last words to him. Something, anything about the last time he saw Charlie. But the latter part of that afternoon remained a blur. From the time he stumbled to the car to the time he woke up in a puddle of his own sweat, about an hour and a half by his estimation, everything had changed.

At first he had thought he was looking in the wrong spot. Still a little bit dazed and incoherent, he figured he might have gone the wrong way or forgotten where they'd been fishing. But then he found their cooler next to a tree, and then Charlie's rod along the bank. His next rationalization was that Charlie had wandered off somewhere. He couldn't be far, Gerald told himself. He'd gone exploring. Or maybe he had to take a leak.

As Gerald stumbled over to the public outhouses near the rental shack, cotton-mouthed and fog-headed, the relentless sun beating down on him, he somehow already knew that he'd never see his son again. He didn't want to acknowledge it, but somewhere deep down he knew it with such finality that he couldn't even bring himself to fear it. Fear was uncertain. This was not.

By the time he'd reached the outhouses, he was gasping for air and his sweat-drenched T-shirt stuck to his back and chest. The old man at the canoe shack was closing up for the day when Gerald asked if he'd seen his son. The young boy with the blond hair and the brown eyes, the one with the light grey T-shirt and the Red

Wings cap. The last clothes Gerald would ever see his son wearing. The man hadn't, not since earlier in the day when they'd first arrived. Looking back now, Gerald regretted not asking the man more questions. Grilling him, forcing him to lie if he had to. Just to hear something positive, anything to stop the incessant spinning of his head and the increasing numbing of his senses. But he didn't want to seem irresponsible. He didn't want to seem like a bad father. He didn't want to be all of the things he knew that he was. So Gerald mumbled something about meeting Charlie back at their fishing spot and walked away with his head down. On the way back, he came across a few anglers, the last of the day; another man with his son, a couple of college-aged buddies with rods and a cooler of beer cans, mostly empty. None of them had seen Charlie either.

In the minutes and hours that followed, Gerald threw the cursed paper bag and its evil poison in the cloudy lake, loaded the car with their gear and phoned the station as soon as his cellphone had reception. He didn't call Janet, thought it would be better to wait until he got home and deliver what could only be the decisive blow to their already rocky marriage in person. He wanted to be there for the anger and the wrath he knew she would throw at him, already craving the shame and guilt she would pour over him.

But much to Gerald's surprise, and private disappointment, it never came. Not in the form of vicious pronouncements, nor in the form of icy silence. The days turned into weeks and the weeks into months. Nothing. Janet's saintly grace was nothing short of miraculous. Through the long days of worrying, wondering, wishing, there was no indication of blame. Through the longer nights of tossing, turning, crying, not a sliver of reproach. Only forgiveness and support.

Gerald realized now that it was the strength of Janet alone that had gotten him through the autumn months that followed. Together they gathered recent photos of Charlie and had them scanned and copied and posted all around the city. Together they organized and participated in search parties in the areas surrounding Booster Lake. Together they took every radio and television interview they could get, pleading with whoever took their son, begging the faceless thief to return what rightly belonged to them. Together they prayed, sitting at the table with the empty space, driving in the car with the empty seat, lying in bed with the empty bedroom down the hall. Together they poured out every last bottle of alcohol in the house. At the time, it was the closest to vindication that Gerald could feel. Every drop that left those bottles and slid down the drain brought him closer to closure, ounce by bitter ounce.

One month passed. Then two. Things with Janet were as good as they'd ever been. There was talk of another child. By four months, they were having regular date nights. Moonlit walks and picnic lunches, just like in college. The talk of another child became more than talk. By five months, the shackles of guilt to which Gerald had confined himself began to loosen. Like the first crack of sunlight after a long, cold winter, the joy and happiness he had hidden himself from began to reappear.

Then, finally, 137 days after the fact, it came.

It's all your fault.

Gerald reached across the counter and twisted the black cap off the bottle of whiskey. For a moment he sat there, a tilt of the bottle away from going back to that place he swore he'd never return. The place he'd condemned for all it had cost him. But Charlie was gone. Janet was gone. Nick was gone. What was left to lose?

He lifted the glass to the neck of the bottle with one hand and poured several splashes of the amber liquid with the other. He lowered the glass to the table and imagined the taste of it, the numbing of his tongue, the warm, cleansing sensation as he swallowed. The way it would make him feel, the way it would make him forget.

With a trembling hand, he brought the glass to his lips and closed his eyes. He took a tiny sip, followed by another. Then a backward tilt of his head and a long swig that downed the rest of the drink. When the alcohol had burned its way down his throat and settled in a warm, tingly knot at the bottom of his stomach he opened his eyes. Then he reached for the bottle and poured himself another.

Chapter 30

Clarence walked down the dingy corridor of his housing unit, a guard's hand at the base of his spine guiding him forward and dictating the pace. Clarence's hands were shackled behind his back, the cold steel of the cuffs digging in to his wrists. In order for his too-big shoes to stay on, he had to shuffle his feet along the concrete floor, drawing stares from the other inmates in his row. He kept his eyes down and moved in step with the guard. When they reached the room at the end of the hall, the same one he had met Dr. Strum in earlier that day, the guard opened the door and led him inside.

Sapp and Burnett were already there. They both had black briefcases at their sides and wore black suits with somber-colored ties. The guard gave them a slight nod and exited without a word. The gnashing grind of sliding steel was followed by a sharp buzz and Sapp stepped forward.

"Clarence. How are you holding up?"

"All right." Clarence remained standing, hands still cuffed, limbs stiff and aching. He nodded at Burnett but neither man spoke.

"Good, good. Did you manage to get any sleep this afternoon?"

"Some."

"Good," Sapp said again, making a move for one of the chairs attached to the metal table. Burnett motioned with his chin for Clarence to take the other. Clarence gave him another nod.

Sapp opened his briefcase and shuffled through a thick stack of papers without making eye contact. "I'm afraid we have to start off today's meeting with some bad news."

Clarence felt his stomach sink. He wanted to ask his lawyer how things could possibly get any worse, but the words were trapped in his chest.

Sapp cleared his throat and appeared to be going over some of his paperwork without really looking at it. "We haven't been able to reach your primary alibi. Natasha Stokes?"

The mention of her name hit Clarence like a kick in the gut. "What do you mean you haven't been able to reach her?" he managed. "Did you try her at work?"

Sapp responded by sliding a sheet of paper across the tabletop.

Clarence hesitated before rotating it with his index finger and reading the half page of scribbles Natasha had left for her sister. Line by line, sentence by sentence, word by word, Clarence read in disbelief. When he got to the end, he picked it up and read it again.

"Now, we've contacted the sister and told her to let us know the minute she hears from Natasha," Sapp said. "For the time being, we'll include her on our witness list and hope we hear from her."

"Hope?" Clarence thought about the last time he saw Natasha. Sitting in her living room, surrounded by the musty smell of old furniture, drinking a Bud, the beads of condensation on his fingertips. Less than forty-eight hours ago. "And if we don't?"

Sapp looked tentatively at Burnett. Back at Clarence. "As of now, she's your only alibi." Another apprehensive pause. "Not having her as a witness could be a crucial blow to our case."

Clarence leaned forward and momentarily forgetting the cuffs on his hands, tried to swing his arms free. He clenched his teeth and felt his cheeks bloom as the jagged steel dug in to his flesh.

"You're telling me my freedom is resting in the hands of a witness and we have no idea where the hell she is? Come on, Byron. You gotta do better than that." He stared directly into the eyes of his lawyer.

Sapp looked away. Burnett remained silent.

"I'm innocent!"

Sapp lowered his head and exhaled. After a moment, he stood up and walked around the table. He crouched next to Clarence and placed his elbows on his knees.

"Clarence. Look at me."

Clarence could feel his blood swelling his veins, his heart battering the inside of his chest. He rolled his shoulder forward and wiped his mouth against the thin cotton of his prison uniform. Sapp stood up and removed a charcoal handkerchief from his breast pocket, wiped the sweat from Clarence's forehead. He crouched down again and rested his open palm across Clarence's left knee.

"I know you're innocent, Clarence. But at this point in the game, it's not about the truth. If it was, we wouldn't even be here." He got to his feet and moved his hand to Clarence's shoulder. His voice was strictly professional now, void of any emotion. "It's about what we can prove. And without Natasha, or any other witnesses,

131

things aren't looking good."

Without looking at Sapp, Clarence could sense the weight of what he was implying. Up until now, he hadn't considered the possibility of being found guilty. Of spending more than a night, two at most, in this wretched hellhole.

He closed his eyes and thought about that cop again, the way he stood over him and kicked him while he was down. He thought about the detectives in the interview room, their contemptuous comments and their insolent stares. He thought about the judge up on his pedestal, the cold and unaffected way he peered down at him and robbed him of his life as he knew it with the utterance of a single sentence. Apparently the justice system didn't believe in misunderstandings.

"Look." Burnett spoke for the first time. "We're not out of this thing. We may not have much, but neither do they. No murder weapon. No real motive. And other than the arresting officer, no witnesses of their own. The onus is on them, Clarence. Innocent until proven guilty."

"Right," Clarence said. "Then why am I behind bars? Why am I in these?" He shook his wrists behind his back, the cuffs jangling like tin cans tied to a string.

Both lawyers shook their heads in what seemed like genuine sympathy.

"I don't know what to tell you, Clarence. The system sucks. It's the reason Jake and I do what we do." Sapp looked at his partner and let out a low chuckle that sounded forced. "Hell. It's the only reason we have jobs."

Clarence didn't laugh. He was focused on a scratch in the center of the table, silently cursing the world for the cruel joke it was playing on his life.

"Anyway," said Sapp, pacing now. "This trial has the makings of World War Three. They're out to get you and they're gonna pull out all the stops. They'll push for an uneducated, all-white jury and I see us getting maybe a couple blacks, tops. So Jake's going to do a lot of the talking at trial. Most of the statements, most of the questioning. The last thing we need is an us versus them sideshow."

Clarence remained silent.

Sapp began gathering the papers from the table and packing

them in his briefcase. When it was full, he clasped the latches and handed it to Burnett. "I'll meet you out there."

Burnett nodded and made his way to the visitor door. He pressed a button and waited for the buzz. He pushed the door open and stepped outside.

"Listen," Sapp said. "I know it's none of my business. And if I'm crossing the line here, I'm sorry."

Clarence continued to stare at the table, his eyes dry and heavy, a dense pain building at the base of his skull.

"I'm not sure if you've mentioned anything to Leslie yet. About Natasha, I mean. But word's gonna get out, Clarence. One way or another, she's going to find out."

The mention of his wife's name brought Clarence back, the looming prospect of doing what he needed to do suddenly dwarfing the gravity of everything else going on around him – the suffocating sensation of the concrete walls closing in around him, the unyielding steel digging into his wrists, the erratic circumstances that had put him here. He bowed his head and nodded, more to himself than to Sapp.

"All right, then. Take care of yourself, Clarence. And hard as it may be, keep your head up." Sapp smiled at him and started toward the exit. "Every now and again, the good guy does actually win."

Chapter 31

By the time Sugar reached Shaughnessy Park, it was going on six o'clock. The dreary, low-hanging clouds had washed out what was left of the late afternoon sunset. The only light came from the faint shimmer of crystallized snow beneath a dull, frowning half moon. As usual, the park was abandoned.

While Sugar could still remember Shaughnessy as the place he and Reggie wasted away the weekends and summer holidays of their youth, the park had devolved in to little more than an unofficial dumping ground and occasional drinking spot for teenagers with nowhere else to go. Its once-vibrant play structures were corroded by rust, the sports fields and network of walking trails spoiled by neglect. Frozen snow sat atop the meshless basketball rims and rotten picnic tables like a thick layer of dust.

When Sugar had left his house, he hadn't intended on coming this far. His original plan was to ditch the gun in a dumpster or a garbage can, maybe toss it down the grate of a sewer. But every time he stopped to dump it, he'd heard footsteps, or voices. Too spooked to make the drop, he'd carry on in hurried steps, head down, drawstring bag clutched tight against his shoulder, until he found himself at the park entrance.

Sugar headed immediately for the riverside trail. The other option was a narrow, pine-darkened path fringing Redwood Cemetery. Through the swelling dusk, he could make out countless objects scattered along the borders of the park; black garbage bags, piles of damp, rotten leaves, stacks of old, used tires, heaps of wood and shingles and unwanted scraps of furniture. The blue steel trash barrels were overflowing and the wind was having its way with the excess, tossing and turning fast food wrappers and faded newspaper pages across the open field. Aluminum cans and shards of glass stabbed through the snow and glimmered in the moonlight.

The trees, which stood like row upon row of attentive soldiers, seemed to have taken their last breaths; they were stripped of their bark and their leaves, grey and naked against the December wind. The silhouettes of their broken branches lay scattered around the trunks, large and gnarled like elephant tusks. On the far east side of the park sat the carcass of a burnt out seventies model Ford. Its original color had been replaced by reddish-yellow rust and all of its lights and windows had been smashed out, leaving the front of the car with a hole like a mouth, toothless and gaping. As Sugar approached the car, it seemed to be grinning at him, the last living thing in the park and in need of a friend. Sugar looked away, scanning, searching, until he saw a row of leafless shrubs about a hundred yards away.

He left the gravel path and cut across an open plot of snow-dusted grass the size of a football field. Out of the cover of the trees, alone in the center of the field, Sugar shivered. The wind was whipping now, slicing and biting at his cheeks. He rubbed his hands together and tucked them in the sleeves of his hoodie. He lowered his head and began to run, the screaming wind drowned out by the crunch of packed snow and dead leaves beneath his heels.

The shrubs near the river were grey and barren, their branches jutting out like tangled bones in every direction. Not much cover, but they'd have to do. He got down on his knees and scanned the park. Still empty. He slid the bag off his shoulder, desperate to finally rid himself of the nagging burden inside.

His fingers were numb and he had trouble with the icy zipper. He curled up his bare hands and blew warm air on them, wiped at his runny nose and his frozen cheeks. Just as he got back to work on the zipper, he heard the crackle of snapped branches. He dropped the bag and got to his feet just in time to see a squirrel scrabble up a nearby tree. He took a deep breath and cursed himself for being such a baby.

He crouched down again and decided to ditch the entire package, bag and all. He shoved the backpack into the bush and took off running, away from the outstretched branches, arms thrashing, legs flailing, heart slamming against his chest, not looking back. He reached the entrance of the park out of breath and gasping for air. Up ahead, he could see the warm glow of streetlights. He turned his back to the darkness and went toward them.

Chapter 32

Gerald was sitting at a corner booth in the back of Monk's Tavern with a clear view of the front door. Every time it swung open, he tensed up and glanced at the Heineken clock above the bar, hoping it was and wasn't her at the same time. He'd arrived nearly a full hour earlier than they'd agreed on. He felt more comfortable being the first one there, sitting and waiting, building up a sort of home court advantage. Besides, it gave him time for a quick drink.

Aside from Gerald and three college-aged guys in jeans and sweaters sitting at the bar-side stools, the restaurant was empty. Gerald stirred the remains of his Jack and Coke, mostly melted ice, with a little green straw and downed it. He caught the bartender's eye and signalled for another, stealing another glance at the clock over his shoulder: twenty-five after seven. He chewed on the straw and watched the flat-screen television suspended above the bar. 1-0 Wings, midway through the first.

The bartender, a thirtyish white guy with a blond faux-hawk and studded earrings in both ears, came over with his drink. Gerald thanked him and looked back at the clock. 7:29. Back at the television. Still 1-0. He removed the straw from the glass and downed the drink in two big gulps just as he heard the front door open. A gust of wind swirled beneath the table and nibbled at his legs and he heard the swish and crunch of the James Street traffic. The door closed and, for the first time in ten days, Gerald saw his wife.

He watched Janet straighten her hair with her gloved hands and tuck it behind her ears. She scanned the room until he caught her eye and started over. She was wearing blue jeans with a hooded North Face jacket that he recognized and a pair of high brown winter boots that he didn't. The rubber of her soles chirped as she crossed the hardwood planks, the bartender and all three guys at the bar checking her out every step of the way. When she was within a couple feet of his table, Gerald got up from his chair on wobbly legs.

Janet's face was emotionless and it looked for a moment as if she might ignore his open arms and walk right past him. To his relief, she stopped and leaned into him. The shell of her coat was cool and he could smell the crisp pine scent of winter on her skin. The embrace was brief and awkward and Janet was the first to let go.

"I'm so sorry about Nick," she said. God, he missed that voice. She removed her gloves and her coat and sat down in the stool across from Gerald.

Her hair was longer than he remembered, her eyes larger. That impossible bright green. For the first time since she'd arrived, she made eye contact with him. She must have seen the lack of sleep and excess of whiskey in his face.

"You've been drinking."

He let out a low chuckle and immediately regretted it. He had difficulty holding her gaze and shifted his eyes to her hands. He noticed her nails were painted a dull shade of white. She was wearing her wedding ring.

"Been a hell of a couple days," he said.

Janet sighed and shook her head.

"Come on, Janet." He waited for her to look at him. She didn't. "I fucked up, I know it. Come on, Janet, look at me. I'm sorry, OK? Can you please look at me, at least?"

She folded her hands, her ring disappearing between the knuckles of her right hand, and exhaled a long, heavy breath. When she looked up she scanned the room without really looking. Glanced at the guys at the bar, the bartender behind it, the television above it, the empty rocks glass on the table next to his elbow.

When she finally met his eyes, her irises were dark green, almost black, and unblinking. "I never should have agreed to this."

"Please, Janet. I'm sorry." Gerald was standing now. He reached for her arm but she pulled it away. "I need you, Janet. I need you so bad."

Janet slid her stool out from under her, the abrupt scrape of metal on wood drawing the attention of the men at the bar. She grabbed her jacket from the coat tree and pulled it over her arms one sleeve at a time. She shook her head again, a trace of sympathy etched at the corners of her darkened eyes.

"Six months, Ger. Six months down the drain." She zipped up her jacket and reached for her gloves. "You know something? I actually thought we might be able to work things out. Then you go

137

and do...this."

Gerald could feel his throat catching, the area behind his eyes swelling. He was aware that the bartender and the college kids were still looking in their direction.

He turned his back to them so he was facing Janet's shoulder. "I didn't throw it all away. It's one mistake. Please, babe. Just give me a chance here."

Janet rotated and placed her gloved hands on his shoulders.

"This was your chance, Ger. You know I had Alison drop me off here?" She dropped her hands to her side and her eyes to the floor. "I was planning on coming home tonight."

"You still can. Just come home and everything will be OK, you'll see. We'll work this out."

She looked up at Gerald's face for a second or two before moving toward the exit.

He took a step after her, grabbed her by the elbow. She broke free without looking at him and walked faster.

"You still can," he called after her, arms spread at his sides. "Come on, Janet. Please."

She didn't stop until she reached the door. She paused for a moment and Gerald waited for her to turn around. She never did.

*   *   *

After three more drinks, Gerald decided to call a cab.

He climbed in the back seat, weightless and numb, and gave the driver his address. The traffic was light and the wind was howling. Building by building, darkened street by darkened street, Gerald watched the city blow by him like an angry blizzard.

By the time the taxi crossed the bridge and pulled onto Washburn, Gerald's buzz had faded, replaced by a steady pulse behind his temples. The bars and restaurants and office buildings of downtown had been replaced by two-story Victorians, big and dark against the pale moonlight. Rooftops were ridged with frost and front lawns shimmered silver like frozen ponds.

As they neared Gerald's street, he ordered the driver to stop and turn around, directing him back to the freeway and instructing him to get off a couple exits later. When they hit Marshall, they

138

turned left. A block later, Gerald saw what he was looking for and asked the driver to pull into the parking lot.

Gerald stumbled out of the taxi and balled up his hands against the wind. He crossed the lot and entered through the turnstile, grabbed a small red basket from a stack along the wall and headed straight for the back corner. The fluorescent lighting was bright and the floors were slippery and smelled as if they'd just been wiped with bleach. Aside from an overweight black woman behind the counter, he was alone in the store. He found the whiskey and picked up four bottles of JD, placing them one by one in the basket. He paid for them with his credit card and exited through the turnstile carrying the bottles under his arms in paper bags.

He stepped into the blistering wind and crouched on the sidewalk, taking temporary cover behind a trashcan. He pulled one of the bottles from a paper bag and twisted the cap off. He raised it to his lips and took a three-second swig, warming his insides immediately. He replaced the cap, returned the bottle to the bag and stood up. He took a deep breath of the icy air and walked back across the parking lot toward the taxi.

Chapter 33

When Sugar opened his eyes on Monday morning it was just past eight. What little of the weekend he hadn't slept away, Sugar spent losing himself in movies and video games, until the details of Thursday night were nothing more than faded shards of his subconscious.

The sounds of the gun were less torturous now, the images of the blood less violent. The only evidence that the events of Thursday night weren't merely a series of graphic nightmares, or one of the countless R-rated movies he'd watched, was the unrelenting pain in his left side. Tempting as it was to stay in bed for the third straight day, he knew he couldn't hibernate in his room for the rest of his life. Impossible as it seemed, he knew he had to do something.

He eased himself out of bed and pulled the left leg of his plaid boxers up and over his hipbone. Even against his dark skin he could see the bruise there, the circumference of a hockey puck, the color of an eggplant. He poked it with his finger and shuddered, a jolt of pain springing up his spine. He limped across the room to his closet, found a clean pair of sandblasted jeans and a red Ecko T. Applying most of his weight on the rickety banner along the wall, he descended the stairs one tentative step at a time until he reached the landing.

The empty hook where his mother hung her coat told him she was out again, the kitchen's state of disarray that she probably hadn't been home all night. Her glass ashtray sat in the middle of the table like a centerpiece, a small mound of grey and white ash and yellowed cigarette butts cresting the lip. Dirty plates, crusted bowls and smeared glasses were spread across the kitchen counter and piled haphazardly in the steel sink.

He flipped on the old AM/FM radio next to the microwave and fiddled with the dial and the antenna until the rap station came in static-free. He opened the fridge and surveyed his options. Mustard and ketchup in the door; a half empty bottle of no-name Cola on the top shelf; stale pizza from who knew when, and a crusty bottle of hot sauce on the bottom. He closed the fridge and tried the cupboards. Wedged between a box of generic rice crisp cereal and a jar of pasta sauce, he found a can of pork and beans. He rinsed a fork and devoured them cold, straight from the can. When he finished, he looked under the sink for dish soap and, finding none, grabbed a cup full of powdered laundry detergent. He filled the sink with hot water and scrubbed the dishes, wiped the counter and the table and swept the kitchen floor. He tied off the overflowing garbage bag, scribbled a note on a napkin and left it on the counter by the front door.

*　　*　　*

Outside, the cloudless sky was electric blue, the sun suspended high above the neighborhood like a brilliant white bulb. A pristine sheet of snow covered the ground and shone like pulverized crystal. Sugar raised his forearm to his brow and squinted through the swarm of black blots the sun was throwing at him. When his eyes adjusted to the brightness, he crossed the street and walked past the nearly empty parking lot of his complex, deciding to take the long way. Though he was certain about what he had to do, he was in no hurry to do it. Once he got where he was going, once he crossed that line, he knew there would be no turning back.

Sugar made his way up Tyndall, past the Catholic school and the public library. As he neared the high school there were more people out and about, mostly young mothers and groups of kids bundled up in parkas and snow pants. Some were playing tag, others spread across the ground forming snow angels. A few of them were attempting to make snowballs, astonished and disappointed when the brittle snow crumbled in their mitts and slid through their hands like flour. When he was standing on the street across from the row house he was looking for, he stopped and took in the big blue sky, the warmth of the sun on his cheeks, the smell of the crisp clean air filling his nostrils.

A woman pushing a stroller was approaching, the wheels gliding like blades across the icy sidewalk. Sugar stepped aside and saw she was more girl than woman, no more than a year or two older than him. They exchanged quick smiles and she continued down the sidewalk, Sugar watching until she became a tiny red speck on a sprawling white canvas.

141

He crossed the empty street and walked up cracked wooden steps to a small, sheltered stoop. It was cooler there, out of the sun, and Sugar blew into his hands. He squared his shoulders and knocked.

When Kelvin came to the door, he held a smoking joint between his index finger and his thumb. His navy Yankees cap was tilted sideways atop his head, his thick gold "KJ" chain hanging across his chest like a Christmas ornament.

Kelvin took a step back and raised the burning joint to his lips, took a drag. He stared at Sugar with even eyes. When he didn't say anything, Sugar asked if he could come inside. Kelvin held his gaze and took another puff before easing the door open and stepping to the side. Sugar squeezed past him and stood in the narrow entrance.

It was warm inside the apartment. The air was sticky and dense, the musty smell of weed creeping out from behind the walls and beneath the floorboards. Sugar followed Kelvin down a short, carpeted hallway and they turned left into the small, cluttered living room. Kelvin motioned to the ancient green sofa with the joint.

Kelvin was against the wall, half leaning, half standing. His slim black forearms were folded across his abdomen, his bony shoulders slouched forward. His head was tilted back, resting against the wall and his face was blank. The TV on the wall beside him was set to MTV, muted. On the floor beneath it sat a PS2, a brand new X-Box 360 and a black CD tower full of movies, music and video games. He took one final drag of the joint and dropped it in the mouth of a Pepsi can on the floor beside him.

"So?" he finally said and walked over to his white wooden rocking chair. "What up?"

"I wanna get in the game." The words sounded strange to Sugar as they left his mouth, but not as strange as he expected they might. There was a finality to them, an unaffectedness that suggested he'd always been meant to say them and was just now getting around to it.

Kelvin ran his long fingers across his lips, underneath his chin, up and down his cheekbones. His eyes were locked on Sugar. He blinked a few times before speaking.

"You?" he said. "Wanna get in the game?"

Sugar shrugged, then nodded.

Kelvin leaned back in the rocking chair and Sugar watched his lips transform from a thin straight line to a small smirk to a full-on, beam-of-white smile. He shook his head and laughed, clapped his hands together a couple of times.

"Lil Sugar Sinclair wanna get in the game," he said, still laughing. "Thought I'd never see the day."

Sugar eased back in the softness of the sofa. He wasn't sure what to do next, what to say. So he folded and unfolded his hands, looked around the room, waited.

Kelvin picked up a remote control from the chair beside him, pointed it at the TV and the screen went black. He leaned forward and the wooden rockers scraped against the floorboards. His face was pensive now, the smile gone from his lips. He gave Sugar a slight nod. "Reggie'd be proud."

Sugar absorbed the words like a gut punch, felt them surge through his body until they settled in the pit of his stomach with a thud. Sitting there, on Kelvin Jackson's green couch, about to surrender his dreams, to throw away his life to begin dealing drugs, Sugar knew that his older brother would be anything but proud.

There's a better way, he could hear Reggie telling him. You don't have to go down the same path that I went. Sugar felt the familiar sting of guilt and sadness he got when he thought about his brother, but this time there was a tinge of something else. Something cold and fierce. The admiration he was used to feeling for his brother was replaced by an unsettling contempt.

There's a better way? Sugar wanted to scream. A better way? If there's a better way, then show me. Show me, Reggie! That's right, you can't. You can't because you're fucking dead. You're dead and gone and I'm all alone to deal with this fucked up world and I don't know what else to do. Don't you dare tell me there's a better way, Reggie, don't you fucking dare.

"Sugar, man?"

At the sound of Kelvin's voice, Sugar became aware he was leaning forward, hands sweaty and clenched, finger nails digging deep into the soft green fabric of the sofa. He loosened his grip and placed his palms flat on his knees. He stared at the blank television screen against the wall.

"You OK, yo?"

143

Sugar couldn't answer. He was lost in the reflection of the screen, the face looking back at him darker and younger than he was used to seeing.

"Sugar?" Kelvin got up from his chair and crouched beside him, squeezed his shoulder.

Sugar wiped his face and exhaled. "Yeah," he said. "I'm fine."

Kelvin motioned for Sugar to slide over to the middle of the couch and sat down beside him. The smell of marijuana from his clothes was strong and Sugar slid farther, until there was a full cushion between them.

"What you now, fifteen?" Kelvin asked, his Timberlands propped up on a blue milk crate.

Sugar nodded. "And a half."

"Right around when I got started. Lookin back though, I wish I woulda gotten in a lot younger, y'know? Work when I want, sleep all day, party all night, nobody to answer to but my own self. And the green," he said, head bobbing, narrow eyes moving from the TV to the video game consoles to the boots on his feet. "The green ain't bad neither."

"You ever been busted?" Sugar asked.

"Nah, man. There been times the five-oh come up on me, no doubt, but I ain't never been charged or nothin." He shifted in his seat and the springs beneath him chirped. "That's the beauty of it, man. Everybody know what's goin down, but they don't waste their time on jugglers like us. Long as you be holdin less than an onion and you don't do nothin stupid, ain't shit to worry about."

Sugar nodded and averted his eyes, wondering what an onion was, not wanting to ask, feeling relieved when he didn't have to.

"Zip. Oh-zee. Ounce. Get caught with less than that, they just take it from you or make you throw it down a sewer or some shit. Got a G more'n that, though? One single G more?" Kelvin held up the index finger of his right hand and studied it for a moment before pursing his lips and shaking his head. "You be goin for a ride."

Sugar remained silent, trying to remember how many Gs were in an O.

"Like I said, though. You smart about it, ain't nothin to worry about." Kelvin got up from his chair and turned his hat forward, pulled it down until the brim covered his eyebrows.

"Let's bounce."

Sugar planted his clammy hands in the cushions and pushed himself up, a dart of pain shooting through his thigh.

"Where we goin?"

"Where you think?" Kelvin was beside him now, and placed a hand on his shoulder. He nudged him forward, led him across the small living room and down the dank hallway without another word.

When they reached the front entrance, Kelvin opened the door to a wall of sunlight. Sugar winced and stepped out on to the front stoop, Kelvin right behind him.

Chapter 34

The only light in the cell came from a single bulb surrounded by a protective cage of wire. It hung from the center of the ceiling, flickering like a wounded firefly and giving off an intolerable buzz, which after five days and five nights, Clarence had still not found a way to ignore. Just another monotonous reminder of his monotonous existence.

He was sitting at the edge of his cot, staring at the wall of his cell, thinking about the world beyond it. In the time since he had last stepped foot in that world, it had become a place completely separate from himself. It was still out there, he knew, but he was no longer a part of it. The world out there belonged to his wife, it belonged to his children. To his lawyers, and to the men who stood guard outside of his cell and swept the corridors while he slept. To the cop who had arrested him that night and changed his life forever.

Clarence realized now that even when he had been a part of that world, it had cared very little for him. It did not miss him, it did not need him, and it was certainly not waiting on him. With or without Clarence Sanford, the sun would continue to rise every morning and the sun would continue to set every evening. Depressing as that seemed, at least to be part of that world was to be part of something. In here, he was nothing among nothingness.

Clarence felt a sudden chill. As he reached for his blanket he heard a voice from outside his cell.

"It's better not to think about it."

Clarence jerked his head around, momentarily blinded by a series of white blots hovering between him and the source of the voice. He strained his eyes until they adjusted to the light and a figure on the other side of the bars came slowly into focus. The figure appeared to be half man, half child. He stood at least a head taller than Clarence, and had a good hundred pounds on him, but his immaculate, clean-shaven face was that of a freshman.

"Excuse me?" Clarence said without moving from the bed.

The man-child motioned his head toward the ceiling, revealing a thick neck decorated with a sprawling and intricate tattoo of what appeared to be a spider web. The green of his prison garb told Clarence he was a trustee, the metal dinner cart he was pushing that

146

it was four o'clock.

"The world," he said. "The more you be thinkin about all you missin out there, the slower the time go."

The man took a step toward the steel door and extended his paw of a hand through the bars. His sleeves were rolled up to his elbows, his thick black forearms corded with veins. "Griff."

When Clarence made no effort to stand up, the man called Griff pulled his hand back through the bars and dropped it to his side.

"I know who you are," he said, a slight smirk creasing the corners of his mouth. "You that cop killer."

Clarence felt his face darken and his jaw tighten. When Griff didn't say anything more, he shook his head. "It's not like that. I'm innocent." He knew the moment the words left his lips how stupid they sounded, like claiming celibacy in a whorehouse.

"Ain't we all." Griff crossed his arms across his chest and chuckled.

Clarence looked down at the floor and remained silent.

"You know you a hero in here, right?"

Clarence looked up, surprised to see honesty in the man's face.

"For real, man." Griff ran the tip of his tongue across his lower lip. "Not a person in here ain't put here by the po-lice."

"How does anybody even know who I am? I've barely left my cell."

Griff smiled. "Welcome to the cut, man. Everyone know everything."

He lifted a plastic orange tray from the cart and placed it in a steel shelf built into the front of Clarence's cell.

Clarence shifted on the cot, but remained seated.

"What are you in for?"

"Me?" Griff had a half-moon smile plastered across his youthful face. "I really am innocent."

For the first time he could remember since being inside, Clarence heard the sound of his own laughter.

"Nah, man. Got pinched for possession." Griff pushed the tray through the slot and stepped back behind the cart. "This time of year, though? I'd rather be in here than on the streets, y'know what

I'm sayin? Warm place to sleep, decent meals. Keep shit straight, do my time, be out just in time for spring."

"This your first time?"

"Locked up?" Griff shook his head. "I done spent eight years in state before this. Manslaughter." He said it with no emotion, no change in his tone. As if he were giving Clarence directions.

"Stupid kid, made a stupid mistake, y'know?" He shrugged and dropped his eyes to the concrete. "Every day for those eight years, I thought about how I killed a man over a couple hundred dollars, a lousy bag of rock. Promised myself I wouldn't go back to that life. Then, when I get back out I'm so far behind, y'know? Everything so different out there, so fast and shit. Less than a year, I lasted."

Judging by the youth in his face, Griff couldn't have been older than twenty-five, thirty tops. Almost a third of his life, the whole of his adulthood, spent locked up. Clarence couldn't imagine eight years in here. It was hard to imagine another eight days at this point. Maybe it got easier with time, maybe you got used to it. Maybe you just woke up one morning accepting that this place had become your reality.

Griff cracked his knuckles and looked at Clarence. "But it's like I said, man. Easier when you stop thinkin bout life on the outside."

Clarence nodded, believing it was true but not understanding how it was possible.

"Anyway, good meetin you, man." He gripped the handle of the cart and unlocked the wheels with the toe of his shoe. "Mouths to feed, know what I'm sayin?"

"Yeah," Clarence said.

Griff took a step forward and then paused. "One more thing," he said.

"What's that?"

"You really are innocent? I'd be keepin that shit to myself, y'know what I'm sayin?"

Clarence nodded and watched as Griff pushed off down the hall, the rubber wheels of the cart squeaking along the floor in front of him.

Chapter 35

Trinity Temple was a mammoth of a building on the west side, spanning half a city block alongside a ribbon of the Rouge River. Not yet two years old, the church was another reminder that no matter how dire the economy, or how impoverished the community, there was always money for big, expensive religious institutions, their holy crosses sprouting from the dilapidation around them like roses in a landfill.

As Gerald approached the church, the streets were overflowing with vehicles, parked and crawling, and busy with foot traffic. Entire blocks were cordoned off by marked cars and yellow ribbon and uniformed officers directed traffic at every corner. Gerald pulled his Taurus forward and followed the emphatic hand gestures of an officer into the football field-sized parking lot behind the church. He found a spot behind an F-150 and crossed the freshly cleared pavement with his forearm shielding his face from the sun.

The sprawling grey facade of the church was stark and grim. Whether it was the way the shadows hit the stone, or the fact that he had come to associate churches with mourning, the building looked to Gerald like a massive tomb. Over the years, churches had become the kind of place he would cross the street to avoid passing, the very mention of them sending chills down his spine and rushing forth unwanted memories, awakening uncomfortable feelings of pain and loss and suffering. Like hospitals and cemeteries.

Gerald walked up the bevelled steps and was greeted at the immense front entrance by the cold handshakes and somber faces of unfamiliar officers in full uniform. The front foyer was filled with hundreds of people, a barely audible murmur of hushed voices filling the vast space. Everyone was dressed in either black or DPD blue. He removed his sunglasses, hoping the Visine he had picked up on the way over had taken care of the aftereffects of his three-day binge. He walked among and around the mass of mourners with lowered eyes, shaking the hands of fellow cops as he went, politely thanking the ones he knew for their condolences.

Across the room, next to the sanctuary entrance, Gerald spotted John Clifford. Without Ramos by his side, he barely recognized him. With his dark hair slicked back, his solid black suit and his shiny black shoes, he looked more like a lawyer than a homicide detective. His back was against the wall and he was surveying the room with the intensity and determination of a sniper. When he caught sight of Gerald and gave him a curt nod, Gerald dropped his head and pretended to not see him.

Gerald entered the sanctuary doors at the far end of the foyer to the flowery scent of burning incense. The angular pews were swallowed by a sea of navy blue, the outer walls lined with reporters and video cameras. Gerald found the reserved seating for his precinct in the third row and sat in the rigid pew beside Alden Brown, a black officer around Nick's age. They shook hands and exchanged knowing looks. Neither man spoke.

The stage in front of him was lined with thick white candles in tall glass votives. Off to one side was the casket, draped in an American flag and surrounded by bright bouquets of red, yellow, pink and purple. A blown-up photo of Nick, smiling and in uniform, stood on an easel beside it. The pulpit was flanked by two rows of folding chairs – one for high-ranking officers and politicians, the other for Nick's family. Already seated, front and center, was Virginia Reese. Her small children were dressed in black and seated on either side of her. She was wearing a black button-up blouse and a long black skirt that came halfway down her bony shins. Her long blond hair was resting on her shoulders, shining like a halo around her narrow, ashen face. Her eyes were the eyes of defeat, seeped in pain and anguish and fatigue. Looking at the three of them sitting there, Gerald felt a throb of remorse.

We got him.

In the days since he'd shown up on the Reeses' porch and given Virginia the news that shattered her world, Gerald had replayed that lie in his head over and over again. Through the days of drink and the nights of restlessness, all he could see was Virginia's face. That look of relief and comfort when he told her they'd caught her husband's killer. As bad as the lies were though, he knew the truth was even worse: Nick's killer was still out there. And nobody was looking for him.

Virginia turned her head and Gerald averted his eyes before she could find them.

The din of the crowd suddenly died down and Gerald watched

150

a short man with a neatly groomed goatee cross the stage. He adjusted the microphone to chin level and gripped the wooden edges of the pulpit. Save for his skinny neck and the balding head atop it, his slight frame was completely hidden.

"Ladies and gentlemen, if you'll please be seated." The power of the pastor's voice belied his stature. It was firm and deep and carried throughout the temple like a roll of thunder. Gerald looked around at the bowed heads and blank faces and felt as though all the air had been sucked out of the room. Despite the thousands of bodies in the room, it felt cool.

"My friends," the pastor began. "We are gathered here this morning in the memory of Nick Reese. Nick was taken from us in the line of duty, serving his community. As we remember Nick today, I ask that we keep his family especially in our thoughts and our prayers. His lovely wife Virginia, and his beautiful children, Casey and Abby. Also his father, Joseph, and his brother, Nathan. And his parents-in-law, James and Linda. As the family struggles and grieves at this very difficult time, may our sympathy and the love of our Lord comfort them."

An utterance of Amens filled the congregation and Gerald risked another glance toward the stage. Casey and Abby looked lost up there, among the grieving adults, their faces blank and stricken, their dull eyes searching the room for answers that wouldn't come for years, if ever. Virginia sat with her hands folded on her lap, her face hollow and expressionless. She wiped at a tear from her cheek and looked out at the congregation. Gerald wasn't quick enough this time, and her eyes locked in on him.

He wanted to look away, to run and hide, but he couldn't move. They were the only two in the room and everything was silent. The pastor was still speaking, but his voice had become a barely noticeable drone of background noise. Gerald stared into Virginia's sad blue eyes and wished he could tell her, with a look, how sorry he was. For her loss. For her children's loss. For lying to her, and for robbing her of the truth she so desperately deserved.

But no such look existed, so he went on staring at her hopeless face. She tilted her head and gave him a weak and fleeting smile and he felt something within himself crumble. Before he could return the smile, before he could do anything at all, the sorrow returned to her face and she looked away.

When Gerald could finally move, finally breathe, he looked back toward the pastor. His hands were still gripping the pulpit, his eyes intense and lively as he spoke.

"… not a job, but a calling," he was saying. "What Nick did for you, for me, for his community and for his city as a whole, is a true testament to what kind of man he was. Nick was an exemplary officer of the law, yes, but above that, he was a special human being. A man of selflessness, of bravery, a man of courage. For every time an officer of the law steps foot on those streets, out among all that is wrong and evil in this world, he is well aware of the risk and the peril. Yet he continues to go out there, willingly, to stand up for what is right and what is good in this world. Day in and day out for the past five years of his life, Nick went out there and put it all on the line. And ultimately," the pastor paused and scanned the room with unblinking eyes, "he paid the highest price doing so. He sacrificed his life.

"As a police officer, Nick's job was to uphold justice and keep the streets safe. And as the Psalms say, 'Blessed are they who maintain justice, who constantly do what is right.' How ironic it is that he was killed in an act of the unnecessary violence he spent his life trying to thwart. How utterly unfortunate that a man whose job it was to uphold the justice and the safety of his community, was taken from us in the most unjust of manners." The pastor paused again, closed his eyes for a moment and folded his hands on the bridge of the pulpit.

"In times of such tragic loss and unjust travesty," he continued, "it is easy, natural even, to get angry. Thoughts of vengeance creep into our minds. But as I stand here before you, I warn you: this is the work of the enemy. Beware these evil thoughts. For we cannot focus our energies on a justice that we cannot provide. Justice belongs to God, and God alone. So I ask you, take comfort in knowing, that in this life and the next, justice for Nick will be served. Focus not on what has been taken from us, but on what Nick Reese has given us, what he has left us. Remember Nick by honoring him, and honor him by remembering him." The pastor bowed his head and folded his hands. "May God bless you, Nick. And may you rest in peace."

The room was silent. Every rustle of tissue, every sob and sniffle, every awkward shift in the wooden pews was magnified, the sound of each carrying through the sanctuary and hanging in the air for what seemed an eternity.

Finally, Lieutenant Alexander made his way toward the vacant spot behind the pulpit. He stood behind the microphone and cleared his throat.

Gerald watched as his precinct leader's lips began to move, but didn't hear what came out of them. He was no longer in that room. He was outside of himself, eyes focused again on Virginia.

Her head hung like the withered bulb of a flower, her slender shoulders trembling as she held a sodden tissue to her face. Seeing her, at that moment, fraught and empty and frail, looking as though the slightest contact would shatter her, the slightest of breezes would swirl her up and toss her around like a doll, Gerald could think of nothing but justice.

Justice for this woman, who would wake up every morning, struggle her way out of bed and go to work and raise her children and attempt to move on with her life one difficult day and one impossible night at a time. Justice for these children, who would go through life asking where's daddy, what happened to daddy, why's he gone and when's he coming back, trudging through the most important years of their lives without a father. Justice for Nick, who hours from now would be buried in a wooden casket six feet below the frozen surface of Redwood Cemetery.

Gerald shifted his attention to the brass on stage: Alexander's lips moving, nothing coming out; Graves sitting tall in his chair, unaffected and unattached; a half dozen others in perfectly pressed uniforms, hats resting on their knees and minds elsewhere, on to the next case maybe.

They may have moved on, Virginia. They may have given up on your justice, but I haven't. I won't. I'll get him for you, Virginia. I'll get you your justice. And not the justice the pastor spoke of, either. Not this other-worldly, next-life, divine bullshit form of justice that you have to wait for and may or may never receive. Real justice, Virginia. Here and now justice, this-life justice. Justice you can see and taste and breathe and feel. The type of justice that would make handcuffs and twenty-five to life seem like a walk in the park.

153

The type of justice that will allow you to put your head on your pillow at night and fall asleep knowing that the man who took your husband, the man who took your children's father, was taken care of.

We got him.

I'm sorry, Virginia. We didn't get him. We didn't.

But I will, Virginia, I will. If it takes the rest of my life, I'll get him. I promise.

Chapter 36

"How much longer?" Sugar asked. He and Kelvin had been walking almost half an hour, Sugar constantly two steps behind, when he finally gathered the courage to speak up.

The sun was high and bright and most of the snow had turned to puddles of slush. His Nikes and his socks were soaked through to his ankles, his neck and back slick with sweat.

Kelvin pointed across the four lanes of traffic to the other side of Seven Mile. "There."

They were standing in the empty parking lot of what used to be a Marathon station, the only remnants of its existence a faded blue sign high above the concrete slab where the pumps used to stand. The building itself, or what remained of it, was boarded up with wooden slats and plastered in faded graffiti.

Only a couple of miles from where Sugar had lived his entire life, the neighborhood was completely foreign to him. It was more commercial than residential, though by the looks of it most of the businesses that had once operated there were long gone. Nothing left but deserted lots and rundown buildings, the odd detached home which may or may not have been occupied.

There was a break in the traffic and Kelvin took off.

"Come on," he yelled over his shoulder when he was halfway across the road.

Sugar ran after him, the melted snow in his shoes swishing beneath his heels and between his toes. He made it to the other side out of breath, the horns of another wave of traffic blaring behind him. He bent over and rested his forearms on his knees, gulping for air. Each mouthful was thick with gasoline and exhaust fumes. He stood up and spit on the sidewalk.

Kelvin had his hands on his hips and was breathing just as hard as Sugar. Traffic continued to cruise by them, the tires of trucks and cars and buses cutting through the puddles and spraying dirty water up along the curb. They took a step back and Kelvin motioned toward a bench. It was on the corner, next to a squat brick building and a pay phone.

They sat down as the traffic light hanging above them turned red. The traffic ceased and Sugar could finally hear himself think.

The green and white street sign at the corner told him they were on Camden Street, the black and white arrow below it that it was a one-way. He could see now that the building beside them was a liquor store. Despite its rundown exterior, it appeared to be open. On the corner across from them was a vacant lot surrounded by a rusty chain link fence topped with cyclone loops of razor barbed wire. Weeds the height of children and the color of ash poked through the links and hung out over the sidewalk.

"This is it?" Sugar asked, still gasping for air.

"What you expect?" Kelvin said. "Flashing lights and a giant sign says, 'Buy Dope Here'?"

"I dunno." Sugar shrugged. "Just looks kinda, I dunno…dead."

"May be, man, but people lookin to score? This where they come. Buds, crack, smack, ice, anything they need they find it here."

"Where – "

The light turned green and Sugar's words were swallowed by the roaring and splashing of the passing vehicles. Kelvin stood up and Sugar followed. They turned left at a street named Inkster and walked away from the traffic. The noise behind them faded to a barely audible rumble and Sugar tried again.

"Where the dealers at?"

Kelvin motioned with his chin down the street.

Sugar could see now there were kids lining both sides of a one-block stretch of street, ten or twelve of them in total. They were back from the curb, standing beside trees or sitting on benches or leaning against the stained brick walls of the surrounding buildings.

"Come on," Kelvin said. "Lemme introduce you."

He continued down Inkster at his usual brisk pace and Sugar again found himself struggling to keep up. The one-way traffic approaching them was sparse, most of the vehicles moving slowly and with their windows down. Sugar could see the kids were stepping toward the curbs and calling out to them, "You need?" and, "I got it!" Most of them were his age or younger.

"I dunno man," Sugar said. "Maybe this ain't such a good idea."

Kelvin stopped and turned to face Sugar. He opened his mouth and it appeared he was about to say something. Instead he closed his mouth, shook his head, turned around and kept on walking.

Sugar remained where he was. He watched as a car pulled alongside the curb on the other side of the street and one of the kids, lanky and dressed in a red and white Adidas track suit, got up from a bench and went over to it. He leaned in the window, reached in his pocket and made an exchange with the driver. In a matter of seconds, the car was gone and the boy was back on his bench.

By the time Sugar looked back at Kelvin, he was halfway down the block. There was a guy straddling a blue bicycle next to him, his arms resting across the chrome handle bars. Kelvin said something to him and they both looked at Sugar, smiling. Sugar felt himself shrink under their gazes and considered turning around. Turning his back on this whole idea and just going back to life as he knew it. But then Kelvin waved him over and he was trapped. He stood motionless for another moment, the penetrating stares temporarily immobilizing him. He finally lowered his head and slowly made his way toward them.

"Yo, Ozzie, this my boy, Sugar. Reggie Sinclair's little bro." Kelvin reached out and wrapped his fingers around Sugar's shoulder, pulled him closer. "He wanna get started. Think you can hook him up?"

Sugar could feel Ozzie eyeing him up and forced himself to stop staring at the sidewalk. Ozzie appeared to be nineteen, maybe twenty. He was clean-shaven, his face serious and unremarkable. He stared at Sugar for another few seconds before pulling out a cellphone and turning his back to him and Kelvin. He spoke in a low voice and turned back around, returning the phone to his pocket.

"Follow me."

They waited for a break in the traffic and crossed the street, Ozzie on his bike, Kelvin and Sugar following on foot. When they were on the other side, Ozzie hopped off his bike and pushed it beside him. He led them down a narrow alley between two buildings. They walked single file, stones and broken glass crunching beneath their feet with every step. Melted snow dripped from the rusty fire escapes in a tick-tock rhythm and gathered in puddles beneath the spouts of the buildings' eaves troughs. They were out of the sun now and Sugar found himself shivering.

When they reached a rotten wooden fence at the end of the

alley, Ozzie leaned against it. The minutes passed and the three of them stood in silence, Sugar stealing the odd glance at Kelvin and Kelvin ignoring him. Then Ozzie's cellphone buzzed and a young guy dressed in a black do-rag and leather jacket came from the alley. He handed Ozzie a paper bag without a word and kept walking. When he was out of sight, Ozzie took a couple steps along the fence and pulled on a pair of creaky two-by-fours. When they popped loose, he dropped them to the ground and motioned for Kelvin and Sugar to follow him through the opening.

On the other side of the fence, they were surrounded by loose tires, rusty engines, splintered pallets, shells of old cars. The lot was one giant puddle, blotched in spots by rainbow-colored pools of oil and scattered islands of trash and dead grass. On the far side was the rear wall of a red brick building with barred windows and "Super Auto Sales" stencilled along the top in faded white spray paint.

Ozzie led them to an old gutted Plymouth without doors and they sat on a slat of soiled cardboard covering the back seat. Ozzie removed the paper bag from inside his coat and handed it to Kelvin.

"As usual, the first package on me," Ozzie said. "After that, all the risk be yours."

"It's all good," said Kelvin, looking over at Sugar. "He's good for it."

"A'ight, I'm out." Ozzie climbed out of the car and bumped fists with Kelvin. Then he winked at Sugar. "Good luck, little man. I'll tell the others to be expectin you."

Sugar stared at him with blank eyes and nodded. He watched as Ozzie made his way back across the lot and stepped through the opening in the fence.

"A'ight." Kelvin reached inside the paper bag and pulled out a small clear baggie packed tight with a cluster of weed. "This here a dime bag, sells for ten bucks. Each package you get gonna have sixteen of these in it. When the package run out, you should have one-sixty. One-forty goes to Ozzie, rest is yours. Except for this first one. This one, you keep it all. You feel me so far?"

Sugar nodded, his mind swimming at the thought of a hundred and sixty dollars in his pocket.

"Only three rules. Ready?"

Sugar shifted in the seat and nodded.

"One," Kelvin said, the dime bag dangling between his middle finger and his thumb. "Ozzie always gets his cut. You lose it, you get jacked, you give wrong change, whatever. Ozzie gives you a package, he always gets his one-forty." He stared at Sugar and raised his pinkie so his hand made the symbol of devil's horns, the baggie hanging from its mouth.

"Two. You sell only in the designated area. Back on Inkster, between Camden and Sherbrook. You get caught pumpin Ozzie's shit anywhere else, it most likely to be the last thing you ever do.

"And three? Keep your numbers up. To Ozzie, you just another juggler. You can't keep his product movin, he'll find someone who can." Kelvin lowered his hand and shrugged, gave Sugar a matter-of-fact smile.

Sugar tried to process the flood of information Kelvin was throwing at him, but his mind was still working on the numbers.

"So how many these packages can I sell in a day?"

"Depends. Some of our boys be movin eight to ten a day. Startin out though? I'd say two, maybe three."

"Two or three?" Sugar wasn't sure he heard him right.

"Ain't much, I know. But everybody gotta start somewhere. It's where I started, where Reggie started. Hell, it wasn't too long ago Ozzie was sitting right here, nothin but a single package to his name. Now he runnin this entire block, twenty-one years old."

Sugar didn't hear the last part of what Kelvin said. He was busy doing and redoing the math in his head. Two to three packages was forty to sixty dollars. A day. Four-twenty a week. Eighteen hundred a month. Dollars.

"Who knows? Could be you one day." Kelvin laughed and nudged Sugar on the shoulder. "Lieutenant Sugar Sinclair. Got a good ring, don't it?"

Kelvin finished unwrapping the paper bag and began handing Sugar the dime bags one at a time. "Here. Put these in your pockets."

When all of the baggies were in Sugar's jeans, Kelvin crumpled up the paper bag and threw it on the floor of the car. He slid out and rapped his palms against the roof.

"Let's go," he said. "Rule number three."

Sugar shifted his weight from foot to soaked foot, trying to keep the blood circulating. He was standing on Inkster, between a bus stop and a fire hydrant. There were two boys farther down the street, about his age. When Sugar had come over, they'd given him a slight nod and introduced themselves, but now, consumed by an anxiety that grew stronger with each passing car, he couldn't remember their names.

Sugar tried to keep his mind on the money, the opportunities it could provide him. Just get through the first sale, the first day, the first week, he told himself. Save up enough cash to get out of Detroit, to go somewhere he could stop looking over his shoulder. Maybe get a real job and find his own place, send Ma birthday cards and extra money when he had it. Come home for Christmases.

But standing there, on a street corner in an unfamiliar part of the city with drugs in his pockets, it wasn't that simple. There was still the in-between part, the getting-there part. And Sugar realized now, for the first time, that he had to actually go through with this. It was too late to turn around now. He was too far in to go back to the life, the neighborhood, the home that up until fifteen minutes ago was all he knew.

"You got one, rook."

The voice startled him. He turned to see the taller of the two boys pointing at a black Cadillac creeping along the curb toward them.

"It's all you," the boy shouted. "They ask for anything other than green, just send em forward and we'll take care of em."

Sugar watched the car ease forward, squinting against the reflection bouncing off its windshield. When it came to a stop directly in front of him, the passenger window was already down. There was a white man in his thirties or forties in the driver's seat, hands on the wheel, eyes forward. Sugar swallowed the golf ball-sized lump in his throat and moved toward the car. He crouched down and leaned in the window. There was a twenty-dollar bill lying on the passenger seat.

"Give me two," said the man, staring straight ahead.

Sugar kept his eyes on the money and reached into the right

pocket of his jeans. He fumbled with the plastic baggies with sweaty hands until he had two between his fingers. He pulled them out and placed them on the seat before picking up the twenty. By the time he had the bill in his pocket, the Cadillac was halfway down the road.

Sugar looked up to see Kelvin running across the street, a beaming smile plastered across his face. A smile Sugar hadn't seen since they were kids.

"That's how we do, boy! You on your way for real!" Kelvin slapped him on the back and punched him in the shoulder.

On my way, Sugar thought as he looked over Kelvin's shoulder at the oncoming traffic. And ain't nothin gonna stop me.

Chapter 37

Gerald threw his leather coat across the worn, checker-patterned sofa and slumped down beside it. The springs groaned and the cushions gave way around him until he was almost sitting on the ground.

The scene surrounding him was chaos. One side of the basement was dominated by a massive wall-to-wall bookshelf, the plank shelves bowing beneath the weight of paperbacks and hard covers of all sizes. The other side of the room was taken up by a long wooden table with folding metal legs. It was covered with a half-finished jigsaw puzzle of what appeared to be the old Tiger Stadium, pieces clustered and scattered around it in a recklessness that appeared almost organized. On the drywall behind the table hung dozens of already-finished puzzles, mostly cityscapes and historical buildings, many of them in black and white. Every other flat surface in the room, including the floor, was covered with books, magazines and newspapers plastered with yellow post-it notes. Behind him, another long table supported a massive aquarium filled with colorful fish – orange, blue, red, yellow – flitting their fins, dipping and diving among lush greenery and bright white coral. The whisper of the cycling water and the fluid motion of the fish had a soothing quality Gerald hadn't experienced for as long as he could remember.

Across from him, on the other side of what he could only guess was a coffee table, sat Archie Ziegler. Despite his years, Arch still looked as young and fit as the day he retired. His shoulder-length hair was a bit thinner, and his firm, wiry frame had expanded some in the middle, but his deep blue eyes still shone with the life of a much younger man. At the moment, he had a content smile on his face, lips slightly curved. His hand was wrist-deep in a red plastic bowl resting on his lap.

"So," Gerald said. "This is what I have to look forward to in retirement? Reading and puzzles?"

"Nah." Archie said. "That's just the months with 'R' in em. Rest of the year you get to golf."

Gerald smiled. Arch had always had that easy way about him, a nonchalance that Gerald sometimes envied. Though he was old

162

enough to be Gerald's father, Arch had always felt more like a friend.

"Sure you don't want popcorn?" Arch asked. "Come on, I'll make some fresh stuff."

"I'm good," Gerald said.

"How bout a smoothie? Or a milkshake?" Arch was half-standing. "I got this new blender? Thing can turn a hammer to shreds. World's best shakes, hands down."

"Seriously, I'm OK."

Arch sat back down and shrugged. "Your loss."

Gerald couldn't help but laugh. God, it felt good to laugh.

Arch was deep in his burgundy leather easy chair with his feet propped across an avocado-green ottoman. He had moccasins on, worn brown leather with a trim of white fur around the ankle, along with khaki cargo shorts and a black Pearl Jam T-shirt. Even when he had been on the streets, you'd never take Archie Ziegler for a detective. More like a writer, or a professor. Maybe an artist, or even an architect. But not a detective. And definitely not a detective who'd put in his twenty-five, and then another seven, a detective known throughout the county as a law enforcement legend. Maybe it was that unassuming appearance, that cool personality that made him so successful at cracking cases with information he had no right knowing. People trusted him, people told him things. In his prime, he'd had a stable of sources and CIs around the city that made Columbo look amateur. Despite his reputation and the countless options it afforded him, however, he'd never gone beyond detective. Never wanted to. The streets were his life, where he belonged.

"Didn't see you at the service this morning," Arch said.

As quickly as it had disappeared when Gerald sat down in Arch's basement, the burden of the day returned at the thought of Nick's funeral.

"I was in and out," Gerald said. "Didn't feel much like stickin around, you know?"

Arch scratched at his thin, reddish beard. He tilted his head back and stared at the ceiling tiles, as if deciding whether or not Gerald's response was acceptable. Finally, he looked back at him and nodded. The next question was more difficult.

"How you holdin up?"

There was some concern behind his words and Gerald knew immediately what he was really asking. And judging by the glint in Arch's eye, the slightest tinge of disappointment on his face, Gerald could see he already knew the answer.

Despite their ties with the department, it wasn't through work that Gerald and Arch had come to know one another. It happened, instead, in the dimly lit basement of an inner city church filled with thick clouds of cigarette smoke, sipping weak instant coffee from Styrofoam cups. It had been early in Gerald's career, less than a year in, when he walked down that dingy stairway and into that smoke-filled room, nervous behind the curious stares, trying to convince himself he didn't belong there. He took a seat in a folding metal chair next to the man he recognized as a homicide detective from The City. They exchanged nods and ten minutes later, the first words Gerald heard from the detective's mouth were: "My name is Archie, and I'm an alcoholic."

Now, more than a decade later, sitting on Arch's couch, under the burning scrutiny of his gaze, Gerald knew his friend was asking him if he was still on the wagon.

He said the words Archie already knew, his eyes fixed on a knot in the beige berber carpet between his feet.

"I slipped." Gerald shook his head, all of those dark, familiar feelings that had coerced him into twisting the cap, tipping the bottle, taking the sip, rushed back to him in a sudden surge. He swallowed hard.

"It's just with Janet leaving, and then what happened to Nick…" He shook his head again, aware of the inadequacy of his excuses. He'd screwed up, plain and simple.

When he finally built up the courage to meet Arch's face, he saw it was fixed with an understanding frown, a frown that said he'd been down that dark road himself, more times than he'd like to admit and more times than he'd like to remember.

For a long while neither of them spoke. The fish tank behind Gerald sounded like a waterfall. He could feel perspiration beading on his forehead and at his temples. Finally, Arch leaned forward and put his elbows on his knees, steepled his fingers.

"What happened to Nick? It's a horrible, horrible thing." He let the words hang there for a moment. Looked Gerald square in the eyes. "But it's not your fault, man."

"I know." Gerald could hear the shortness of breath in his voice. "It's not that."

Arch raised his eyebrows. Remained silent.

"I arrested the wrong guy."

When Archie didn't say anything, Gerald continued.

"This Sanford guy? The guy I collared? His registration on the car, his wallet inside, but it wasn't him. The guy from the car definitely wasn't the guy I arrested. Different clothes. Smaller, younger."

"You're sure?"

"Sure as I'm sittin here."

Arch collapsed his hands and folded them across his lap. He was thinking, Gerald knew. Trying to put it all together, trying to get the pieces to fit.

"So our doer? The real one, I mean. He's driving a car that doesn't belong to him, panics when he sees five-oh, tries to get away, happens to be packin. Nick gets too close and he decides to pop him."

Gerald nodded.

"And meanwhile, the real owner of the car, this Sanford, he just happens to be in the area. It's after midnight, it's thirty degrees and it's blowing snow, a damn near storm, and he's out walking?" He leaned back in his chair. "Sounds like a carjacking."

"Bingo," Gerald said. "According to Clifford and Ramos, Sanford says he was forced out of his car at gunpoint a few blocks away. A couple of kids."

Arch ran his fingers through his hair. "Who else have you told?"

Gerald shrugged. "Everyone. I met with Graves the day after, told him everything. Clifford and Ramos know too. And Victor Anton."

"The new DA?"

Gerald nodded.

"And?"

"And," Gerald said, "he's going ahead with the charges against Sanford. Thinks with my testimony it's a slam dunk."

Arch tilted his head toward the ceiling and appeared to focus on something up there for a few seconds. Then he blinked and looked back at Gerald.

"Are you gonna do it?"

"Does it matter?" Gerald could hear the bitterness in his voice. "If I testify, I help put an innocent man away for life and Nick's killer goes free. If I don't, they take their chances in court without me and Nick's killer still goes free. Either way, he's still out there."

Arch seemed to study Gerald for a moment. Then he looked at him with knowing eyes. "You're gonna try and find him yourself, aren't you?"

Gerald pursed his lips and nodded.

"And you want my help."

Again, Gerald nodded.

Arch scratched at a patch of stubble on his cheek. "On one condition."

"Anything."

"The next time things get…slippery?" He raised his eyebrows and Gerald felt himself shrink. "You call me. Any time, day or night. No excuses."

The only thing keeping Gerald from looking away was the sincerity in Arch's eyes. He managed a weak nod.

"Good," Arch said, the beginnings of a smile creasing his face. "In that case we can talk business. What do you have for me?"

"Zip."

"Nothing?"

"Nada. Other than what Clifford and Ramos said about the kids."

Arch sighed. "I'll see what I can do. No guarantees, but check back with me tomorrow night."

"Thanks. In the meantime, I'll hit the bricks and bang on some doors. Maybe there's some eyes or ears out there." Gerald reached for his coat and struggled out of the grasp of the sofa.

Arch rose from his chair and met Gerald in the middle of the room. They gave each other a quick hug.

"Thanks again Arch, I owe you one."

"One? You owe me a hell of a lot more'n one. And one of these days I'll be around to collect."

"Yeah, yeah," Gerald said as he made his way to the stairway.

166

"You know where I live."

"Hey, Ger?" Arch called after him.

"Yeah?"

"Good luck."

"Thanks," Gerald said from the bottom step. "I think I'm gonna need all I can get."

Chapter 38

The visiting room was four white brick walls and a row of booths divided by a dirty Plexiglas partition. Each booth consisted of a single stationary stool and was separated from the next by a thick slab of wood with a black telephone receiver attached to it.

It was hot and humid and had the sour, salty smell of a men's locker room. There was an air of restless expectancy – the spasmodic shuffling of feet, the fluttering din of lowered voices. The conversation was idle and tedious, a mechanism to ease the anxieties and pass the agonizing minutes until the inmates would see their visitors – the wives, the mothers, the children, the only ties they had left to the outside world.

A buzzer sounded and Clarence looked through the smeared glass as a single queue of mostly black and mostly female visitors filed through the door in the back corner of the room. Halfway down the line, behind an overweight woman with a nest of curly copper hair and a young mother dragging two kids by their skinny wrists, he saw Leslie. She moved slowly and tentatively, scanning the row of cubicles with lowered eyes. When she spotted Clarence, she gave him a weak half smile and dropped her head. By the time she reached the stool opposite him, her smile had disappeared and she seemed to be shuddering.

In the three days since the arraignment, Leslie seemed to have lost weight and aged a couple of years. Her lips were cracked and colorless and her eyes, usually bright and lively, were glazed over and rimmed by puffy pockets of black. Her hair was uncombed and hung stringy and loose around her shoulders. Behind it all, Clarence searched for a sliver of the woman he had married, the woman he shared two children with. He found nothing.

He tried his best to maintain eye contact as she removed her coat and folded it across the stool beneath her. When she took her seat and met his gaze he smiled. After a moment of hesitation she smiled back, but it wasn't the smile he knew. The pleasant, playful smile he had come to know over the years, the very one that had helped get him through the darkest and loneliest hours of the past two nights, was replaced by that same flimsy, half smile he had never seen until two minutes earlier but now seemed to shape her mouth so naturally.

They sat there, looking at each other's faces through the dirty glass. Clarence picked up the telephone receiver and waited for Leslie to do the same. At first, no one spoke. Nothing but the hollow hush of dead air and the faint transmission of the background chatter.

Since he last met with Sapp, Clarence had thought of nothing except telling Leslie about Natasha. Agonizing, anticipating, convincing, reasoning. Lying awake at night, torturing himself and brooding over what to say and how to say it, rehearsing the words and imagining her reaction. And now, here they were. Her she was. Sitting in front of him, Leslie, thin and old and weak, looking as though she'd endured a lifetime of disappointment and that the next piece of bad news would be the final hit she ever took, the blow that ruined and destroyed her beyond repair. Every scrap of courage Clarence had gathered over the past seventy-two hours, every ounce of resolve he had built up suddenly evaporated.

After an eternity of looking into his wife's lifeless eyes, the hand holding the receiver growing limper and the lump in his throat growing denser, Clarence finally found his voice.

"Hey, Les. How you been?"

"All right, I guess. Work gave me some time off." Her voice was distant and metallic, as if it were coming through two tin cans attached to a string. "How about you? Looks like your head's almost healed."

"Yeah, it's gettin there. Should be good as new in another couple days."

She nodded and said nothing. Just sat there, one hand holding the receiver, the other splayed across the battered tabletop. Clarence could see that her slender hands were brittle, the webs between her fingers and thumbs white and callus and the nubs cresting her fingernails chewed raw. The diamond of her wedding band sparkled for an instant beneath the fluorescent lighting before she curled her hand into a ball and it disappeared.

"So," Clarence said. "How are Michael and Sonia? What have you told them?"

"Rod and I told them the truth last night." She dropped her

eyes and shook her head. "It's all over the news, Clarence. Your name, your photo. We had no choice."

"You told them it was all a mistake, right? That they made a mistake and that I'd be home soon?"

She nodded.

"How'd they take it?"

"Not great. Sonia was up all night, crying. She finally fell asleep in our bed around three."

"And Michael?"

She shrugged. "A little better, I guess. No tears, but he's been pretty quiet. He spent most of the day in his room."

Clarence couldn't begin to imagine what his children were feeling, what they were thinking. Didn't even want to try.

"Can you bring pictures of them when you come on Wednesday?"

"Of course."

"And one of you."

A hint of a smile began to form at the corner of her lips but disappeared just as quickly. "Sure."

"Rodney been around much?"

"He's with the kids right now." She stifled a yawn and wiped at her swollen eyes with the heel of her hand. "I kept them home from school today. Mom and dad are coming up tonight, too."

"That's good," Clarence said. Studying his wife, it seemed in some ways that he'd seen her only yesterday, but in others that it had been years. She was right in front of him, perhaps eighteen inches away, but she had never felt more distant. Connected by a lousy jail telephone line, separated by everything else. They lived in different worlds now, and Clarence wondered how long it would be before they became different people. How long until Leslie became a stranger to him. Some woman that visited him for fifteen minutes twice a week and talked to him about things and people that he had once known but long since forgotten.

"So," Leslie said. "How is it? In here, I mean. What's it like?"

Clarence shrugged. "Routine, routine, routine. Up at four, breakfast at five, lunch at eleven, dinner at four, lights out at ten. One hour in between to shower, clean up, walk my unit. Rest of the time I'm locked up in my cell."

"What do you all day?"

"Not much," Clarence said. "Eat, sleep, read. The days are long and slow. Feels like I've been here forever."

"The food?"

"Pasta, beans. Lots of cakes and cookies. It's like they're trying to fatten us up or something, Hansel and Gretel-style. Feed us to the guards."

Leslie smiled. Not the weak half smile this time, but the real, Leslie Sanford smile. "I miss you, Clarence."

"I miss you too, Les. I miss you so much."

For a moment they sat there, staring at one another in silence and all of the horrors and sorrow surrounding their circumstances seemed to melt away. Clarence captured the image of his wife's smile in his mind's eye and held it there, storing it away, something telling him that as long as he had that image everything would be OK.

"Have you met with Byron lately?"

Byron. The case. Natasha. Reality. All of a sudden it came flooding back to him and he could feel himself drowning beneath the weight of what he had to tell his wife.

"Clarence?"

He could feel her eyes moving across his face. Studying, examining, looking for something but scared of what she might find.

"What is it?"

"Huh? Oh, nothing. It' just that, it's just...I met with him yesterday."

"And?"

Clarence hesitated, for a fleeting moment considered telling her. He loved her, she loved him. They'd find a way to work it out.

"Not much new. Looks like it'll come down to my word against that cop's."

"What?" Leslie said. "Are you serious? He said the other night there'd be no problems, that it wouldn't even go to trial."

There was a flicker in her eyes that lit up her entire face and the youth that had been washed out by fatigue momentarily returned. Her grip on the phone had tightened and she was sitting up straight in her stool.

"You're innocent, Clarence. How can they do this?"

"I don't know." Clarence said, almost to himself. "It'll be OK,

171

though. Believe me, everything will be fine."

"Fine." She shrugged her shoulders and the color in her face was again replaced by a mask of exhaustion. She lowered the receiver and tossed her head back, revealing the dark smoothness of her throat. "How's it gonna be fine, Clarence? It's been four days already. Four days. What...how..." She buried her face in the palms of her hands.

"The truth will come out," Clarence said, reciting Sapp's words, but for the first time finding himself doubting them. "Sooner or later it has to."

"Sooner or later." She said, averting her eyes. "I don't...I'm not sure how long I can go on like this."

There was nothing sufficient he could say, so Clarence remained silent. He stared at the faint outline of his reflection in the glass before him and wondered how it had come to this. Why it had come to this. Was it some inevitable twist of fate that his entire life had been leading up to? Was it some form of punishment, a penance for the transgressions of his past? Or for his unfaithfulness? Or maybe it was all just one big joke the world had decided to play on him, God winding up and giving him a big, fat slap across the face for no particular reason other than that He could.

"Five minutes." The voice over the PA system crackled from the overhead speakers.

Leslie lifted her head and dabbed at the edges of her eyes with her knuckles. Clarence clenched his jaw, focused all of his energies on holding back his own tears.

"Well," she said.

"Well."

"I guess I'll see you Wednesday, then." Clarence nodded.

"You need to talk before then, you call. Anytime. If you hear anything new..."

Another nod.

"OK, then." That flimsy, half smile again. "Love you."

"Love you, too."

Leslie stood and began to place the receiver in its cradle.

"Les?"

She paused and brought the receiver slowly back to her ear.

"Don't forget those pictures."

Chapter 39

Cutter's Corner Grocery was at the corner of Jarvis and Powers, three blocks east of Sugar's housing complex. Other than the small OPEN sign in the bottom right corner of the front window and the black iron bars shielding the door, the store could easily be mistaken for another house on its block of identical two-story, red brick standalones. Inside, however, the main floor had been converted to four crowded aisles separated by rigid metal shelving stocked with everything from canned food and diapers to boxed wine and jumper cables.

It was just past six o'clock when Sugar stepped inside, the little bell above the door announcing his arrival. The buzzing fluorescent lights were in stark contrast to the tombstone dusk outside and Sugar blinked away the stabbing reflections from the scuffed eggshell floor beneath him. He took in the competing smells of bleach, stale beer and pepperoni sticks. There were a half dozen customers in the store, most of them standing in a crooked line with empty hands and hanging heads, waiting their turn for cigarettes and lottery tickets. Sugar grabbed a tarnished wire basket from a stack beside the entrance and slipped through the crowd, nodding politely at the defeated faces as he moved among them, trying to control the relentless tugging at the corners of his own mouth.

In the hours following his first sale to the man in the black Caddy, Sugar had learned the names of the other boys, Richie and Damon, and they passed the afternoon chatting and laughing and taking turns making sales as the basketball sun above them faded and dropped, lighter and lower, finally dissolving in the western skyline to their backs and sending them their separate ways.

Sugar had ended up selling another five dime bags, all without having to move more than ten steps from his perch atop the bench at the corner. The resulting haul was seventy dollars, the bills rolled to the size of a cigarette and wedged beneath the elastic of his dampened sock. It was all his, every penny of it. It was forty dollars more than Sugar had ever had to his name at one time.

As he wandered the aisles, plucking items from the shelves, not looking at the prices printed on the tiny green stickers, resisting the impulse to go crazy, there was a lightness in his head and his body that he hadn't felt in years. It felt as if a massive anchor had been removed from his neck, and instead of fighting and gasping for air at the bottom of the ocean, he was now floating atop it, safe within a boat, buoyed by the water and calmed by the sudden revelation of knowing how to swim. It was a feeling so thrilling, so magical, that Sugar swore to himself he would never sleep another wink, desperate to embrace it for every possible second, scared that if he closed his eyes it would be gone the next time he opened them, never to return.

By the time he had gone up and down every aisle twice, the mob at the counter had dwindled down to a single man wearing a stained blue jacket and rubber boots. The forty of OE in his hands was slick with condensation. Sugar got in line behind him and nearly choked on the foul fumes of urine and wet dog. He took a step back and looked up at the clock behind the counter, hoping Ma would be home when he got there, unable to remember the last time they'd had dinner together.

When the man finally dug enough loose change from his pockets to pay for his beer, he walked out of the store, mumbling under his breath, and Sugar stepped to the till. He reached in the basket and, one item at a time, began emptying its contents on the counter. A box of Lucky Charms, a jug of milk, a loaf of Wonder Bread, a carton of eggs, a package of hotdogs, two boxes of Kraft Dinner. When the basket was bare, he opened the ice cream freezer next to the counter to a blast of frosty air and the welcome smell of chocolate and dug around until he found a tub of Ben & Jerry's Chocolate Chip Cookie Dough, Ma's favorite. He added it to the pile on the counter.

The cashier, a middle-aged man with elephant ears and rotten teeth, acknowledged him with a curt nod and began bagging the groceries as he manually punched the prices into his ancient cash register.

"That be all?"

Sugar nodded.

The man ripped the tape from the register and pulled it to within a couple inches of his scrunched and squinting face.

"Twenty-three fitty," he said.

Sugar looked around the empty store before bending down and pulling the wad of cash from his sock. He unrolled the soggy bills and slid a twenty and a ten through the opening in the glass.

The man took the bills and Sugar walked the wire basket back to the stack at the front door, intentionally averting his eyes from the rack of newspapers. To this point, he'd managed to avoid any media mentioning the murder. Another week or so and another story would steal the spotlight and dominate the headlines. Until then, what he didn't know couldn't hurt him.

Sugar went back to the counter for his change. He clutched the paper bag of groceries close to his chest, thanked the man with a smile and left the store with a jump in his step.

Within a block of home, Sugar heard his name. He turned his head long enough to see Deon, running down the street, his worn sneakers smacking against the icy concrete. Sugar slowed his pace, but kept moving toward home.

"Yo, Sugar." Deon was beside him now, his heavy breaths coming in staggered gasps. "I was just on my way to your place. What's goin on, man?"

Sugar kept walking. He wasn't in the mood.

"Nothin, man." He answered without looking at Deon, quickening his pace without making it obvious. "Just on my way home."

"Where from?"

Sugar stopped and looked at his friend. For the first time, it occurred to him how immature Deon seemed. All the questions, all the time. Just like a little kid.

"Had some shit to do."

"Here." Deon slipped the straps of Sugar's backpack off his shoulders and handed it to him. "You left this in class the other day. Your books are inside."

"Thanks," Sugar mumbled, taking the bag and depositing the bag of groceries before slinging it over his shoulders.

"What happened Friday?" There was genuine concern in Deon's voice. "Why weren't you at school today?"

Sugar looked at his friend of eleven years, his fragile body swimming in an oversized coat and baggy black Dickies, his wary face drooping like melted chocolate.

175

"I was sick."

"You OK now?"

Sugar took one more look at his friend and shook his head. He turned back in the direction of his house but managed only a step before he felt a feeble grasp at his wrist. When he turned around again, Deon's mouth was wrenched open, his eyes hopeful.

"You mad at me or somethin?" He looked at his feet as he spoke, kicked at a chunk of frozen snow. "Seems like you been avoidin me."

"I'm not avoiding you, Deon. It's just that…it's just, don't it feel like we're gettin left behind?"

Deon tilted his head but remained silent.

"You know, like everyone around here is growin up but us? You see how they treat us at school, man. It's like we don't even exist."

Deon said nothing.

"Come on, man. What do we do? We sit around, watch movies, listen to music. That's kiddie shit, man. It's time to grow up."

"Like how?"

"When's the last time we hung out with anybody? Besides each other, I mean. Went to a party or some shit like that?"

Deon appeared to wince at the question. "Parties? What are you saying, you want to start drinkin, gettin high all the time? What about making something of our lives?"

Sugar's pity for his friend was suddenly replaced by anger. It pissed him off how young Deon sounded. What pissed him off more though was that less than a week ago, he knew he sounded exactly like him. Smart and level-headed, above all the shit the other kids did. Sugar kicked at an empty soda can and watched it jump the curb and slide beneath a parked car.

"Are we though, Deon? Are we makin somethin of our lives? Cause the last time I checked we were just two broke ass kids with nothin goin for us. Maybe we don't get drunk every weekend, but what *do* we do?" He could hear his voice crack as he spoke. "I'm sick and tired of being a nobody. Ain't you?"

Deon stared into Sugar's eyes, helpless, searching desperately for something. Then, looking like he'd been kicked in the stomach,

176

he shrugged and threw his hands in the air.

"Whatever, man. It's your life."

Sugar held his gaze for a moment before turning his back to him. He made it halfway down the block when he heard Deon's voice again.

"See you at school tomorrow?"

"Probably not," Sugar called without looking back. "School's for tools."

Chapter 40

Gerald climbed the rickety steps and scanned the red brick facade on either side of the front door. The unit number, made of iron and faded to the color of charcoal, dangled from a single screw on the left; the rusty black mailbox, lidless and overflowing with weathered envelopes and faded flyers, hung on the right. Like most of the houses he'd visited that morning, it had no doorbell.

Gerald raised his hand and knocked three times, the thin glass rattling beneath his gloved knuckles with each rap. After thirty seconds, he pulled his hat tight against his head and knocked again. He knew these people were home and it was just a game they played. He had no choice but to play along.

Just as he was about to give up and move on to the next one, he heard a raspy voice from above.

"Whatchyou want?"

Gerald looked up to see a middle-aged woman peering through a second-floor window. She had a leopard-print kerchief wrapped around her head and skin the color of fresh soil.

"Morning ma'am. If you don't mind, I'd like to ask you a few questions."

The woman poked her head out the screenless window and glanced down the street in both directions, as if she were crossing a busy intersection.

"You with the po-lice?" The first thing they always said.

"Yes ma'am. Shouldn't take more than a couple minutes of your time."

"I don't know nothin," she called down. The second thing they always said.

"If you could please just come on down for a minute, I'll be out of your hair before you know it. Just a couple questions, ma'am. I promise."

"I ain't got nothin to say to the po-lice." The woman looked down the street one more time, slid the window shut and disappeared behind a sun-stained floral curtain that had probably been hanging there since the seventies.

Gerald looked up, beyond the frosted shingles and past the soot-spewing chimneys, toward the sky. It was vast and dull, the

178

color of ash. Four days after the fact, he knew his chances of finding Nick's killer were slimmer than slim. Potential witnesses were unlikely to be reliable and, given that the victim was a white cop from The City, even more unlikely to be forthcoming. The only reason Gerald went on banging on doors and freezing his ass off was knowing that if he didn't do it, no one else would. He was Nick's last hope.

Gerald followed the sidewalk to the next unit, the last in its row. What was left of the slush from the day before had frozen into jagged shards of ice and it crunched beneath the heels of his heavy leather boots. Within a minute of knocking, a black woman appeared at the door. Late fifties, early sixties, she was crouched over a gnarled wooden cane with a knobby handle. Her frizzy hair was the color of snow, the better part of her wrinkled face consumed by a squat, pear-shaped nose. Spotting the beige hearing aid buds sprouting from both of her ears, Gerald tried to mask his dejection with a polite smile and introduced himself.

"Come on, then," the woman said, tugging at his forearm and pushing the door closed with her cane. "I ain't payin to heat the whole damn neighborhood."

She led him to a small kitchen off the main hallway and motioned to the closer of two vinyl-backed chairs at a circular table. The twin fluorescent tubes directly in the center of the ceiling emitted an irritating buzz and bathed the linoleum floor and laminate counter tops with harsh light and rigid shadows. Gerald sat down slowly, careful to conceal the Glock lodged in the waistband of his jeans while the woman hobbled toward the counter and started a pot of coffee.

Gerald removed his gloves and folded them neatly atop the burgundy tablecloth as he took in his surroundings. The living space was clean and cozy and smelled faintly of cinnamon. Judging by the woman's age and the lack of clutter, he figured she lived alone.

"How do you take it?" The woman had her back to him, her weak voice barely audible above the clanging of glass and silverware.

"Black," Gerald said. "Please."

He watched the woman reach for a cupboard above the stove and pour a splash of something from a brown bottle in one of the

179

cups. He averted his eyes as she turned around and approached the table, one tenuous step at a time. The bony fingers of her left hand were curled around her cane, those of her right expertly balancing a silver tray topped with a pair of white ceramic mugs filled to the rim. When she reached the table, she set the tray between them and took a seat.

For a moment they sat in silence and stared at the steam rising from the bowels of their mugs. The liquid in Gerald's was oil black, that in the old woman's a full shade lighter.

"So," Gerald said. "As I mentioned, we're investigating a crime that occurred in the area on Thursday night."

"What kinda crime?"

"An officer was killed in the line of duty. You may have heard about it on the news?"

She shook her head. "I don't read no newspapers. Haven't owned a television since the nineties, neither. What I don't know can't hurt me."

"Don't blame you," Gerald said. "Maybe you remember something out of the ordinary from Thursday night, though? A suspicious vehicle, strange sounds, anything like that?"

"Thursday." The woman concentrated on the tablecloth and repeated the word under her breath several times, the wrinkles on her forehead multiplying. She raised her head and shook it again. "Not that I can recall. I keep to myself, mostly."

"You're positive you didn't hear gunshots, sirens, anything like that?"

"May have." There was a lack of interest in her tone. "Hear it so often, it don't even register no more. It's like I said, the world out there ain't of no concern to me."

Gerald reached for his coffee, which was no longer steaming, and took a sip. It tasted slightly burnt, but he'd had worse. Before he could think of his next question, the woman spoke.

"Used to be a time I'd sit out on my stoop at night. Visit with the neighbors, watch the kids play ball, race up and down the street on their bi-cycles. Those were the good days, before the neighborhood went to hell in a hand basket." Her pale grey eyes had taken on a faraway look and she seemed to be talking more to herself now. "Hand delivered straight to Satan, it was."

180

Gerald continued sipping on his coffee. While he felt a tinge of sympathy for the woman, he couldn't keep himself from thinking, You reap what you sow. He didn't blame the woman personally, but it wasn't until all the blacks had invaded Crookston that the problems started.

"Lost both my boys, less than a year apart," she continued. "Shot dead, both of em. One in broad daylight, not a stone's throw from where we're sittin. Right out front his own home."

Gerald felt a pinch in his chest and looked at his hands. He tapped his fingernails on the coffee cup, gripped it to the point he thought it might shatter between his palms.

"Y'always think your kids'll be the ones to bury you," she continued, "not the other way around."

The surge of emotion was suddenly too violent for Gerald to contain, the memories of Charlie too strong for him to ignore. He could see his son as a newborn, wrapped tight in a powder blue hospital blanket, the nurse handing him over for the first time, Gerald holding him close and taking in his teardrop eyes and his baby powder scent. He could see him at two years old, standing behind the rubber tee, gripping his foam baseball bat, swinging and connecting with the ball for the first time, looking up at his parents with those same teardrop eyes, searching for approval. He could see him at five, first day of kindergarten, orange T-shirt and navy shorts cut just above the knee, clutching the straps of his Power Rangers backpack, his sun-kissed face fixed with nerves and fear and excitement. He could see him last Christmas, kneeling in front of the tree, ripping and tearing at the wrapping paper, his tongue sticking out the side of his mouth the way it did when he was deep in concentration, screaming and jumping to his feet with a joy so pure and uncontained when he found the Red Wings jersey inside. And he could see him six months ago, up to his ankles in the warm waters of the turquoise lake, seven years old, growing so fast now, fishing rod dangling at his side, the relentless sun beating down on his freckled back.

Gerald opened his eyes to discover they were damp. He wiped at his flushed face with the sleeve of his coat and was hit with the brief scent of salt.

"Officer?"

Gerald forced the emotion down his throat before lifting his head.

"I'm sorry," he managed. "But I really should be going."

He stood up and gripped the back of the chair. When he found his footing, he made his way back down the hall. The woman followed him without a word.

When he had his hand on the doorknob, she reached out and touched his elbow. He forced himself to turn around and look at her face.

"I hope you catch him," she said.

"Thank you, ma'am. I hope so too."

Gerald opened the door and the woman dropped her hand from his elbow.

"They never did catch them that killed mine," she said.

Gerald stood with his back to her for a moment before stepping out into the sunless afternoon.

Chapter 41

When Sugar arrived home, he found the front door unlocked and the kitchen light on.

"Ma?" he called as he slipped his shoes off and placed his backpack on the counter. "I got supper."

Hearing nothing, he crossed the kitchen and poked his head in the living room. Judging by the lingering smell of too-strong perfume and the accumulation of beer cans scattered across the coffee table, he'd just missed her. Probably off to the neighbor's, maybe Bingo if there was any welfare money left. He turned the light off and swallowed his disappointment.

After a moment of standing in the darkness of the empty room, he went back to the kitchen. He put a pot of water on the stove and found places in the empty fridge and among the bare cupboards for the groceries. Then he emptied his sock and his pockets, spreading the cash and remaining dime bags across the kitchen table. Sugar knew, with equal parts apprehension and acceptance, that this was it. For better or worse, his life had been reduced to forty-five dollars in crumpled bills and another ninety worth of weed. But it was like Kelvin had said: eat or be eaten. And though he knew with undeniable certainty that his appetite would never be satisfied, Sugar figured he may as well eat.

When the water was boiling, he went over to the stove and turned it down to medium. He dumped in a couple shakes of salt and reached for a package of KD. As he began pouring the noodles into the pot, he heard a knock at the door. Probably Deon, he thought. Either here to offer an apology, or maybe expecting one himself. Sugar scooped the cash and the baggies from the table and shoved them in his pockets.

When he walked to the door and peeked out the window his heart stopped. On the other side of the door, planted in the center of his stoop, stood a white man that Sugar knew could only be a cop. He wasn't in uniform, but between his confident stance and the complacent look on his face, he may as well have been flashing his badge. Sugar ducked down and took a deep breath.

"Shit," he muttered to himself. He considered staying down there, on his knees, hidden behind the door, and pretending no one was home. Waiting it out until the cop gave up and went away. But the kitchen light was on and, besides, he knew he'd probably been spotted when he looked out the window. His best option was probably just to surrender, give it all up once and for all.

Sugar was still crouching, heart racing, one hand frozen to the knob, when he heard another knock. Three raps, sharp and heavy. He managed to get to his feet and, after another deep breath, pulled the door open. The chill of the night sliced at his face and a sudden gust of wind nearly tore the doorknob from his trembling hand. He kept his eyes low and tried to make himself invisible. The man outside remained still, the black leather of his jacket bleeding into the murky dusk behind him. He reached for his breast pocket and Sugar felt himself flinch.

"Officer Dawes," the man said. He now held a copper-plated shield between his black-gloved fingers. "Your parents home?"

Though Sugar had little direct experience with the police, he knew they were the enemy. They were the ones that took his father from him, the ones that tore his family apart. But standing there, a foot and a half away from this cop, the closest he'd ever been to one, Sugar was unable to muster the hate he knew he was supposed to feel for him. He was too nervous, too consumed by the debilitating fear coursing through his body. All he could manage was a feeble shake of his head.

The cop took a step forward and poked his head through the doorway, forcing Sugar to retreat further into the kitchen. His foot got tangled in the mat and he stumbled. Chest hammering, knees trembling, he steadied himself against the counter.

"Mind if I come in?" The cop already had one foot in the door. "Cold as hell out here."

Before Sugar could answer, the cop took another step inside and slammed the door on the howling wind. Everything went silent.

"Thanks," he said. He took his gloves off and rubbed his hands together.

Out of the gloom of the night, the cop didn't appear as old as Sugar had originally thought. His face was tired and worn, but his dark brown hair and matching goatee were thick. The contours of a solid chest and thick arms were visible beneath his layers of clothing. His wolf-grey eyes were exploring the kitchen, slow and methodical, seemingly devouring every detail in the room.

"Who all lives here?"

Sugar was still leaning against the counter. He swallowed the gob of saliva that had built up in the back of his mouth.

"Just me and my mom. She gone right now."

The cop shifted his eyes to Sugar, gave him a stiff smile.

"That's all right. Maybe you can help." He stamped his snow-crusted boots on the ratty mat and nodded toward the kitchen table. "Let's sit."

Sugar inched away from the counter and wobbled toward the table, his legs feeling like spaghetti. He slid out a chair, but instead of joining him at the table the cop walked around the kitchen, his black boots squeaking as he went. He stopped to look at the window above the sink, the pot on the stove, the random collection of magnets plastering the fridge. After completing a lap around the room, the cop finally made his way to the table and sat down across from Sugar.

In the moments of silence that followed, Sugar could feel himself melting under the scrutiny of the cop's silent grey stare. His neck and forearms were slick with perspiration and he held his breath, suddenly aware of the surrounding noises – the off-key hum of the fridge, the faint whisper of the heat register, the steady rush of blood between his ears. Finally, the cop averted his eyes and Sugar felt himself exhale.

"Reason I'm here," the cop said, "is there was a shooting the other night. Right around the corner from here."

Sugar wondered if this was his cue to confess, his last chance to come clean before they dropped the hammer. He imagined an entire squad waiting on the street, bursting through the door at a moment's notice, guns drawn, barking orders at one another and throwing him against the wall, cuffing his hands behind his back and marching him down the sidewalk to a waiting squad car like they did his father. Sugar searched the cop's eyes for a look of expectancy, a hint of intimidation. Finding neither, he remained silent.

"Anyway. We're canvassing the area, looking for witnesses. Anybody might remember something that might help us with the case." The cop pulled a pen and a notepad from inside his coat and laid them across the table in front of him.

Sugar felt a swell of relief. He allowed himself to breathe again and flexed his fingers.

"So I just have a couple questions here," the cop said, flipping pages in his notebook. "Five, ten minutes tops. That all right?"

Sugar nodded.

"OK. Let's start with some info about yourself." He reached for the pen, clicked it open. "You got a name?"

"Sugar. Sinclair."

The cop's hand hovered above the notepad, the pen fixed between his fingertips. He looked up at Sugar, raised his eyebrows.

"Sugar your real name, or that a nickname?"

"Real." Sugar paused, cleared his throat. "After Sugar Ray Robinson."

The cop jotted something down, his head bobbing in time with his pen strokes.

"Hell of a fighter." The cop looked back up at Sugar. It may have been the light, but the grey in his eyes seemed a little bit bluer. "You like boxing?"

Sugar shrugged, careful not to let his guard down. "Not really. My dad did."

The cop nodded and opened his mouth to speak, but stopped himself. The wind outside was still thrashing, the window frame above the sink trembling on its metal rail. Sugar tried to relax, but he could still feel the sweat tingling his back and neck like a swarm of mosquitoes.

"How old are you?"

"Fifteen."

"High school?" The cop sounded surprised.

"Redford."

"I think your water's ready," the cop said.

"Huh?" Sugar followed the cop's line of sight and saw a steady stream of foamy white water cascading over the lip of the pot and sizzling on the bright orange element. He jumped up, banging his knee on the edge of the table, and staggered over to the stove. He turned it off and dumped the steaming water down the drain.

"Feel free to eat," the cop said from the table. "Really, I don't mind."

Sugar looked down at the pile of white noodles, bloated and slick with moisture, suddenly aware of the fact that he hadn't eaten since breakfast. No wonder he was feeling so weak, so lightheaded. Tempting as it was to wolf something down, he wanted the cop gone as fast as possible. He covered the pot with a lid and walked back to the table, trying to mask the pain in his knee.

"It's a'ight," he said as he sat back down. "I'll eat later."

"Your call." The cop shrugged and leaned back in his chair. "Now, back to Thursday night. Where were you? Home?"

There was no threat in the cop's tone, nothing to suggest a set up. Sugar nodded.

"Doing what?"

"Sleeping."

"Upstairs?"

Another nod.

"Do you remember seeing anything, hearing anything out of the ordinary that night?"

Sugar took his time, pretending to think back. He recalled something Reggie had told him once about lying: it was better to concede something small and irrelevant than to deny everything.

"I heard shots," Sugar said. Slow, cautious. "Woke me up."

"Do you remember what time this would have been?"

Sugar shook his head. "Didn't look. Just heard the shots and went back to sleep."

"Just like that? You hear shots right outside your window and you fall back asleep like nothing happened?"

"Happens all the time." Sugar shrugged and left it at that, hoped it was enough.

The cop leaned over and wrote something in his book. "How many?"

"Shots?" Sugar shrugged. "Three, maybe four? Happened so fast, it's hard to say."

"What did they sound like?"

"I dunno, loud? Like firecrackers."

"How much time between shots?"

Sugar could feel the cop's eyes on him, studying, probing. "Can't remember."

"Were they all together? Spread out?"

"All together, I think."

"All together. You're sure?"

"Yup."

The cop looked up from his pad. "You're sure, why didn't you say so when I asked the first time?"

Sugar felt the sweat pooling beneath his arms and across his lower back. The cop's eyes were focused on him again, untrusting and intense. He shifted in his chair and looked down at the table.

"I forgot."

The cop went on staring at him. After thirty seconds or so, seemingly satisfied, he continued.

"You hear anything else?"

"No."

"Did you look out your window at any point? See anything?"

"Unh-uh." Sugar risked a look up at the cop. "Like I said, hearing shots round here ain't no thing."

"But these ones were close, right around the corner. Didn't occur to you to get out of bed and look out the window?"

The cop's tone had changed. Like he knew more than he was letting on. Relax, Sugar told himself. If he was here to take you away, he would've done it by now. Keep your answers short, and don't say any more than you need to.

"Guess not," he said.

The cop dropped his pen on the pad. He rubbed at his eyes, the ropy blue veins on his hands dancing beneath swollen pink knuckles. When he looked back up, Sugar thought he saw disgust in the cop's blue-grey eyes, but it may have been defeat.

"What about around the neighborhood? Or at school?" he said. "You hear anything about what went down?"

"Not really. Just that…" Sugar heard his voice catch. "Just that a cop got killed."

"Nobody out there bragging about it?" The cop half-smiled as he said it, but there was something like pain in his voice.

Before Sugar could answer, the front door swung open. The thud of the knob crashing into the wall was followed by a burst of icy wind and the jarring rattle of glass and the squealing of rusty hinges. Sugar and the cop turned their heads at the same time.

"The fuck is this?"

Ma stood in the doorway, holding a can of Pabst Blue Ribbon in one hand, steadying herself against the door with the other. Her eyes were wild and bloodshot.

"Everything's all right, ma'am. I'm with the police." The cop stood up and Sugar felt all the air go out of the room. "I'm just gonna need you to calm down for a second."

"You let him in here, boy?" She was looking at Sugar, and he lowered his eyes. "You let a fuckin po-lice in our house?"

"Now, ma'am…"

Ma slammed her beer can on the counter and extended a shaky index finger toward the cop.

"You," she said. "Get the fuck out my house."

The cop took a step forward, palms open and facing upwards. "Listen. Ms. Sinclair. I'm gonna need you to…"

"Don't you fuckin Ms. Sinclair me. Only time you come round's when you need somethin, when it's one your own gets killed." Her words were slurred, her voice rising. "Where was you when it was my boy got shot, huh?"

The cop stood still, lips parted. He looked helplessly between Sugar and his mother a couple of times before finally reaching in his pocket and pulling out a card. He scribbled something on the back and placed it on the kitchen table.

"You think of anything else, you give me a call," he said to Sugar.

Sugar averted his eyes and didn't look up until he heard the front door open swing shut. Ma stumbled past him, muttering under her breath about the goddamn pigs. When she reached the fridge, she stopped. She turned around, walked back to the counter, grabbed what was left of her beer and passed Sugar with little more than a shake of her head and a look of disgust before disappearing into the living room.

189

Chapter 42

Gerald sat in the semidarkness of his living room with a tall glass of iced tomato juice in his hand. His worn leather recliner was positioned directly in front of the fireplace and he watched the orange-white flames slither and whirl behind the glass, their gentle warmth stroking against the soles of his bare feet. The forty-two inch plasma screen to his back was set to a digital music channel, the surround sound speakers transmitting an acoustic version of Neil Young's Powderfinger.

While a scalding pot of coffee and twenty-five minutes under the strongest, hottest shower he could handle had thawed the numbness from his body and rid his bones of the stony chill they'd absorbed throughout the day, the skin on his cheeks and throat was tender and raw and there was an uncontrollable pulsing in the tips of his fingers. There was also a relentless grinding in his gut that he knew had nothing to do with the weather or the thirteen weary hours he'd spent enduring it.

Lost in the shuddering glow of the fire, Gerald's mind was consumed with one thing and one thing only.

Charlie.

The thoughts of his son had first been triggered earlier that afternoon, sitting at the kitchen table with the old woman with the Bailey's in her coffee. The mention of her two dead sons had blindsided him, fast and fierce, like an unexpected slap in the face. And while a prompt departure from her home and a long lunch in his car had been enough to temporarily push the unwelcome memories to the fringe of his consciousness, nothing could have prepared him for the onslaught that followed.

From the moment he stepped into that battered, two-story end unit on the east corner of the projects and laid eyes on the anxious kid with the innocent face, the feelings he'd fought so hard to suppress charged back at him like a full scale assault.

Sugar.

With his baggy blue jeans halfway down his ass and his baseball cap pulled down over his left ear, he was the typical urban teenager – black and poor and paranoid, weighed down by a glacier-sized chip on his shoulder. In short, everything Charlie was not.

Still, just as the smell of scotch made him think of the grandfather who'd passed away before he had a chance to meet him, and the way Janet's eyes always reminded him of Ireland even though he'd never been there, there was something indefinable about the kid that screamed Charlie.

Something in the way his body language was both guarded and engaged, the way his youthful eyes revealed an unspoken understanding of the world and all its faults well beyond his years.

And then there was the smile. The kind of smile you felt more than you saw, that was special because you knew how rare it was and how much meaning it carried. The kind of smile that transformed a room and everything in it and struck you with a disarming pang of privilege merely to be in its presence.

The slamming of the back door made Gerald jump. He dropped his feet from the ottoman and straightened in his chair. He held his breath at the sound of heavy footsteps trodding across the tiles of the kitchen floor and finally exhaled when he heard the fridge open and the rattling of jars and bottles.

He swivelled his chair to see Archie entering the living room with a plate in his hand and a mouthful of food. He was wearing a red and black trapper hat with the earflaps hanging down. A manila envelope protruded from the pocket of his olive-colored parka.

"Help yourself," Gerald said.

"Would've, but you're outta ginger ale." Arch set the plate and the envelope on the coffee table and took the leather loveseat across from Gerald. He removed his hat and his parka and dropped them in a crumpled heap beside him. "Pizza ain't bad, though."

"Glad you like it."

Arch took another bite and settled back in the sofa.

"So," he said when he was finished chewing. "How'd it go?"

Gerald shrugged. He thought about the steady dose of slammed doors and scornful sneers, the overwhelming defeat of knowing another day was gone and he was another step behind in the search for Nick's killer. With his back to the fire, the room seemed darker, colder. He didn't answer Arch's question.

"That bad, huh?"

"How about you?"

Arch leaned forward and with two fingers pushed the envelope across the table toward Gerald.

"What's this?"

"That," Arch said, "happens to be a statement of occurrences from the night of December fifth, signed by one Clarence Sanford."

Gerald pulled a stack of paper from the folder and began leafing through it. "How'd you get this?"

"You know the rules," Arch said. "I tell you, I have to kill you."

"It's like a goddamn novel," Gerald said, squinting through the dimness of the room and sliding the stack back in the folder. "Give me the Cliffs Notes."

"Basically the guy claims he was driving home from his girlfriend's – and yes, he's married – when he gets carjacked at Webb and Weaver. Didn't get many details on account of all the snow and the fact he's shit scared, but he does claim to remember there were two of them. One with the gun was young, seventeen, eighteen, tall and skinny, dressed in dark clothes. He didn't get a good look at the other."

The driver, Gerald thought. "What else?"

"Who do you think I am, Santa Claus?"

"Cough it up, old man. You could have told me that over the phone."

Arch smiled and folded his hands behind his head. "The good news first, or the bad?"

"I could use some good right about now."

"Say it first."

"Say what?"

"You know what."

Gerald clenched his jaw. "Archie Ziegler is the king."

"The king of what?"

"The universe."

"Come on, say it like you mean it."

Gerald inhaled and heard the rattling of mucus in his lungs, felt a shot of fire beneath his ribs. "Archie Ziegler is the king of the universe," he said with more conviction.

"There." Archie smiled. "Was that so hard?"

Gerald walked around the sofa and sat on the edge of the coffee table, stared into Arch's glowing face. Waited.

Arch reached into his breast pocket. He pulled out something small and shiny and tossed it to Gerald.

Gerald turned the Zippo over in his dry, calloused hands. He flipped it open, sparked it, stared at the flame for a moment before snapping it closed.

"KJ. Not exactly the rarest initials," he said. "And that's assuming it's even a name."

"I know," Arch said. "That's the bad news."

"What's the good, then?"

"I found some matches."

Gerald felt hopeful. "How many?"

"Six hundred and seventy two."

Gerald hoped Arch was joking but could tell from his face that he wasn't. He looked at the ceiling and felt the balloon of buildup deflate around him, the heaviness of the day settling in his skull and filling the room around him.

"Great." Gerald shook his head. "So all I have to do is knock on six hundred seventy two doors and case closed, we got our guy."

"Not quite."

"What do you mean?"

"Well," Arch said. "Narrow the search parameters based on the few things we know about the suspect, and the number of doors is substantially smaller."

"Such as?"

"For starters, when you reduce the search to males between the ages of sixteen and twenty, you're down to one fifty five." He was having fun now. "When you narrow those down to a twelve block radius surrounding the scene of the carjacking, the number goes down even more."

Gerald felt a flicker of hope. "How many?"

"Guess."

"Come on, Ziggy. How many?"

Arch reached into his pocket and slowly pulled his hand out, his thumb and two fingers formed in the shape of a gun. He waggled them a couple of times before pointing them at Gerald.

"Three? You narrowed it down to three?" Gerald felt his limbs come to life.

Arch settled back in his seat and licked his lips. "Now we

can't get ahead of ourselves here. First off, we don't even know KJ is a name. Second, we – "

"I don't care," Gerald was standing now, the blood pumping through his legs. "You got a list?"

Once again, Arch reached into his pocket, this time producing a folded square of loose leaf. He unfolded it and laid it on his lap. "First one's named Kendall Jyles. Sixteen years old, junior at Redford High. Clean sheet, never so much as a misdemeanor.

"Next, we got Kyrie Johnson. Seventeen, senior at St. Jerome's."

"The catholic school?"

Arch nodded. "He's an interesting one. Comes from a decent family, captain of the football team, volunteers regular down at the homeless shelter on Watt. Thing is though, the volunteering ain't exactly voluntary if you know what I mean."

"Community service?"

Arch nodded. "Got pinched for possession last Halloween, a hundred and fifty hours and six months probation."

"Anything since?"

"Not that he's been busted for."

"What about the last one?"

"The last one, if I was a betting man, would be our definitive front-runner. Kelvin Jackson, turned seventeen last month, also enrolled at Redford. He's in the system early and often, fingered and questioned for everything from arson to grand theft auto. Thing is, he's never been charged. Kid's either real good or real lucky."

Gerald smiled. "You got addresses?"

"What do you think?"

Gerald leaned forward and extended his open palm.

Arch handed him the sheet of paper, and Gerald stared into the fire, feeling for the first time that he might have a chance.

"Gerald?" Arch's voice snapped him out of his trance. "Yeah?"

"You thought about what you're gonna do if you find this guy?" Gerald remained silent for a moment, still staring into the hungry yellow flames of the fire.

"I haven't." He turned around and looked his friend in the eye. "I honestly haven't."

194

Chapter 43

Gutless.

That single word, those seven letters, meaningless now, a mantra recited to the point of exhaustion, continued to play over and over in Clarence's head.

Gutless.

Gutless, gutless, gutless.

It was as if the word had become a living, breathing part of his surroundings, an extension of his solitary existence, white noise, there but barely, like the droning repetition of a leaky faucet, half lulling him to sleep, half keeping him awake.

He was lying flat against his rigid mattress, motionless, enveloped in the rusty odor and the suffocating humidity of his cage, his torso wrapped like a mummy inside his thin grey sheets, staring up at the dull grey ceiling. His eyes were dry and felt as if they'd been gouged with sandpaper.

Since his visit with Leslie, he hadn't slept. Measuring the elapsed time not by clocks or the rising and setting of the sun, but by the stringent and invariable routine of tasteless meals and patronizing headcounts, Clarence figured it had been between twenty-two and twenty-four hours.

The harder he tried to banish his wife from his thoughts, the clearer she became. Sitting across from him, ghostly and frail, smiling at him with a smile that was not hers and speaking to him in a voice he did not recognize. Rising from her stool, turning her back on his unfulfilled intentions, floating toward the exit, the unspoken truth lingering between them in the invisible limbo of the visitor's room.

As the mind-numbing minutes bled into torturous hours, self-reproach gave way to sheer and utter regret. He'd had the chance to go through with it, the opportunity to come clean, and he'd blown it. Now she was going to hear the truth from some hotshot cop or some big-mouthed reporter and see him for the lying, cheating coward that he was. Any and all chances of forgiveness and reconciliation, remote as they already were, would be lost forever. Gut. Less.

A subtle presence in the hallway caused Clarence to stiffen. At once he became aware of the grainy film coating his throat and his mouth, the stiffness in his rigid knees and balled up fists, the crusted layer of sweat between his back and his sheets. The softest sound of staggered breathing, the faintest scent of soap.

Without lifting his head, Clarence knew there was a set of eyes on the other side of the bars, sizing him up, daring him to turn around and return the gaze. It was one of the games they had started playing with him: seeing how fast they could break him. Oftentimes they would just stand there with their contemptuous and intimidating smiles, staring holes through him, eye fucking him until he caved. It was only when he felt brave enough to try for a minor moral victory, to feign ignorance and attempt to rob them of their satisfaction by playing dead, that they would start in with the name calling. Cop killer. Bitch. Nigger. Combinations and variations thereof, often in concert with one another, a vicious onslaught that did not cease until he acknowledged them. Young, old, black, white – it didn't matter. They were all in on it. And no matter how many times he played the game, Clarence knew it had only one possible ending. Him breaking down, weary with shame and degradation, looking at the floor in defeat like a broken dog. Them, cocking their heads and casting a final prideful smirk in his direction, once more establishing their reigning superiority.

The guard cleared his throat and dragged his nightstick across the steel bars, filling the cell with the eerie sound of an out-of-tune xylophone. Finally, reluctantly, Clarence raised his head from the pillow. The guard was familiar: big, bushy eyebrows and skin so black it was nearly blue. He stood just beyond the bars, hands on hips, his shadow spilling into the jail cell, a shade or two darker than the pale grey of the battered concrete floor. Clarence looked away from the guard's sober face, focusing instead on his pressed black uniform, his thin grey tie, his faded gold chest badge.

"Get your bitch-ass up," the guard said, reaching for his keys. "You got a visitor."

*   *   *

Squinting against the flickering blaze of the overhead lights, Clarence could make out the profile of Byron Sapp. He was slouched over the metal table in the center of the attorney booth,

196

head down and shoulders sagging. With his listless posture and his rumpled charcoal suit, he had the appearance of a much older man.

Clarence took his time crossing the room. His lawyer didn't look up until he reached the edge of the table.

"Clarence. How are you holding up?" Sapp gave Clarence a tight smile and motioned for him to take the empty seat across from him.

Clarence remained where he was and folded his arms across his chest. His joints were still stiff and felt as if they might crack. "I think I'll stand."

Sapp exhaled.

"Suit yourself." He shuffled the sheets of paper in front of him, stacking and restacking them with unsteady hands before looking back up at Clarence. "Sorry to show up unannounced like this."

Clarence waited. He could feel the lumps of stress clustered along the tight slab of muscle wedged between his shoulder blades. When it became clear he had no intention of speaking, his lawyer continued.

"I know we had a scheduled appointment for tomorrow, it's just that…"

"What is it, Byron?"

Sapp opened his mouth. Hesitated. His eyes roamed the room as if the answer might be etched in the concrete of the walls.

"What is it?"

Sapp's pupils went still and he forced himself to look up at Clarence. He placed his hands flat atop his stack of paper and cleared his throat.

"I think we should make an offer."

"What do you mean an offer?"

"Now hear me out here, Clarence. I've spoken with the DA and they may be willing to offer twenty-five for a guilty plea. You'd be…"

"Twenty-five years?"

"You'd be up for parole in twelve, maybe ten. Considering the charges we're up against, this is a very fair offer."

Clarence steadied his legs enough to take a step forward. He rested his open palms against the cool edge of the table and looked down at Sapp.

"You want me to plead guilty to something I didn't do?"

No answer.

"Byron?"

Still nothing.

"I'm innocent, Byron."

Finally Sapp sighed.

"It's like I said before. It's not about whether or not you did it. It's about the facts, the evidence. And frankly, right now, they hold all the cards." Another sigh, a shake of his head. "I know it's not what you want to hear right now, but there it is."

"If their case is so strong, why are they offering a deal?"

"It's cleaner, costs less money. Less mess."

"What if Natasha turns up? What about all the character witnesses you said we could use?" Clarence was embarrassed by the desperation in his voice.

Sapp responded with another sigh.

"You were supposed to have me out of here by now, Byron." Then, before he could stop himself: "What kind of lawyer are you, anyway?"

Sapp's sagging shoulders went rigid and he jerked his chin in Clarence's direction.

"What kind of lawyer am I?" He clenched his jaw and pointed a finger at Clarence. "I'm the kind of lawyer that has his client's best interests in mind. The kind of lawyer that knows when to fold a hand. The alternative here is life in prison with no chance of parole, Clarence. Life."

Clarence held his lawyer's solemn eyes for a moment, the reverberation of that final word ringing through his ears.

Life.

He closed his eyes and wondered for the thousandth time if he was trapped in some kind of never-ending nightmare. Then he stood up straight and took a deep breath. The air was stale and tasted like metal. He tilted his head skyward and made his way to the nearest wall.

"Listen, Clarence…"

Sapp's voice trailed off, Clarence dragging his hand against the cold, stubbled concrete that confirmed it was all real.

After several minutes of pacing the perimeter of the room, he made his way back to the table. Sapp hadn't moved. His back and shoulders were square to the steel chair, his jaw fixed in a rigid frown.

Clarence crouched over the edge of the table so the skin of his sweaty forearms stuck to the surface, his eyes level with those of Sapp.

"Look at me, Byron."

Sapp shifted in his seat, but his eyes remained downward.

"Look at me!"

Sapp ran his fingers across the top of his skull and squeezed the bridge of his nose before slowly shifting his eyes toward Clarence. The room had gotten warmer, the damp air tickling his neck and forehead.

"I'm gonna ask you this, and I'm only gonna ask it once." Clarence heard an edge in his voice that scared him.

Sapp blinked once and nodded.

"Do you think I did it?"

Silence.

"You think I did it."

"I didn't say that."

"Then tell me you believe me, Byron. Tell me you believe I'm innocent."

"It doesn't matter what I believe."

"It does matter." Clarence said. "It matters to me."

Sapp dropped his head and shook it, just the once. Then he stood up, gathered his files and slid them in his briefcase. He brushed past Clarence and left the room without looking back.

Chapter 44

While the faded wooden signs at either entrance of the parking lot referred to the complex as The Brower Projects, it was known to police and residents simply as The Reds.

One of the last remaining subsidized housing projects in Crookston, the complex was flanked on the east and west by large, empty parking lots and on the north and south by taller, newer apartment buildings whose shadows blanketed The Reds almost permanently. It consisted of four rows of fifty rust-colored tenements, each divided into an upper, a lower and a basement apartment unit. Each unit remained constantly occupied, some by legitimate tenants, others by vagrants and squatters. It was common for two, sometimes three generations to live under one roof, as many as a dozen people crammed into a tiny three-bedroom unit.

As Gerald parked his Taurus next to a nineties model Blazer in the east lot, he fought back an involuntary gag reflex he had come to associate with The Reds. While he'd visited the projects dozens of times over the years, there was one incident that always stuck in his mind, branded on the back of his brain like an unwanted tattoo.

It had been a couple Augusts ago, in the midst of a relentless heat wave, when he and Nick were first-on-scene to a reported OD in a rundown basement unit. It was the first time Gerald had smelled a crime scene before he'd seen it, assaulted at the entrance by the sour stench of death and decay, which – despite plenty of fluids and a healthy dose of Vick's Vapor Rub – had both him and Nick spewing their lunches all over the concrete steps. When they finally managed to step inside, they found single mattresses spread across every inch of the floor, tattered and stained in blood, urine, feces and who knew what else, sixteen of them in all, including the one in the bathtub. Spent syringes and cracked vials were strewn across the floor like miniature land mines and the smell of old trash and spoiled food were almost as bad as the bloated body they found rotting, face down, in the back room.

Gerald got out of his car and shuddered against the cold as he made his way across the parking lot and down the empty sidewalk, among the rows and rows of crumbling red brick, watching the unit numbers descend one at a time. When he reached number 27 he located the entrance for the lower apartment and paused beneath the small flat roof. The unit looked like all the rest – one of about two hundred bleak and battered facades, crammed together like headstones in an overrun cemetery.

Gerald's first two leads of the day had turned out to be busts. The first KJ – Kyrie Johnson – had suffered a broken leg in a basketball game a few weeks earlier and was confined to the use of crutches; the other – Kendall Jyles – was a porky motherfucker, too big to fit in a car, let alone get out of it and run.

And now, this dilapidated tenement in the heart of The Reds was his last hope – like the last cast of the day, a dry and withered minnow dangling from the end of a rusty hook. Hard as he tried to block it from his mind, the possibility that he may never find Nick's killer seemed once again very real. And the truth was, he now realized, that he didn't know what scared him more: knocking on the door and staring Nick's killer in the face, or once again coming up empty, turning back around and living with the burden of knowing a ghost was still out there somewhere, faceless and haunting.

Gerald looked up at the splintered wooden door. There was a small window in the center, covered from the inside by a black garbage bag. He finally walked up the three tiny steps and rattled the glass with his knuckles. A few seconds later, he heard footsteps.

The kid in the doorway was scrawny, a shit-eating, catch-me-if-you-can grin plastered across his face. His long arms hung at his side like a pair of ropes, and his legs were like telephone poles. Gerald's gut instinct, the one he'd learned to trust over the years, told him that even if the kid wasn't yet a killer, he had the capacity to be one. There was a cold emptiness in his eyes that suggested zero empathy.

"Yeah?" The kid's voice was laced with an exaggerated tone of annoyance. He couldn't have been more than eighteen, but the sparse patches of peach fuzz above his lip and along his gaunt cheekbones told Gerald he was trying to appear older.

"Kelvin Jackson?"

"Depends on who's askin?"

"Name's Gerald Dawes." He held out his hand, but when the kid didn't take it, he pulled it back and shoved it in his pocket.

201

"You five-oh?"

Gerald nodded.

"Off duty." He unzipped the front of his faded leather jacket and opened the flap, revealing his badge. "Just wanted to ask you a couple questions. Off the record."

The kid scoffed. "Ain't nothin off the record with five-oh."

"So you are Kelvin Jackson."

"What's it to ya?" There was a challenge behind the kid's eyes, more sinister than playful.

"Well, for starters, I need to know who I'm about to be taking in on possession charges."

"Possession? Man, you crazy."

"The stank comin from inside your place tells me otherwise. It's enough to me give me probable cause to search the place right now. You know what that means, right?" Gerald squared his shoulders and crossed his arms. "Don't need no warrant or nothin."

The kid looked at him, eyes narrowed.

Gerald knew it was risky feeding him complete bullshit. Growing up in a hood like The Reds, learning from a young age the ins and outs of the system, some of these kids knew the law better than the cops did. But he also knew that in Crookston it wasn't about the law. It was about doing whatever you had to do to get what you wanted. It was about survival. And it went both ways.

"On the other hand, I could look the other way. Turn my ass around and be out of your life forever, like I was never here."

The kid muttered something under his breath and shook his head.

"What's that?" Gerald said.

"I said, what you wanna know?"

"Depends on who's askin. You Kelvin Jackson, or not?"

The kid shrugged. "Say I am."

Gerald shrugged back. "Fair enough."

He flipped up his collar. The wind was biting at the skin on his cheeks, still raw from the day before, but he refused to ask Jackson if he could step inside. He was in control here and he couldn't afford to look weak.

"I'll get straight to the point, seeing how busy you are and all. We're looking for information about the cop killing that went down the other night."

Before the kid could catch himself, Gerald saw the look of shock in his eyes. It was fleeting, and he did well to recover as quick as he did, but Gerald caught it.

"I don't know nothin," Jackson managed. His voice was steady, but he was avoiding eye contact.

"Nothin," Gerald said, nodding. "Nothin at all. A cop gets killed a couple blocks from your house, in your hood, and you know nothing about it. Come on, Jackson. I may be a cop, and I may be white, but I'm not stupid. Stop wasting my time."

"Look," Jackson said, most of the defiance gone from his voice now. "All I know is a cop got hisself killed over in The Flats." He scanned the parking lot for a couple of seconds before looking at Gerald. The front door was still open and he was leaning against the inside wall about a foot from the entrance, out of the wind.

"What you care for anyway?" he added. "I thought y'all pinched somebody on that already?"

"Yeah, well," Gerald said, "you know how it is. We still gotta go through with the investigation. Tie up any loose ends, you know. Cross our t's and dot our i's."

"He the right guy though, right?" Jackson asked the question too quick, too much expectancy in his voice.

As the two of them stood there, Gerald considered how to play it. The kid obviously knew about the shooting, and about the arrest. Sure, it was all over the news, but it wasn't exactly common for a black teenager in the ghetto to read the papers. Not unless he had a personal interest in the case.

Gerald fingered the inscribed Zippo in his pocket and considered using it, hitting the kid while he was off balance. Better to save some ammo, he thought, in case this thing went to the trenches.

"Pardon me for saying so," Gerald said, "but you don't quite strike me as the type to keep up on current affairs."

The kid shrugged it off. "Last time I checked, takin an interest in your community ain't a crime." That shit-eating smile again.

Gerald pursed his lips. How he'd love to wipe that smile off his face, and then some. Instead, he took a long, deep breath, felt the frigid air gripping his lungs.

"And why exactly have you taken such an interest in this particular case?"

"Just a concerned citizen, I guess."

"Between you and me?" Gerald said, taking a half step closer to the door and lowering his voice. "We're starting to go in another direction on this. Not much evidence against the guy we collared. His car was involved, yeah, but apparently it was hot. We got wits sayin there were two perps." Gerald leaned in even closer, waited for Jackson to look at him. "Young guys. Young and black."

Gerald was staring straight into Jackson's long, narrow face as he said it, and he felt a surge of satisfaction when it once again registered a momentary tremor of surprise.

Jackson began to look at the ground, but caught himself and maintained uncomfortable eye contact with Gerald.

"Why you tellin me all this?" There was no bravado left in his voice, no more defiance in his eyes.

"Oh, I don't know," Gerald said. "Just figured since you're such a concerned citizen and all, you might wanna be kept in the loop." He kept his eyes level with Jackson's, willing them to reveal whatever information lay beneath the surface of his flushed cheeks and his nervous half-smile.

"Well, thanks for that," Jackson said coolly. He was standing tall now, looking down at Gerald, with his hand on the knob. "Sorry I couldn't be more helpful, officer, but I really should get goin. Shit to do and all."

Gerald nodded. "Thanks for your time." He reached in his coat pocket and pulled out a business card. "In case you hear anything."

Jackson took the card without a word. He gave Gerald a bitter smile and took a step back into the narrow hall. He closed the door and left Gerald standing alone in the cold and bitter wind.

Chapter 45

In his mind, Sugar was good as gone. His third day on the corner and he'd already pulled down about one-eighty. Average of sixty bucks a day times six days a week was three-sixty, four-twenty if he worked Sundays. A little over sixteen hundred a month.

Despite the numbing cold, Sugar felt a rush of warmth at the realization that come March, maybe even February, he'd be home free, riding a bus with three Gs in his pocket, off to a better place to start a better life.

Sugar had no idea what time it was, but what little sun there'd been earlier in the day was now washed over with a dull haze tinting the entire neighborhood a dark shade of blue.

The traffic had begun to slow, and the filthy puddle of slush covering the street was beginning to freeze over. The only sign of life from the surrounding buildings were the ribbons of pale grey smoke coming from some of the roofs, rising from the rotting tin and disappearing into an endless blanket of grey that stretched as far as he could see.

Though there was no wind, the air felt like cold metal and Sugar could see his breath when he exhaled. Tonight, he vowed to himself, he'd finally get a proper winter coat. Even bundled in his thickest hoodie, a dark grey Adidas with light grey stripes, a size too big, and two layers of long-sleeved Ts beneath it, he could feel the frigid air pinching at his flesh. His hands were shoved deep in his pockets, massaging the rolls of bills between his fingers and his thumbs.

The rev of an engine, followed by the violent crunch of tires on ice, snapped Sugar back to reality. He saw the quick flash of headlights and gave the driver a nod as he took a step toward the street. When the silver Beemer pulled alongside the curb, Sugar saw two men inside, both middle-aged, both white. The passenger window was already lowered and Sugar squatted so his eyes were level with those of the passenger, who wore a dark grey jacket and had black sunglasses resting on top of his head. The driver was staring forward with one hand on the steering wheel, the other holding a cellphone to his ear.

Sugar acknowledged the passenger with a brief nod.

The man pulled two tens from his pocket and held them out toward Sugar. Sugar kept his eyes in the car as he reached into the pouch of his hoodie. In one fluid motion, he palmed two dime bags, reached through the window, shook hands with the passenger and exchanged the baggies for the bills. The passenger gave him a quick nod and the car took off.

Back on his corner, Sugar could feel himself smiling as he watched the Beemer's taillights disappear. He couldn't help but think about Deon and all the other suckers who'd spent all day sitting in a classroom. Ma, it turned out, had been right all along. All those times she'd told him to get a job, to grow up and be a man, to stop wasting his time getting a so-called education that would only benefit the middle-class white folk who could afford college.

All those days at Redford High, wandering alone and aimless down the halls, a total stranger to the classmates he'd grown up with for the past decade, seemed so distant now. And for what? To sit behind a desk all day and listen to a teacher that didn't know him from the kid beside him and take notes on something he'd have to study, memorize, and be tested on, only to forget it the next day and start all over again. To finish one grade at a time, only to one day stand on a podium surrounded by people he'd never see again, wearing an oversized purple gown with a matching cap and accept a diploma he'd probably throw straight in the trash.

On the one hand, Sugar felt superior to all his classmates for figuring it out before them. On the other hand, he felt ashamed because it had taken him so long. He was embarrassed by his foolish hopes for something better for himself. He was black. He was poor. He grew up in Crookston. Fate had been knocking on his door since the day he was born, and he'd finally gathered the courage to let it in. Like his father, like Reggie, like the thousands before them and all of those to follow, this was it for Sugar.

As the minutes passed, the sky grew darker. That last moment of the afternoon, before dark blue faded to black, seemed to come and go without warning. Sugar always forgot over the course of the long, lazy months of summer and fall how fast it got dark this time of year.

A few lights had come on in the neighborhood, their dingy glow pushing through stained windows and peeking around the edges of bent blinds and frayed curtains. The traffic had died down to the occasional vehicle, none of them in any rush to get wherever it was they were going, coasting down the middle of Inkster, their headlights bouncing carelessly off the darkened windows, their tail pipes leaving white snakes of exhaust slithering toward the darkness above.

Fifteen more minutes, Sugar told himself, his hands now in the pouch of his hoodie, playing with his last two baggies. If he didn't sell out in the next fifteen minutes, he'd call it a day. He looked up at the grey sky, through the maze of telephone wires, where a single crow circled overhead, a speck of black dipping and diving above and below the jagged skyline.

Another set of headlights appeared from around the corner at Sherbrook and Sugar smiled, hoping this was it. He blinked away the spots of white in his eyes and made out the silhouette of a dark SUV coming toward him. He took a step toward the curb and saw it was a black Suburban, its windows tinted almost as dark as the paint.

When the vehicle was within a couple feet of Sugar it slowed, almost to a crawl, and veered toward him. Slowly, the Suburban scaled the sidewalk until it was directly in front of him. Standing on the curb, Sugar was eye level with the roof of the truck, but he felt like a midget beside it. It was like a sleek black wall had gone up in front of him and there was no way around it. For what seemed like minutes, the Suburban just sat there.

Above the hum of the idling engine, Sugar could hear the faint but familiar beats of a rap song coming from inside the truck. He tried to look through the window but couldn't see past the glare of his own reflection bouncing off the black tint, so he looked down at the jagged pyramids of snow at his feet. One uncomfortable second followed another and Sugar wanted to ease back, step away from the road.

The music coming from inside the Suburban suddenly went silent. The engine was still on, but its steady drone was drowned out by Sugar's heavy, staggered breathing. He was aware now that his hands, which were balled into fists at his sides, were sweating. He hoped whoever was inside the Suburban couldn't see the nerves that had taken control of his body, the fear that he knew was etched in his face.

Just then, the street to his right went dark and he saw a flash of door swing open.

By the time he knew what was happening it was too late. There was a hand around his throat, another pushing against his chest. He could feel his feet being driven backward, scrambling and tripping over one another, the death grip around his neck the only thing keeping him from falling. Sugar tried to focus his vision but all he could see were blurs and flashes of black. He could faintly hear himself screaming but it could have been coming from inside his head. Just as he had the overwhelming sense of free fall, he felt the crushing slam of concrete against his shoulders. Every ounce of oxygen drained from his body and his head was filled with a sharp blast of light.

When he managed to open his eyes he saw through a bleary fog the face of Kelvin Jackson. He tried to blink the image away, but every time he opened his eyes there it was. Dark and serious, washed over by the shadows cast from his black hood, the only sign of life the white slits of his stony eyes.

Still pinned against the concrete wall, Sugar looked down and saw Kelvin's forearm pressed against his collarbone. Their faces were so close Sugar could nearly taste the strong, sour stench of something alcoholic escaping from between Kelvin's dark purple lips.

Over Kelvin's shoulder, Sugar could see through the open passenger door of the Suburban the shadowed silhouette of the driver slouched behind the wheel. The faint orange ember of a cigarette or a joint was moving slowly in time with music that Sugar couldn't hear over the pulse of rushing blood between his ears. He focused on that glowing speck in the darkened vehicle, hoping if he stared at it long enough and hard enough that it might somehow transport him someplace else, away from this. Whatever this was.

Kelvin, who had eased the pressure of his stiff-arm but remained standing directly over top of Sugar, still hadn't said a word. Sugar felt fully exposed beneath the weight of his stare. His head was swimming in the sweet strong odor now, his stomach feeling both heavy and hollow.

"Look at me." Kelvin's voice was barely above a whisper but the severity of its tone gave Sugar chills.

Sugar blinked away the burning cherry coming from inside the Suburban and shifted his line of sight until it landed on the creased shadow just above Kelvin's eyebrows. He couldn't bring himself to look any lower; to make eye contact would be to confess to the unknown sin he was being accused of, to concede what little dignity he had left.

"I said look at me."

Sugar continued to stare straight ahead, locking his eyes on a shimmering bead of sweat in the center of Kelvin's forehead. He inhaled a deep gulp of icy air and tried not to wince as it sliced through his ribs like a burning blade.

A flurry of motion at waist level broke Sugar's concentration. He looked down in time to see a flash of black. Kelvin's arm came up, and before Sugar had a chance to turn his head he felt something cold and rigid digging into his cheek.

"You been talkin to the cops?"

Sugar felt his body go limp. The cop in his kitchen seemed so distant already, so surreal. When was that anyway? Yesterday? The day before?

"Answer the question," said Kelvin, "and I won't have to use this."

The barrel of the gun was tracing the contours of Sugar's chin and cheekbones now, its icy muzzle firm against his skin.

"They came by," Sugar managed. "But I didn't say nothin."

"Who came by? When?"

"Some cop. But I swear, Kelvin, I never said nothin."

"I said when."

"I dunno. Two nights ago, I think."

"White guy? Goatee?"

He couldn't remember for sure, but nodded anyway.

Kelvin dropped the gun to his side and his eyes to the ground. For what seemed like a full minute he stared down at the laces of his white Nikes. Finally, without a word, he raised the gun, took a step forward and swung at Sugar's head.

Before Sugar could react, he was sprawled across the sidewalk. He was numb from the neck up and the neighborhood around him was coated in a black fog.

"Next time it's loaded," he heard Kelvin say.

Over the high-pitched ringing in his ears, Sugar heard the slam of a door followed by the rev of an engine. From his stomach, he watched as the hazy taillights of the Suburban disappeared down the street and around a corner.

Chapter 46

"Let's make this quick."

Victor Anton motioned to a young waitress at the next booth over and pulled his cellphone from a clip on his belt.

"Fine by me," Gerald said. "I got somewhere to be myself."

"So." Anton was scrolling through his phone now. "What is it?"

"I think I may have a suspect in Nick's murder."

Anton put his phone on the table and looked at Gerald.

"You told me if any new evidence were to come up, you'd consider taking the case in a different direction," Gerald said.

"And you think that means going out and doing your own investigation, like you're Encyclopedia Brown or something? You're not even a detective, Dawes. You're barely above a meter maid."

Gerald felt his jaw clench. It took everything within him to keep from reaching across the table and knocking the pompous grin off Anton's face.

"OK," Anton finally said. "So what? You got a confession?"

Gerald took a deep breath and was momentarily calmed by the aroma of strong coffee and fresh cinnamon rolls. "No confession."

Anton moved his head up and down in slow, deliberate nods. "OK, no confession. A murder weapon, then. You bring it along with you?"

Play nice, Gerald told himself. He's your only hope.

"No weapon either. But I've spent the past couple days canvassing the area of the murder, talking to potential witnesses. Anyway, this one kid, Kelvin Jackson, he seems to know – "

Anton interrupted him by raising his hand.

"We've been over this, Dawes. We already have a suspect. And a damn good one, at that. I should be working on the case instead of wasting my time meeting you in coffee shops and listening to your Hardy Boy hunches."

The waitress arrived at the table and Anton ordered a coffee, two creams and two sugars. Gerald downed what was left of his tomato juice and asked for a refill.

When the server was gone, Anton leaned forward and shook his head.

211

"It's like I said before. Unless you get me something better than what we have, I don't want to hear about it."

"All I'm hearing is that you'd rather put an innocent man on trial than go after the truth, Vic. It's bullshit."

"Jesus, man. Listen to yourself. You need to stop taking this so personally."

"This isn't about me," Gerald said. "Never has been."

Anton pulled his shirt cuff back and glanced at his gold-plated watch. He looked back up at Gerald and lowered his voice when he spoke.

"I'm gonna say this, and I'm only gonna say it once, so listen good. In a minute or so, I'm gonna get up and walk out that door. Way I see it, we never had this conversation. You show up at trial in a couple months, you get up on the stand and you answer the questions the way I want them answered. You answer the defense's questions the way I want them answered. You're up there less than an hour, then you get to go home. We get our conviction, we get one more bad guy off the streets. Everybody's happy. Understood?"

Whether Anton knew it or not, he was essentially offering Gerald a license to kill. The problem was, now that it was within his grasp, the idea of using it terrified him; as much as he wanted justice for Nick, he found himself scrambling for any excuse not to go through with it.

"How bout if your star witness decides to tell the truth on the stand? That no, he couldn't identify the suspect in the courtroom, and that no, he couldn't be sure it was the same man he saw fleeing from the Infiniti that night. That, in fact, he was pretty damn sure it wasn't the same guy. What then, huh? You still like your chances of a conviction then?"

Anton wiped his lips and folded his forearms across his chest. "Is that a threat?"

Gerald didn't answer. Just returned Anton's stare.

"Because it sure as hell sounded like one. And the last time I checked, an officer who's supposed to be on stress leave, but is instead interfering with an ongoing investigation, isn't in any position to be making threats. Especially when the person he's threatening has the chief of police on his speed dial." He removed his hands from his chest and laid them open on the table, as if he were revealing a well-played full house.

Gerald looked down at Anton's outspread hands and then over at his cellphone.

"Go ahead," he said with a nod of his chin. "Cause to tell you the truth, I'm getting pretty sick and tired of the bullshit. I'm starting to think that blowing this whole thing wide open isn't too bad an idea. Sure, it might cost me my career. Hell, it might cost me more than that.

"But fuck it," Gerald continued. "I've already lost my son, my marriage. I've already lost twelve fucking years of my goddamn life to this job. So go ahead and make the call."

When he looked back up at Anton, something in his face had changed. The light in his eyes had dimmed and his cocky smirk had been replaced by a thin-lipped frown. Whether or not he believed Gerald was bluffing, Gerald knew he would never call him on it.

"All right," Anton finally said. "We've obviously gotten ourselves into a difficult situation here. But just because we're after different things doesn't mean we both can't win."

He fidgeted with his tie and cleared his throat.

"I see no problem with you continuing your little investigation. And I also see no reason for anybody but the two of us having to know about it," he said. "In the meantime, me and my team will continue working the case against Sanford. You find a better suspect, and some real evidence, we drop the case and go in a new direction.

"Trial's set for early April. If you don't have anything by then, you probably never will. We go ahead with Sanford and you testify against him."

When Gerald didn't say anything, Anton leaned forward.

"I see this as a win-win, Dawes. What do you say?"

Gerald stared at Anton for a moment before getting to his feet and pulling on his coat.

"Like I said, I got somewhere to be." He pulled a ten from his pocket and dropped it on the table. "Coffee's on me."

Chapter 47

By the time Gerald found the restaurant, he was fifteen minutes late. He'd tried to arrive before her again, but the place was impossible to find. It was a newish Mexican joint with minimal signage, barely visible among the shops and other restaurants on the crowded one-way.

When he finally spotted it, wedged between a used bookstore and a Chinese take-out place on the second floor of an old brick building, Gerald made his way up the stairs and through the swinging front door. The smells of sizzling beef and southern spices were strong and the room was dim.

Gerald stood in the narrow entrance and squinted until his eyes were accustomed to the semi-darkness. Before he had a chance to step inside, he was greeted by a young girl with heavy makeup and too many facial piercings to count.

"Reservations?" she asked, tonguing a silver stud in her lower lip.

"I was supposed to meet someone. I'm not sure if she's here yet."

"Short brunette, pretty?"

"That's her," Gerald said.

The girl nodded and turned her back to him.

Gerald followed her past the lively Mexican wall art and the colorful piñatas, through the crowded tables and chairs of the main dining area. The place was nearly full, bustling with the sounds of laughter and silverware and background salsa music.

Janet was sitting alone at a small square table sipping something red and icy through a straw. There was a single white candle burning in the middle of the table.

When Gerald was within a couple of steps, she stood up and gave him a hug. It was close but brief, and when she pulled away, he found himself wanting to hold her longer. For an awkward moment he stood at the edge of the table with his arms extended and watched her sit back down.

"What can I get you to drink?" the girl asked after he took the seat across from Janet.

"Just a water, thanks."

She nodded and walked back in the direction of the entrance, leaving the two of them together for the first time since Monk's Tavern, the night after Nick was killed.

Janet's hair was down around her shoulders, the way Gerald liked it. Her eyes were green as ever, shining in the faint glow of the hanging lights above them.

She was wearing a red ribbed turtleneck with a gold necklace – an anniversary gift he'd given her early in the marriage. Gerald found his gaze wandering toward her hands, which cradled the oversized martini glass, and felt a tinge of relief when he saw she was wearing her wedding ring.

She caught his glance and smiled back.

"You look great, Jan," Gerald said. "I miss you."

She smiled. "How you been?"

"Better, I guess."

"Are you back working yet?"

"Probably not till the new year. Gotta get my head straight, you know? I'm not even sure I've processed everything that's happened yet."

Janet shook her head and stared into her drink.

"I can't imagine what you must be going through. I'm so sorry I haven't been there for you."

Gerald began to speak, but she shook her head. She pursed her lips, inhaled deeply. Opened her mouth several times only before closing it, seemingly searching for the right words.

"I...I'm sorry for leaving like that, Ger." Her head was still down, her dark hair hanging just above the salted rim of her glass. "And I'm sorry about what I said."

It's all your fault.

The memory of the words hit Gerald like a slap in the face. The thought of them stung even more than when she'd first said them. It *was* his fault. All those times he'd blamed himself he didn't think it could get any worse. But he'd been wrong: his wife blaming him was much worse.

"I didn't mean it, Ger. It just...it just came out." She grabbed his hands across the table. "I'm sorry."

Every bone in Gerald's body urged him to jump across the table and take his wife in his arms and hold her like he'd never let

215

her go. To make everything go back to the way it was. The way it was before what, though?

Gerald knew deep down that this wasn't just about Charlie. There had been a strain on their relationship long before that, a faceless force they both knew was there but were too proud, or perhaps too scared, to acknowledge. The constant bickering. The increasingly heated arguments about his job. The money, and what they spent it on. Sure there had been good days, weeks even. There had even been times when things seemed almost right again, on the verge of being the way they were when they were first dating. But for as long as Gerald could remember there had been something missing between them.

So he didn't jump across the table. He didn't take his wife in his arms and hold her like he'd never let her go. Instead, he just sat there. Wondering where the years had gone and what had become of them.

"Gerald?"

He knew she wanted him to say it was all right, that he was sorry too, that she was forgiven.

What came out was, "Why then? If you didn't mean it, why?"

"I don't know. Just the stress, I guess. The frustration." Her grip on his hands tightened and he could feel her fingernails pressing into his damp palms. "About…you know. Not being able to get pregnant."

Gerald exhaled and tilted his head back. The white stucco ceiling looked almost yellow in the dimness of the room. He watched a thin banner of candle light dance across it.

"I wanted another child just as bad as you, Janet. You think you're the only one who was frustrated?"

"I know. I'm trying to apologize here."

Janet loosened her grip and caressed the tops of Gerald's hands with her thumbs. "Charlie adored you, you know that? He absolutely adored you."

Gerald stared down at the tangle of hands in the center of the table, trying to ignore the swelling in his chest. The tears were almost there now, small burning pools just beyond his aching eyelids. He forced himself to not blink.

"Who am I?" Janet's voice brought him back. He looked up to see her head tilted back, her eyes crossed, a straw shoved up each nostril. She had a goofy smile plastered on her face, weak and disarming at the same time. Just like Charlie. She'd always been so good at that – lightening the mood, easing the tension. Making it seem like everything was just the way it should be.

Gerald felt the pressure in his chest dissipate and couldn't contain the smile he felt breaking at the corners of his mouth.

"He always did have his mother's sense of humor."

She nodded her chin toward him. "And his father's smile."

There it was again, that little grin. Everything was going to be all right, that smile was telling Gerald. He felt his wife's eyes on him, patient and expectant. Waiting for him to tell her that he forgave her and loved her and that everything could go back to normal now. But he knew it wasn't that simple. Not this time. Not until he could look at her without thinking about him.

"What are we doing here, Janet?" he finally said. It came out colder than he'd intended.

For the first time that evening, her big green eyes registered a look of concern.

"What do you mean?"

"I mean us. You and me. What is this?"

"We're doing what any couple who's been married thirteen years would do. We hit a rough patch and we're working through it."

Before Gerald could respond, a waitress arrived at their table with Gerald's water. She glanced down at the menus, which hadn't been opened yet.

"Ready to order?"

Gerald answered her without looking up. "Another couple minutes."

"Sure thing."

When she was gone, Gerald adjusted himself in his seat and took a long sip of water.

"It's more than just a rough patch, Janet. Can you even remember the last time you were happy? With this? With us?"

Janet closed her eyes and raised her hands to her face, masking it with her slender fingers. Her gold ring sparkled in the candlelight, the diamond dancing like a firefly in the dimness of the

217

room. Her shoulders trembled and her head wavered from side to side.

Gerald stood and walked around the table. He sat on the red padded seat and put his arm around Janet's shoulders. She leaned into him and began to sob.

He stroked the outside of her arm with one hand and brushed the hair from her forehead with the other. She felt like a child in his arms, small and fragile and scared. The heaving of her body was slow and controlled, almost rhythmic. Gerald sat in silence, stroking her arm and brushing her hair.

When she stopped shaking, he grabbed a serviette from the table and handed it to her. She dabbed at the corners of her eyes and wiped the tears from her face.

The two of them sat there for several minutes in complete silence. Gerald removed his arm from around her shoulders. He dropped his head and folded his hands across his lap as if in prayer. Janet was staring into the glow of the candle now, her arms wrapped around her shoulders like a shawl.

Without taking her eyes off the flame, she spoke.

"What happened, Ger?"

Between the indifference in her voice and the renewed calmness on her face, there was nothing to indicate she had just been crying. Her eyes were dry and bright as ever, no longer green, but bronze in the flickering reflection of the flame.

"I don't know," he said. "But whatever it is, we both know it didn't happen overnight."

"Doesn't make it any easier though, does it?"

"No," he said. "It doesn't."

Gerald felt a sense of comfort in the silence that followed. It was reassuring somehow. Resolute.

"So that's it," Janet finally said, more to herself than to Gerald. She was still staring into the burning flame.

"Yeah." The pain of what was happening was offset by the inevitability of it. "I guess that's it."

Janet tore her eyes away from the candle and she gave him a half-hearted smile. She stood up and grabbed her coat from the hook next to the booth. When she reached for her purse, Gerald grabbed her arm and looked up at her eyes, which were green again.

"For what it's worth, Jan, I do love you. I always will."

She leaned toward him and squeezed his shoulders. She kissed him on the forehead and he closed his eyes, inhaling the tangy sweetness of her breath, absorbing the warm moisture of her lips pressed against his skin. He didn't open his eyes again until he knew she was gone.

Alone at the table, Gerald dipped the tips of his finger and his thumb into his half-empty glass of water and squeezed the wick of the burning candle. It made a hissing sound and filled his nose with the smoky scent of sulfur. It was suddenly dark in his private corner of the restaurant. Gerald sat in the darkness for a moment. Then he stood up and left.

Chapter 48

The burden of the day worked its way from the top of Gerald's head and through his temples until it finally came to rest atop his knotted shoulders. As he approached the freeway, he considered going home, but knew he couldn't do it. That big empty house full of fading memories was the last thing he needed right now. He was restless and his head was buzzing. He was trying to comprehend the significance of what had just happened, to take it all in. The pierced hostess, the flickering candle light, the glow of Janet's bright green eyes. It all seemed so vivid. Yet it couldn't be true, this couldn't be the end.

As the city lights grew brighter and the traffic grew denser, Gerald was unable to think of anything else. They'd been through it all together – the good, the bad and the brutal. Over time, it was as if Janet had become a part of him, like another limb. An extension of himself that he couldn't function properly without.

From the day she stepped into his life, Gerald had experienced an internal calmness he had never felt. At last, he was at peace with himself and the world around him. Deep down, though, he had always felt it was too good to be true. That she was too good for him and everyone knew it but her. It often felt like one long waiting game, silently counting down the days until she'd finally figure it out.

Now, seventeen years and countless memories later, the game was over. It had come to a crashing halt, and from where Gerald was sitting there were no winners.

Mile after mile, off-ramp after off-ramp, the city outside Gerald's window passed by in a single stretch of nothingness. The traffic around him blended into the roads, their lights nothing more than a succession of tiny red blips on a black screen. He had lost track of where he was. Both hands on the wheel, ten above the speed limit, windows up, radio down. Nothing but him and his thoughts. When he finally looked up and saw an exit sign he recognized, he took it. What he needed, he decided, was a drink. Just one. Just to clear his mind.

As he decelerated around the ramp and merged with the northbound traffic, he rolled down his window. The blast of frigid air cleared his head instantly. There were single flakes of snow falling lazily from the sky now and Gerald hit his wipers. He reached for the dial on the dashboard and flipped through radio stations until he heard Jimmy Page in the middle of his Dazed and Confused solo. He turned up the music and picked up speed again. He could already feel the alcohol tingling his tongue. That first sip, ice cold and bitter, was always the best.

*　　*　　*

By the time Gerald reached the Silver Spur's parking lot, he could almost taste it. Back in his younger years, he'd been a regular here. After nearly every shift, early, late or graveyard, he'd retreat to one of the long tables near the back of the bar and drink until he felt the familiar comfort he no longer felt in his own home. The Spur was a place for him to get away, to escape the horrors of The Job, the horrors of the city around him, one drink at a time, until his stress was replaced by numb indifference.

Gerald realized now that those early years, those long afternoons and endless evenings spent in the Spur had been the turning point for him. All through his late teens and early twenties, he had kept his drinking under control. Sure, he liked to tie one on occasionally, but who didn't? He never binged, he never drank more than he needed to, and he never drank alone. There was even a period of about a year when he first met Janet that he rarely drank at all.

But then he'd become a cop. A couple of beers after work became the routine, and before long it went from one or two to the better part of a six-pack. When the empties started to pile up and Janet began to comment on it, he switched to the hard stuff. Sometimes vodka, sometimes gin. All that mattered was how much better the medicine made him feel. When it felt that no one in the world could truly understand what he was going through, the bottle was always there, waiting.

When Charlie was born, he'd tried to cut back. He would drink only a couple nights a week, and when he did it would only be two or three. The truth was, Charlie had given him a new reason for living, a second wind in the marathon that had become his life. A duty, a purpose, an opportunity to give his son the kind of father he himself had always wanted. But soon enough, the joy and privilege was buried by the burden of responsibility.

It was right around the time he started drinking heavy again that he met Archie Ziegler. From the moment Gerald met him, he was amazed by this man, this cop, who talked so openly about his drinking. His disease, he called it. He didn't beat around the bush, he didn't shift blame and he didn't seem to be ashamed of it. He was an alcoholic and he was trying to get better, plain and simple. The honesty was surprising to Gerald, but also scary as hell. For the first time it made him feel accountable for his actions, forced him to face the issue he'd up until then swept under the carpet and go toe to toe with the demon he'd grown accustomed to casting off to the darkest recesses of his deepest closet.

Gerald looked up at the flashing red sign. The "U" in the name was still out, had been for as long as he could remember. Every part of him wanted to open the door and get out of the car. To walk across that lot and order a drink and begin the process of forgetting. Instead, he just sat there, clinging to the desperate hope that he wasn't still the same scared and insecure twenty-something that used to park in this very lot and drink until his troubles and worries disappeared.

He reached in his pocket and pulled out his cellphone. He could smell the sweat coming from beneath his heavy coat and felt his hands beginning to shake. He dialled Arch's number. It rang seven times before going to voicemail.

The snow was coming down thick and swirling now, blocking out the moon and the stars. Gerald could feel the warm air from the heater blowing on his feet. The driver's window was rolled down halfway and the inside of the windshield had begun to fog up. He turned off the ignition and stared at the falling snow.

As much as he still couldn't stand the cold of a Detroit winter, he didn't mind the snow. There was something peaceful about it, the way it fell from the sky and accumulated on the ground, still and white as far as he could see, sparkling in contrast to the blackness of the night. Something about all that snow reminded him of an unseen balance in the world and reassured him that nothing, no matter how strong or horrible or violent, could last forever.

He followed the descent of individual snowflakes, falling from the sky like wounded butterflies, floating and fluttering until they hit his windshield. Some of them fell so slowly it was as if they were deliberately trying to prolong their finite existence, seemingly suspending themselves in midair to delay their inevitable demise. But in the end, they would eventually all surrender to gravity and submit to the same fate as those before them, one second floating and fluttering and the next second diving and disappearing into a sea of white obscurity. Like humans, Gerald thought, snowflakes own but a moment in time, each as insignificant as the next, only to disintegrate when their time is up. Some lasted longer than others, but in the end they all dissolved into nothingness.

Gerald watched as the beads of water streaked down his windshield and couldn't help but think back to the season's first snowfall. The night Nick was killed.

He felt a sudden surge of guilt in the pit of his stomach. Here he was, feeling sorry for himself and wallowing in self-pity while Nick's family was suffering, while Nick's killer was roaming the streets. He thought about the promise he made himself at the funeral. He thought about his meeting earlier that day with Anton, and his visit to Jackson's place. A Zippo engraved with the initials of a punk kid with a bad attitude wasn't much, but at the moment it was all he had.

A blast of cold air rushed through the open window and Gerald shuddered. He shook his head and started the ignition, put the car into drive and, without looking back, drove out of the parking lot. He turned the radio on again and cranked the volume. He headed east until he hit the freeway and turned west toward Crookston.

Chapter 49

Sugar cut across the old, abandoned railroad tracks running through Ritter Park. The snow was falling now and the dampness of his clothes had begun to sink into his bones. His imitation Timberlands were soaked through, his feet numb. The bitter taste of blood was still fresh in his mouth and his lip felt swollen and tender. He had no idea how bad it was, but he knew from the throbbing in his head that it wasn't pretty.

He walked as fast as his weary body allowed, desperate to get back home, collapse beneath the scathing needles of a hot shower and retreat to his room. Climb in his bed and get under the covers, escape the day and hide from the world and everybody in it.

Head down, he crossed Forsythe and turned left on Lester. The thin layer of snow covering the ground was beginning to crystallize, becoming slicker with every step. To keep from slipping, he moved from the street to the narrow boulevard separating the curb and the sidewalk. The crunch of dead grass and rotten leaves beneath his boots was all he could hear. It made him aware he was the only living thing as far he could see.

When he reached the corner of Lester and Munroe, he stopped. The streets were empty in every direction. Turning right on Munroe would take him up to Watt, which would lead him to Spence, and eventually home. If he continued straight though, he'd be able to cut through the playground and save five, maybe ten minutes. A thousand times he'd taken that route, but tonight it had him feeling uneasy. He was still rattled from Kelvin's attack, and with the snow blocking out the moon and the stars, the playground would be pitch black.

Before he could make a decision he saw the flash of headlights to his right. The car was still a block or two away, headed in his direction. Momentarily startled, Sugar dropped his head and turned right, toward the oncoming vehicle. This area, this time of night, he didn't want to draw attention to himself, but there was something oddly comforting about no longer being all alone out there.

Halfway down the block, the car passed him on the other side of the road. Sugar kept his head down. Without looking back, he sensed the car slowing down. Stop sign, he told himself. You're being paranoid again. Fighting the urge to look back, he shoved his hands deeper in his pockets and picked up his pace.

As Sugar approached the end of the block, he heard the sound of rubber gripping snow. With each step he took, the sound got louder, closer. He felt his body tense and his first instinct was to run. Instead, he moved to the far edge of the sidewalk and kept moving, trying as hard as he could to keep his shoulders square. Glancing sideways, he could now see a pale yellow glow on the snow-covered street beside him. He forced himself to keep looking forward, to try and remain calm as he felt his breaths and his steps getting quicker. He could sense the car moving gradually closer to him, the rattle of its engine and the smell of its exhaust looming just beyond the sidewalk.

"Hey!"

Sugar jumped. Tempted again to take off running, he caught his breath and turned his head without stopping. A four-door Ford was pulled up almost against the curb, rolling along at the same pace Sugar was walking. The passenger window was open and through the dark he saw the face of a white man looking at him from the driver's seat. He slowed down, but kept moving forward, one eye on the car.

"Hey," the man shouted again. The car was stopped now and he was craning his neck toward the open window.

Sugar got control of his trembling legs and turned around. Beneath the light of a lamppost, he had a better view of the driver's profile but still couldn't see the details of his face. He concentrated on adjusting his eyes, while at the same time trying not to stare. He was standing on the far edge of the sidewalk, the car idling along the curb beside him, the driver staring through the open window.

"Sugar, right?" The man nodded his head toward him.

Sugar didn't answer right away. He felt at a disadvantage, standing there in the middle of the empty sidewalk, the eyes of the man he couldn't see fixed on him. Sugar moved his eyes across the vehicle, searching for clues. It was a mid-nineties model Taurus, aged beyond its years. It was painted a dark blue but looked almost black under the pallid glow of the streetlights. The paint was old and chipped in spots, stained with dirt and crusted with salt. Rust was beginning to show at the bottom of the door panels and had already

225

eaten through the rear wheel well. A guttural whining sound was coming from the engine, like the distant cries of a wounded animal.

"Officer Dawes," said the man. "From the other day? I was at your place."

Sugar's heart quickened.

"Need a lift?"

Sugar felt a lump in his throat and didn't want to risk speaking. He focused on making eye contact with the cop and slowly turned his head.

"Come on," said the cop as he reached across the seat and pushed the passenger door open. "It's getting late. Let me give you a ride."

Thoughts of jail flashed through Sugar's mind, the end of his life as he knew it. He looked back at the cop and the coldness in his eyes from the other day seemed to be gone. It had been replaced by something more like sadness.

Sugar looked around the empty street once more and stepped forward. He hesitated for a couple of seconds before climbing into the warmth of the car.

"Where's your coat?" asked the cop as he put the car into drive. He pressed a button to close the passenger side window. "It's freezing out there."

Sugar stared straight ahead and shrugged.

The cop looked at him for a moment before turning his eyes back to the road. In contrast to its exterior, the inside of the car was in relatively good shape. The heater was cranked and the radio was on, but turned down low. Sugar could make out little more than a muffled bass line and the occasional murmur of vocals. Some kind of oldies rock.

Plastered to the center of the dashboard was a laminated picture of a kid a few years younger than Sugar, probably the cop's son. Sugar had never met the kid, never even seen him up until now, but he felt a pang of envy. Two parents, a nice home in the suburbs, family dinners around the kitchen table, a closet full of warm clothes. Sugar stared at the photograph in silence for a block or so until they came to a stop sign.

"So," the cop said. "Where you coming from?"

"Just a friend's."

The cop nodded. For the first time, Sugar noticed his clothing. A nice wool coat, black dress pants, fancy black shoes.

"How's your mom doing?"

"Fine."

"Doesn't like cops much, does she?" There was a smirk on the cop's face as he asked it.

Sugar said nothing. He stared into the side view mirror, trying to get a look at the damage on his face without drawing attention to it.

"It's funny I ran into you again, actually," the cop said as they approached Watt. "I had a couple more questions about that night."

Sugar licked his lips and swallowed hard. He stole a glance at the cop and tried to read his eyes. They were still bright, more blue than grey at the moment. He seemed almost indifferent about whatever he needed to ask, zero sense of urgency. If he knew anything, he was doing a good job of hiding it.

Sugar looked at his hands spread out across his lap and folded them. Although the idea of turning himself in had grown weaker every day, it was still bouncing around in the back of his mind. The dishonesty had become something he could taste, smell, feel in his bones. If he could only tell the cop, confess to him as a sinner would to a priest, this would all be over.

Relax, Sugar told himself. If the cop knew anything, he would have said so by now. Stick to your story and you'll be fine.

"Still no word on the street, huh?" The cop was no longer looking at Sugar, but straight ahead at the flakes of snow disintegrating on the windshield.

Sugar shook his head, hoped it was enough.

The cop looked disappointed but not surprised. He nodded his head as if things were going according to plan.

Sugar squeezed his hands together, waited for the next question. None came. He could feel his heart pounding at the door of his chest, certain the cop could hear it too.

They drove the rest of the way to Sugar's complex in complete silence. When they reached the parking lot, the cop slowed down and turned on his blinker. He pulled up to the curb and shifted the gear into park. The engine started to whine.

"You said you go to Redford, right?"

Sugar was already reaching for the door handle. He nodded.

"You know a Kelvin Jackson?"

The question hit Sugar like a kick in the gut.

"No." He knew immediately that he had answered too fast. The look the cop gave him told him he noticed it too. Sugar's cheeks began to burn.

"I mean, I know who he is," Sugar said. "But I don't really know him."

For a moment the cop stared at him. His eyes were calm and blue, though the coldness had returned. After an awkward moment of silence, he nodded.

"All right then, kid. Thanks again for all your help."

"Thanks for the ride."

"You think of anything else you give me a call, OK? You still have my card?"

Sugar nodded. Without looking at the cop, he removed his seat belt and pushed the door open. He stepped outside and slammed the door behind him. As he hurried up the walk toward his house, he could feel the cop's eyes on him. He didn't look back. It wasn't until he got inside that he was able to take a breath.

Chapter 50

For the first time since he'd been in prison, Clarence ate all of his breakfast. The porridge was as cold and lumpy as usual, the toast as dry and tasteless, but today he needed the energy. When he was finished eating, he lowered himself to the cold concrete floor and began doing push ups.

He pushed through the light-headedness and the heaviness in his bones and didn't stop until his shoulders buckled and his forearms trembled. He wiped the sweat from his face with his bed sheet and got flat on his back. He counted out a hundred sit-ups, took a thirty-second break and went back to push ups. He continued this routine until his body was covered in sweat and his muscles were twitching.

He had only fifteen minutes in the restroom, but for once he took his time. He scrubbed and rinsed every inch of his body twice, and for the first time in almost a week he took the time to shave, lathering his face with the cheap cream provided by the prison and pressing the safety blade as close to his skin as possible.

When he returned to his cell, he did another set of push-ups and sit-ups and put on his jail uniform, which he had laid flat beneath his mattress the night before. By the time the guard came to his cell and told him it was time, he hoped he appeared strong and confident and put together.

When Clarence entered the visitor's room, Leslie was already sitting on a stool at the far end, facing forward and staring at her reflection in the glass divider. She didn't seem to notice him until he was in the seat across from her. There was more color in her face today, and white crests of finger nail where there had been only raw cuticles the last time he'd seen her. Her hair, which was loose and hanging at her shoulders, appeared clean and healthy. There was a pair of black leather gloves lying on the table, between her elbows.

Happy as Clarence was to see his wife, the visits had become a struggle. For those fifteen or twenty minutes that he met with her, the burden of his facade was slowly destroying him. He could no longer decide if he looked forward to them because of the scarce semblance of humanity they afforded him, or dreaded them because of the diminishing shards of humanity he knew they cost.

Clarence gripped the receiver and swallowed hard. This was it. It had to be.

Leslie, who was still wearing her coat, brushed her thick hair behind her ears with her fingers and looked at the receiver for a moment before picking it up.

"Hi," she said with a weak smile.

"Hi."

It had been forty-eight hours since he'd last seen her. It felt like a year.

"You look good. You holdin up?"

"I guess. You?"

She answered with a shrug. Looked like she was about to say something, but stopped herself.

Now, Clarence thought. Get it over with.

"Les." He looked his wife over. Expectant eyes, slightly upturned lips.

"Les," he said again. "There's something…something I have to tell you."

Clarence looked over his wife's shoulder as he said it, then around the room and down at the dry, cracked knuckles of his right hand. Anywhere but her face.

"What is it?" Her voice was quiet and soft.

He glanced at her again, averted his eyes.

"It's about the, ah, the other night."

"The night you got arrested?"

He nodded.

"What is it, Clarence?"

He opened his mouth but nothing came out.

"Clarence?" There was concern in her voice now and he could feel her gaze locked to his face.

"I had…there was an alibi. I was with someone that night. Someone who could confirm I wasn't in that car."

"OK." There was uncertainty in Leslie's voice. "Isn't that a good thing?"

"When the police went to question them…to confirm it, they were gone."

"Gone? Who?" She shook her head, almost in disgust. "You're not making any sense, Clarence. Who was gone?"

A moment of silence.

"Who, Clarence?"

For what seemed like an eternity, he didn't say anything. He just sat there, heart beating hard and fast against his chest, head swimming, palms sweating.

Looking into the face of his wife, he didn't know if he had it in him. But the truth was no longer a lingering itch in the back of his mind or an irritating cramp in his gut. It was like a full-blown tumor, weighing him down from the moment he opened his eyes in the morning to the moment he closed them again at the end of the day.

This is it, he told himself.

"Her name's Natasha," he finally said, exhaling deep as he whispered the name.

When he looked at his wife, there was a small crease above her brow and her mouth was slightly agape.

He shook his head slowly and tried to focus his eyes on her own. The sincerity there almost killed him.

"I'm sorry, Les. I'm so, so sorry."

"No, no, no." The receiver dangled from her limp hand and she shook her head, over and over, from side to side. "No, no, no, no, no."

"I'm so sorry."

Leslie finally stopped shaking her head. She looked at him, streaks of black makeup running down her cheeks. Her eyes, though, were clear, unwavering.

Clarence watched helplessly as his wife placed the receiver in its cradle, grabbed her gloves, stood up, gave him one final heartbreaking look, turned around and walked away.

"I'm sorry," he said again.

But she didn't hear him. She was already gone.

Chapter 51

It was still dark outside when Gerald woke up. He took a quick shower, put on a pot of coffee and stood at his bedroom window. The snow had stopped falling sometime during the night, but not before blanketing every inch of the backyard with a glistening sheet of perfect white powder. The green of the pines and the firs was completely covered, their branches sagging from the weight of the snow and drooping at the ends like umbrellas.

Fragments of a dream still lingered in the background of his consciousness, something about that Sugar kid. The details were vague, but he could remember something about a body lying in the snow, cold and blue and coatless.

The aroma of roasted Colombian tore Gerald from the window. After filling the largest mug he could find, he went on staring out the window until the blackness of the sky gave way to a heavy purple and, one by one, the stars began to disappear. The moon was still high, large and looming, though it had changed from bright white to pale blue and was on the verge of making way for daylight.

After a breakfast of cereal and toast with peanut butter and more coffee, Gerald brushed the snow off his Taurus and climbed into the tomb-cold car. The digital clock on the dash showed 7:25.

Gerald arrived at The Reds just as the sun was cresting the roof of the towers on the eastern side of the complex. The sky was blue and clear and the reflection coming off the snow-covered shingles was nearly blinding. Gerald found a parking spot next to a pick-up truck and sat there with the car running.

A few doors down from Jackson's place there was a group of young black men huddled on the stoop. They were passing around a joint in silence, unaware of Gerald's presence or anything else beyond the five-foot radius of their little circle. One of the men tossed the roach to the ground and they all bumped fists. Three of them started down the sidewalk away from the projects while the other stepped inside a basement apartment.

Gerald turned off the car, checked his pockets and crossed the lot to unit number 27. To his surprise, Kelvin Jackson came to the door after only the second knock. He was dressed in jeans and a hoodie and seemed to be wide awake. A thick gold chain with the initials KJ hung from his neck. It took everything Gerald had to suppress the smile forming at the corners of his mouth.

After a moment of hesitation, Jackson pushed the screened door open. Gerald was hit with the skunky odor of pot and he could hear the repetitive beat of rap music coming from behind a closed door somewhere. He locked his eyes on Kelvin and kept them there until the kid looked away.

After staring at the wall for a moment, Jackson looked up at Gerald. He was chewing gum, and Gerald watched his jawline flex with each chomp. There was a faint smell of spearmint coming from beneath his teeth, temporarily masking the stench of the dope.

"You again," Jackson said.

"Me again."

"I'd invite you inside," Jackson said, peering through the open door, "but I only got a minute."

"That's all right," Gerald said. "The stench of that shit makes me sick."

Jackson gave him a dirty look. "What is it this time?"

"Just in the neighborhood, actually. Wondering if maybe you heard anything since we last talked."

"Nah," Kelvin said. "Ain't nothin changed since the other day."

"Interesting," said Gerald, making a point of reaching into his breast pocket.

A flash of uncertainty etched Kelvin's face, but he remained silent.

"What if I told you, seeing as how you're a concerned citizen and all, that we've dropped the charges in that cop-killing case? That we have a new suspect. Young black male, lives somewhere in the neighborhood." Gerald pulled a pack of cigarettes from his breast pocket and turned it over in his hand a couple of times.

Jackson was trying to remain calm, but his body language defied him. He was standing straighter now and the look on his gaunt face had changed from cocky to concerned. All he could manage was a lazy shrug of his shoulders.

Gerald nodded and removed a cigarette from the package.

"Mind if I smoke?" Gerald shook his head and chuckled at his own question. "Look who I'm askin."

Kelvin just stood there with a blank stare on his face, his eyes narrow and suspicious. When he realized he'd been silent for too long he mumbled something and tried to close the door.

Gerald wedged his foot between the door and the jamb.

"Not so fast," he said, patting at his pockets. "You got a light?"

As Kelvin began to shake his head, Gerald pulled the Zippo from his back pocket.

"Never mind," he said. "Got one."

He slid the cigarette between his lips and held out the lighter, going for the kill. When he saw the flicker of revelation in the kid's eyes, he knew he had him. It was a look Gerald knew all too well: one part guilt, one part surprise, a look that said, "You got me. How the hell did you get me?"

Gerald lit the Marlboro and took a long, steady drag. Before he stuck the lighter back in his pocket he made a scene of turning it over in his outstretched hand a couple of times.

"What's the matter?" he said to Jackson, whose face was still frozen in disbelief. "You look like you're gonna be sick."

"Listen," Jackson finally said, his voice weak and uneasy. He had stopped chewing his gum and his eyes were cloudy. "All I know is what I seen on the news. I swear."

Gerald nodded again. He took another drag and exhaled a mouthful of smoke in Jackson's direction.

Part of him wanted to grab the little shit by the scruff of the neck and drag him down to the precinct. Throw him in the box with Clifford and Ramos for an hour and get Anton his confession. Another part of him wanted to take him out to the back lane and empty a clip in the kid's skull. No lawyers, no courtrooms, no bullshit. Eye for an eye.

"All right, then." Gerald stubbed what was left of his cigarette into the brick wall of the apartment and tossed the butt to the ground. "I have any more questions, I'll be in touch."

Jackson gave him a weak nod before closing the door without a word. As Gerald turned his back on the building and headed back toward his car, he was overcome with the strange comfort of knowing that the next time he came back here would be the last.

Chapter 52

Sugar was watching his mother watch television from the old rocking chair in the corner of the living room. She was sitting cross-legged on the couch beneath a pile of blankets. There was a cigarette with about an inch of ash dangling from the corner of her mouth and a can of beer on her lap. She'd been drinking all day. Drinking and smoking and cursing the weather outside.

The TV was tuned to one of those reality shows with all the crazy people living in the same house together. The volume was cranked, bouncing off the walls and the ceiling. Sugar waited for a commercial and got out of his chair.

"Goin to the kitchen, Ma. You want some ice cream?" He'd noticed earlier that it was almost gone, along with most of the other groceries he'd brought home two days ago. Ma hadn't mentioned anything about any of it.

When she didn't answer, he stopped in front of the television and looked at her. She seemed to be ageing by the day. He could remember when the kids around the neighborhood mistook her for his older sister; now she would have no problem passing as his grandmother. The skin on her face and neck was so severely creased it appeared to be on the verge of cracking. Her eyes and teeth were less white than yellow, her greasy hair an unhealthy shade of something close to charcoal. He wondered if his dad or Reggie would even recognize her anymore.

She noticed him staring and turned her attention to the falling snow outside the room's only window.

"You get a job or somethin?" she asked after a long pull on her cigarette.

It was a moment he'd been looking forward to forever – telling Ma that he'd found work, that he'd be able to support her from now on. Like Reggie had. But all the pride he'd expected to feel was overshadowed by the sinking feeling that his days on the corner were over almost as quickly as they'd begun.

He nodded anyway, apprehensive, unsure what he'd tell her if she asked him where. She didn't.

Instead, she took a final drag of her cigarette and dropped it into an empty beer can on the coffee table. She peered up at him through a cloud of smoke.

"Why ain't you workin today?"

Sugar nodded toward the window. "Weather."

She bit her lower lip and shook her head, as if the blowing snow and gusting winds beyond the window were somehow his fault.

"Next time you get paid, don't go wastin it on shit," she said, reaching for a fresh smoke. "Just gimme the cash and let me take care of the shopping."

The commercials ended before Sugar could respond, and Ma shooed him out of the way of the television.

Sugar dropped his head and walked into the kitchen. He flipped on the lights and stood in front of the refrigerator, fighting tears for what seemed like the thousandth time in the past week. His stomach was hollow and he felt as if he were on the verge of collapsing. He placed his open palms against the fridge door and took one deep breath after another.

A knock at the front door made him jump. When his heart slowed down he crossed the kitchen and peeked out the window above the sink. All he could see through the glare coming from the overhead light was a swirling blur of white.

Before he could shield his eyes for a better view, he heard another knock. Three bangs this time, each rattling the glass of the window and the dishes in the sink.

"You gonna get that?" Ma screamed over the voices coming from the television.

Sugar stepped back from the counter and made his way to the door, half expecting to find Kelvin standing on the other side. The draft of a cold wind was coming through the cracks and Sugar rubbed his hands together before slowly pulling open the door. When he saw the cop on his stoop he nearly fainted.

He was wearing a black parka, its shoulders covered in pellets of snow. Behind him, Sugar could see nothing but white. Not the parking lot, not any cars, not any of the surrounding houses. Only swooping swirls of grainy snow, thrown recklessly by the wind in every direction as it whipped between the apartment buildings and around the trees.

Sugar shivered and opened the door wider, allowing the cop to

236

step inside. He gave Sugar a quick nod and stomped his boots on the mat before slamming the door on the vicious wind. The cop appeared nervous, avoiding eye contact and shuffling from foot to foot. Sugar, trying not to stare, noticed he was holding a plastic bag in his left hand.

For an awkward moment the two shifted their eyes from one another to the bag and finally back again. The cop opened his mouth to speak but was interrupted by Ma's raspy voice coming from the living room.

"Who's there?"

Sugar thought about ignoring her but he didn't want her to get up.

"No one, Ma. I got it."

After several seconds of silence, the cop cleared his throat. He looked uncomfortable, as if he didn't know what he was doing there. His lips were pursed and he was staring at his boots, watching as the dripping snow formed in tiny pools on the mat around his feet. He finally raised his eyebrows and extended the bag toward Sugar.

Sugar looked at the bag and hesitated. He imagined the worst – some piece of evidence he left behind at the crime scene, or, worse yet, the gun he thought he'd sufficiently disposed of. Too bulky, he told himself. Relax.

Sugar slowly reached out and grabbed the bag. He held it in front of him with an outstretched arm, like a live grenade that might explode at any second.

The cop took the opportunity to brush the snow off his shoulders and remove his gloves. He ran his hands through his damp hair before blowing warm air into them. He nodded toward the bag.

"I thought you could use it," he said. The awkward half-smile on his face somehow told Sugar it was safe.

He reached into the bag and felt his hand disappear into a ball of what felt like some sort of clothing. He grabbed a handful of the material and let the plastic bag fall to the floor. He could feel the cop's eyes studying him as he looked down at the black jacket in his hands.

Before either of them could say anything, they were interrupted again by the screaming voice of Sugar's mother.

"Who is it?" she called over the din of the television. "What they want?"

Sugar looked down at the coat in his hands, trying to hide his embarrassment. He wanted to thank the cop and tell Ma to shut up, but couldn't find the words for either. When he looked up, the cop's calm blue eyes were locked on him. They were eyes that held no judgment, eyes that seemed to understand.

"You eaten?" the cop asked.

The question surprised Sugar almost as much as the coat.

"Come on," said the cop, placing a hand on Sugar's shoulder. "Let's get outta here."

Sugar studied the cop's face for a moment and decided he was serious.

"What the hell's going on in there, Sugar? I swear to God, if I have to get out my seat you're gonna wish I never had!"

The sound coming from the TV suddenly went dead and Sugar heard the creak of the old sofa. He looked at the coat and then at the cop. He pulled the coat around his body and slid his arms through the sleeves.

"Let's roll."

Chapter 53

"So," Gerald said once he and Sugar had pushed through the blowing snow and climbed into his car. "What do you feel like?"

Sugar shrugged. He was rubbing his bare hands together and staring out the passenger window.

Gerald started the engine and put the wiper blades on full speed. When the mound of snow had been tossed from the windshield, he turned on his lights and eased the car forward.

"I know a great fish and chips joint not too far from here."

Sugar acknowledged this with a slight nod, but said nothing. Gerald pulled out of the parking lot, still grasping to understand exactly what was happening.

When he'd finally given in to the nagging voice in his head telling him to buy the quiet kid from Crookston a winter jacket, he wasn't even sure he'd go through with giving it to him. If he was honest with himself, he was really doing it for himself, wasn't he? Wasn't it merely a vain and pathetic attempt to somehow absolve the guilt he'd been carrying for as long as he could remember?

But six hours later, here he was, shoulder to shoulder with Sugar Sinclair, unwillingly surrendering to the uncomfortable idea that maybe they were brought together by something bigger than themselves.

The snow was coming down in a barrage of pellets and visibility was down to a couple cars' length. Gerald was driving slow, leaning forward in his seat and gripping the steering wheel tight. The wiper blades began to squeak as they worked frantically to keep up with the relentless downfall.

"Sorry bout my mom," Sugar said when they came to a red light. It was the first he'd spoken since they got in the car. "She gets like that sometimes."

"Don't worry about it," Gerald said. "There's nothing to apologize for."

The light turned green and Gerald hit the gas. The tires spun, but the car didn't move. He pressed down on the pedal until the rubber caught concrete and the car finally shot forward.

"It's not your fault, you know," Gerald said once he had regained control of the wheel.

For the first time, Sugar turned toward him.

Gerald motioned with a nod of his chin toward Sugar's battered face.

The kid looked confused for a moment. Then, "You think my mom did this? Nah, man. It ain't like that."

"You telling me she doesn't hit you?"

Sugar didn't answer, just went on staring out the window.

"I've been there, kid." Gerald said. "Except with me it was my dad. Shit happens to white people too, you know."

Gerald noticed the trace of a smirk on Sugar's face, but he said nothing.

The traffic was light and Gerald continued to take his time as they made their way through the storm in silence. When it became clear the conversation was over, he reached for the radio dial.

"Music?" he asked.

When Sugar shrugged, he turned up the radio until it was audible over the furious onslaught of ice and wind. Suddenly, the car was filled with the wailing vocals of Springsteen in his prime.

"You can change it if you want," Gerald said. When there was no response, he looked over to see Sugar staring at the photograph of Charlie mounted to the dashboard. He fought back an unexpected tremor in the center of his chest and turned the radio up.

*   *   *

Milton's Fish and Chips was located between a rundown duplex and an abandoned storefront near the corner of Trent and Gable. There were no windows and it didn't have an "Open" sign. Driving by, one would never even know the restaurant was still in business.

Inside, it had the decor of an old-school diner. The entire back wall was lined with a one-piece counter and alternating orange and yellow bar stools. Atop the counter sat an old-fashioned milkshake machine and a soda fountain, neither in working order. Behind the cash register was a rectangular hole cut in the wall, offering a partial view of the kitchen. The other three walls were covered with ancient newspaper clippings, and the far corner was home to a large turquoise jukebox. It was currently spinning a Supremes tune that

Gerald recognized but didn't know the name of.

Before he made it halfway to the counter he was greeted by Tina. She took a second glance at Sugar, who was a couple steps behind him.

"Lookie here," she said with a smile. "Where you been hiding, Ger? Two specials for yas?"

He smiled back and nodded, leading Sugar to the booth nearest the counter. A few of the other tables were occupied, mostly by single men – some black, some white – dressed in work uniforms. They were all picking at their food or scanning sections of the Free Press and didn't seem to take notice of the middle-aged cop and the teenaged kid from the projects.

Gerald waited until Sugar was seated and took the padded bench across from him.

"Take your jacket off," he said. "Stay a while."

Sugar slowly removed the coat and laid it in a crumpled heap on the bench beside him. He looked around the diner nervously.

"Ever been here?" Gerald asked, knowing full well he hadn't. Sugar shook his head.

"We've been coming here for years," Gerald said. "Cops, that is."

Sugar glanced around the room again and swallowed an invisible lump in his throat.

"How long you been a cop?"

"Eleven years," Gerald said. "Some days it feels like half that, other days like double."

The kid hesitated, wondering perhaps if it was acceptable to ask another question.

"You like it?" he finally said.

"Don't like it, don't really dislike it. It's just a job, you know? Like anything else, I guess."

Just a job. Gerald closed his eyes and thought about Nick. For the thousandth time he saw his partner lying in the bloodstained snow. Just a job.

He forced his eyes open and looked down at his hands. He began to play with his wedding ring, not yet ready to continue the conversation. He was saved from the awkward silence he knew was coming when Tina arrived with two orange trays carrying their food.

She placed them on the table between them and gave Sugar a quick but warm smile.

"Dive in," Gerald said.

Sugar stripped the paper wrapper off of a straw and reached for his soda. Before taking a sip he grabbed a handful of fries and shoved them in his mouth.

Gerald took in the smell of beer-battered fish and oil-soaked French fries and realized he was starving. He cut into a steaming fillet and took a bite. The fish was hot and delicious and he felt as if he hadn't tasted food in days. Between bites, he looked over at Sugar, who had nearly inhaled his entire mound of fries and was now working on his fish. The two of them ate in silence until both were nearly finished.

"Musta been hungry," Gerald said as he wiped the grease and salt from his fingers.

"Yeah. Thanks."

"Consider it a thank you for the other day," Gerald said. "You know you're only one of three people in your entire complex that talked to me? One was senile, and the other was high." Gerald shook his head and chuckled. "That pretty much leaves you as my only witness."

The kid was leaning back in the booth now, and he seemed to stiffen up. Gerald was reminded of the first night they met, the kid sweating and shaking at his kitchen table. Beneath the harsh lights of the diner, Gerald was struck again at how young Sugar looked. With his soft features and undefined jaw, he looked maybe twelve.

As the seconds passed, Sugar became noticeably more nervous.

His body was completely rigid except for his eyes, which were darting around the room like they were following the path of a fly.

"Not much of a witness," Sugar finally said, looking more at the table than at Gerald. "I mean, it ain't even like I seen nothin."

"Right," Gerald said. "But at least you heard the shots. You'd be surprised how a little clue, something you'd think is completely insignificant, could break a case wide open."

Sugar picked up his fork and began to pick at the soggy remains of his fries, dragging them across his plate and through the tiny pools of ketchup. He seemed completely unaware that Gerald was even speaking to him. The way he seemed to instantly transport himself from reality to his own little world reminded Gerald of Charlie when he used to be watching TV or playing video games.

"You know," Gerald said. "I never told you this, but the cop that got killed? Officer Reese? He was my partner."

Sugar's hand froze in midair above his plate. He opened his mouth to speak, but closed it just as quickly.

"Twenty-nine years old," Gerald continued, unable to stop himself. He realized it was the first time he'd talked openly about Nick. With anyone. "A wife. Two young kids."

Sugar was still staring into his empty plate. His face was blank and he seemed to be muttering something to himself.

"All over a stolen car," he mumbled in a voice so soft it was barely audible.

Gerald shook his head. All over a stolen car, he thought. Just a job. The next time he looked over at Sugar, the kid's body had gone limp and he looked as if he might faint.

"You feeling OK?" Gerald asked.

"Huh? Yeah, yeah. Probably just ate too fast."

"You sure?"

Sugar seemed to force a nod. Gerald flipped open his cellphone and checked the time.

"Going on nine," he said. "I should probably get you home."

When Sugar showed no intention of moving, Gerald stood up and placed his hand on his back. His T-shirt was damp.

"You sure you're OK? The restroom's over there if you need it before we leave."

"I'm good," he managed.

Gerald reached for the kid's elbow and guided him to his feet. He weighed next to nothing.

"Come on, let's get you home," Gerald said as he grabbed Sugar's coat from the bench, knowing home was hardly the best place for him.

Oh well, Gerald thought as they moved toward the exit. What can you do? He had nowhere else to go.

Chapter 54

Hour by hour, piece by piece, Clarence could feel himself falling apart. The exhausting transformation from man to shell had reached its inevitable final phase and there was nothing left to do but accept it. Lying in his cot, drained and void of any emotion, he wondered if this was what it meant for a man to lose his soul.

He couldn't remember all the details, just the streaks of mascara and the empty chair. It was enough. It was everything.

In the seven hours since Leslie had turned her back on him, he had tried the house five times and gotten the answering machine on each.

Where was she? Who was she with? What was she doing? What was she thinking?

How recent it seemed that he had been harboring the relentless agony of not telling her, repressing the gnawing guilt deep within. But instead of the relief he had so desperately expected, instead of revelling in the reprieve he had secretly anticipated as a reward for his honesty, he was overwhelmed with a sense of regret.

Had she told anyone? Certainly not the kids; they were going through enough right now. But what about Rodney? Her parents? He would be a new man to them now, if he existed to them at all.

With one swift blow, he had managed to ruin his reputation and lose the trust of the only people in the world who mattered to him. And for what? The temporary, adolescent pleasure of spending two nights a week with a younger woman. An affair that had begun for no good reason other than that he was bored. He could have taken up a new hobby, or bought a fancy new toy. Lord knew he had the money. But no, it had to be another woman.

Staring at the single bulb hanging from the ceiling, Clarence could still recall with clarity the sense of entitlement he had felt. Truly believing that his years of loyalty and faithfulness and respectability, his hard work and his responsible choices, his strident upkeep of all the things that made him the man he had become had somehow earned him the right to neglect all of the things that made him the man he had become.

But what had started out as a little bit of pleasure had turned into a life of lies and deceit, a life of looking in rear view mirrors and carrying changes of clothes in the trunk of his car. It had become too much. That was why he had gone over to Natasha's that night. To end it, once and for all.

But it had already been too late, he now realized. Even if that fateful night had ended differently, he would be in the same position he was in now. Instead of battling his bouts of shame and guilt from the concrete bowels of a county jail, he would be in a corner office overlooking the Renaissance Center; instead of enduring long, sleepless nights in an old, lumpy cot, he would be in a king size bed layered with sheets and comforters. This was, in a sense, more fitting.

Clarence forced himself to his feet and stretched his legs. Pacing his cell, he tried to convince himself that if the roles were reversed he would be able to forgive her. But he simply couldn't imagine the pain and the betrayal she must be feeling right now. Seven years they'd been married, together for eleven. Two children.

No, he thought. There's no chance he'd be able to forgive her.

The pounding in his head increased and he dropped to his knees. He looked around the cold and desolate cell, which had become his home over the course of the past eight days, hoping, searching, praying for a way out.

He looked at the steel toilet and the steel sink. The concrete bookshelf built into the concrete wall. The overhead light housed in its steel cover. The flimsy cot covered in its ragged sheets.

The sheets. Of course.

Clarence buried his head in his hands and began to cry.

Chapter 55

Sugar headed straight for the shower.

He threw his clothes in a pile on the floor and cranked the squeaky faucet all the way to the left. He stood naked beneath the scalding stream of water until it no longer stung. When the shaking became too intense, he crouched on all fours beneath the barrage of burning pellets and watched his chunks of vomit disappear down the drain.

Officer Reese. He had a name.

Up until now, the cop he had killed was just a body. A faceless, nameless body lying in a pool of blood with pale skin and a gaping hole where his throat used to be.

Officer Reese. A body which up until the moment Sugar unloaded the gun on him was a living and breathing human being. A body with a job, a family, a future.

By the time the water flowing from the faucet became cold, Sugar was physically exhausted. He crawled out of the tub and wrapped a towel around his trembling body. He dragged himself to his bedroom and closed the door.

He turned off the light and collapsed in his bed, his body finally succumbing to the gravity of the day. Wrapped in the comfort of his sheets, the images he'd been trying to ignore finally caught up to him. They backed him into a corner and grabbed him by the throat and threatened to pummel him into submission, the result a sharp, devastating collision directly behind his eyes. The still and haunting body of the cop, of Officer Reese. The cold and empty gun that had killed him. The callous threats from Kelvin.

The onslaught was so violent and sudden that Sugar felt he was going to be sick again. Unable to move, he buried his face in his pillow and closed his eyes as tight as he could. He scratched and clawed through the dark and desolate hollows of his past, desperate for the smallest particle of optimism, the tiniest sliver of light by which to escape the horrors of the past couple days. Grasping, digging, digging and grasping and finally clutching at a remnant of pleasure, a shard of happiness from a sunny summer day six years ago.

It had been a perfect July afternoon and they were all together.

Ma, Dad, Reggie and Sugar. The air was warm and moist, a soothing summer breeze gently nudging the snowball clouds across the endless blue sky. They were way up in the nosebleeds at Tiger Stadium, the sea of people beneath them spattered with bright balloons, oversized foam fingers and fluffy pink bouquets of cotton candy. The air was scented with buttered popcorn and barbecued hotdogs. The sprawling emerald field below them was lush and brilliant, meticulously dissected by crisp white chalk lines, the private beach of the infield smack dab in the middle of it all, the bases and home plate forming a diamond of tiny white pebbles in the sand. There was a buzz in the stadium, electric and contagious, and for the first time in his life, Sugar felt he was a part of something special, something bigger than himself.

The game flew by. Sugar followed every pitch, every at-bat, every bullpen change with fervent fascination. He read the program from front to back twice and was shocked at how many black and Hispanic players there were in the game; he'd always assumed baseball was a sport played by white guys not athletic enough to play basketball or football. His dad taught him about Ks and RBIs and errors and sacrifice flies.

By the time Milwaukee's final batter struck out, Sugar's face was flush from the sun and sore from smiling all day. His stomach was swirling with junk food and butterflies. His legs were stiff, his ears ringing, his throat dry. But it was all worth it. The Tigers had won 9-3 and the stadium was humming with happiness and hope and the promise of better things to come.

Sugar climbed out from under his covers, the dim light coming through the window fading fast. He flipped on his bedside lamp and pulled open the drawer of his night table. His fingers slid among the CD cases, gum wrappers, pens and pencils, until they landed on the picture frame he kept there. He pulled it out and wiped at the dust with the corner of his sheet. Tucked in one corner of the black frame was the baseball ticket from that day, in the other Reggie's tenth grade school photo. The picture behind the glass was an old one of his father posing in yellow shorts and a white muscle shirt, hands out front, buried beneath boxing gloves. He had a matching yellow headband and an Afro and black sneakers that went half way up his ankles. He wasn't exactly smiling, but the expression on his face was so casual and non-threatening that it was hard to imagine him ever swinging at anybody with those big gloves on his hands.

Sugar stared at the photos and the sounds of that summer day rushed through his mind as crisp and clear and real as they'd been in the stadium: the voices of twenty thousand strong singing the national anthem, none louder than Dad, eyes closed and black baseball cap fanned across his chest; the thunder cracks of wood when the batters connected, the heavy thud of leather on leather when they whiffed; the deep collective breath of the crowd when a ball was hit high and deep and floated in the blue sky like a UFO suspended in space for eternity; the roar of the crowd for the Tigers' home run and the gasps and boos for the Brewers'.

Sugar's family had been among the last to leave the stadium that day. He could still remember them standing in the bleachers, shoes sticking to the spilled soda and crushed peanut shells beneath him, watching the sun slowly disappear over left field, wanting the moment to last forever. When they finally started making their way toward the exit, Sugar had looked down at the empty stands and the empty field and wondered how something so dead and so quiet had so recently been the source of life and magic and excitement.

Sugar took one more look at the pictures and put them face down on his night table. He felt embarrassed and ashamed of how naive he'd been back then. How he thought that Saturday afternoon would somehow change his life. Looking back now, that day simply was what it was – a single bright spot in an otherwise dark existence. It was the last time he went to a baseball game, or any sporting event for that matter, and it was the last time he stepped foot outside of Crookston.

Exactly seven days later, his dad was gone. Marched off in handcuffs, down the cracked pathway, toward the flashing lights of the police cruiser. As Sugar watched his father get dragged away, his wet face pressed against the screen of the front door, he vowed that he would never end up like him. He'd get an education. He'd be there for his kids. He'd take them to baseball games any time they wanted. He wouldn't get dragged away in handcuffs while his wife and his kids stood crying and screaming at the screen door.

How naive, Sugar thought as he drifted off to sleep.

*   *   *

"Where the hell you think you're goin, boy?"

Ma was sitting at the kitchen table. Her words were slurred, her face worn and tired with drunkenness. Sugar thought about all the times he'd seen her like this; he'd lost count years ago.

"Out," he said, without looking at her. He wasn't in the mood. Not now. Not anymore.

"Don't you turn your back on me, boy. I know you ain't goin out workin."

Sugar stopped at the front door with his hand on the knob. He thought about all those afternoons she wasted away on the couch, smoking cigarettes and drinking cheap beer. Sitting back and waiting for the welfare. Raising her family in the projects, all the while complaining but doing nothing to change it.

Everything in life was a choice. Crookston wasn't the reason for crime and poverty and all the bad things that happened to people, Sugar thought. It wasn't the economy either, or bad luck, or racism. It was choices. Choices that people like Ma made, feeding the system, creating an endless cycle of pain for their kids and their kids' kids.

Sugar turned around and looked at his mother. Her dark eyes were peering at him, challenging, her head tilted slightly to one side. A cigarette dangled from her fingers, burning upwards, slowly filling the room with smoke. The kitchen felt suddenly very small, as if it were closing in on the two of them. Sugar could hear his own breathing above the pounding in his chest. His fists were clenched, tight and sweaty at his sides.

He had the urge to tell Ma that he wasn't useless. That he wasn't an ungrateful, selfish, lazy, good-for-nothing, stupid piece of shit. That he would have made something of himself. He would have, if it weren't for her. He wanted to tell her that there was no chance of that now, and it was all her fault. That he had a killed a man, he had killed a cop, and everything was different now and it would never be the same again. He wanted to tell her all of this, but he couldn't find the words. They were trapped somewhere deep inside him, extinguished and swallowed whole before they ever reached his lips.

249

Sugar finally found his feet and pulled the door open. He stepped outside to the sound of glass shattering against the closed door behind him. He began walking and didn't look back until he reached the corner. He stood there, staring up at the kitchen window until the silhouette of his mother crossed the room and the house went dark.

Then Sugar turned his back to the only home he had ever known and stepped away from it for what he knew would be the final time.

Chapter 56

"I can't believe I missed it," Gerald said. He was deep in his leather recliner, the curling flames of the fireplace at his back.

Arch was seated on the sofa across from him, working on a gyro wrapped in tin foil. It was a quarter to midnight, but he was attacking the wrap like it was his first and only meal of the day.

"You didn't miss anything," he said through a mouthful of food. "You missed it, we wouldn't be sitting here."

Gerald took a sip of tomato juice and shook his head. "It was right in front of me the whole time."

For the better part of the past three hours, Gerald had been trying to convince himself that it couldn't be true, that there had to be some other explanation. But he knew that it was, and that there wasn't.

All over a stolen car.

At the time the kid had said it, the words rolled off Gerald's back. It wasn't until he'd driven home, made his way upstairs, showered away the day's stress and climbed into bed that it hit him like an avalanche.

All over a stolen car.

The information about the car being stolen had never been made public. As far as everyone was concerned, the man behind bars was the owner – and the driver – of the Infiniti.

Gerald stood up to relieve some of the tension that had gathered in the pit of his gut and wandered over to the sliding glass doors that opened up to the backyard. He pulled the ivory curtains aside and stared past his reflection into the blackness beyond his patio.

"This kid, Arch. I just wouldn't think him the type, you know?"

"There's a type?"

Gerald answered with a sigh.

"Remember that kid in Corktown," Arch said. "Summer before last, I think it was? The one with the shotgun?"

Gerald nodded. "What was he, eleven?"

"Yeah. Straight-A student, no history of violence, nothing. Just gets home from school one day and decides to blow a hole through mom and dad. And why not little Fido while I'm at it?"

Gerald cringed at the memory of the gory details, but the lack of emotion in Arch's voice somehow comforted him.

"That was a bad one." Arch rolled his empty food wrapper into a ball and tossed it into a brown paper bag on the coffee table. "Wonder whatever came of him."

Gerald continued staring into the endless depth of his backyard, his eyes slowly adjusting to the darkness. He could make out the stark silhouettes of naked branches grasping for one another and the faded specks of starlight hanging in the navy sky like dirtied diamonds.

"So what are you gonna do?" Arch was at his side now, his hands shoved deep in his jean pockets.

Gerald watched a ghostly trail of smoke rise from a neighboring chimney and followed its ascent above the frosted rooftops and the silver clouds until it evaporated. He tilted his head back and ran his palm across the stubble covering his chin.

"I don't know," Gerald said. He took a deep breath and let out a low chuckle. "I spend all this time looking for Nick's killer and now that I have him on a silver platter I don't know what the hell to do."

Arch remained silent.

"Tell you the truth, there was a time I told myself I'd kill him if I ever found him," Gerald said. He turned his back to the darkness outside and scanned the living room until his eyes fell on a row of photographs above the fireplace. "I dunno, man. He's just a kid for Christ's sake. A goddamn kid."

"Fucked up," was all Arch said.

Gerald tore his eyes from Charlie's most recent school photograph and began pacing the room.

"Any chance they try him as a minor?" Gerald said. "If he came clean, I mean? Voluntary confessions look good, don't they?"

Arch stepped away from the window and pulled the curtains shut behind him. "He killed a cop, Ger. He's done like dinner."

Gerald nodded.

"When I thought it was Jackson I didn't have a problem with it, you know? Wouldn't have lost a night's sleep over it."

"So maybe there's more to it. Maybe our boy Jackson was the

252

triggerman. Maybe the Sugar kid's just an accessory."

Gerald shook his head. "Thought of that already. It doesn't fit. The only reason we're on to Jackson in the first place is the Zippo."

"So?"

"It was found under the driver's seat. Nick was killed by the passenger."

Arch shook his head. He was staring into the fire now. After a minute of silence, "Like I say. Fucked up."

"Fucked," Gerald agreed. "He seems like such a good kid, man. Sometimes you can just tell, you know?"

"Good people make bad choices." Arch turned away from the fire and stared at him.

Gerald wasn't sure if the comment was directed at him, but it stung as if it had been. A familiar pang filled his chest, between his heart and his ribs, sharp and hot. He made his way to his chair and fell into it.

"Any chance he knows you're on to him?" Arch said.

"Can't see how. It was a slip of the tongue, probably didn't even realize he said it."

"No risk of flight then. Why don't you sleep on it? Think it over and give the kid one more night of peace."

"Give myself one more night of peace," Gerald said.

Just then, his cellphone buzzed. He pulled it from his pocket. The number on the screen was blocked.

"Hello?"

For a moment there was nothing on the line but a tinny echo of distant breathing. Sounded like a payphone or a poor cell connection.

"Hello?" he said again.

"It's me." The voice was barely audible but Gerald recognized it immediately. "Sugar."

Gerald nodded his head to catch Archie's attention.

"I need to talk," Sugar said.

"Where are you?"

"Jefferson Plaza."

"Stay right there," Gerald said. "I'll be there in fifteen."

Sugar didn't say anything.

"Sugar?" Gerald said as he got to his feet. "Don't worry.

253

Everything will be OK."

He heard the click of the phone followed by a dial tone.

"Gotta go," Gerald told Arch, leading him to the front door.

"Want company?"

"I think I better go solo on this one."

Arch pulled on his coat and put a hand on Gerald's shoulder. "You need anything," he said. "Call."

Gerald nodded. He grabbed his coat and reached for the door, not liking one bit what was waiting for him on the other side.

Chapter 57

"Lights out!"

Clarence had been sitting on his cot for what seemed like hours. The idea of what he was about to do scared him, but not as much as he would have expected. It had a comforting degree of finality to it. If there was no tomorrow, there would be no more pain.

One by one, the lights in the corridor went out and everything became dark. He listened to the sounds of the prison winding down around him: the creaking and scraping of beds, the groaning and muttering of inmates. The sounds that at one time haunted Clarence's dreams but were now just another part of his wretched existence. After several minutes of waiting, it became quiet.

Wringing the sheet between his dry, calloused hands, Clarence wasn't sure he could through with it. No more pain, he told himself. No more pain.

He got to his feet and twisted the sheet into a long tight coil. He gripped either end of the makeshift rope with trembling hands and wrapped it around his neck, winding it tight and securing it against his throat until he could feel it digging into his Adam's apple. He tied a knot in the front and tightened it the way he would a necktie. He walked to the door of his cell and looped one end of the sheet over the highest bar he could reach, securing it with a double-knot. Sweat was dripping from every pore on his body. He stood there, his head resting against the bars, his clammy hands gripping them tightly. The sheet hung between the bar and his neck with a couple feet of slack. He tested it by bending his knees slightly; when he felt the tug he knew it would do the job. All he had to do was lean forward and let gravity take over.

He wiped the tears from his face and took a deep breath.

Chapter 58

Sugar listened to the dial tone for several seconds before hanging up. The digital clock above the coin slot showed 12:25. Later than he thought.

He put Officer Dawes' card back in his pocket and felt an unfamiliar lightness in his chest. He wondered if it was the feeling of relief, or possibly regret. Either way, it was all over. In fifteen minutes he'd tell the cop everything and he'd be arrested. At the age of fifteen years and seven months, his life would be over.

The Jefferson Plaza parking lot was quiet and empty, its black tarmac dull beneath the tarnished moon, its faded parking lines the color of crusted egg yolk. The L-shaped complex lining the perimeter was built of old red brick, stained by years of neglect and graffiti, and consisted of a dozen or so businesses. A nail salon, a Chinese take-out, a tattoo joint, a dollar store, a pet shop. They were all closed – some for the day, others permanently. Their dark, dirty windows reflected like two-way mirrors beneath the flickering glow of the street lamps at either end of the plaza. The only places still open were a by-the-slice pizza joint and a small Korean-owned convenience store guarded by a wall of steel bars.

Sugar had $3.25 in his pocket and decided he may as well spend it. It wouldn't mean anything to him in a few minutes anyway. He crossed the parking lot, kicking at loose chunks of ice and damp cigarette butts, and realized that his last meal on the outside, the one he'd probably remember in his jail cell for the rest of his life, was going to be a greasy, stale slice of pizza that had been sitting under heat lamps for who knew how long. What a waste, he thought.

Before he reached the sidewalk fronting the pizza place, he heard someone call his name.

"Yo, Sugar! Hold up!"

Shit, Sugar thought. He recognized the voice but couldn't tell where it was coming from. Peering through the darkness of the lot, he could finally make out the figure moving toward him – tall and skinny, bouncing from foot to foot.

The cop would be getting close now, a couple minutes away at most. Sugar kept walking until he was standing directly in front of the pizza place.

Kelvin was only about twenty feet away now. He was jogging, head down and arms pumping. He was dressed entirely in black except for his shoes, which were stark white against the slick black tarmac. Sugar instinctively took a step back and found comfort in the brick wall against his shoulders. His legs had gone rubbery and were beginning to twitch.

As Kelvin approached the sidewalk, he began to slow down. He shoved his hands in his pockets and stepped up onto the curb, stopping a few feet short of Sugar.

"Sugar," he said. His breathing was quick and heavy. "What's up, man?"

Sugar planted his feet and studied Kelvin's face. It was glowing a ghastly shade of green beneath the dirty bulbs of the streetlights. He didn't look angry exactly, but he wasn't smiling either.

"Nothin man." Sugar could hear the fear in his voice and knew that Kelvin could too. "Just grabbin a slice."

"Been lookin around for you all day, man. Where you been at?"

There was a knowing look in Kelvin's eyes, confident and cunning.

"Home, mostly," Sugar said. "Had a killer headache, tryin to sleep it off."

Kelvin nodded. "Stress can do that, man. This been one straight up stressful week, huh?"

Sugar didn't answer. Didn't feel the need to.

"I mean with all the shit that went down the other night. And that cop creepin around our parts and questioning everyone. Killer stress, yo."

It felt to Sugar like time was standing still. He clenched his entire body and held his breath at the sight of each passing car, willing them to turn into the parking lot and sighing in defeat when the red of their taillights disappeared in the distance.

Kelvin took a step forward. He looked directly into Sugar's eyes, a half-smile forming at the corners of his mouth.

"Kelvin." Sugar put his hands out in front of him. "I don't know what's going on here, but it's not what you think."

"What I think is someone with a big fuckin mouth has been

talkin to the cops."

"Listen, Kelvin – "

"No, bitch. You listen." Another step closer. "I got cops on my doorstep every other day, askin me questions, makin me out as a suspect and shit. You make a deal with them? You pin this shit on me?"

Sugar couldn't feel his body. "No, Kelvin. No. I – "

"Where's the gun, Sugar? Tell me where the gun is and I'll consider that maybe you're not trying to fuck me over."

"Shaughnessy."

"Where?"

Sugar tried his best to fight the tears, but knew it was only a matter of time. "In the bushes. In the bushes, in…along the river."

Kelvin was bouncing from foot to foot now, looking around in every direction. He had that nervous look on his face again. The one Sugar had never seen until the cops were chasing them the other night.

"You gotta believe me, Kelvin." Sugar's mouth was dry and the lump in the back of his throat was getting bigger. "I swear, man. It's not what you think."

Kelvin jerked his head around and scanned the parking lot again. Seemingly satisfied, he looked at Sugar with slate eyes and reached inside his coat. The gun was matte black and looked small in Kelvin's gloved hand.

Sugar felt himself try to scream. The lump in his throat surged forward and his mouth opened, but nothing came out.

"I wish it didn't have to come to this, Sugar." Kelvin lowered his head as he said it.

It doesn't have to come to this, Sugar could hear himself saying. I'm turning myself in. I'm leaving you out of it.

"You were like a brother to me."

Kelvin raised his arm and Sugar heard a pop. And then another. And then nothing.

A flood of warmth filled Sugar's chest. Falling to his knees, he watched Kelvin turn around and run. He watched through a wall of fog as the black silhouette got smaller and darker, the shimmering of bright white sneakers bouncing off the concrete.

The warmth in Sugar's chest spread through his stomach. His

arms and his legs tingled, then went numb. He felt weak and tired and slumped to the cold concrete below him, landing on his right side, looking out at the empty parking lot. He was in a tunnel now, surrounded by darkness. His breathing was loud in his ears and seemed to be coming from outside of his body, hissing like a popped balloon.

After what seemed like an hour, he heard the echo of footsteps somewhere in the distance.

He lay on the cold hard floor of the tunnel and couldn't move. His heart was beating slowly and deliberately now, each pump of blood producing another surge of warmth. He tried to reach for his chest but couldn't lift his arms.

The footsteps were closer now. A faint light flickered from above. The footsteps stopped.

Someone was standing over him now.

Another flicker. Officer Dawes. His eyes were blue and wet with tears.

I'm sorry, Sugar said. I'm sorry. He said it over and over and over. I'm sorry, I'm sorry, I'm sorry.

Each breath was shorter now, each gulp slower and more painful. His mouth was dry and each gasp for air burned from the top of his throat to the bottom of his lungs. His eyelids felt heavy, so, so heavy. He could no longer hear the hissing of his breath or the pumping of his heart.

I'm sorry.

He inhaled once more and felt a sharp blast of air enter his lungs. He gasped for another breath, but it didn't come. He tried to say sorry again, but it didn't come. He felt his body go cold and limp and everything went black.

Chapter 59

Two minutes too late.

Kneeled over Sugar's lifeless body, Gerald cursed the traffic he hadn't passed and the red lights he hadn't run. He could have stopped the shooting, controlled the bleeding at the very least. A matter of minutes, the difference between life and death.

Sugar's cheeks were still warm, his lips still pink. He'd taken his last breath, a single desperate gasp from the bottom of his lungs, mere seconds ago. Gerald's heart was still galloping, his arms weak and quivering from pumping and pumping on Sugar's chest until there was no blood left to pump. He could feel the sweat at the top of his head and the back of his neck beginning to freeze. He held in his wet, sticky hands the jacket he had gifted Sugar, bullet-pierced and soaked in blood.

The wails of sirens in the distance were growing louder. It seemed like hours since Gerald had called 911, but according to his watch it had been less than four minutes. He got to his feet and looked down at Sugar. His mouth was open, his eyes closed. From the neck up, he looked like a sleeping child, exhausted after a long afternoon of play. The faded beam from the streetlamp and the slightly brighter lights coming through the window of the pizza place gave his skin a yellow glow, almost angelic. He began to wonder how his Charlie had looked in his final moments but stopped himself.

The sirens were screaming now, within a block or two. Gerald wiped his bloody hands on a dry section of the coat before laying it carefully over Sugar's frail body. There were still no signs of life coming from the pizza place, though the fluorescent OPEN sign was flashing and the smell of fresh dough was creeping through the entrance. Gerald was considering going inside when the first cruiser pulled into the far side of the parking lot, followed directly by an ambulance and another cruiser.

Gerald knew that within ten minutes the parking lot would be a circus of vehicles, cops, media, EMTs, CSIs and yellow tape. Frankly, he didn't want to be around to see it. He'd seen enough of Crookston for one night. He'd seen enough of Crookston for a lifetime.

He put his head down and stepped off the curb toward his car. As he pulled onto the freeway, he passed a pair of cruisers, their wailing sirens cutting through the cold of the night like an alarm announcing Armageddon. He tried to catch a glimpse of the drivers but they were going too fast.

He knew exactly where he was headed, but he wasn't in a rush to get there. He decided to bypass the freeway and go through the heart of Crookston, the way he knew Kelvin Jackson would take home.

Chapter 60

Guns don't kill people, people kill people. It's what Gerald's first partner, Randy Mason, used to always say. Gerald still wasn't convinced.

In all his time working the streets, he had fired his gun only twice. Neither time could he recall making the conscious choice to pull the trigger. When you held that gun in your hand, it took on a life of its own; that trigger controlled you, it owned you. The primal urge to squeeze was so strong, so innate. It was as if your finger were being manipulated by some invisible magnetic force.

Sitting in his car with his seat reclined and his eyes glued to Kelvin Jackson's front door, Gerald remembered wondering, as a rookie, eleven years earlier, if the feeling of power the gun gave him would ever subside. It never had. There was still something about the raw heft of steel in his hand, the sleek coldness of it against his palm, the way his index finger curved perfectly around the trigger.

The temperature outside was hovering just above zero, the wind howling beyond the windows like the mournful cry of desperate children trying to get inside. Gerald had the heat cranked, the vents aimed directly at his outstretched hands, the edges of the windows fogging up around him. His Glock, fully loaded, was resting on his thigh. He'd been sitting this way for nearly forty-five minutes.

After leaving Jefferson Plaza, Gerald had made it to Jackson's place in six minutes flat. He'd tried knocking, unsure exactly what he would do, what he was prepared to do, if the punk answered. Not surprisingly, he did not. A part of Gerald wanted to hit the bricks, search every street on every block and every nook and cranny in between until he found the bastard. But the rational part of him knew that Jackson had to return home at some point. And when he did, Gerald would be ready.

The minutes were crawling. Hard as he tried, Gerald couldn't erase Sugar's face from his memory. His innocent baby face, shining in the glow of the streetlight. His gaping oval mouth twitching ever so slightly as he struggled to spew his dying words.

I'm sorry.

Thinking about the last words anyone would ever hear the kid say gave Gerald chills. He knew they had been meant specifically for him. A final confession, an ultimate release of the burden he'd been carrying since the night he killed Nick.

To rid his mind of death, Gerald turned on the radio. He flipped through the commercials and late night talk shows until he found a vaguely familiar pop tune from a few years back.

Peering over the steering wheel, Gerald watched as an ancient Galaxy came to a stop in front of a unit a few doors down from Jackson's. The slam of the passenger door was followed by a middle-aged black man stumbling across the parking lot. He steadied himself against the frame of a front door while searching for his keys, eventually finding them buried in a coat pocket. After nearly falling over and working at the lock for more than a minute, he finally pulled the door open and staggered inside.

Gerald shook his head and adjusted the volume. The pop music continued to roll, commercial-free, each song sounding so similar that Gerald didn't notice when one ended and the next began. But at least it was passing the time. Gerald glanced at the clock. Twenty-five after one.

More than an hour since he'd parked.

Despite not having slept in more than twenty hours, he felt wide awake. The aftershocks of adrenaline were still pulsing and thoughts of Kelvin Jackson arriving home kept him alert. He looked down at the gun on his lap and again wondered if he had the resolve to go through with it, to do what needed to be done.

Nick was dead. Sugar was dead. An innocent man was behind bars. He had all the motivation he needed. It would be up to the gun to decide.

One forty-five. The complex was quiet as a tomb. The granite sky was completely overcast. The temperature was still dropping, the wind still thrashing. Gerald's eyes were getting dry and itchy from the stale air circulating in the car, but he dared not blink. Any minute, he kept telling himself. He'd grown tired of pop music and settled on a call-in talk show debating the Lions' chances of making the playoffs: having to finish the season 3-0 and needing help, the general consensus was slim to none.

Finally, just before two o'clock, Gerald saw movement in the northeast corner of the lot. A figure blanketed in black stepped between a pair of parked cars and continued toward the housing units. Gerald recognized Jackson's lanky frame immediately and killed the engine.

Jackson was walking quickly and looking over his shoulder every couple of seconds. Gerald knew he had to make his move before Jackson got inside, or he could be in for a long night of cat and mouse. He waited until the kid walked past his car and had his back to him.

Slowly, Gerald sat upright. He gripped the door handle and, with as little pressure as possible, nudged it open. Jackson was only a few feet from his front door now. With his baggy clothing, it was impossible to tell if he was still packing, but Gerald knew it was more than likely. He eased out of the car. Without taking his eyes of the center of Jackson's back, he disengaged the safety on his Glock. He left the car door open and took a couple of delicate steps forward, careful to avoid the chunks of ice scattered across the concrete. He made it about halfway across the lot, to within twenty feet of Jackson, when he missed a step and heard a crunch beneath his foot. Jackson heard it too.

The kid spun around and faced Gerald. They were close enough that Gerald could see the surprise in his eyes. He raised his Glock and pointed it at Kelvin's chest.

"Hold it right there, Kelvin!" The echo of Gerald's voice bounced off the brick walls like a gunshot.

Kelvin stared at him. Frozen. His hands were empty. His eyes were locked on Gerald's Glock. Gerald suddenly found himself hoping to God he wouldn't have to squeeze the trigger.

"Take it nice and easy and nobody gets hurt," Gerald said, taking a tentative step toward Jackson.

The kid's eyes were darting around the parking lot now, searching in desperation for a potential escape route. Finding none, his gaze returned to Gerald's gun. The lights from some of the surrounding homes were coming on now, the heads of inquisitive neighbors filling the windows.

Slowly, Jackson raised his arms and lowered his head. Gerald inched his way toward the boy until he was close enough to hear his muffled whimpers.

"Put your hands behind your head," Gerald said. He was

behind Kelvin now, the gun pressed gently against the base of his bony skull.

With his finger resting on the trigger he thought about how easy it would be.

Jackson's shaking hands finally came around to the back of his head and he dropped to his knees. Gerald's trigger finger was steady but anxious. He imagined the pop, the mess, the satisfaction.

"Please," the kid whimpered. "Please."

Gerald took one final look at Jackson's scalp before returning his gun to its holster. He unclipped the cuffs from his belt and slid them over Jackson's skinny wrists until he heard the final click.

"It's over, Kelvin. It's all over."

Gerald pulled his cellphone out of his pocket and dialled nine-eleven. He left Jackson kneeling on the curb and took a seat on the stoop behind him. He didn't want the kid to see him crying.

Chapter 61

When Clarence woke up, he saw his sheet lying in a twisted pile on the floor beside him and knew that he hadn't been dreaming. His clothing was soaked through with sweat, his skin damp and clammy.

He could tell from the dead silence of the jail that it was still at least an hour until first count. He slowly got to his feet and stretched his aching joints. He spread out on his cot and felt, for the first time since that night, a smile forming at the corners of his mouth.

Nothing had changed since yesterday, but he felt different. The desperation of last night, crawling that close to the edge, had shown him that he alone owned his life. They may have control over it, but he owned it; they may hold the rope, but he held the noose.

The buzzer sounded and Clarence heard the hollow click of his lock. The DEP, a short Latino whose name escaped him, addressed Clarence by his inmate number and he stood.

"Warden wants you in his office," the DEP said. "Stat."

Clarence slipped his laceless shoes over his bare feet and followed the Latino down the empty corridors in silence, the two men's alternating footsteps echoing off the concrete walls. He had never been to the warden's office and wondered what was going on. They navigated a maze of grey, vacant hallways and dank stairwells until they finally came to a door labelled "Warden C. McLean." Clarence had seen McLean only once, and had never exchanged words with him. He had heard virtually nothing of the man, a ruler from behind closed doors.

The DEP knocked three times and they waited. Clarence could feel the sweat beading along his hairline, his cuffed hands unable to do anything about it. After a moment, the heavy door swung open and the warden ordered the DEP to remove Clarence's cuffs before closing the door on them. Clarence stood there, feeling foolish, looking around the small and scarcely furnished office, unsure if he should shake the man's hand.

He was surprised to see Sapp seated on a leather couch along the wall. He was dressed to his usual professional standard and had his left leg folded neatly over his right. Clarence made brief eye contact before going back to scanning the room. When the warden finally extended his hand, Clarence shook it and allowed himself to breathe.

"Please," said the warden. "Take a seat."

Seeing no chairs, Clarence took the cushion next to Sapp. His lawyer greeted him with a pat on the shoulder. The hint of smile on his face put Clarence at ease.

The warden walked around a large wooden desk covered with file folders and stacks of paper. Once he was seated, he got straight to the point.

"The reason you're here this morning, Mr. Sanford, is that there's been a development in the case against you." The warden's voice was even, his face stone. Every word seemed to drag on longer than the last.

Clarence allowed himself, for the briefest of moments, to imagine the news he'd dreamt about for the past nine nights.

"Apparently the police department has a new suspect in the crime for which you've been charged."

The hope rose again in Clarence's chest, and this time he couldn't push it back down. He felt his heart rate quicken and became aware he was perched on the edge of his seat. Hours seemed to pass.

"Consequently, all of the charges against you have been dropped."

Clarence felt his bones go numb and his flesh begin to tingle. He looked at Sapp, whose smile now covered half his face.

"You'll be released this afternoon," Sapp said.

Sapp stood, and when Clarence found his legs several seconds later, he joined him. He locked his arms around his lawyer's shoulders and squeezed as hard as he could.

"You're going home," Sapp whispered into Clarence's ear. "You're going home."

Chapter 62

When Gerald stepped in the room, five men dressed in dark suits stopped mid-conversation and stared up at him with somber faces. Harriston Graves and Victor Anton were seated next to each other on the right side of the oval table. The other three he didn't recognize. He gave the group a courteous nod and eyed the only empty chair at the table, a black leather roller to the left of Anton. Before he took it, Graves introduced him to the strangers.

At the head of the table was Judge Norman Barlow, a tiny old man with a firm handshake and a serious face. To his right, across from Graves and Anton, sat Byron Sapp and Jake Burnett. They were Sanford's attorneys, one black, one white. Gerald didn't bother trying to remember which was which. Both wore scowls of contempt and neither rose from their seats when they reached across the table to shake Gerald's hand.

Gerald could feel five sets of eyeballs on him as he rolled out the chair next to Anton. He sank into his seat and focused on the pristine polish of the table. His head was light from lack of sleep and too much coffee. By the time Kelvin was arrested and Gerald had answered all the detectives' questions, it was almost four in the morning. He'd laid in bed for a couple of hours, but couldn't shut his mind off; according to his rough calculations, he was approaching thirty hours without sleep.

Judge Barlow broke the silence with a sigh.

"All right. Now that we're all here," he began, shifting his eyes toward Gerald, "let us get to the matter at hand."

He made a point of looking up at the chrome-plated clock at the front of the room and added, "Let's make this quick. I'm backed up as it is."

One of the lawyers, the black one, spoke next. "Works for us. The sooner this travesty of justice is resolved, the better." He was staring directly at Gerald.

"Now, now," Barlow said. "We're all here for the same thing, counsellor. There's no need to get hostile."

"I apologize, your honor," said the lawyer. "It's just that my client has been locked up for a crime he did not commit for nine days now. His immediate release is of the utmost urgency."

268

The white lawyer nodded his narrow head in agreement.

"That's why we're here, Mr. Sapp." Barlow spread his hands across the table, like a magician who had just made the rabbit disappear. "Why don't we start with Captain Graves?"

Graves leaned forward in his chair and glanced at the stack of paper in front of him.

"Early this morning, at approximately oh-two hundred hours, we apprehended a new suspect for the December fifth murder of Officer Nick Reese."

"And he confessed?" the black lawyer asked, earning him a stern look of disapproval from Barlow.

When Graves was certain it was safe, he continued. "He confessed to being there that night, but claims it was a friend that did the shooting."

"And where's this friend?" The lawyer was leaning forward in his chair now, his voice high with a sense of urgency.

Graves looked from Judge Barlow to Gerald to Anton. Finally, he addressed the man who asked him the question.

"He's dead, Mr. Sapp."

The room was consumed in silence. Gerald saw Sugar lying there. His face, the coat, the blood.

"Dead?" Sapp said. "As in murdered?"

Graves nodded. "Maybe I'll let Officer Dawes take it from here."

Hearing his name caught Gerald off guard. He blinked Sugar out of his mind's eye and looked around the room, stopping when his gaze fell on Judge Barlow.

"Go ahead, Officer Dawes. Why don't you start from the beginning? From the time Mr. Sanford was arrested." The judge's tone revealed both genuine interest and a hint of accusation.

"Well," Gerald began, "shortly after I arrested Mr. Sanford, I began having doubts that he was the one who killed Nick, I mean Officer Reese." He looked at his hands as the name passed his lips.

Before he could continue, the black lawyer named Sapp interjected. "Doubts? What kind of doubts? Why didn't you come forward?"

"Enough, counsellor," said the judge. "Let the man speak and save any questions for the end."

269

Sapp shot Gerald a dirty look before lowering his head like a scolded schoolboy.

"So as I was saying," Gerald returned Sapp's glare, "I was pretty sure I'd arrested the wrong guy. That Officer Reese's real killer was still out there somewhere."

He hesitated, shook his head. "And no, I didn't come forward."

He stole a look at Graves and Anton. Both were shifting nervously in their chairs, their cheeks a shallow shade of pink. Gerald knew it was what they wanted to hear, that if he admitted to coming forward IA would have to get involved and a never-ending shit show would ensue. Besides, he wanted to save a bit of leverage in case he needed it later on.

"I was scared and felt horrible, but I had no idea what to do. So I sat on it."

When no one said anything, Gerald took it as his cue to continue. "So after a couple of days, I sort of started my own investigation. I came across some evidence and, long story short, it led to a couple of suspects. Two kids actually.

"Last night, one of them called me and told me he was ready to talk." The images were creeping up on him and he had to take a deep breath before he continued. "It's clear to me he's about to confess, but when I get there I find the kid's body." His tiny, cold, dead body.

"The friend," Sapp said. "The friend killed him."

"I knew it was him right away," Gerald said. "He's had a few run-ins with the law and the next one probably meant some time. So he got rid of the only link."

Gerald shrugged his shoulders; it was a room full of people who dealt with death on a daily basis.

"So this kid," Sapp said. "That's who we have in custody?"

Gerald nodded. "I went to his place after I called nine-eleven. Ended up waiting almost two hours before he got home. He surrendered and I called for backup."

"And he's admitted to being there the night Officer Reese was killed?"

Gerald honestly didn't know. All he'd been told since leaving The Reds earlier that morning was to be at this meeting. He looked past Anton and caught Graves' eye.

"Yes," Graves said. "He corroborated everything. Stealing the car, his friend shooting Officer Reese, murdering his friend, everything. Statement was signed this morning."

"So our client's innocent," Sapp said, as if that settled everything. He turned toward Judge Barlow.

"When will he be released?"

The judge sighed and glanced down at his notes.

"All charges have been dropped. You can head over to the jail now. I'll have the paperwork sent within the hour."

Sapp rose from his seat, and the white lawyer followed.

"Well. That puts an end to one of the most abhorrent injustices I've ever witnessed." He walked around the table, his sidekick at his heels, and turned around when he reached the door. "Oh, and gentlemen. This will definitely not be the last you hear from us."

The four remaining men held their breath until they heard the thud of the heavy oak door.

"Well, gentlemen," Barlow said. "I have a feeling this is about to get real messy."

"It was my fault, your honor." The words came easier than Gerald had expected. He would have loved to see the reactions to his right, but fought the urge to glance over. "Any negligence was completely my own, not that of the department."

The judge nodded. "Very commendable of you, officer. I'm just grateful this all got sorted out before it went to trial."

He looked up at the clock, seemingly decided he had another minute or two to spare.

"How do you plan to deal with the media?"

Graves shrugged. "The grounds for arresting Sanford at the time were sound, the evidence supported our charges. The way we see it, one of our officers just happened to stumble upon some information which led us to the real killer."

Us.

Gerald clenched his jaw and stared a hole through the wall behind Barlow.

"We're talking about a cop killing here," Anton said. "As far as the media's concerned, all that matters is we got the right guy. They'll forget about Sanford before the sun goes down."

"Works for me," Barlow said. Another look at the clock.

"Now if you'll excuse me, gentlemen, I have to take care of that paper work. Feel free to use the room as long as you like."

Barlow disappeared behind the door without another word and it seemed as if all the air from the room followed him. Neither Gerald nor Anton nor Graves said a word. The only sign of life coming from any of them was the muted popping sound coming from Anton cracking his knuckles beneath the surface of the table.

"We appreciate your discretion with the details, Dawes," Graves finally said. If there was any sincerity in his voice, Gerald couldn't hear it. "I think you'd agree the less we say, the faster this will all go away."

Gerald stood up, ready to leave, hoping to never see either of them again.

"We got Nick's killer," he said. "That's all that ever mattered."

"With the added bonus of getting two more hood rats off the streets," Anton said. "Two parasites with one stone."

Gerald felt his arm begin to move before he knew what was happening. Because of where he was standing, it was more of a jab than a punch, and he didn't get as much behind it as he would have liked. Still, when he heard the raw crack of bone on flesh and saw the blood trickling down Anton's chin, he felt a rush of satisfaction. He looked down at Anton, who was covering his face with both hands, and at Graves, whose mouth was hanging open.

Gerald reached into his breast pocket and placed his badge flat on the table, staring into Graves' disbelieving eyes.

"You'll have my gun by the end of the day."

Chapter 63

Clarence stared at the swirling snowflakes beyond the frosted window. They were fat and delicate, like the night he got arrested. High above the jagged barbed wire of the security fence and the smudged green tips of evergreens, the sun shone a brilliant white. The bright blue sky extended forever in every direction, the occasional low-hanging cirrus coasting across its otherwise blank canvas.

It was the same sky as it had been before Clarence got locked away. The same today as it was yesterday as it would be tomorrow. Yet seeing it for the first time in ten days, it looked somehow different. More visceral, more alive. He got the sense he could reach out and touch it, hold it in his hand like a living, breathing thing.

Clarence stood and stretched his arms high above his head. There was still a tiny part of him that believed it wasn't true, that it could all come crashing back down on him at any moment. That the world wasn't quite done playing its games with him, that it had saved the mother of cruel jokes as the grand finale.

He leaned his forearms against the cool pane of the window and scanned the jail yard. The inch or so of snow covering the tarmac was clean and pure and untouched, a perfect sheet of shimmering confetti. There was no one out there, nothing but a half dozen meshless basketball nets perched atop tall steel poles, their white metal backboards reflecting the sun's rays like mirrors in the sky.

Clarence squinted into the sunlight and focused on one of the basketball poles, transported suddenly to a bitter winter day in his childhood. There were five of them, maybe six. They were on their way home from school when they gathered around a bus stop and one of the Martin brothers, Donnie probably, pulled a fiver from his pocket and offered it to whoever stuck their tongue on the steel pole. They all looked at each other, volunteering one another, razzing one another, until finally Clarence threw his arm in the air and said he'd do it.

They yelped and hollered as he gripped the pole with his mitted hands and psyched himself up. After at least a full minute of the others chanting, and at least a half dozen false starts, he leaned

273

in, stuck out his tongue and poked it toward the frosty steel. Almost immediately, he began flailing his arms in sheer panic. The group continued to howl, their bodies shaking with hysteria, until Clarence's muffled whimpers grew louder and his eyes began to brim with tears. Still giddy with excitement, the boys continued to laugh, jokingly suggesting they leave him there.

Finally, once the laughter had faded to a series of nervous chuckles, Donnie stepped behind Clarence and gripped his shoulders. His cheeks were wet with tears, the tip of his tongue numb and swollen. His hands were wrapped around the pole, his chin resting against the icy steel. Suddenly, his eyes went wide and Donnie yanked.

Twenty-some years later, standing in a room in the Wayne County Jail, Clarence could still feel the surge of pain and see the spurt of blood dripping down his chin. He cringed at the memory and tore his eyes from the jail yard.

Clarence heard the door slam shut behind him and turned around. Byron Sapp took a seat at the oval wooden table in the center of the room and placed a tower of paperwork in front of him.

Clarence's mind was numb and he paced the room in an attempt to rid himself of the lingering images of the icy pole. When he was beside Sapp he looked down at the stack of papers.

"Is this it?" he asked.

"This is it," Sapp said. "You're officially a free man."

The words rolled around in Clarence's head and he stared down at Sapp without really seeing him, his lawyer's voice a hollow echo in his mind. It seemed to Clarence he was looking in on a dream, experiencing everything through a filter. The moment was very real to him, but somehow just out of reach.

"Why don't you take a seat, Clarence?"

Clarence felt his legs move, but not toward the table. He found himself at the window again, staring out at the clean white snow and the bright blue sky.

"Listen, Clarence," Sapp said. "I really hate to rain on your parade, but the fact remains this whole situation could have been avoided. The DPD abused its power and we're gonna make them pay."

Clarence went on staring out the window. High above the hazy tree line on the other side of the steel fence he could see the speck of a bird among the fluttering snowflakes. It soared with such ease, its movement almost imperceptible. Clarence didn't allow himself to blink as he followed its flight path, steady and hypnotic. It seemed to glide across the sky so effortlessly, so efficiently, as if it were travelling in slow motion. Not a single wasted wing flap.

"Clarence?"

"No," Clarence heard himself say.

"No?" The sound of a chair dragging against carpet. "No what?"

"People make mistakes, Byron."

"This was not a mistake, Clarence." Sapp's voice came from directly behind him now. He went on about wrongful arrest, excessive force, inexcusable injustice.

Clarence continued to stalk the seemingly aimless speck in the sky as it hovered just above the tree line. The bird would occasionally descend, but only for a moment, and never out of sight.

Wrongful arrests paid well, Clarence could hear Sapp saying. The city would likely settle before it ever got to court.

The bird tilted, revealing for the first time its massive black wingspan. It dove toward the treetops and levelled off before tilting again and disappearing behind the wall of green.

"Talk to me, Clarence. Say something. Say anything."

"People make mistakes," Clarence said again.

"Suit yourself," Sapp finally said, gathering his briefcase and leaving the room.

When he heard the door close, Clarence tore his eyes away from the tree line and continued staring at the falling snow.

www.ingramcontent.com/pod-product-compliance
Lightning Source LLC
Chambersburg PA
CBHW070727280626
47159CB00023B/2852